EDUCATING CALLIE

SECRETS OF FROST BOOK ONE

EMMA JAYNE MILLS

Text Copyright 2017 © Emma Jayne Mills
All rights reserved.
Please do not participate in or encourage piracy of copyrighted materials in violation of the author's rights.
Purchase only authorised editions.
This book is a work of fiction. Names, characters, storylines and incidents are either products of the author's imagination or used fictitiously and any resemblance to actual persons, living or dead, is entirely coincidental.

Cover Design: RebeccaCovers
Formatting: Pink Elephant Designs

For the ones who live in darkness, never give up on the light.

PROLOGUE

DUBLIN, IRELAND, 1993

Declan Murray followed the stranger into the shadows of the Temple Bar nightclub. He'd been watching the man for some time, with suspicions regarding his identity. This evening, he'd gained the confirmation he was seeking. He waited until the man seated himself in a darkened corner of the club, his face masked from view, and ordered two tumblers of whiskey from the barman. Setting the two glasses on the table the man occupied, he slid into the seat alongside him.

"Do you know who I am?" Declan asked, looking straight ahead, at a dance floor that writhed with the bodies of young, horny clubbers.

"Aye," the man answered, picking up the glass and gulping a mouthful of liquid fire.

It was no surprise to Declan that the man knew him. Most of Dublin knew him, or at the very least, his name and reputation.

"Then we're on equal standing because I also know who you are." Declan rubbed his chin thoughtfully. This was a delicate situation that required carefully treading. While he didn't fear him, this man was dangerous in an entirely different way to Declan.

"I doubt that," the stranger answered, not taking his eyes off the pretty blonde directly in front of their table. She couldn't see them in the dimly illuminated seats but the lights on the dancefloor lit her up like a firework.

Declan leaned in, whispered a woman's name in his ear and sat back, triumphantly watching the man stiffen.

"I also know what you do and what you've been doing for quite some time. I know what happened to the last young lady you followed and where you left her when you were finished with her. I know what you'd like to do to *her*." Declan tipped his chin to the blonde girl on the dancefloor, who was now gyrating distastefully on the hip of a man she didn't know. "I know that in a few days, the gardai will find another body. She'll be laid out for them, probably beside a stream or in a clearing in the woods, not buried, or hidden. She'll be dressed in a white nightgown, with a crown of dead flowers on her pretty little head. But perhaps the most interesting thing I know is that they're onto you. You left them a clue and it's only a matter of time."

"What do you want?" The stranger hissed, breaking his cool, calm persona.

"You need to get out of the country, and I need your services," Declan said, smiling.

"I'm not a contract killer." The stranger downed the whiskey and moved to leave.

"This isn't a contract. It's long term. A mother with an illegitimate child on the way. Watch and wait, until the child is born. Only the mother dies. Make it look like one of yours, I think you'll find she's your type."

"When is the baby due?" The man's interest was sparked.

"Six months." Declan waited while his companion appeared to be mulling over his decision, all the while not taking his eyes off the dancing girl. "The child will be taken care of when the mother is gone, you needn't concern yourself with that."

"What if I say no?"

"I have low friends in high places. A whisper of your name in the right ears will place you on their radar in seconds. That same whisper could also ensure you'd be left alone to continue adding as many whores to your collection as you like, indefinitely. You've two choices, accept my offer, or leave and pretend we never met. The second comes with consequences." Declan paused for effect, letting his words to sink in and enjoying the control he had over this big man who was wreaking havoc across the country yet couldn't evade Declan Murray. "If you leave here tonight without accepting my offer, the police will be on you before your feet hit Grafton Street. Accept my offer, and you can go on as you were. A new start, back in your home country. For my part, I will ensure you remain well and truly off their radar. Once the job is done, you're free to continue your life as you wish but will no longer have my protection. Do we have a deal?"

"Done."

"Grand. I'll be in touch with details." Declan shot the remainder of the whiskey and stood to leave. "Oh, one more thing."

"What?"

"Find another one." Declan gestured to the blonde on the dance-floor. "She belongs to me."

CHAPTER ONE

"There is a crack in everything; it's how the light gets in."

— LEONARD COHEN

CALLIE

I have cracks, more than my fair share, but no light gets in. Only darkness. The darkness seeps through my cracks like thick, black ink, leaving no room for light inside me. I cover my cracks and I cover the darkness. If you didn't know me, you wouldn't know they were there. I perfected the art of hiding them a long time ago. The *real* people in my life, the ones who see me, they know about my darkness. They know it's there even though they can't see it. They do what they can to help me heal. So, I project light. I do it for them, so that I may see them smile. I don't feel the light. I never feel, not truly. I live in the light, but the darkness lives in me.

THE TEACHER

The monotony of existence can only be appeased by observing its own sweet decay. I have endured long, torturous years, waiting for life to arrive at this moment. Death after unsatisfactory death has failed to give me the closure I need to end this game, completing the circle that began to form years ago. Its arch has been achingly slow in movement, although I found the anticipation exquisite.

My companion covered my tracks until the work he asked of me was done. Not that it mattered, by the time our agreement ended, I had become adept at covering my tracks. That isn't to say, I won't still use him to my advantage. My reluctance in assisting him may have been obvious, but I must admit, without his beginnings, I would have no end. And what an end it promises to be. At last, the time has come.

She is alone. Vulnerable as she runs, blinded by tear-filled eyes, towards the forest. Anyone who has lived in this town as long as she has, is aware of the dangers that lurk in the forest at night.

The good policeman, who thought to play detective, almost caught up with me once. He wasn't quite clever enough to engage me in this game though. He got too close and I dealt with him. Taking him out, along with his interfering wife, was a simple task. I had no need to toy with them, merely to remove them both from my path like a fallen log. Their daughter was always my focus. Her mere existence brings a perfect end to my years of circling, scheming, and watching. Now, she will pay the price for their actions and after she has done so, she will redeem them and all who came before them. Sweet Callie will be my long-ago promised reward. I have waited patiently for her and now she will finally be mine. Completely. No longer will I have to share her affections with others. It is time for her lessons to begin.

CALLIE

I don't know why I headed for the woods that night. Something in the vast darkness, lit only by a blanket of snow, and a yearning to be alone, called to me from within the cluster of trees. I needed to hide; from my memories, my emotions, and my anger, but mostly from him. His incensed voice lingered in my ears, demanding that I let him explain. I didn't need an explanation. My ears had heard every vicious word thrown at me with an anger I'd never before seen from him. There was nothing he could say that would validate his actions.

I'd never been much of a runner, the relay race on school sports day was my limit and I was well past school age. So, scarpering cross country in the dark wasn't the best idea I'd ever had. My clumsy feet caught on a tree root and I lost my balance. Tumbling to the ground in an ungainly heap, my head collided with the exposed root.

"Shit!"

I let out a groan and reached up to rub the bump that was already forming on my temple. My fingers scraped through a wet patch on my skin and my hand came away sticky. *Perfect!* The crack of a twig snapped by a heavy tread echoed around me. I twisted my head, staring wild eyed into the night, thinking it was him. It wasn't. I wish it had been.

I remember waking, blinking to clear my vision, and struggling against the drowsiness that loitered, threatening to pull me back under. My body screamed with a dull ache and my head throbbed. Snow drenched clothes had dried stiffly on my body, restricting my movement as I willed my limbs into a sitting position. Through a blurry haze, my eyes slowly became accustomed to the blinding darkness that enclosed me and I took in what I could make out of my surroundings. It looked like a cellar. It smelled like a cellar. Damp and musty, an earthy scent that revealed I was no longer above ground. I was trapped, held in what was nothing more than a cold, grey, concrete tomb.

There was a chill in the room, but that wasn't why my body began to shake. I panicked. It seemed the most obvious reaction. I was in no fit state to be thinking straight, so, I went with panic. A tiny voice somewhere deep inside told me I ought to be screaming for help. I didn't. I figured anyone who was likely to hear my shouts wouldn't be friendly. That was attention I didn't want. So, I continued to process my situation, rubbing my arms to calm myself and taking slow, deep breaths.

"Stay calm, Callie," I whispered, watching my breath puffing into the empty air. "Just stay calm and you can figure this out."

My dad, when he was alive, always taught me to take notice of life. *Look for the things that others might miss, find the clues that help to answer your questions.* That wasn't so easy to do when you were in full on panic mode, but I looked around the room anyway, detailing what I could. A small window sat in the stone wall, above my head, just below the ceiling, it was probably at ground level on the outside. The frame was just about big enough to squeeze through if, unlike me, you were tall enough to reach it. The glass had been roughly painted over in black, but it still allowed a sliver of light into the dim room. It was daylight out there. The last thing I remembered was running through town. It had been dark, and I'd veered off into the woods. I'd been held here overnight, at the very least.

"Okay, that's question one, Callie. You can do this," I urged myself on, imagining my dad's voice in my head.

The thin, green, stretch of material on the camping cot that I sat on was supposed to serve as a mattress. It gave little comfort. Not that I could have found comfort in anything. There was a pillow; stained brown, without a case, and a scratchy, grey, woollen blanket, folded neatly at the end of the bed. I briefly considered wrapping the blanket around me, to warm me from the chill, but a quick sniff told me I didn't want that thing anywhere near my body.

A jug of water and a glass sat on a small stool next to the bed. I reached for them, greedily, pouring a glass so quickly the water spilled over the edge and splashed onto the concrete floor. I drank deeply, emptying the glass in seconds, then replaced it and stood. My body trembled and I threw my arms out to the sides, stabilising my balance. The room tilted in my vision. I paused on the spot for a few seconds, allowing my body to get a grip of itself. Then, stretching out almost blindly and finding the walls to guide me, I moved slowly around the room.

My stomach flipped and the water threatened to reappear when my eyes landed on the chains. They cascaded down the wall—where they were attached with hooks— and pooled in a rusty heap on the floor. Turning away from them, I continued to explore the room. I don't know what I was looking for, I just needed to feel as though I was doing something. I couldn't sit and wait for him, whoever *he* was, to come back. I needed to move. My heart stalled at the sight that met me when my fingers finally hit a light switch. On the wall, in red paint, was a message for me. *Is it paint?*

"*Yes, it's paint, Callie.*" Again, my dad's voice whispered in my mind, not allowing me to consider that it could be anything else.

> "*Sweet Callie, you are my reward.*
> *It all ends with you. You will be my last.*"

"Question two. Fuck!"

This was where the others were. The realisation hit me in a rush of clarity. Now, the killer had me. I was going to die. A tsunami of panic and anger drenched me, threatening to drown me where I stood. My body shook again, only this time it was anger that won the battle. How dare he? How dare this maniac take all those women and treat them this way?

My breaths became shuddery pants. I heaved in, trying to breathe deeply again, but my lungs refused to co-operate. My efforts only succeeded in bringing on another dizzy spell, driving me to my knees on the cold, hard floor. I gulped in the cold air, my throat barking its fight at me, as I braced myself on hands and knees.

The killer had evaded the police for months. They hadn't found a single clue to his identity, leaving them baffled. He was careful, meticulous. He left nothing behind. My brother, Cameron, along with his fellow police officers, speculated that they hadn't heard of anyone leading the police on a merry dance in this way since *The Yorkshire Ripper*, which was unimaginable. All the advances in technology since those gruesome murders in the eighties were proving useless in the search. How could that be?

This killer left a string of women's bodies in the areas surrounding the small town where I lived, killing them only after subjecting them to torturous injuries. There was gossip that he was also responsible for many more similar murders, spanning at least ten years, spread across the country. It seemed there was no rhyme or reason to his killings. The only similarities being that they were women in their early twenties. He mutilated them all in the same way, before slitting their throats and leaving them to bleed to death. That detail had never been released to the press, but Cameron let it slip to me. Their bodies were left unhidden, laid out as though they were sleeping. Each one was dressed in a long, white nightgown that didn't belong to her and wore a crown made from dead flowers. He chose a different flower for each woman, another detail kept from the press.

Cameron was involved in several of the searches for the missing women. His smiling face formed in my mind and my breathing slowed, bringing peace, and anchoring me long enough to regain my composure. He wouldn't survive if anything happened to me. I knew, because I wouldn't survive if it were the other way around. I thought of my friends too. Friends who had been there for me through every up and down life threw in my direction. They gave me the strength to carry on, when I wanted so desperately to give up. Then there was Jase. He would blame himself because we'd argued. I'd run from his temper and he had chased, yelling into the night. I had people to live for.

I stood, pulling myself to my feet with more strength than I felt, and ventured towards the steps that must lead the main house. I climbed them as stealthily as my aching limbs would allow, cringing and pausing on every creak and murmur the wooden stairs made. The last thing I wanted was to alert my captor to the fact that I was awake. Reaching out, I closed my shaking fingers around the doorknob and turned it slowly. I didn't truly expect it to be unlocked. That sick feeling in the pit of my stomach resurfaced when the latch clicked, and the door opened away from me. It was too late to turn back and await my fate in the cellar. He was there, in front of me.

I never saw his face; he kept it covered under a black balaclava. Only his eyes were on show, leaving me no hint of his identity. His body was big, sturdy, and muscular. This was a man who stayed fit. He sat at a circular, pine table, in a large kitchen, both his hands resting flat on the surface. He wore black, leather gloves and his eyes were trained on me. They tracked my every move, every breath, every blink, but he didn't speak. He never spoke. I thought about edging closer to the door, my eyes flicking back and forth between him and a door that I assumed led outside. My fight returned to me, whether through hope or desperation, I didn't know, but I wondered if I could outrun him. All I had to do was get to a window or door and break the glass. I'd do it with my bare hands if I had to. He continued to watch my movements, his unfeeling gaze never moving from me. There was nothing in his eyes, they gave away no hint of feeling or emotion. Those eyes terrified me and despite my silent planning, I was rooted to the spot in fear.

Slowly, he stood, dressed all in black, and moved to open the fridge. I watched him, confused, as he arranged salad and pieces of cooked chicken on two plates, with gloved hands. He always wore gloves; I don't think I ever saw him without them. When he was finished, he placed the plate on the table, moved a chair out and gestured for me to sit. I didn't move. He came to me, grasping my arm, surprisingly gently, and steering me to the waiting chair. I sat, warily eyeing him and he pointed at the plate. If I ate, would death come more quickly? Did I want that? To get it over with quickly. Or did I want to stall him and give myself a fighting chance?

Suddenly frustrated, I picked up the fork he'd set down and stabbed a piece of cucumber with it. I shoved it into my mouth and chewed angrily. I wanted him to talk, tell me what he was planning to do with me, what he wanted from me. Anything. He merely sat opposite me at the table and watched me as I ate; his own food left untouched. Finally, and probably unwisely, I lost my temper. Slamming my fork down, I stood. The chair toppled and fell back when I pushed it away from me with my legs.

"No!" My cracked voice shouted at him. He didn't move, didn't even seem surprised at my outburst. "I'm not doing this. Who are you? What do you want? If you're going to kill me, just get it over with!"

He shook his head and stood. His movements slow and careful, approaching me on silent steps. He was taller than me and stooped, to look down into my face, as he drew closer.

"No?" I asked. He shook his head again. "No, you won't tell me who you are? No, you won't tell me what you want, or no, you aren't going to kill me?"

More head shaking.

"No to all of it?" I guessed, my voice wavering.

A nod.

"You're not going to kill me?"

He shook his head and placed his hand on my arm again, this time steering me out of the kitchen, along a narrow hallway towards another door. Peeling paint, faded damask wallpaper, and elaborate ceiling coving told of what a grand and beautiful house it once was. The kitchen had been recently decorated in warm yellows and was clean and bright. This hallway, however, looked as though nobody had walked its cracked, tiled floor in decades. He opened a door and gestured inside to a bathroom. A shower, sink, and toilet were crammed into the tiny room. The shower was a new addition I thought, but the rest looked as though it had merely been cleaned and the walls painted a stark white.

"You killed the others," I stated, holding onto my bravado. A nod in response and another gesture towards the bathroom. "You want me to use the bathroom?"

Another nod. He then pointed to another door, before stepping across the hallway to open it and waving his hand in that direction. I could make out the end of a bed through the gap.

"I should go in there afterwards?"

He nodded. Bile rose in my throat, leaving behind that sickly, sore throat feeling, at the thought of what he may be suggesting. I knew the other women had been subjected to horrific violence, but my brother hadn't divulged whether they were sexually assaulted. There had been no mention of it in the news reports and that gave me a sliver of hope but didn't fully ease my mind. The thought that he implied he wasn't going to kill me did nothing to calm my fears either; there were worse things than death.

He nudged me into the bathroom and closed the door behind me as he left. I let out a sigh, pushing back the tears and leaned heavily against the door. There was no lock and no window. No way out, other than the door I'd come through. Feeling helpless, I turned on the shower as hot as it would go, peeled off my filthy clothes, and stood under the scalding water. I let the familiar cherry scented shampoo and conditioner calm me for a few minutes, before allowing my mind to acknowledge that they were the exact same products I used at home. With the sudden knowledge that this might be someone I knew, I sank to the floor of the cubicle, drew my legs up against my chest, and wrapped my arms around them. There I stayed, unable to cry, my mind numb, until the water ran cold.

Questions plagued me when my mind began to work again. Had he watched me and found out what products I used? Or did he know what products I used because he was someone close to me? I shook my head and banished that thought quickly. I refused to believe anyone I knew was capable of this. The water began to cool, and I stepped out of the cubicle. The soft, pink, fluffy towel seemed out of place in the unadorned white bathroom. It didn't fit with the serial killer chic the rest of the house had going on. If anything, it reminded me of Dana, and if I hadn't been in such an awful position, I might have smiled at the thought of my girly friend.

I opened the bathroom door and dared a look around the small hallway. There was no sign of him, but I could hear movement in the kitchen. Moving quickly to the bedroom, I found a pair of black dress trousers and a pale pink blouse, with a frilled collar, laid out on the bed. Next to it lay plain white underwear and a pair of pink ballet flats. Not anything that I would usually wear, but a quick check told me they were all in my size. The thought of the faceless man picking out clothes for me wasn't one I wanted to linger on. *Stay active, keep your mind busy*, my dad's voice nagged in my head. That way, I might actually avoid insanity. Insanity might have been a better option. I dressed quickly, not wanting him to come in and find me naked and looked around the room, trying to pick out the details.

The cracks in the ceiling, peeking through the slick coat of white paint, gave away the room's failed attempt at cosy décor. We hadn't gone up any stairs and judging by the size of the room I was in, it had once been a living or dining room, when the house had seen better days. The window was draped with heavy, green, velvet curtains. I picked up the edge of one, pulling it back and looking at the window. It was painted black. Surely, someone could see that from the outside. They had to realise that wasn't normal. Who in their right mind painted their windows black? Please let him have observant neighbours, I thought, continuing to scan the room.

There were creams, perfumes, and make-up, all brands that I owned, even if I didn't use them. My boyfriend, Jase, had a thing about buying me expensive perfume and cosmetics. I had quite the collection, but I rarely wore it, except for one particular brand that was his favourite. The bottles and jars were organised neatly on an ornate, white dressing table with gold gilded edges. There were silver plated hairbrushes and a hand-held mirror to match. A pink velvet cushioned stool sat underneath the table. All very Victorian and weirdly placed. Perhaps, given the circumstances, I shouldn't have found any of it odd. This was a serial killer's lair, after all. What did I know about what classed as weird for a man like him?

I opened the wardrobe to find it full of new clothes and shoes. All in the style I assumed *he* must prefer. The bedding was white. There was a patchwork bedspread, in shades of pink and cream, folded neatly across the end of the bed and the bed itself was adorned with lots of throw pillows, in yet more pink. I wasn't a fan of pink. In fact, my dad had often joked that I should have been born a boy. I could play football and climb trees with the best of them, and always preferred the company of boys, sharing most of my brother's male friends even now. My best friend was a boy I met when we were in preschool and we'd grown up together. I was *that* girl— the one who always hung around with the boys, because girls were too much hard work.

In an alcove, nestled between the wall and a white brick chimney breast, was a bookshelf containing nothing but classics. I ran my fingers along the spines of *Pride and Prejudice*, *Great Expectations*, and other such works, along with several poetry anthologies. A sage green armchair, with a beige cashmere shawl draped over the back of it, sat next to the bookshelf. Ordinarily, I would have been excited about a find such as this. A cosy little reading nook, where I could hide away for hours, blocking out the real world. Here, my idea of heaven disturbed me beyond my wildest dreams. That was the moment I knew, with clarity, that he had been planning this for a very long time. This room was set up for someone to stay in permanently. A soft knock sounded at the door. I froze and watched the doorknob, it didn't turn. He didn't enter, and I didn't tell him to. When the knock came again, more demanding this time, I took it as my cue to leave the room.

Taking a few deep breaths, preparing myself for who knew what was to come, I opened the door and walked a few steps out of the room. I needed to pull myself together and start thinking straight. There had to be a way out of this. I couldn't allow myself to think about all the other women who hadn't escaped. I needed to be the one that found freedom. In the shabby hallway, he was pulling on a heavy, winter coat. Was he going out? This could be my chance. Something told me he wouldn't be stupid enough to just leave me loose in the house, but I could hope. Hope would be my salvation. Cameron always told me I was the strong one and I silently vowed be exactly that now. I would get back to him.

THE TEACHER

I sit at this bar, feigning outrage that my lady is missing. None of them have even the slightest inkling that she is safely with me, where she belongs. A man can never find what is under his nose; my Mother's words were never truer than in this moment. The townsfolk are gathered. They come together in their time of need, supporting each other in between searches for their lost princess. She has been with me for two days. She slept peacefully for the first twenty-four hours. I sat by her side and regarded her tranquil face. Now, observing as they suffer is almost as satisfying as watching my sweet lady sleep. They all look up in unison each time the door opens. This time her brother enters the bar.

He carries a look of distraught exhaustion. His shoulders are slumped, and his head hangs low. I soundlessly congratulate myself on my ability to make him feel pain, too. Yet more penance for the crimes of his elders. It seems only proper that the entire family pay the price. How else will they learn from their mistakes? The twins may not remember the woman who started this journey, but they are her legacy and the game she began will end with them.

"Cameron," I address him. "Any news?"

"Nothing new." He rubs a hand down his stubbled face and moves towards the band of misfits awaiting him.

"Re-fill?" asks the young bar tender, from behind the bar. He isn't the landlord. He is no more than a nameless face to me, despite his being here as long as I have been coming here to drink. My lady is familiar with him, of course, but he matters not to me. Fortunately for him, he has no part to play in this performance.

"One more." I push my glass towards him and continue to watch my lessons sinking in.

I realise, with a secret, satisfied smile to myself, that this time my lessons are affecting the entire town. I have taken their sweetheart. She is the ray of sunlight in this dull little town and now she is no longer theirs. Everything has finally come together, the events of years past and a clandestine conversation in a Dublin nightclub, have finally come to a head. The initial game may have played out years ago, but the reigns were passed to me to do with as I wished. I chose to continue along this seductive curve. I couldn't have planned it more perfectly. I no longer have to pretend to like the people she calls friends, in order to stay close to her. She is solely mine at last.

CALLIE

I was alone. He put me in the bedroom, not tied or chained. Just as I began to hope he was a bumbling fool; he produced a key and locked the door behind him. Did he really think I wouldn't try and escape? I heard the front door click as he locked it and waited a few minutes to make sure he wasn't coming back, before I started hammering on the window and yelling for help. I had no idea if I could be heard, it didn't stop me. I screamed until my voice was gravelly and my throat sore, because I had to try. I didn't know how long he would be gone, so I was fast and loud.

After what seemed like hours, I was all screamed out. My throat felt as though I'd reached a hand down it and yanked out my vocal cords, scratching the fleshy walls with my nails along the way. My knuckles were scratched and bruised from thumping the window, the door, and the walls. With my heart pounded in my chest, I looked around the room for something, anything, I could use to break the glass.

"The stool!" I picked it up and threw it at the window with every ounce of strength I had left. It fell to the floor with a dull thud, having had no effect. "That was fucking pathetic, Callie!"

Swallowing the sob that threatened, I picked it up again and moved closer to the window. I swung the stool. This time not letting go and making sure the wooden legs hit the glass. The window cracked, not much, but it was a start. I hit it, over and over again, until finally the glass gave and fell from the frame in sharp slivers. Not thinking about the jagged edges still embedded in the frame, I leaned through the window as far as I could and screamed as loudly as my broken voice would allow. A sharp pain gripped the crown of my hair and the sweet smell invaded my senses again.

Pain. Hot, intense pain in my arm, dragged me screaming from oblivion. He was there. Sitting on the edge of the bed and I was back in the cellar. The bed had been moved to the other side of the room, and the rust encrusted chains were now tightly fastened and digging into the skin around my wrists. His icy eyes, peeking out through the balaclava, held a slight sparkle that told me he was smiling, as though he hadn't just dragged the tip of a knife down the length of my arm. There was a flash of familiarity in that look, but it was gone as quickly as it had appeared.

The blade burned another trail along my shoulder and down my arm, ending just above my wrist. His cuts weren't deep enough to cause any real damage, barely enough to draw blood, but it hurt. It really hurt. He lifted the knife and pressed it against my cheek, just below my eye. The tip gradually pressed harder into my face and I felt blood creep across my skin. He lifted the knife and placed it in another spot, next to the corner of my eye, pushing it into my skin once more, before covering my mouth with that stinking rag.

Sweet oblivion.

The black, serrated, hunting knife was against my other cheek when I was startled from sleep again. My body froze in fear, terrified that my movement might drive him to something much worse. He drew the sharp point down my cheek and across my chin, ending in the dip below my bottom lip. Then he left. It was as though he were just there to wake me for the day ahead.

For a moment, I didn't move. I lay on the bed, shaking. My body was twisted at an odd angle, to allow for the shackles that were still tight around my wrists and hanging from the wall behind me. When I rose, slowly, the cuts on my arms re-opened and the dried blood cracked, letting fresh blood trickle through. *Is this what happened to the other women?* Somehow, I knew what they had gone through was worse than this. Sudden grief for them overwhelmed me and I doubled over, laying my head on my knees, and sobbed for the women he had killed. Strangers with whom I would eternally share a connection. I don't know why I didn't cry for myself, perhaps there was still hope clinging to the edges of my despair.

The door opened. I straightened, stiffly. He laid a black, floor length dress over the end of the camp bed, then came towards me with a key in hand. He slowly unlocked the metal cuff from my wrist. His actions were of someone who cared that I was hurt, softly rubbing the skin where the rough edges had cut into it and drawn blood. Lifting my chin with his gentle touch, he pointed to the dress, then to the door at the top of the stairs. Then he turned and left. I felt sick. All fight left me, and I knew I had to go along with him. I couldn't face that knife again.

He wore a black dinner suit that night, with a white shirt, black tie, and the balaclava. I stopped in front of him and looked directly into the steel eyes. He avoided my gaze and with fast movements, reached out to snatch my arm. He dragged me, roughly, down the hallway, and into the bedroom. Stopping in front of the mirror, he hauled me in front of him and lifted my chin from behind. His grip was tight, forcing me to look at my reflection. All trace of the tenderness he had shown before had evaporated. His grip tightened on my chin and he jabbed a finger at our mirror images.

I looked at my sorry reflection with indifference. My appearance shocked me, but I couldn't find an outward reaction. My cheeks were covered in tiny cuts. One long one ran from underneath my left eye, all the way down to my chin. Dried blood covered my face, resembling trails of red tears falling down my cheeks. There were long, angry, red lines streaking down both arms. My hair was matted and there was dry blood at the edges of my hairline. I looked horrific and felt even worse.

With his eyes on mine in the mirror, he ran his fingers along the marks on my arm. I tried to turn my head away, but his grip on my chin refused to relent, silently demanding that I continue to watch. When he got to the marks on my face, he leant forward, rested his covered nose against my neck and inhaled deeply. His intimate touch caused my stomach to roll, but there was nothing in it to bring up. Then silently, always silently, his gentle touch returned, and he led me from the bedroom, down the hall into a dining room. The table was set for two.

THE TEACHER

My lady deserves the best and I will ensure she has it. As you will come to see; I am not the villain of this piece. I am merely beginning my life with the lady I was destined to be with. Teaching is a calling set deep within me, as much a part of my survival as breathing. I am comfortable in the knowledge that I do the right thing. Mother taught me well and the gentleman she created has honoured her memory in return. Sharing my work with the world is a privilege denied to many like me.

Do not mistake my words for a confession. I seek no forgiveness, nor would I accept it. I have no need for it. I am not a serial killer, you see. Serial killers receive no reward. I have mine. I have served the women of this world and now, I will be rewarded.

I wish I could tell her she looks stunning as I lead her to the dining table and seat her at one end. My voice will give away my identity though and she isn't ready for that information yet. That time will come. This evening, I will treat her as the lady of the house should be treated. I am aware that it is a premature action on my part; she should not occupy that seat until her lessons are complete. She must earn her place, but this evening I wish to indulge myself. I have waited so long for her to join me and I hope, if I give her an idea of the life we may live together, she will fight my lessons less.

The closing wounds and dry blood on her skin serve as a reminder that she must obey me. The sight of it excites me. One day, when her lessons are learned and she no longer has to carry them with her, I will take her out in public. I will be the envy of every man around us. She will choose me. Of that, there is no doubt.

I lift the domed, silver lid on the platter in front of her, before pouring her a glass of the finest wine and taking my own seat at the head of the table. She stares at me, her hazel eyes rounded and wild, beautiful in her despair. I gesture to her plate and she lifts her cutlery, slowly, pain marring her features. Her lessons may cause her discomfort now, but she will soon be pain free.

CALLIE

I hammered on the tiny cellar window. He left again. He flew up from the table and dragged me down the stairs by my hair, throwing me roughly on the floor of the cellar when I refused to eat. Then he covered my face with the rag. The effects of whatever he doused it with had worn off and I was finally able to move around. It must have been hours since he'd left me there and judging by the little reaction to the noise I was making, there was nobody nearby. I wanted nothing more than to lie down and quietly slip into oblivion, making it all go away, but I couldn't give up. I was a fighter, the way my parents had always taught me to be. I pummelled again with my fist, breaking the window was my only hope. I punched at the thin glass relentlessly with the heel of my hand, until finally it cracked. Gasping in shock, I continued hitting it, desperation and hope fuelling my energy levels. I knew my hands were ripped to shreds; blood covered them and crawled down my arms, but there was no way I was stopping. I kept going, until at last, I had enough space to crawl through.

Jagged edges of the windowpane clawed at the dress I was still wearing, catching, and ripping it as I shoved my way through. The glass tore further into my arms and legs, but I ignored it and dragged my bare feet out onto snow covered ground. I looked around, attempting to get my bearings, and rose to my knees, hands buried in the snow.

My prison cell was nothing more than a shell from the outside. It was the kind of place that hadn't seen life in generations but once housed a rich family. An old, unloved place that nobody noticed anymore, and kids told ghost stories about. I doubted anyone even knew it was there. Climbing roses, that had once been full of blooms, now crawled like zombies over the front of the house. Wild ivy invaded the walls and tangled in the guttering. The chimney stack had long since crumbled and there were gaps in the roof tiles. Every window on the top floor was boarded and each one on the ground floor painted black. Turning my attention away from the house, I saw that I was surrounded completely by tall trees, their bare branches heavily laden with snow. This wasn't an area of the forest I recognised. I was in the middle of nowhere.

"Shit!" I cursed to myself.

I pushed to my feet and began to move as quickly as my shaky legs would allow. My bare feet didn't register the icy surface they felt, my fingers didn't acknowledge the biting wind. I left a trail, but I couldn't muster the energy to cover it as I went and hopefully, the still falling snow would disguise my tracks soon enough. My energy was low, but I pulled on the thoughts of my brother and my friends to keep me focused. I'd gotten out of there, all I had to do was keep moving.

I never knew how long I was out there, and it hasn't occurred to me to ask since. The snow became heavier and darkness had fallen when I thought I heard the sound of male voices. I was freezing, broken, dehydrated, and quite possibly hallucinating. A flash of light through the trees had me hunkering down behind the nearest bush. *What if it was him?* I whimpered and allowed my body to collapse from fear and exhaustion. I could just lie there and let the snow cover me, he wouldn't see me then. I would probably die from hypothermia, but that had to be better than what he had planned for me. If I was going to die, I would do it on my own terms. Loud, muffled voices and footsteps in all directions interrupted my thoughts.

"Shush! Too loud, my head hurts." I don't know if I managed the words.

Light. Blinding me.

"Turn it off!" I think I whispered.

More shouting. *Was that my name?* Footsteps rapidly drawing near. *Don't let it be him. Please don't let it be him.* A sharp intake of breath, then gentle hands under my shoulders and knees. I flinched. The pain made me dizzy.

"No more," I croaked, my dry lips cracking with the effort. "Please, no more."

"Shh, CeeCee, don't talk. I've got you. It's over, baby." A kiss on my forehead. I knew that voice. I loved that voice.

"Callie?" A new voice called. I knew that one too.

"It's her, Cam." The first voice was deep, comforting.

I inhaled weakly; my body shook with the effort. A familiar male scent filled my nostrils and I knew I was safe. Not that it mattered, the darkness had still found me.

My anger smouldered as I stormed through the snow, and along the dark street of the small town I lived in. I ran as fast as I could, away from the one person I thought would love me forever. I didn't stop to acknowledge the distant calls chasing me down the old cobbled road. I was angry, confused and hurt.

I wasn't dressed for charging through ankle deep snow at midnight, but that hadn't occurred to me. Would it occur to any woman who walked into her boyfriend's flat, after a busy Friday night tending bar, to be greeted by him, drunk as a skunk, and spouting abuse at her? Telling her it was time to give up her job and be at home for him at the end of the working day. He was tired of coming home to an empty house. He was sick of seeing her behind that bar, other men drooling over and flirting with his woman, thinking they might stand a chance. He didn't want her smiling for anyone but him or coming home smelling of beer, and other men's aftershave. She had to stop with the independence crap and settle down with him once and for all. He'd waited long enough. She didn't need to go to work, that was for him to do. He would take care of her and she would take care of him, the way a woman should. That's how it was going to work from now on.

I screamed at him that he had become an over-bearing, possessive moron, and I couldn't live like that. Then, I stormed into the night in a fit of rage. I didn't stop to hear him call out my name or his excuses as I ran, on auto pilot, not thinking about the direction I was going. If he really wanted to find me, he'd know where to look. Or would he? I had to admit, after six years, I'd recently begun to wonder if Jase had any clue about me at all. Things hadn't been right with us for a while, I knew that, and I'd been thinking of breaking up with him. But he'd always been part of me, and I couldn't bring myself to let go, desperately clinging to the idea that one day MY Jase would come back to me. Not this jealous, control freak, that had to know my every move and barely let me out of his sight. I don't know when or why he became that way. Maybe it had always been there, hiding subtly under the surface. I just knew he'd changed, and I couldn't carry on like that.

I huffed to myself and began to rummage through my pockets for my gloves. Damn, it was cold. No gloves. Of course, I always forget my gloves. It was a running joke among my friends. They all bought me gloves for any occasion that came up. Christmas, birthday, Sundays! My brother religiously carried spares and a couple of my friends were forever giving me theirs to wear. Because "Callie always forgets her gloves."

It wasn't until I registered how cold my hands were that I noticed the snow had gotten considerably heavier. I could no longer see the ground in front of me. I looked up, turning, realising with a sigh of relief, that I was outside Greg and Dana's front door. I lived on the other side of town and common sense, plus my over-protective brother's lectures, told me I ought to get inside. The snowfall was rapidly becoming more blizzard like and before long I wouldn't be able to see my hand in front of my face. Greg and Dana were two of my oldest friends, they would be more than happy to let me in at this time of night, to crash on *their sofa. Ha! Dana would probably turn into some girly sleepover from hell, especially when I told her about my fight with Jase. I could deal with that for one night. I lifted my hand to knock on the door and Jase's voice hollered behind me.*

No!

I ran again, towards the woods. The snow covered the exposed tree root and I never saw it coming. I never saw the man, or the rag either. I never saw anything after my world went black.

I woke with the remnants of a scream on my lips and sat bolt upright in bed. Looking around the room, frantically, I grabbed at my wrists, checking for chains.

"Hey, it's alright, Cal. You're at home. You're safe. It was just a dream," my brother crooned in my ear. I struggled to gain control of my shaking body while he held me and rocked me gently in his comforting arms.

The nightmares began exactly one week after my escape. I'd wake with the metallic taste of blood in my mouth, the scent of chloroform in my nose, aching and drenched in sweat, like I'd fought a battle in my sleep. Cameron or Jase were always there to pull me from sleep and hold me afterwards. They whispered soothing words to me and told me I was safe until I calmed down.

I wasn't safe. No woman was safe. Because *he* hadn't been caught. The police searched the house and had watched it constantly since my escape, but they'd learned nothing about him. They couldn't even find any records of who owned the place. Every trace of ownership had been erased from existence. It was just a derelict shell, left to ruin. They coated my house in dust while looking for fingerprints, or anything at all, that might give away the fact that he'd been there. Cameron attempted to hide that from me, but I already suspected myself. How else had he known so much about me, right down to my clothing size, unless he'd been in my house? They found nothing. He disappeared without a trace. No more women were taken. No more women were killed. Perhaps, that should have soothed me, made me feel safer, but it didn't. Nothing did. Because it didn't matter that the killings had stopped, he was still out there, and I knew in my gut that one day he would come back for me.

In the weeks and months after my abduction, I did everything I could to make sure my brother and my friends didn't suffer because of my darkness. *"How are you?"* fast became my most hated question, but I answered them when they asked. I never gave them everything. That wasn't theirs to suffer. They needed to hope that I would be okay. So, I gave them that hope, when hope was really a punishing bitch who had sentenced me to life, when I should have died with the others. I dutifully talked to the counsellors because it was what was expected of me, but I never felt as though it helped. It couldn't change the fact that I would remain under his control until he decided to end it. Nobody else could take that away. Only he could make that decision.

I allowed them all to think I was getting better. When I look back, I'm not sure I ever really fooled them, but we played the game. For a while, I even felt like I was winning. They did what they could to keep things normal for me. Each one of them going out of their way to make life fun and happy, to distract me from the fact that he was still out there. Maybe they were distracting themselves too. I'm sure it played on their minds, as well as mine.

Jase reluctantly went back to work a few days later, after refusing to leave my side while I was in hospital. We didn't speak about the argument or about the problems we had in the months that had led to that night. We simply fell back into our routine; we were together, just like we always had been. Not that I was complaining, the old Jase was back — mostly. The one I'd known and loved all my life. Apparently, my being tortured by a serial killer, almost dying of hypothermia, and overdosing on chloroform had brought him to his senses. He was still full of talk about our future. He chatted incessantly about how he was never going to lose me again, and how we were going to have our very own happy ever after, but the over-bearing, possessiveness was gone. He was determined to spend his life making me happy.

I didn't want the things he was promising, but the darkness had taken over me and I hadn't argued. I didn't have it in me. Deep down, I knew nothing about our relationship had been resolved. Those Neanderthal ideas came sneaking back in bit by bit, when I was too wrapped up in my darkness to notice. So, I clung to Jase as the cracks formed, desperate for comfort, for something I knew, to pull me from the gloom. He had always been there, and I wanted that familiarity. I needed him. I knew it was selfish and bad for us both, but I couldn't let go. At least, not yet.

CHAPTER TWO

CALLIE

ONE YEAR LATER.

I was running again. moving as fast as my legs would carry me, through the freezing January night. You'd think a girl would have learned her lesson. Not this one. I let him back in and here I was, storming along the same street, fuming once more, after another confrontation with Jase. Only this time, it was different. This time, there was no argument. I didn't stick around long enough for an argument. This time, I'd arrived at his place after work and found he wasn't alone. No, my wonderful boyfriend was naked, with one of our best friends, and neither of them were holding anything back!

Jason Montgomery. I'd thrown away another year of my life on him. Conned myself into thinking he'd fixed me. Picked up all my pieces, put me back together, and sealed all the cracks. He hadn't. He'd covered them with tracing paper and masking tape, so they were almost gone, almost unseen, but never really that far from the surface. I knew only I could seal them, but I'd spent the last year fooling myself into thinking Jase could do it for me. My cracks were still there. My darkness was ever present.

I blocked out the shouts that chased me through the snowstorm. A glance at my clothes told me I wasn't dressed for the weather and a flash of déjà-vu hit me. I halted, skidding on the snow. Slush and ice flew up, drenching my jeans and panic threatened to floor me. I turned on the spot. The exact spot where it had all gone wrong last time. The place where I'd changed direction because of Jase's shouts and gone running into the hands of a maniac. *No!* This wasn't going to happen again. *He* was gone. *He* wasn't here anymore.

Doing my best to calm my breathing, I knocked on Greg and Dana's front door. I thumped loudly with my closed fist, knowing that they had to hear through two doors. I leaned back, to look at the windows, trying to see if there were any lights on inside. The house they bought when they got married was actually an enormous old barn at the edge of the woods. It was in complete disrepair and needed a lot of work to make it even remotely habitable. Through their own blood, sweat and tears (and a fair amount of mine and Jase's too) they turned it into two luxury apartments, one upstairs and one down. Their intention was to rent out the upstairs loft type dwelling as a second income. The entrances to both places were in a hallway just inside the main front door. They hadn't yet gotten around to fixing up separate doorbells.

"Dana?" I bent to lift the letter box and called through it. "Dana, Greg? Are you guys there? I need you to let me in!"

"CeeCee!" Jase called me from further down the street. *Shit!* He'd heard me. I thumped incessantly on the door.

"Please be home, please be home, please be home," I chanted to myself, as Jase's running footsteps thumped on the snow-covered footpath.

THE TEACHER

She stops suddenly, gathering her wits about her. She gets her bearings and I know she has remembered herself. She will not, much to my disappointment, put herself in further danger this evening. She hammers on a door, calling out and looking around her, anxious and wary of the dark. If only she would realise what she is to me. How important she is. Nobody means more to me than her. Without her, there is no reason for my work, she is the muse behind the artist.

My chance is gone for tonight. No matter, I can wait. After all this time, it will be special when we are reunited. Not that we were ever parted, not completely. Next time, I will reveal my identity to her. She took that joy from me before. She will know my story and the part she has played in my voyage. In reality, it is our story. She will know how her family influenced my craft and gave my life lessons more meaning than I ever imagined possible. I am not only the monstrous creation of my mother; I am the culmination of years of destruction. She will learn every intricate connection in this cursed town.

My attention is diverted from my lady, when her flame haired friend curses loudly and slams the door behind her. Turning to spit at the closed door, she stomps off into the night. Such a dirty mouth. She is vulgar and loud, like the others. This one needs to be taught how a real lady behaves. As luck would have it, I have room for another student, and it has been some time since I used my skills for teaching.

I follow her, silently...

CALLIE

I lifted my hand to bang on the door again, but never made contact. The door opened and I fell through, collapsing in a heap at a pair of bare feet.

"Fuck!" I mumbled, getting to my feet, and brushing the snow from my saturated jeans. My dad had always despaired at my foul language when he was alive, but my mum had been as bad, so there wasn't really much he could say. I liked to swear. "Greg listen, Jase is going to be here any minute, you can't let him in. Oh—" my words trailed off when I finally looked up at the figure in front of me. "—you're not Greg."

I was rendered mute, as my eyes clashed with those of possibly the most beautiful man I had ever seen. In my defence, I was pissed off with my boyfriend, not blind. There was something in his eyes though. A darkness that was recognised instantly by my own. I saw it only fleetingly, before the barrier went up, but it couldn't be mistaken, not when I was so familiar with it. There was definite flicker of recognition from him too. He saw my darkness in that spilt second, when my guard was down.

"No," he answered, his mouth forming a cocky smirk. "I'm not Greg."

He blatantly looked me up and down and I quivered under his gaze, my stomach somersaulting like a schoolgirl's. He curved his body around me, to close the door against the blizzard outside. His arm brushed against my shoulder and I didn't sniff him. I truly didn't, but his masculine scent didn't help with my loss of speech. No word of a lie, he smelled bloody amazing. Like the air after a storm, clean and fresh, with a subtle hint of chocolate on his breath. Let me tell you, when a man smells like chocolate, a woman is going to stand up and take notice.

I can only imagine what I must have looked like, all covered in snow. I gave myself a quick once over, fidgeting with my jeans and pulling at the black t-shirt with the *"Irish Rover"* bar logo on. Snow coated my hair and I could feel my clothes, wet from the melting snow, clinging to my body. At least the t-shirt wasn't white, that was about the only thing I had going for me though. I'd taken my coat off when I arrived at Jase's, having my own key, and left it in the hallway before going into the living room. That's when I'd seen *them*. In my red haze, I'd left without it.

"Erm, is he here? Greg, I mean, or Dana? Wait, who are you and what are you doing in my friend's house?" I demanded, suddenly realising I ought to question this situation, like the good policeman's daughter that I was.

He could be anyone. Gorgeous men could be raving lunatics too.

He could've had Greg and Dana bound and gagged somewhere, ready to kill them and wear their skin as a memento. *Okay, breathe.* My own experience plagued my mind so much that I exaggerated every scenario I found myself in. Or maybe, I just read too many books. Hmm, are too many books really a thing? *Focus, Callie!*

"I could ask you the same question," he replied.

He was still smirking. His mouth kicked up at one corner and his eyes sparkled with amusement at my expense. I balled my fists, digging my nails into my palms and decided I was going to wipe that smirk off his pretty face. *Arrogant much?* Who did he think he was? Standing there, all bare foot and smouldering, in his navy blue, checked pyjama pants and a faded *Rolling Stones* t-shirt, with the sleeves cut off. The shirt showed off his perfectly toned arms and the low sides gave a glimpse of his obviously muscled torso. His hair was all messy and sticking up in different directions, like he'd got out of the shower and just run his hands through it. Not that I was looking, obviously. Although, I might have complimented him on his awesome taste in aging rock bands, if my head had been in the game.

"Are Greg and Dana here? Do you know?" I sighed, deciding to go with it and assume he actually knew them. I would lull him into a false sense of security, then strike while he wasn't looking and rescue my friends. *Yeah, I'm going with the book thing.*

He raked a hand through his dark hair, making it even messier and just a little bit adorable, and glanced towards Greg and Dana's door. "They're not back yet. Some belated New Year's work thing of Dana's, I think. I'm Adam, Greg's cousin."

"Shit, that was tonight." I remembered how excited Dana was when she forced Olivia and me to go shopping with her for *"a most spectacular outfit"* for tonight's celebrations. Dana was a beauty therapist and had been invited to a big event hosted by her bosses, who owned a chain of beauty parlours across the region. She was especially excited because she'd recently been promoted to manager at the salon she worked at, here in town.

I narrowed my eyes and craned my neck to look up at Adam. Greg's cousin. I had a vague memory of meeting two of his cousins when we were kids. They didn't look alike, but an echo of a conversation with

Greg came back to me. He was talking about his cousin, who would be moving into their upstairs place. Something about him taking over from the old police sergeant, at the station in town, where Greg and my brother both worked. *Oh...*

"Adam... um, yeah..." I waved a finger around as though I remembered. "Greg told me about you. I think maybe we met once, years ago..."

"Ok, well, this would be the part where you tell me who *you* are." He raised his dark eyebrows at me. Neither of us got chance to say anything else, because someone called my name and banged on the door.

"CeeCee!" Ugh! The name Jase had called me since we were kids was no longer a comforting sound to my ears. "I know you're in there. Please, baby, we can work this out. It wasn't what it looked like."

I cringed, listening to Jase whine his weak, clichéd defence, through the door. Wasn't what it looked like? So, you weren't actually buried balls deep inside my friend, whose legs were not wrapped around you and locked tight at the ankles? Of course not, my mistake.

Adam reached out a hand to gently lift my chin and gain eye contact with me, a question on his features. I shook my head; silently hoping that he would step into his role as a police officer and not let on that I was there. He nodded once and pointed to the door that led up to the loft apartment.

"Go up," he whispered. "I'll deal with him."

His thumb brushed my bottom lip as he took his hand away and I frowned. Could I trust this man? He was my friend's cousin and a police officer, that had to count for something. Greg was one of the kindest, most genuine men I knew, and I was going with my gut that it ran in the family. Something about Adam put me at ease. I let out the breath I was holding and nodded at him. Jase knocked again, obviously not intending to give up and go away. I felt Adam's hand on the small of my back, when I moved around him to go upstairs. He pulled the door closed behind me, blocking Jase's view of the stairs. When Adam opened the outer door, I paused at the top of the staircase to listen.

"Cee—" Jase began.

"I don't know who you are, mate, but you've got the wrong house."

Adam's deep voice had a serrated edge to it. He was confident and authoritative, letting Jase know in those words that he would take no crap.

"I know she's here. There's nowhere else for her to go. Who the fuck are you?" Jase growled, angrily. "Where's Greg? Is she hiding in there with Dana?"

"I'd watch your tone if I were you," Adam warned, his own tone eerily calm and focused. It was far more threatening than Jase's angry growls.

"Look, I just want to find my girlfriend. We had a stupid fight and she ran away from me."

"Running away tends to suggest she's scared of you," Adam stated, dangerously. "Did you hurt her?"

"What? No! I'm worried about her. She's probably in there right now, tearing me to shreds with that friend of hers. You know what women are like." I could imagine him standing there, a hand on the back of his neck, the way he did when he was stressed or irritated.

"It's late to be banging on doors and yelling in the street, don't you think?" Adam responded, sounding bored.

"I don't give a shit what time it is. I need to talk to CeeCee. Can you just go and get her?" Jase's temper flared. I heard it in his voice.

"I recommend you go home and calm down, before you do something you'll regret." Adam remained completely calm.

"Is that a threat?" Jase fumed.

"No, it's a warning. Sergeant Adam Butler, just taken a position at the local police station. I don't think we've met." Adam's air of confident dominance sent thrills though me that I should not have been feeling.

"Fuck!" Jase groaned. "Look, I don't want any trouble."

"Well, that's fortunate, because I won't put up with trouble in my town," Adam stated.

"I just really need to see my girlfriend, right now."

"Not going to happen," Adam told him, with finality.

Silence and what I assumed, not being able to see them, was a stand-off, ensued. Then I heard the front door close and the sound of bare feet padding up the wooden staircase. I wrapped my arms around my waist and moved towards the huge floor to ceiling windows at one end of the loft. They overlooked the woods beyond. I loved those woods. Jase and I had spent hours walking in them with his family dog when we were love-sick teenagers, desperately trying to grab alone time.

We officially got together since we were sixteen. For seven years, I believed there would never be anyone else for me. Jase and I had known each other all our lives. We grew up as neighbours, just toddlers when his family moved in next door to mine. When were five, he held my hand because I got upset during our first day at school. When we were eight, Jase gave me a plastic ring from a Christmas cracker, and told me he was going to marry me one day. When we were ten, he went on holiday with his family, and brought me back a necklace made from string and shells he'd gathered on the beach. When we were twelve, he started to sneak in my bedroom window at night, and we watched movies, and talked in hushed voices. When we were fourteen, he started to hold my hand at every opportunity he got. When we were sixteen, he officially asked me out and called me his girlfriend. When were seventeen, we gave our virginity to each other and promised to love each other forever. For seven years, we had been together as a couple; as friends, three times that. Seven years of my life just gone.

"So, can I assume you're CeeCee?" Adam's gravelly voice sounded behind me.

"Callie actually," I sighed, turning towards him. Adam cocked his head to one side and raised an eyebrow at me, that questioning look again. I shrugged. "My name is Callindra. Everyone calls me Callie or Cal. Well, mostly. Everyone, except Jase. When we were like, three years old, he couldn't pronounce Callie. It came out Cowie and it made me cry. So, our parents taught him to call me CeeCee, because my middle name begins with a C too. He never stopped. Sorry you asked?"

"Not at all. Hot chocolate?" Adam flicked the kettle on without reacting to my ramble.

Taking a mug from the draining board beside the sink, he washed it out and set it down next to the kettle. Then he disappeared, through the floor to ceiling *Union Jack* curtain covering the hallway, that I knew led to the bedroom. After a couple of seconds, he came back out, holding a navy sweatshirt and a pair of grey jogging bottoms.

"Here, feel free to use the shower to warm up and put these on. Your clothes are soaked. Bring them back out and I'll throw them in the dryer." He held out the clothes towards me.

"I should go," I said, hurriedly, unable to hide the flush that reddened my cheeks. "I appreciate your help. Really, I do, but I should leave you in peace."

"Nope," he said, shoving the clothes at me, compelling me to take them as he towered over me.

"Nope?" I raised my eyes to look at him, grasping at the clothing, and hugging them to my chest before they fell to the floor.

"Nope." He smiled and it lit up his face for a split second, the quickly fell away again. I wasn't staring. Well, maybe a little bit. "I can't let you go anywhere in this weather, it's not safe."

He was still in police mode; all serve and protect. Seriously, I had enough bossy males in my life to last me a lifetime. I grew up as one of the boys, joining in on equal terms. Once we hit our late teens, it seemed all the men in my life caught the protective bug. As much as I loved them all, one more wasn't going to fly.

"I'm not staying here!" I shivered and his smile returned, becoming a grin, like he found my attitude cute.

"You're freezing and I'd be a shit copper if I let you go back out there. I'm *not* a shit copper! You have my word, you're safe. I'll even show you my warrant card, so you know I'm who I say I am. Change your clothes, drink the hot chocolate I'm going to make for you, warm up. When Greg and Dana get back, you can go downstairs and spend the night with them." He dropped heaped spoons of chocolate powder into the mug, not looking up from what he was doing. What he said was how it was going to be, he was confident of that.

I huffed and he chuckled to himself, while I made a show of stomping away, and locking myself in the bathroom. He was right, I knew he was. It was already past midnight. Greg and Dana wouldn't be out much longer, I'd go downstairs then. Plus, my only route home took me past Jase's place and I wasn't ready for that. Relinquishing control, I quickly peeled off my wet jeans, pausing when I realised my mobile wasn't in the back pocket, where I normally stashed it. There was nothing I could do about it, so I took off my t-shirt and pulled on Adam's clothes. They were huge on me, obviously. The bottoms were way too long in the leg for my 5'2 frame. Thankfully, they had a drawstring waist and I could tighten them. They were still loose, but they wouldn't fall around my knees when I walked. I rolled the cuffs up at the ankle for good measure. The vintage *Nike* sweatshirt practically hit my knees, but it was warm and soft, and it smelled good.

An overwhelming sense of comfort and security swept over me. I instinctively knew I was safe with Adam. The way he'd got rid of Jase, coolly and calmly, without even needing to know what was going on, made me feel at ease. I was a naturally strong person, especially after what I'd been through in the past. I fought my own battles and stood on my own two feet, but after the night I'd had, I figured I was entitled to a little bit of damsel in distress syndrome.

"So, Callie? Callie what?" Adam asked, doing a double take when I came back into the living room.

He liked seeing a woman wearing his clothes. The way his eyes intensely raked up and down my body told me as much. Working in a pub for the last few years had given me quite an insight into human behaviour. Adam owned me with a look, drinking in every detail and branding me where I stood. The whole *"she's wearing my clothes"* thing was one of those male fetishes I would never understand. I looked like a toddler playing dress up in her dad's tracksuit, but I liked the way he looked at me.

"Wilson," I supplied, pretending not to notice his scrutiny, and turning to look around the loft.

I hadn't been up there since I helped Dana with the last of the decorating. A cricket bat, a baseball cap, a box of vinyl records, and a few other personal additions told me he'd begun to make his own mark on the place. The empty shelves we put in the living area now held a handful of books. I itched to run my fingers over the spines and find out who he read. Was he a guns and bombs, war stories man, or did he read the classics, maybe he preferred sci-fi? Or dinoporn, I'd heard that was a thing now. *Please don't let him read dinoporn.*

Dana and I decided to leave the red brick walls mostly bare, thinking it looked cool. On the wall behind the TV, however, we'd hung a bunch of American road signs and other memorabilia that we found in mine and Cameron's attic. My mum had collected it all on her travels. There was a *Las Vegas* sign, a *Coca Cola* one, and a *route 66* road sign too. A stab of pain ran through me with the memory of my mum and her obsession with all things America. I could have done with a hug from my mum that night.

"I thought I'd heard your name mentioned somewhere else today. You're Cameron's sister," Adam stated, nodding to himself. He made no indication of whether he knew more than that. I ought to have realised he'd already met Cameron. That meant there was a good chance he did know a few things about me.

"Yeah, that's me," I answered, quietly.

"Take a seat." He indicated the brown, leather sofa. It rested on a large, Aztec patterned rug, in the middle of the room. In front of the sofa, sat a coffee table that Greg had made from disused pallets, and we both moved towards it. "I met Cam today, he couldn't stop talking about his little sister."

"Little? Is that what he said? I'll give him little! We're bloody twins! Twenty-two minutes between us and he thinks he can claim older brother status. I don't bloody think so!" I blustered, before taking a breath. "So, you're his new boss?"

Adam laughed at my mini rant. "Technically, I'm his boss, but I prefer to think of us as a team. I'm pretty sure he wouldn't want you running around, alone and upset, in the middle of the night. Especially not in this weather. Not after—" his voice trailed off and his eyes met mine, uncertain. *Yep, he knew.*

"It's fine, what happened to me is no secret. You would have to know about it, I suppose. This is your town now and you work with my brother. Even if you didn't, you'd have heard about it sooner or later, around here. But for the record, I'm not upset. I'm fucking angry!"

Adam got up and grabbed a bottle of brandy, from a cupboard in the kitchen. Sitting back down, he unscrewed the cap and splashed some into the mug of hot chocolate.

"Aren't you having any?" I asked.

"There's only one cup in the place at the minute. I haven't had time to shop for that kind of thing yet," he explained. I hadn't spoken to Greg or Dana for a few days, so I didn't know when he arrived, but he obviously hadn't been there long.

I picked up the cup and took a sip before passing it to him. "It's a big cup, we can share."

A hint of a smile quirked at the corner of his mouth and he took the cup. His fingers, brushing against mine, shouldn't have made my stomach flip in the way they did. I think he felt it too, because he snapped his eyes up to meet mine when we touched. We both looked away as quickly as we'd looked up.

"Do you need to ring Cameron?" he asked, after taking a sip and handing the cup back.

"I think I dropped my phone, somewhere out there in the snow." I shrugged and waved my hand around indicating outside.

Technology and I weren't exactly bosom buddies. I lost mobile phones frequently. Sometimes, I forgot I even owned them. That was when I could be bothered to figure out how they worked. Cameron was forever nagging me about it. Texts and calls were my limit, anything beyond that and I was clueless.

He reached across to the coffee table and slid across his own phone. "Use mine. His number is in there."

"Nah, it's ok. He'll want an explanation for me not being with Jase and when I give it to him, he'll flip his switch and go looking for him. Best he doesn't find out until tomorrow. He wasn't expecting me home after work tonight, so he won't know any different if I stay with Greg and Dana."

Adam nodded. "Jase won't try and call him, to find out where you are?"

"He wouldn't dare. I mean, they're friends, but Cam is over-protective where I'm concerned. Jase wouldn't go to him over this. He wouldn't want to have to explain why I ran off and left him."

"Understandable. Cam being over-protective, I mean. Feel like talking about it?" He moved closer to me on the sofa when I handed him the cup of hot chocolate. I knew his eyes were searching mine for that hint of darkness he'd recognised in them earlier. He was curious, but my shutters were up, and they were staying up.

"There's not much to say. I caught my now very much ex-boyfriend, going at it with one of my so-called friends. I got mad and ran out of there. Found myself here, thought Greg and Dana would be home, hammered on the door, fell at your feet," I summarised quickly.

He flashed a quick grin at my rambling. "You don't have to make light of it. It's got to hurt."

"I'm not about to go dumping all of my crap on you. I don't know you. You might be Greg's cousin, and I trust him and Dana with my life, they're like family. So, yeah, that pretty much makes you family too, that's kind of how we work around here, but we don't know each other yet. You're probably sitting here, wondering how the hell you ended up with a crazy woman sitting on your sofa, in the middle of the night. And now I'm rambling. I do that. Just tell me to shut up." I looked up, to find him smiling down at me. He reached out, as if by instinct, his fingers tucking my snow-soaked hair behind my ear and away from my eyes.

"I'm sorry you had to see that tonight, Callie," Adam said, quietly, showing me a flash of his own darkness again. He knew pain. Pain that he carried with him, papering over the cracks it formed in the same way I did.

"Thanks, but it's okay. It's kind of been a long time coming. If it hadn't been for the whole *kidnapping by a serial killer* thing, we likely would have broken up a year ago," I told him, in the laid back, nonchalant manner I'd perfected since the darkness came.

"So, it's over?" His fingers trailed to the end of the strand of hair he'd lifted.

"Hmm?" I murmured, distracted by his touch.

I didn't feel an urge to flinch away from his touch, in the way I still did with my friends sometimes. Occasionally, I even pulled away from Nick, who was my closest friend. The men in my life had perfected the art of subtle, slow movements around me, so as not to spook me and send me tumbling into a memory I didn't want. There was a sense of familiarity about Adam, about us, like old friends reuniting after a long separation. Perhaps, it was the knowledge that we were both enclosed in darkness, that we both had malfunctioning cracks, that should have let the light in, but didn't. Could you recognise something like that in a person and bond with them so quickly?

"Jase? Is it over? Or, will he turn up on your doorstep, with chocolates and flowers, begging forgiveness?" Adam asked, passing the cup back. His eyes never left mine, both of us searching, knowing the darkness was beginning to tie us together somehow.

"If he does, he'll prove once and for all, how little he actually knows about me." I shook my head, breaking the intense eye contact. "No, we're done."

"Not a hearts and flowers type of girl, then?" he asked, smiling, and trying to make light of the situation. He was distracting me. Over the last year, I'd become an expert at recognising such techniques and perfected a few of my own.

"I just think it's a no brainer. Every girl likes chocolate and flowers, right? Like there's nothing more to a woman than that. It requires zero thought on the man's part. I mean, if you're going to do it, at least take the time to find out her favourites." I held out the cup.

"You finish it." He grinned cheekily, flashing his perfect teeth at me. "So, what does it take to win the heart of the lovely, Callindra Wilson?"

"Know me," I stated.

"Explain?" he asked, curiosity in his tone.

"Well, notice things about me. Simple things. Like, what makes me laugh. How I drink my tea. My favourite books. How I always, *always* forget my gloves. Notice the things I love doing but never make time for and help me to make sure I do them."

"Like what?" He bent his leg and turned slightly towards me, resting his elbow on the back of the sofa. He propped his chin in his hand and gave me his undivided attention.

"Watching the sunset. Looking at the stars. Days out at the seaside. Listening to loud music and dancing like an idiot," I listed. "Finding the perfect gifts for my friends and family. My parents had this rule when it came to Christmas and birthdays. We'd have to give each other something we'd either made, found, or spent no more than a fiver on. It taught us to think about the person we were giving presents to."

"Little things make a big difference?" He reached out to play with my hair again.

"To me they do," I answered with a shrug. "I don't need expensive jewellery and meals in posh restaurants. I want a look, a hug, a kiss, magic words, a squeeze of my hand, *every* day. Diamonds, flowers, and chocolates mean nothing compared to that."

"No champagne and roses then," he concluded, with a nod, and I couldn't help but feel he was filing it away, for future reference.

"I'd rather a man turn up on my doorstep with beer, pizza, and an action movie!" I laughed, looking up at him.

"Woman, is it too soon to fall in love with you?"

"Yes. Entirely. It would never last this early on in our relationship," I answered, with another laugh, feeling comfortable and at ease.

"Ok, I'll wait until tomorrow."

"Tomorrow could work," I yawned.

I instinctively leaned into him when he shifted, to put an arm around my shoulders. The action felt natural, like friends, snuggling up together for a night in front of the TV. There was no awkwardness, just a tranquil silence, as I rested my head on his shoulder and sat in his embrace. My mind stopped racing and became still. My constant paranoia calmed and for the first time in a year, I relaxed.

I woke to find my head resting on a firm, toned chest. I'd slept all night, without a nightmare sending me screaming from slumber in the early hours. Even with Jase in my bed, that rarely happened. Sturdy arms were clamped around my waist. Our legs were tangled together underneath the weight of a blanket, which, I assumed, Adam had thrown over us at some point.

I peeled my eyes open and looked around, groggily piecing together the events of the night before. We'd talked way into the night. I told Adam things I would never have dreamt of telling any other person I'd just met. I never gave details to anyone outside my little bubble and yet, Adam now knew things about me that no stranger should.

He already knew mine and Cameron's parents were killed in a car accident, when we were eighteen— apparently, he and Cameron had quite the bonding session too— and I'd actually spoken freely about it to him. I confided that I couldn't bring myself to walk into their bedroom since they died. I stood at the door, my hand on the handle, but never went in. Their deaths were when the first of my cracks appeared.

He tentatively asked me about the abduction, telling me what he already knew, from Cameron and the police reports. I filled in some of the blanks for him. That was something I only really spoke to Cameron and my closest friends about. Even then, not in detail. The only reason my brother knew as much as he did, was because he'd insisted on being present at all the police interviews that followed my escape.

Adam told me about his decision to move to Frost Ford for a fresh start, after the death of his brother, in a bodged armed robbery. He revealed that he blamed himself for it, because he hadn't been able to get to the scene quickly enough. Since his brother's death, he'd struggled to find his place in the world. No longer feeling at home in the town he'd grown up in, he distanced himself from friends he'd known all his life and lost the joy in his job he'd once had. When Greg called, to tell him about the position opening up in the station here, he'd jumped at it.

We shared parts of the darkness that raged within us both. He acknowledged my cracks, and I his, and they somehow became a thread linking us together. His were different than mine, but no less painful. He told me he buried his darkness deep within him somewhere, so people he cared about couldn't see it. I told him I pretended mine didn't exist, for the people I loved.

Then, it seemed I had sprawled out all over him and used him as a body pillow. Serious *"Oh shit!"* moment pending. I cringed with embarrassment, as I lifted my head and looked up at him.

"Good morning, snow angel."

He was awake, looking down at me, through long, dark lashes. Seriously, no man should have eyelashes that long. His hair was a cute mess of waves across his forehead. Not that I was looking at him that way, obviously, but he did look a little bit gorgeous. Typical man, waking up looking fantastic, when I probably looked like I'd been dragged through a hedge backwards. Not that being dragged through a hedge forwards would have made it any better. I never had understood that saying.

"Morning," I murmured, before attempting to sit.

He loosened his arms, allowing me to move freely. I sat up, stretching, and running my fingers through my matted hair.

"How are you feeling this morning?" He groaned and stretched out his long body, as best he could, on the cramped two-seater sofa.

"I'm fine." I nodded and stood up quickly. "Sorry, for using you as a pillow."

"It was my pleasure." He grinned when he stood and moved to look out of the window. "Looks good out there. The snow has stopped. We never really saw much snow down south."

"I should get going," I mumbled, looking at the floor, awkwardness enveloping me.

"Stay and have breakfast, tea at least. Then I'll walk you to the station. Cam is on duty this morning, if I remember the schedules right." He ran his hand through his hair and moved towards the kitchen.

"Do we have to share a crockery and cutlery, as well as cups?" I attempted to joke my way through the awkwardness he didn't seem to share.

"Afraid so, Angel," he nodded, while muttering to himself about getting the place sorted out. He flicked the switch on the kettle and disappeared into the bathroom.

"You know, we have a ton of extra stuff at the pub, we're in the middle of replacing it all. Nothing fancy, but it's all in good condition. I know Mick wouldn't mind if you took it off our hands," I called towards the closed bathroom door, busying myself by washing out the single mug.

"That's ok, I'll get around to shopping at some point," he said as he came out of the bathroom.

"Seriously, I know how many hours you lot spend at work. Unless you're prepared to let Dana do it for you, you'll never shop. Everything will be pink and fluffy." He grimaced at the thought of Dana shopping for him. We both knew it would be all dainty hearts, furry cushions, and pink flowers. "Besides, we're only going to donate it all anyway. It's boxed up, ready to go, we can just drop it off here instead. I mean, you'll probably spend most of your time eating at the pub anyway or live off takeaway, like Cam tries to get away with. But at least you won't have to share cups with crazy women, who batter your door down in the middle of the night. Unless, you don't want second-hand stuff of course. Shit! Sorry, I didn't think of that." He was smiling at me again and I realised what I'd done. "I rambled, didn't I?"

He laughed, full on threw his head back and laughed, and I loved the sound of it. It made my heart beat a little bit faster, and that fluttery feeling danced around my tummy again.

"You rambled a little bit. It's cute. I have no problem with second hand. I'll take the pub's cast offs, thank you. How do you take your tea?"

"Strong, no sugar, a tiny splash of milk," I supplied.

"Hmm, maybe I'll only ever need one cup when you're here, we seem to have that in common too," he pondered. There's no way I silently high fived myself at the idea that he naturally assumed I'd be there again. I didn't. Cross my heart. *Ugh! Get a grip, Callie.*

"Ha! How about coffee?" I quizzed, conversational wizard that I was.

"Black. No sugar," he answered.

"Same!" I grinned, pulling my dry clothes out of his tumble dryer. "I'm gonna go change."

"Keep the sweatshirt, you'll need it out there this morning," he called after me.

"Thanks!" I closed the bathroom door behind me and listened to him clattering around in the kitchen.

My brother immediately went into hyper protective mode, when he saw me walk into the police station, with Adam. He shot up from his desk, his anxious eyes scanning me from head to toe for injuries. I cut off his questioning instantly and gave him a brief explanation of the events of the night before. Leaving out most of the finer details. I wasn't about to announce to a full police force, small though it may be, that my boyfriend had been sticking it in my best friend. I would give him all of it later, except for the Adam phenomenon, because I wasn't entirely sure what that was about, myself. Dodgy female hormones, I was guessing.

"Can we talk about this later, at home?" I pleaded and pulled off the hat, throwing it on Cameron's desk, in exasperation.

"Oh, there'll be plenty of talking. I know you haven't told me everything Cal," Cameron snapped. He yanked my own gloves from his pocket and took my hands to remove Adam's. "These Adam's?"

I nodded. Cameron pulled me into his arms and squeezed tight. He didn't care that my head was squashed between his chest and his arms. Brothers never care about that stuff, it's funny to them. Short girl problems.

"Can't breathe, Cam," I stammered, slapping him on the back to let him know.

"You should grow some more! Thanks for taking care of her, Sarge." Cameron let go of me and handed Adam his gloves, looking over the top of my head at him.

"Standing right here, Cameron!" I snapped.

"No problem. Listen, go easy on her, mate, she's had a shitty night." Adam lowered his voice and they turned their backs to discuss me, because apparently, neither of them could see me, standing right there. I crossed my arms over my chest and sent them a death glare.

"Morning, Callie?" Greg questioned, when arriving to begin his shift. He frowned at my presence. I visited them at work, but never this early. "Everything alright?"

"Yeah, Greg, I'm okay, just had a crazy night. I met your cousin though. He's pretty cool," I told him, brightly.

"Yeah, he's one of the good 'uns. I always knew you two would hit it off."

"You did?" I gave him a frown of my own. That memory of having met Adam before resurfaced.

"Yeah. How did you ended up running into each other? He only got here yesterday." Greg's light brown hair was gelled back and perfectly styled, so it didn't fall into his eyes. I always felt an urge to stick my hand in it and mess it up.

"I bumped into him while I was looking for you and Dana." Bumped. Ha! I'd practically thrown myself at the man's feet!

"Everything alright, cous?" Greg called over to Adam, his frown deepening, while he removed his coat and gloves.

"All good," Adam confirmed. He and Cameron ended their surreptitious conversation and joined us.

"What's going on, Cal?" Greg wanted to know, but I'd noticed the look of annoyance on my brother's face, when he turned back to face us.

"Cam," I sighed.

"I'm going to kill him," Cameron announced, bitterly and I knew Adam had filled him in on Jase's actions. *Fantastic!*

"Who're we killing, buddy?" Greg was on board with Cameron's murder plot, like a good friend should be.

"Jase fucking Montgomery!" Cameron growled angrily.

"Shit!" Greg groaned, turning to me. "What did he do?"

"Amy," I supplied, simply.

I didn't know what to think about Amy's part in the whole thing. She was supposed to be my friend. What kind of friends went after each other's boyfriends? I was no idiot. I knew Jase got a lot of female attention; he was a good-looking guy. But attention from my friends? That was something I did not want to think about.

"Seriously?" Greg's eyes went wide. Then he was by my side wrapping me up in his arms and planting a kiss on my hair.

"Walked right in on them." My voice was muffled under Greg's arms, but he didn't squeeze as tightly as Cameron, so I could still breathe, and he could still hear me.

"Shit, Cal, I'm sorry. He's an idiot!" Greg muttered and I could hear anger in his voice, he rubbed my shoulders gently, then released me. "Didn't know how good he had it!"

Adam caught my eye. *"Okay?"* He mouthed, the word silently at me. I nodded and smiled, then mouthed the same word back, before he disappeared into his office.

"I'm going home, Cameron," I informed my brother.

I was desperate for a hot bath, my pyjamas, woolly socks, and the tub of *Rolo* flavoured ice cream I had stashed at the back of the freezer. I know, ice cream in January, but it was my comfort food, no matter what the weather was doing.

"Not on your own, you're not," my brother snapped. "Give me an hour and I'll take you."

"Cam, I can walk home by myself," I argued, getting frustrated.

This was how it was going to be for a while. The price I would have to pay for running off into the night, for the second time in a year, and not letting him know where I was. My brother was about to go into over-protective hyper drive. Yes, that's a thing.

"No!" Cameron was adamant. He sat down and turned his attention back to the paperwork on his desk.

"I'll take her home." Adam re-appeared in the doorway, having changed into his uniform.

I looked at him, really looked at him, for the first time. A day's worth of dark stubble graced his chin, shrouding his face in darkness. A long, straight nose led a path to a full mouth, with lips that naturally turned down slightly, making it seem as though he was constantly pissed off. He pulled off the mean and moody look to perfection. And yet, among all the darkness, the brightest, most sparkling, sea blue eyes, shone out at me. He was tall. That, I had already noticed. But then, everyone was tall compared to me. I wasn't quite the *"Oom-pah Loompa"* Nick and my brother would have me believe I was, but I was shorter than average, and Adam was *really* tall. Even underneath his bulky uniform, I could see that his body was lean and toned, but I didn't think it came from hours in a gym. It was different than that. He smirked, catching me blatantly checking him out, and I grinned, guiltily.

"You don't have to do that," I told him, blinking and diverting my gaze to the floor. "You've done enough. "

"I wasn't planning on hanging around the station for long this morning, anyway. I need to get out and show my face around town. We'll pick my car up on the way past my place and drive the rest of the way. The snow ploughs were out early this morning, so the roads are clear." He did the *"what I say goes"* thing again and I found I didn't actually want to fight him over it.

"Thanks," Cameron agreed, as though I had no part in the conversation. Looking from Adam to me he added, "If that dick shows his face, you don't let him in. You're done with him, Callie!"

"He won't. He'll be in hiding for days. You don't need to worry; I've got no desire to speak to him." I leant forward and hugged my brother. He was an over-protective pain in the arse, but he was my over-protective pain in the arse, and I knew I couldn't do life without him. "I'll be fine."

"I'll try and get away early tonight, so we can talk." He returned my hug.

"I'll look forward to it," I groaned sarcastically. Adam rested a hand on the small of my back and steered me towards the door.

"Love you, tiny twin," Cameron called.

"Love you, tall twin," I replied.

We picked up Adam's white Jeep, from outside Greg and Dana's house, and I directed him the rest of the way to my house. I spent the quick journey mentally thanking my lucky stars that Jase's parents no longer lived next door. They moved to a smaller place when he and his brother left home a few years earlier. The house Cameron and I grew up in was a white, wooden fronted place, with steps leading up to a wrap-around porch. It stood out among the old English, red brick houses in Frost Ford. Our mum had taken great delight in the fact that it was different to the rest. I think I inherited my resistance to following the crowd from her.

Adam stood in the doorway, frowning, when he was leaving. We'd wasted an hour, sitting on the mis-matched wooden stools at the island in the kitchen, sharing a single cup of coffee and joking that cup sharing was going to be our thing.

"What?" I asked.

"I'm just trying to figure out how many times I can legitimately turn up here to check on you, before it becomes stalker like. You know, since you lost your phone in the snow, and I can't just take your number, and ring you," he said, thoughtfully, a half smile lighting his features.

"Well, let's see. I think the man who found a crazy woman on his doorstep, rescued her from her ranting ex-boyfriend, gave her his clothes, and made her hot chocolate with brandy, all during a blizzard, has earned himself an open invitation. Don't you?" Although our house already had an open invitation to all our friends, I thought I should make it clear that now included him.

"I'll take that." He grinned. I moved forward to hug him, tiptoeing, and draping my arms around his neck.

"Thank you, Adam," I whispered into his neck. He leaned down and looped his arms around my waist, pulling me tightly against him.

"You're welcome, snow angel." He moved back slightly and planted a gentle kiss on my forehead. "I'll see you soon."

I scanned up and down the street, before I closed the door. The feeling of being watched had begun to sneak up on me again that morning. It had eased in recent weeks, allowing me to lose some of the paranoia I'd carried with me since the abduction. This time, I couldn't seem to shake it.

THE TEACHER

Once again, my lady is surrounded by her friends. They flock to her, desperate to take care of their fragile little bird. I know better. There is nothing fragile about her. She beat me at my own game. That does not take fragility, that takes strength, guts, and determination.

My days will be taken up with teaching for a while. I will not be able to pay as much attention as I would like to my lady's activities. Annoying and yet, the red head bleeds prettily. This pleases me. It appeases my call to teaching and draws me to her. I waited too long to take another student, but it was a necessary break.

The fact that she is so wonderfully unpredictable in life, means that her absence is likely to go un-noticed longer than average, giving me more time to work on her lessons. It is my intention to ensure she knows what she did to my lady is unacceptable. She must learn from this. Pain will be her lesson. She will suffer. And then she will die.

CALLIE

My mind wandered while I waited for Cameron to get home that night. I really needed to make sure he and I talked before he saw Jase. He might be a liar and a cheat, but Jase was clever. If Cameron even threatened to lay a finger on him, Jase would have him on an assault charge before he could blink, putting my brother's career on the line. I like to think Cameron was more sensible than that, but he'd been known to be a bit unpredictable in the past. He and Jase had come close to blows several times over the years, when Cameron thought Jase wasn't treating me properly. Thankfully, the fact that they had been friends for so long, always seemed to stop them from taking it too far. Somehow though, I didn't think my brother classed Jase as a friend anymore.

The last thing I wanted, was for our friends to feel as though they had to pick sides. Things were going to be weird for a while and I hated that it was because of me. I'd caused them enough upset in the last year. There were eleven of us that had more or less grown up together. Cameron, Nick, Jase, and I had been friends since pre-school. We met Greg, Dana, Olivia, and Vinnie at primary school and then Nate, Luke, and Amy at secondary school. We did almost everything together, always had each other's backs, and never let anyone come between us. Now, because of Jase and me, that was all going to change.

My friends all had their own issues. I think it's what brought us together and kept us so tightly involved in each other's lives. We're all broken in some way. The fractured parts cancel out the half-healed parts and somehow it binds us together. That mutual acceptance is what allows us to be there for each other. The knowledge that we can crawl through the dark tunnels of our lives because, no matter what, we will always have each other to lean on.

"I talked to Mick; you've got next week off. He'll be over to see you tomorrow night, after closing. I want you to take a couple of days off college too. I'll keep Jase away from you, don't worry about that—" Cameron began talking at me, the second he came through the door, after work. No, hello, how are you? Forget hyper drive, he'd skipped every stage along the way and forged, full steam ahead, into situation critical. Melt down imminent. *Fanbloodytastic!*

"Cam, I'm fine. I'm not going to fall apart over this. I'm perfectly capable of going to work and college," I argued. "And *you* are going to stay the hell away from Jase!"

Ignoring my Jase warning, he put something in the fridge in the kitchen, and came to sit next to me. He pulled me to him, draping his arm around my shoulders, and spoke with his chin resting on my head.

"When you walked into the station this morning, I knew instantly something had happened to you. All kinds of shit ran through my mind, sis, especially after last year. What if Adam hadn't been there? You had no phone, were you just going to keep running blind? How long before you ended up in the woods to avoid Jase? And you know what kind of fucked up shit that put in my head. You scared the crap out of me, Cal. So, you're just going to have to let me do the big brother thing for a while, okay?"

I resisted the urge to roll my eyes and nodded instead, letting him get it all off his chest. I was well aware that, although he sounded over dramatic, all kinds of alternative scenarios had worked their way into his head, over the course of the day. Cameron knew as well as I did, that the people you loved could be taken away from you in an instant, and it affected him greatly.

"It's not even the break-up, you know? You can handle that. It won't be easy, but it's been a long time coming. Everything came back to me today, every single second of the time you were missing. If Adam hadn't been there last night, I wouldn't have known where you were this morning. I thought you were with Jase and everything was fine. You could have died out there, in weather like that. I wouldn't have had a clue where to start looking. What do I do then? What the hell do I do, without you? You're all I've got left, Callie. *You* keep me going. We both know you're the strong one here. I can't do this life thing without you. I don't *want* to!" He finally stopped for breath, after doing a little rambling of his own.

"I'm sorry, I wasn't thinking. I was so angry. I just wanted to get far away, as fast as possible." I poked a finger into his side. "And hey, you're strong, too. We get each other through this life thing, just like we always have."

Cameron and I had always been close. I don't know if it was a twin thing or just a case of siblings who actually liked each other. The deaths of our parents, in a car accident, had bound us even tighter. At eighteen years of age, Cameron and I were left with nothing but each other to rely on. We had no surviving Grandparents or long-lost Aunts and Uncles. Mum was an only child and Dad's only sister died when we were babies. So, with little other choice, we picked up the pieces of our broken family, and built a life without the people who had brought us into the world. It was hard, there were moments when we wanted to give up, but we kept going.

Cameron went through his training for the police force, following in our Dad's footsteps. Before we lost them, I'd always wanted to travel and go abroad to study. Now, the mere thought of not being near my brother had my heart in shreds and my stomach in knots. Instead, I found a job in the local pub and eventually went to college nearby.

After working at the pub for a couple of years, Mick convinced me to reduce my work hours and go to college part time, to take courses related to the hospitality industry. The mortgage had been paid on our parent's house when they were alive, so, between us, Cameron and I managed to cover the bills and stay in the house after they were gone. Neither of us would have wanted to give it up. They also left us an inheritance in savings accounts that we'd barely touched. Neither of us felt the need to do anything with the money.

For five years, Cameron and I built our lives back up, with the support of a very close group of friends, Jase included. Times like that were when living in a small town, where everyone knew your business, was a bonus. We leaned on each other. When I broke, he fixed me. When he broke, I fixed him. It had been far from easy, but we'd done it and we both knew our parents would be proud of us. I also knew neither one of us could have done it without the other.

"Okay," I sighed, no longer wanting to talk about it. "So, if you're going to put me under house arrest, the least you can do is ply me with take away and alcohol!"

Cameron grinned. "Way ahead of you, tiny twin. The beer is in the fridge and the curry should be here any minute. Wussy chicken korma, for you!"

"Did I ever tell you how awesome you are?" I lifted my head from his shoulder and looked up at him.

"Not today." He grinned, picking up the TV remote and flicking to the movie channels.

"You're awesome." I smiled, snatching the remote from his hand.

"And you're short!" He snickered and grabbed the remote back when I slapped him in the chest.

CHAPTER THREE

CALLIE

Cameron stayed true to his word, keeping me under house arrest in the days that followed my *"sleepover with the hot bobby"* — which was what Olivia and Vinnie had taken to calling it. I tried explaining that nobody used the word *bobby* to refer to police officers anymore, but they thought it sounded good.

My nightmares only granted me one night of respite with Adam and returned with a vengeance. I hadn't slept for longer than three or four hours a night. Mick, my saviour, came over to entertain me with pub gossip, and good whiskey, when he could, but he still had the pub to run, and was currently down his right-hand woman. Olivia and Vinnie both worked, as did Greg and Dana, and my other friends. As for Nick, he'd gone A.W.O.L. He'd called me on the house phone, many times, so I knew he was alive and well, but I hadn't seen him. That was unusual for us. Nick had too many responsibilities to disappear, whatever was going on with him had to be serious.

I spent the days reading my newly bought books, but I was a quick reader and soon ran out. I was up to date on all my college work, after emailing my tutor to get him to send me the assignments I'd missed. I cleaned the house from top to bottom, rearranged the furniture several times, and spent a really fun morning filling three boxes with Jase's stuff.

I boxed up the clothes, and other bits and pieces, he kept in my room, along with his aftershave, the t-shirt I wore to sleep in, photographs in frames, and all the little souvenirs of our relationship. I took the key to his place off my keyring —which had been left on the front porch, with my jacket— and threw it in one of the boxes. That's when the tears came again. Don't get me wrong, I wasn't about to go running back to him, but it felt weird that he wasn't around. Seven years is a long time to be with someone. Especially, when you got together so young and hadn't spent any of your adult life not being one half of a couple. Aside from that, Jase was my friend first. For as long as I could remember, he'd been part of my life. Despite the end, most of my memories of Jase were good ones, and I missed him. All the time alone gave me ample opportunity to mope about him.

His lips met mine and his fingers snaked into my hair, to pull out the band holding my ponytail up. He ran his digits through the dark strands as it fell around my shoulders. I sighed happily and he gently rubbed the spot where it had been gathered, knowing my scalp would ache, from my hair being tied back tightly all day. I leaned into his touch, loving the feel of his hands in my hair. His tongue slipped past my lips and the kiss deepened. I moaned with pleasure, when he slid his other hand underneath my top and undid my bra. His hand found its way around the front and his thumb teased my nipple to a peak. I moaned again; his touch was my addiction.

"Hello, gorgeous," *he greeted me with a smile and a sensuous kiss, when I climbed into his car.*

"Hello handsome," *I answered, when he pulled back to watch me finish what he'd started. Twisting in my seat, I shoved my hands under my t-shirt and fiddled with the straps on my bra.* "I cannot wait to get this thing off, it's killing me!"

The first thing I did when he picked me up each night was take my bra off. There's no better feeling, than taking your bra off at the end of the day, and Jase loved to watch the show. He sat back, with a lop-sided grin on his gorgeous face, his honey coloured hair falling messily into his eyes, as I pulled the straps of my bra down my arms. I reached underneath the front of my shirt to pull the bra out, before stuffing it into my bag. I'd just finished work. It was the middle of summer. I was hot and sticky and couldn't wait to get home for a shower.

"I will never get tired of watching you do that." Jase winked at me and I smiled back, while I buckled my seat belt.

He pulled the car out from the curb and began to drive slowly down the street, tapping the breaks intermittently, every few seconds. A wicked grin appeared on his face and he kept glancing back and forth, between me and the road. I looked at him and stifled a laugh.

"I know what you're doing," I told him sternly, feigning anger.

"Don't give me fake angry face," he said, continuing to tap the breaks, his hazel eyes now fixed to my chest.

"Jase!" I growled, still not really angry.

"I can't help it," he laughed. "They bounce when I do that!" His foot touched the break again and he lowered a hand to his crotch. "See what you do to me? We need to get home. I'm so fucking hard for you, Cee."

"You wouldn't want me right now, I'm sweaty," I laughed. He continued to drive normally, resting a hand on my thigh, and squeezing lightly.

"We can shower," he suggested, moving his hand higher.

"Hmm, shower sex sounds good," I sighed and opened my legs for him.

"Love you, baby," he said, his hand finding its mark through my jeans and pulling the zip down.

"Love you too," I replied, pushing my hips down in my seat and closing my eyes.

"Pull yourself together, Callindra Cecelia Wilson!" I scolded myself in the mirror, snapping out of the memory.

I hurriedly pulled my dark brown hair into a messy ponytail, deliberately pulling harder than I normally would, to bring my mind back to reality. For a long time after the abduction, looking at myself in the mirror was something I couldn't bring myself to do. I couldn't see my face without also seeing *him*, standing behind me. Thankfully, unlike the nightmares, that hadn't lasted very long, and I studied my reflection now. The scars, from the knife marks on my cheeks, had faded to almost nothing over the last year, and I no longer caked on the concealer to cover them. Minimal make-up had always been my thing and I was glad to get back to it. A few faded white lines covered my arms, and of course, there were the deeper marks on my wrists.

On the whole, I considered myself lucky, to have come out of my ordeal with very few physical reminders. I'd done some damage to my vocal cords, caused through prolonged screaming. It left me destined to spend forever sounding like I had a severe case of tonsillitis. Olivia and Dana assured me it was sexy as hell, but I found it frustrating. Not being able to raise your voice loud enough, to be heard over the music, wasn't ideal when you worked in a busy pub. The doctors told me it would improve over time, but I'd never have my old voice back. He would always have that part of me. Still, I was alive. The others weren't and I tried to focus on that, rather than let myself linger on the rest.

Having looked in the fridge, and found it practically bare, I decided a trip to the supermarket was in order. A girl couldn't live on ice cream and vodka alone. Well, not permanently. So, I pulled up my big girl pants, and decided to go and see Cameron at work, to get the car keys from him. I pulled on black jeans, a long sleeved, grey, off the shoulder sweatshirt, wound a thick black scarf around my neck. I'd do, I shrugged at my reflection. Grabbing my jacket, I shoved my purse and keys in my pockets, and I was ready to go.

Cameron and I shared our dad's old land rover. He'd taken it to work that morning, in an attempt to keep me in the house, and away from *"psycho ex boyfriends"* as he'd put it. I was tired of his caveman routine though and needed to get out of my prison. The sun's rays pushed through the gaps in the clouds, letting the light through. I trudged through the snow-covered streets of Frost Ford town centre, towards the station. Shaking off the feeling of being followed, I stuffed my paranoia, and my hands, into the pockets of my leather biker jacket, because guess what I'd forgotten? The police station was almost opposite Mick's pub, *The Irish Rover*, right in the centre of the High Street. Next door to the pub, was Nick's tattoo parlour, *W. Ink*. He was incredibly talented. His clients booked months in advance and came for miles to be inked by him. The neon in the window was on and I silently reminded myself to hunt him down at some point soon.

A little further down the street was *"Denver & Sons"* the garage belonging to Nate's dad. Nate also worked there, since training to be a mechanic when he left school. He would take over the business completely when his dad retired. Nate and I shared a love of American muscle cars, my mum's influence on my part. A few years earlier, he found an old *Mustang* at a car auction and bought it. It needed a lot of work and he'd completely overhauled the engine and re-sprayed it all himself. It had taken him forever. I smiled and waved, when I spotted him climbing out of the beast, outside the garage. I loved that car as much as he did, she was a beauty. He waved back and made the universal *"call me"* hand signal in the air. I gave him a thumbs up with one hand and pushed open the door to the police station with the other

It was a small, old fashioned looking station. The main reception desk sat at the front and was the first thing you saw when you entered. The pc's desks and filing cabinets were arranged behind it and there was an office to one side. A hallway led off to other rooms and the cells, at the other side. Small town, small police force. It wasn't as though we had a high crime rate to warrant anything larger. As long as you overlooked the whole serial killer thing, obviously. Everyone in town knew each other and each other's business. Even the less savoury members of the community knew not to shit on their own doorstep. I couldn't resist a furtive glance over to the door and what I knew to be Adam's office. His name now proudly graced the glass in the door, and I could hear his muffled voice inside; he was obviously on the phone to someone.

"Hey, Cam, can I get the car keys? We need food, dude," I said, walking towards his desk in the office, at the back of the main reception.

Cameron looked up at me, inspecting me, searching to see if I was okay. I smiled, brightly. With a sigh, he leaned back in his chair, stretching his arms above his head. Then reached down and rummaged around his coat pockets for the car keys.

"You want a coffee, Cal?" Greg stood up from his own chair, opposite Cameron.

"Yeah, I have time," I answered. I perched on Cameron's desk, facing him, and crossing my legs at the ankles. "Anything you want me to get?"

"Usual," he shrugged. "I can shop before I come home though, you don't have to. You look tired, sis."

"Not sleeping will do that to a person."

He didn't need to know how bad it was. Of course, there wasn't much fooling him. He knew better than most, being the one who came running, when he heard my screams in the night, and talking me back to reality when the nightmares took hold. What he didn't know, was that I never went back to sleep after I told him I was fine and ushered him back to bed. I laid awake, mind racing, until the sun came up. Closing my eyes only brought visions of the darkness. The thick, black, poisonous darkness, swimming through my veins, searing me from the inside.

"What's keeping you awake?" Greg asked over his shoulder, as if he didn't already have a good idea.

"Life and nightmares. All the good stuff," I supplied, taking the cup of black coffee from Greg.

He put Cameron's usual white and as much sugar as you can fit in the cup on his desk, before sitting back at his desk with his own drink and spinning his chair to face me.

"You should drink camomile tea before bed. Dana swears by it," Greg offered helpfully, folding, and turning a piece of paper on his desk repeatedly.

"I prefer hot chocolate, with a generous slug of brandy!" I winked at him.

We were laughing when the door to Adam's office opened and he stepped through. Oh, did he know how to wear a police uniform. Tall, dark, and handsome just wasn't a big enough description for this man. His scowl brightened when he saw me, and a smile replaced it.

"Angel," he greeted me, and I didn't swoon at the open use of the nick name. Nope. Not a swoon in sight. He didn't attempt to hide the term of endearment, nor did he show any embarrassment in using it. It was what he had decided he was calling me, and he didn't care who knew, or what they thought.

"Adam," I smiled back, sipping my coffee, and failing miserably at hiding the fact I was eyeing him up.

"Are you drooling over my cousin, Callie?" Greg teased, grinning at me.

"I'm heartbroken, Greg, not blind," I admitted with a shrug.

Greg laughed and threw a paper aeroplane at me. I chuckled as it hit the top of my head and skidded to the floor. Cameron bent forward to pick it up and threw it back at Greg. Adam winked at me, ignoring their antics, and perched on the edge of Greg's desk. He crossed his arms over that rock-hard chest of his and I wondered what he looked like without the shirt. Did he have a six pack of abs and those V lines, that made ordinarily intelligent women's brain cells turn to mush? Our eyes locked and held for what seemed like an eternity, the rest of the world paling into insignificance around us. Then my brother's voice snapped me out of my little dreamscape.

"You know what you need to get?" Cameron poked me in the leg with the car key.

"What?" I snatched the key and pocketed it in my jacket, before he could poke me again.

"A new phone!" He raised his eyebrows at me; he'd been on at me for days.

"Yeah, I suppose I should." Another paper aeroplane hit me, and I smirked at Greg.

"And I'll super glue it to your arm, so you can't lose it next time you decide to go off on a little adventure, in the middle of the night!" Cameron took out a pair of my gloves from his desk drawer. "Better yet, I'll put a tracking app on it."

"What's a tracking app?" I held out my hands, to let him put the gloves on me, switching the coffee cup from hand to hand, as he did so. Then, he flicked my leg. "Ouch! You're such a bully, Cam!"

"Right, you look bullied, don't you?" he said, blandly. "A tracking app is to let me know where you are, so you can't go running off again. I should have put one on you years ago."

"You want dinner tonight?" I asked, deciding it was time to leave.

Pushing up from the desk, I handed my barely touched cup of coffee to Adam. He took it and drank, his eyes not leaving mine over the top of the cup. Nope. Not swooning. I mentally drew a no swoon zone around myself and built the walls really, really high. Impenetrable!

"Yeah, I'll be home," Cameron replied, as I walked towards the front of the station.

"See ya's later," I called over my shoulder.

Greg giggled like a girl, when another paper aeroplane hit the back of my head. I spun on the spot and gave him a special wave with my middle finger.

"Bye, Angel," Adam's deep timber rumbled behind me. I put a roof on my impenetrable no swoon zone and kept my smile to myself.

"I knew you'd go for her, cous," Greg murmured as I turned my back.

"Don't forget to use your cushion, so you can reach the pedals, Hobbit!" Cameron called.

"Comedian!"

I killed two excitement challenged— and somewhat creepy, when my paranoia snuck out to play— hours wandering around the supermarket. Once home, I changed into red tartan pyjama bottoms, thick, knitted socks, and an old *Guns n' Roses* t-shirt that was my dad's. I collapsed into my favourite armchair, in front of the roaring fireplace, with a tub of strawberry cheesecake flavoured ice cream, and my current book. I was back to feeling sorry for myself.

After the shopping trip, I spoke to Mick. He was ecstatic when I told him there was no way I was taking any more time off work, and that I'd be in next night. Being Friday, it was always a busy shift and I needed that distraction again. Tonight, however, I was a mess. I just wanted to escape into my book with my comfort food and pretend the world as I knew it didn't exist for a few hours. Books were my escape, and escaping was something I did often, since the abduction.

Cameron was pretty easy going about my book hoarding problem. I had hundreds of them, lying around the house, in piles. It used to drive my dad mad. He'd yell at me to pick them up and threaten to throw them out. I always laughed at him, knowing there was no way he would ever do it. Mum would never have let him, because she was just as bad when it came to her own books.

Tonight, I needed that escapism. Tonight, I needed to pretend that

Jase Montgomery had never existed. Never been a part of my life. Never broken my heart in the most horrible way. I just couldn't get him out of my head though. Even my latest book boyfriend, despite being a hot as sin fallen angel with actual wings, just wasn't cutting it for me. Falling into a memory came easy.

Jase and I were in my room, sprawled across my bed on our stomachs, schoolbooks strewn around us. We were supposed to be doing homework. Well, I was. Jase had just thrown his pen at the wall and announced he was done for the night. I ignored him as he began kissing, nipping, and licking his way up the backs of my bare legs. It had been a warm spring day and I was wearing denim cut off shorts. He told me my legs had been driving him crazy all day. He paused, to lick a circle around the back of my knee. I squirmed and giggled. He gave a moan of appreciation in response and continued his way up my leg.

"I should give you a love bite right here." He poked a finger into the flesh of my left bum cheek.

I laughed. "Can you concentrate, please?"

"I am concentrating." I could hear the grin in his voice but refused to turn and look at him. "Concentrating on distracting my girlfriend."

I still got butterflies in my stomach when he called me that, despite having been together almost two years. Seventeen may be young to be in love, but I knew how I felt. Jase was it for me. We were good together and I didn't need anyone else. He trailed his fingers up and down the backs of my thighs lightly.

"Is it working?" His voice was suddenly right by my ear, his hand drifted further up to squeeze my hip, as he bent to kiss the side of my neck.

"No," I lied. "Go and get me a drink."

"In a minute," he groaned and climbed over me, covering my body with his, and tugged gently on my ponytail to get my attention. "Take a break, a sexy break."

"Jay, I need to finish this," I argued, but not doing very well at refusing him.

"Do it later." He pressed his groin into the tops of my legs, letting me know what he wanted.

Since we'd decided, a month ago, to take that final step in our relationship, Jase had become insatiable. Not that I was much better myself. I had a gorgeous, very attentive, and adventurous boyfriend. What girl wouldn't make the most of that?

"Soon," I mumbled and shuffled around on the bed, now well and truly distracted.

His weight shifted and I shrieked, when he playfully sank his teeth into my bum cheek, through my shorts. I whipped my head around to see him climbing off the bed.

"Ten minutes, Cee. I'll give you ten minutes. Then you're all mine." He left the room, smiling like the cat that got the cream. He knew I wouldn't turn him down.

"Alright, twin?" Cameron called, snapping me out of my Jase induced stupor, when he came through the front door. "I brought Adam home for dinner."

"I made lasagne. Hi, Adam." I gestured to the countertop in the kitchen and feigned interest in my book. Our house was open plan and all on one level, so wherever we were, we could still see each other.

"Angel, how are you doing?" I felt Adam's eyes taking me in, looking deeper than he was letting on. Noticing. Seeing the things that others couldn't.

"Fine. I'm fine. You? How're you finding life in Frost Ford?" I rambled, more out of politeness than actually wanting to make conversation.

My memories of happier times with Jase had put me in a sour mood. I put my head back in my book and managed to regain interest, when I realised that I was almost at the end and it was going to be explosive. How could I not have been concentrating on this?

"Good," he answered, nodding, and taking the beer Cameron handed him.

I lifted my eyes from my book and glanced at him quickly. He latched onto my gaze and refused to let go, holding it, and narrowing his eyes at me. He saw the cracks opening. He knew I wasn't okay. I could fool the others, even Cameron, to a certain extent. I could put on a show and let them think I was better than I was. There would be no fooling Adam. He could see straight into the very core of my darkness. There was no hiding from him, and I didn't know how I felt about that.

"Hey, Cal, did you eat?" Cameron asked, rummaging around in the kitchen.

"Hmm? What? Oh, yeah, I ate," I replied, breaking my staring match with Adam long enough to answer.

"Dinner? Only this lasagne hasn't been touched?" Cameron stopped what he was doing to look at me.

"I made it for you." I looked back at my book. I was almost at the end, just a few more paragraphs. Then it happened. The book ended on a cliff hanger. Seriously, who does that? Now I had a year to wait for the next one.

"Oh! Oh! Oh!" I screeched. Adam's head snapped up in my direction.

"We call that a nerdgasm. She has them often," Cameron explained to Adam, who nodded slowly. "Callie, what did you eat?"

"Ice cream," I said, looking at him out of the corner of my eye, to gage his reaction.

"Callie!" Cameron was annoyed.

"What? Ice cream can be dinner. It was strawberry cheesecake flavour. Strawberries are fruit— Cheesecake has cheese— Fruit and cheese can be dinner. I ate dinner," I reasoned, with a shrug.

Adam and Cameron exchanged a look. I don't know what it meant. Probably something along the lines of *"she's hopeless what shall we do with her"* or *"do you want to put her out of her misery or shall I?"* Whatever it was, I'm sure they knew what it meant, I didn't need to.

"Right, I'm heating this lasagne and you'll eat with us. Do you want salad, Cal?" Cameron asked

"Nah, I had fruit," I murmured, sticking my head in my book again, re-reading the end, to make sure I hadn't missed anything.

Cameron muttered something under his breath and Adam laughed. That's when I realised my brother had some kind of man crush thing going on, with his new boss.

CHAPTER FOUR

CALLIE

The fact that they were dead, probably should have rung alarm bells, but I ignored each of the single red roses, that appeared on my doorstep for five days running. I assumed it was Jase's idea of a sick joke. Some kind of symbolistic nod to our dead relationship. I ignored the boxes of truffle filled chocolates too. They went in the bin unopened, lest my brother see them and flip his lid. It was plain to me that Jase was trying to get my attention. If the idiot couldn't remember that firstly, I didn't like milk chocolate, and secondly, my favourite flowers were gerberas, whether alive or dead, then I wasn't giving him my time.

Flowers reminded me of my parent's deaths. The house had been filled with them for weeks afterwards, tokens from well-wishers. I remember the day I lost my shit and stormed around the house, screaming, and shouting that none of it mattered. A bunch of dying weeds would never make a difference. I'd thrown them all out in my fit of rage. Jase was there that day. He'd talked me down. You'd think he'd remember something like that. Although, even if he had remembered those things, I don't think I would have budged. Seven years too late and all that.

Our laughter came to an abrupt halt and Mick's body stiffened beside me. The smile dropped from my face like lead, and my eyes met Jase's familiar gaze, across the bar. It was early in the evening, I was working. Cameron, Adam, and Greg had come in for a drink after their shift ended. We were joking around while it was quiet, mostly my brother and I bantering, while the others laughed at us. It was too early for Vinnie or any of the door staff to be in, so Jase had been able to walk right in without a drama. Not that he was barred, just that Vinnie wouldn't have let him in without a warning, at the very least.

"Say the word, love. His feet won't touch the floor," Mick offered, in his Irish brogue.

"*Okay?*" Adam mouthed at me, eyeing Jase as he walked towards the bar. He winked when I nodded and mouthed the word back.

I *was* okay, until I glanced at my brother's furious expression and my dinner threatened to perform an encore. Cameron was under the impression he'd somehow managed to keep Jase away from the house over the last week. He hadn't called the landline and if he'd been ringing my mobile, I wouldn't have known. Jase stopped opposite me at the bar and leaned towards me slightly, hands in the pockets of his faded blue jeans. He was wearing a grey hoodie, underneath his black, leather biker jacket. His entire outfit screamed bad boy. He knew damned well I loved that look on him.

"Cee, we need to talk," he said, quietly. I blanched at the use of the shortened version of my name. "I've been blowing up your phone all week, babe."

"I lost it," I blurted and frowned, not really knowing why I'd explained myself to him. "I have nothing to say to you. Please stop with the flowers and shit, okay? I don't want them."

"What flowers? CeeCee, look, I've got plenty to say to you, so maybe you could just listen? Let me explain." The irritation is his tone was obvious.

Cameron's head snapped up and he took a step towards Jase. I threw a panicked look towards Mick, who put a hand on my shoulder to reassure me. I knew none of the others would allow anything to happen between Jase and my brother, but it made me nervous all the same.

"My sister said she doesn't want to speak to you, Jase." Cameron glared through his words.

"And *I* said, she can listen!" Jase snapped, his eyes not leaving mine.

I flinched slightly at the threat implied in his voice. I'd never seen Jase act that way before, but a quick glance at Greg and Cameron told me they were both familiar with this side of him. I'd always know he could take care of himself, but he wasn't confrontational. He didn't pick fights. At least, not around me. A complete stranger stood in front of me and it scared me.

Greg stepped up beside Cameron, so that they were obscuring his view of me. "You need to leave, Jase."

Jase looked past them both, at me. "Cee, I made a mistake. A drunken, stupid mistake. Are you seriously never going to get over it? You can't hold one night against me forever, babe. Shit, it wasn't even a night. It was a few minutes and I haven't thought about her since. *She's* not the one on my mind, Cee, *you* are. It's always been you. This is *us*, baby, come on. We're forever."

"Please go, Jase," I said quietly, desperately fighting back the tears that threatened.

I still loved him, I realised it in that moment. Even after what he'd done, I still loved him. There was going to be no quick, dignified demise to our relationship. I don't know how I managed to fool myself into thinking I could just walk away from him. This wasn't going to be easy. We were going to be messy, we were going to hurt, and there was going to be a lot of crying.

"NO!" Jase leaned over the bar, reaching for my arm, but Mick was faster than him. In the blink of an eye, he moved me behind him, placed one hand on the bar and vaulted. He cleared the bar in one fluid movement, and landed in front of Jase, causing him to stagger back a step.

"You're leaving now, Jason. Let's not have any confusion in the matter," Mick said, his voice low and threatening. Jase wasn't short, by any means, but Mick had inches and brawn on him. "This is *my* pub and I don't take kindly to folks upsetting my staff. So, you're going to either walk out of here under your own steam, or I can assist you. The choice is yours."

Jase glared back at him, standing his ground. Adam moved in beside Mick, taller than all of them and intimidating in his stance.

"You heard the man." Adam's voice held the same low, menacing tone that Mick's had.

"You again? What are you, her bodyguard?" Jase snarled.

"Callie has made it clear she doesn't want your company. You need to leave her alone." Adam gave the instruction in no uncertain terms.

"This isn't over, CeeCee. *We* aren't over!" Jase looked at me and I lowered my eyes because if I kept looking at him, I would break. "Will you please just listen to me?"

"How about you listen to me? Carefully, because I don't like to repeat myself." Adam took another step towards him and levelled him with a look. "You fucked up. What you had is gone. She's not *yours* anymore."

"You're not going to come near her again," Cameron added, stepping up beside Adam. "You're not going to attempt to contact her. You're not going to look in her direction. I'll make this official if I have to, Jase."

Realising he was fighting a losing battle, Jase turned on his heel and left without another word. I looked from Cameron to Adam and back again. Cameron was visibly fuming. He bounced on the balls of his feet, hands fisting at his sides. He was seconds away from following Jase and laying into him, and Adam looked as though he wouldn't be far behind. I wiped the tears from my face with the sleeves of my checked shirt and rapidly pulled myself together.

"You can't go after him. Your jobs will be on the line if you even threaten him. You both know that. Please?" I implored them both.

"Okay," Cameron mumbled after a few seconds.

"Adam?" I looked at him, he nodded once, but I got the feeling it was only to placate me.

"And you!" I pointed at Mick. "That thing, where you jumped over the bar? Totally hot!"

"So, that's how it is, I see. He gets totally hot and we get told off like naughty schoolboys? How does that work?" Adam joked.

"Erm...I really don't need to be told I'm totally hot by my sister, buddy." Cameron frowned into his empty glass, as if wondering how it got that way.

"Granted, that would be weird, but thanks wouldn't go a miss." Adam winked at me.

"I'll buy you both a beer to make up for it," I compromised, picking up Adam's empty pint glass to re-fil it.

"Ahem, I was there too!" Greg piped up, a mock look of hurt on his face.

"Yeah, but you're sensible. You didn't look as though you were going to follow him out the door, drag him down a dark alley, and break both his legs." I silently thanked every star in the sky that they hadn't.

"Face actually. I was thinking face," Cameron said, humourlessly, while I poured all three of them a beer.

"So, totally hot, eh?" Mick grinned at me.

"Yeah, Micka, totally hot," I laughed and took a sip from Adam's beer when he pushed it towards me.

I woke late the next morning, with a pounding headache. Staying after work with Mick and the others hadn't been my best idea. I did manage to get a few more hours of alcohol induced sleep than normal, before the nightmare kicked in though. I roused in the night, convinced there was someone outside my window, but wasn't about to get out of bed and check.

Cameron came running, locking my window, and assuring me there was nobody out there. I don't know how he always managed to anticipate my nightmare. He was almost always there before I woke myself from them. Maybe it was a freaky twin thing. Maybe I made a lot of noise when I had the dreams. Whatever it was, I felt bad that he was now getting the brunt of my nightmares.

Jase had taken a lot of that pressure off him, being the one I spent almost every night with. He was good at it too. He told me it was his job to keep me safe, that he had failed me once, and would never allow anyone to hurt me again. Instead, he had ended up being the one to hurt me. Now, he was gone, and my poor brother was getting less sleep than me. Cameron never complained or made it seem like a burden. He just pulled me close to him and whispered soothing words, until I calmed down. He must have been exhausted.

I stumbled from the kitchen, where I'd made myself a mug of strong black coffee, surprised by a knock on the door. I stopped in the middle of the room, staring at the door. It was odd, because none of our friends ever knocked. They just yelled *"Incoming"* and walked right in.

I wondered if Jase would knock now, or just come in, and suddenly wished Cameron hadn't already left for work. I opened the door, cautiously peeping through the gap, and breathed a sigh of relief when I saw Adam. Not that Adam improved my morning mood. My parents often said I was evil in the mornings. Cameron was well rehearsed in noiselessly leaving a cup of tea on my bedside table and making sure he was on his way to work, before I surfaced.

There are a few things you should know about me. One, as much as I try to be cheerful and upbeat, morning Callie is not a very nice person. Two, if you turn up at my house, be prepared to take me as you find me. If that means I'm in my pjs, then that's what you'll get. I mean, it's not like I'd answer the door naked. I've just never been one to get stressed because you caught me without a bra, or before I've dragged a brush through my hair. I'm just not that girl.

"Cute," Adam observed, giving me the once over from under hooded eyes.

"Hmm?" I looked up at him, bleary eyed and bad tempered.

"Stripy socks, I like them. And the erm, pyjamas?" He grinned and pointed a finger, waving it up and down my body. "That sweatshirt has never looked better."

I followed the line of his finger and looked down at myself. The sweatshirt I blindly threw on, when I got out of bed, happened to be the one Adam had given me. It was covering my pyjama shorts, making it look as though *all* I was wearing were the knee-high socks, and his sweatshirt. No wonder he looked pleased with himself. I rolled my eyes, instantly regretting it, when the thudding in my head became louder, and my stomach rolled.

"Right," I grumbled, lifting a hand to my throbbing head.

"Aren't you going to ask me in?" he asked, the grin going nowhere.

He was thoroughly enjoying the fact that I was wearing his clothes again. Well, newsflash buddy, I was cold, and your sweatshirt was convenient. It had nothing to do with your smell making me feel all warm and fuzzy. Absolutely nothing. Probably.

"Come in," I said, curtly and pushed the door open, sweeping my arm out, theatrically.

I closed the door behind him, and he followed my yawning, shuffling, grumpy ogress into the kitchen area. Of course, he was once again looking hot in his uniform. Not a hangover in sight for him. He stood, hands in the pockets of his black trousers, inspecting me.

"Everything alright?" I asked, narrowing my eyes, and cocking my head to one side. Needless to say, my patience was not at its strongest in the mornings, and I was in no mood for guessing games.

"Everything's fine. I just wanted to make sure you were okay. After yesterday, with Jase."

"Why do you look like that?"

"Like what?"

"That!" I pointed at him. He frowned, confused. I gestured to myself. "Look at me."

"Believe me, I have been," he murmured, huskily.

"I look like shit! My hair is a bird's nest. I smell like I fell asleep in a bath of whiskey. My tongue feels like the Sahara. I could clean my teeth with bleach today and my mouth still wouldn't feel clean. There's a demon inside my head with a fucking drum kit, and I'm not even wearing my own clothes."

"I like you in my clothes."

"I don't *care* that I look like shit, Adam, that's not the point." I lifted my hands to my hips, giving him an accusatory look. "Why aren't *you* hungover? Because I'm telling you, if you're one of those special unicorns who doesn't get hangovers, I'll have to re-evaluate our friendship."

"I stopped drinking," he admitted with a smile of realisation. I hadn't noticed him stop, but then, I *had* been wasted. "I had to work this morning, needed a clear head."

"So, you *do* get hangovers?"

"Sorry, I don't," he admitted.

"I don't believe this. How can you be this perfect? There has to be something wrong with you!"

"I'm far from perfect, Angel."

"How exactly? Hmm? Tell me!"

"Well, I have really ugly feet." He pointed to his boots. "They're big, and hairy, and my second toe is longer than all the others."

"You've got hobbit feet?"

"Yes," he confessed.

"Good!" I snapped. "What do you want?"

"Well, I'm guessing you haven't bought a new mobile, for me to call you on. So, I thought I'd make the most of that open invitation. Assuming it still stands, of course?" His smile wavered, and I noticed he was fidgeting. He actually looked nervous. Huh, I unnerved Mr Cool. How about that?

I rubbed a hand across my forehead, forcing myself to become fully awake. Morning Callie wasn't being very nice to him. One of my other friends would just tell me to shut up, but he was still being polite. Sighing, I grabbed his jacket sleeve and tugged him over to the kitchen island, where I pushed my cup towards him.

"Sorry, I'm really not a morning person, especially when I'm hungover. Your invitation still stands. It always will."

"I'm glad and I noticed. You hid it well that morning at my place, though." He sipped the coffee, the smile back in place.

"I was using my manners then. We're past that stage now. I mean, I slept on you the first night we met. Literally draped myself all over you and wrapped my legs around you like a body pillow. I don't think we need to be polite anymore. You can tell me to sod off if I'm being a bitch." I met his gaze and managed a weak smile back. His own smile grew at my words and he licked his lips, his eyes flicked to my bare legs. He looked good today, I decided. He did every day, but today he looked extra good. He smelled good too. *Ugh! Stupid female hormones.* I reached down to the shelf under the island, pulled out a box and unceremoniously dropped it onto the counter. "I *did* get a new phone."

"You haven't even turned it on yet." He raised an eyebrow at me, inquisitively.

"I tried." My defence was weak. Actually, it was non-existent. "It's just, I get bored of all that techy stuff, really quickly. I can just about mange to send a text message. I tend to just leave these things lying around, until Cam or Liv take pity on me. It's charged, Cam did that."

"Give it here," he laughed, shaking his head at me.

"Oh, I didn't mean—" I began.

"How else am I going to get your number?" He stopped me before I could finish. "Ringtone?"

"Anything?"

"Anything," he confirmed.

"Doctor Who!" I grinned; ignoring the warm fuzzies that appeared, when I realised Adam wanted my phone number. Because, duh, he was my brother's boss, and I was Cameron's next of kin, of course he wanted my number. *Definitely not a fuzzy moment, Callie!*

"I should have known," he said and asked for the Wi-Fi code.

I watched him tap away at the screen for a few minutes, before telling me he set the *Doctor Who* theme tune as my ringtone, and the *TARDIS* landing for the text message tone. He played them both back to me. Unable to contain my excitement, I clapped my hands in delight and threw my arms around him, announcing he was officially the coolest phone setter upper in the history of ever! I didn't miss the way he buried his face in the crook of my neck and inhaled the scent of my hair, but I didn't acknowledge it either.

We shared coffee and chatted, while Adam continued to fiddle with my phone, downloading the apps that I told him I used. Not that there were many. I had the social media accounts, but I rarely used them. I didn't like all the random messages from people I didn't know. Then there were all those people from school, who never spoke to me back then, and wouldn't speak if we bumped into each other in person now, so were definitely only being nosey online. All my friends were in my life in person and that was the way I liked it.

"Cam says you have nightmares, about the abduction," Adam

ventured. Our heads were bent close together over the top of the phone, his hair brushing my temple.

"I spend my nights chained to a wall, in a dark cellar, while a psycho in a ski mask cuts me to ribbons with a hunting knife. Such fun!" I laughed, sarcastically, reaching out and spinning the phone with my finger.

Adam didn't gasp in shock or pity me. Neither did he chastise me for making light of it, the way most people did when I joked about my dreams. They hated that. Instead, he nodded in understanding and told me about his own nightmares.

"I used to have nightmares about my brother's death all the time. Sometimes, I'd get there in time to save him, only for the gun man to kill someone else in his place. Other times, it's a full-on flashback of the entire night." He placed his hand over mine and stopped my phone spinning action.

"How did you make them stop?" I asked, ready to give anything a try.

"Actually, I think you did." He looked up from our joined hands, meeting my eyes with a thoughtful gaze. I ignored the fact our faces were within kissing distance, even when his eyes strayed to my lips.

"What do you mean?" I frowned, taking my hand from under his and moving back an inch.

"I was still having them every night, until you landed on my doorstep. That night, with you in my arms, was the first full night's sleep I've had in over a year. Haven't had a nightmare since."

"I didn't dream that night either," I confessed. "Maybe we chased each other's nightmares away."

"Maybe. Only I obviously wasn't as good at the task in hand as you were, since yours came back." He looked down at the phone and picked it up, his fingers once again tapping away.

"Well one night's reprieve was better than nothing, believe me." I looked down at my hands, I was now turning the cup in circles. "Best night's sleep I've had in ages."

"I see your darkness, Angel." He put the phone down and reached out again, stilling my hands with his own, and bringing my fingers to his lips, to place a light kiss on them.

"I see yours too," I whispered, meeting his eyes with tears in mine.

"Drop the walls. Let me in." His hushed words whispered over my knuckles as he spoke.

"I will if you will," I bargained.

"I'll make you a deal. We both drop the barriers and battle our darkness together." He leant forward, lowering my hand to kiss my cheek.

"Deal." I leaned in to let his lips skim my cheek, pausing for a moment with my forehead resting against his.

His darkness brought light to mine. We became connected through a shared blackness that reminded us to live in the light. It was a deal I knew I could keep, one that I didn't hesitate to make. Adam wouldn't allow me to hide, even when I wanted to. I needed that. Relief filled me at the thought of having someone I didn't have to pretend with. I lifted my head and we held each other's gaze for a moment. His eyes lowered to my lips, his lids hooded, and I stilled, caught in the moment. Then he blinked and moved back. He reached to pick up my new phone, swiping the screen, and tapping something out on it.

"All done. I added my number and texted myself yours." He handed me the slim, silver phone and took his own from his pocket, just as it beeped. I watched him save my number, frowning at the name he entered.

"Snow Angel?" I asked, with new-found light heartedness.

"That's what popped into my head when I saw you for the first time. You were completely covered in snow. It looked as though you'd been lying in it, making snow angels." He smiled at the memory.

"I must have looked a complete wreck," I mumbled, looking away, embarrassed.

"No, you didn't." He lifted my chin with his fingers. "You don't have to look away from me. Always give me your eyes, Angel."

"I'm afraid of what you might find there," I admitted.

"I'm not," he smiled his reply.

I'm not saying it's down to some higher power. Who knows if that stuff exists? My mum always believed though, that people were given to each other at the perfect time in their lives. She said there were no random meetings or coincidences, it was all set out on each individual's path of destiny. She would tell us my dad was sent to her at just the right moment, any earlier and she wouldn't have been ready for him. I wondered if she had sent Adam to me.

THE TEACHER

The red head cries out, she struggles against the chains, and those ugly purple boots of hers scrape the floor. I smile, though she cannot see the happiness she brings me. The tip of the knife rests on her cheek, her movements halt, and I observe with fascination as the fight leaves her body. A woman's struggle is a beautiful thing, especially when she believes herself undeserving of her punishment.

"Wait, just stop, please. Listen—" she begs, and I regard her silently, allowing her the moment she craves. A moment that will make no difference to her predicament, other than to entertain me. "We can come to some sort of arrangement. You know, one that makes the knife unnecessary."

"You offer your body as a means of survival?" My silence is broken. I am no longer concerned if she recognises my voice, there will be no turning back for her after this. A woman who offers her body is no lady.

"I won't tell anyone, I promise. I don't even know who you are." Her tears flood from her once sparkling eyes. "Please don't kill me."

"You are unreachable." I am disappointed in my student. "Your body is a vessel for depravity and deception. There is no teaching a whore, it is entrenched in you."

The act of rape, a defilement of the most brutal kind, is one I would never lower myself to perform. Sex is evil, a repulsive act contrived by women to control men. A lady would never offer her body in any situation. She should remain sacred.

The knife sears a ragged path along her cheekbone and her blood seeps through, mixing with her tears. I will replace the sparkle in her eyes with death. Her fiery hair will contrast prettily against the white of the gown I have reserved for her. Innocence will return to her in eternal slumber, though not before she learns the error of her impure thoughts and lewd suggestions. The time to finish her education approaches.

My identity is the only secret I keep during my lessons. Everything else is knowledge I give freely. To reveal my face would give them the closure they do not deserve. They slip into darkness with unanswered questions that will haunt their dreamless sleep. However, I think I will reveal myself to her before the end. She ought to know her teacher's identity. That way, I can be sure she knows the reasons for her schooling. Her death will be a gift for my lady.

Me: Got a new number. You know what to do. C. xx

Nick: Who the hell is this?

Me: Callie, dipshit!!!

Nick: Thank fuck for that. I thought the lemurs had found me.

Me: It's only a matter of time.

Nick: You doing ok?

Me: No. Cam has me under 24-hour surveillance. Come break me out.

Nick: Soon, Moonbeam.

Me: Miss you, Sunshine.

Nick: Miss you more.

Me: Don't tell the lemurs that. They're very jealous creatures.

Nick: I take it back. I don't miss you at all. In fact, who are you again?

CALLIE

The Irish Rover was the only pub in Frost Ford and Mick's roguish charm was a hit with everyone in town. He claimed he was the Irish Rover, when he re-named the pub. The murky path of life sent him running from his hometown in Dublin at the tender age of seventeen. Eight years later, he turned up in Frost Ford and immediately decided he was staying. He spent two years re-modelling the pub, and building a reputation from scratch, completely turning it around. It was now a roaring success. Our town had been crying out for a venue like the one he created. Customers came from nearby towns, as well as our own. I started work for him about six months after he took over the place.

Mick and I needed each other at that point in our lives. We'd both gone through trauma. Events that were beyond our control had blown everything we knew out of the water. For me, it was the death of my parents. For him, something that only he can tell you about. We needed a new focus and direction, and we found it together. Mick and I clicked instantly, becoming close friends. He was easy to be around, he didn't judge, gave the best advice, and always made me laugh. He'd approached me several times about taking on a manager's position for him. I wasn't comfortable with the level of commitment that came with a managerial position, while I was still at college, so I turned him down. He still taught me practically everything to do with running the pub and I loved working with him.

That night, Mick and I were busy re-enacting the dance routine from *Dirty Dancing* behind the bar. The place was busy, but the customers were happy to wait for their drinks, while they laughed at our antics. We'd developed a reputation for performing, and playing games while we worked, and it kept the customers entertained. Our friends usually turned up at some point during the night. I thrived on nights like that, when the bar was packed, and everyone was laughing, and having fun. It made the darkness disappear for a while and it was easier for me to live in the light.

"We're re-choreographing the lift part!" Mick hollered over the music.

As the song came to an end, Mick picked me up, threw me over his shoulder, and slapped me on the backside, before spinning in a circle, and putting me back down. I wobbled on my leopard print ankle boots. Dana talked me into buying them on our last shopping trip. I'd resisted at first but now I loved them, even if I wasn't as sturdy on them as my biker boots.

"Back to work, love. Pints to pull. Money to earn." Mick moved to serve a group of people who had just come in. He walked down the right side of the bar, pausing to ring the bell and announce a free juke box until last orders.

I untangled the necklaces I wore, while I wandered down to the other end of the bar, towards Malcolm, one of our regulars. He'd just sat down on what we considered his personal bar stool. My friend, Olivia, sat next to him. Nobody sat on that stool apart from him. When he wasn't there, it was left empty. Mick often joked that the stool had moulded itself to Malcolm's arse. He even had his own glass behind the bar. Every night at the same time, in he strolled, sat on his stool, drank his three glasses of Jameson's, and chatted to everyone around him, before setting off home. He was always happy, never a bad word for anyone. It was people like him who helped make the pub what it was.

"How are you tonight, Mal?" I set his whiskey down on the bar. Malcolm and his wife were friends of my parents and had been a fantastic support to Cameron and me after they died.

"All the better for seeing your pretty face." He smiled and picked up his glass. He tipped it towards me and nodded once, before wetting his lips with the liquid. "How are you, Callie? We missed you around here last week."

"I'm good, thanks. Give me a shout when you're ready for a re-fill." I tapped the bar top beside his glass and moved onto the next customer. We both knew he wouldn't have to shout for a re-fill. Mick and I would keep an eye on his glass, and one of us would automatically fill it when he was ready.

"Hey, Cal, heard you're back on the market? How about a drink next week? You know we could make beautiful music together." Matt, the lead singer for *"Frost"* —a band who played regularly at the pub—

called to me from the other end of the bar. Being local boys, they always drew a big crowd when they played in the Rover.

"How about I book you boys for next weekend and we don't have this conversation again?" I flashed a grin at him, knowing he was just messing around, having a joke with me. It was all part of the banter I loved that came with working in the pub.

"Friday night, honey, it's a date!" He winked and raised his glass to me. Ziggy, their drummer, nodded in my direction and held a thumb up, confirming they would be there the following weekend.

"That's what I like to hear, Matty. Now, go and put me a tune on that juke box." I left the Guinness I'd poured for another customer to settle, and prepared the rest of his order, before topping it up.

"I've got the perfect song for you," Matt replied and began moving through the crowd.

"Callie, when you've got a minute, sweetheart." A busty blonde unwound herself from my brother and waved her glass in my direction. I nodded back to acknowledge her. I didn't know her name, but I knew her face and her drink.

Nights like that always went quickly and it was soon time to clear the bar at the end of the shift. Cameron, having disappeared earlier on, to avoid his admirer, came back in just before last orders. He was sitting at a table with Adam and Mick, looking uncharacteristically miserable, while I finished clearing the bar. Underneath the overprotective streak, my brother was generally a light-hearted person and spent a lot of the time joking around. When he wasn't all smiles, I knew there was a problem.

"Hey, sis, you up for hanging out with Jack tonight?" he called across the bar. Knowing he was referring to *Jack Daniels* generally meant he'd had a bad day. My good mood immediately plummeted. If Cameron was down, I was down with him. Definite twin thing. "Adam and Mick are coming back to ours, you in?"

"Always," I said, wiping down the bar top. "Rough day, bruv'?"

"That's putting it mildly," Cameron mumbled, downing his beer, and slamming the glass down on the table. I gave Adam a questioning look and he grimaced, shaking his head. I nodded in understanding, knowing to let it lie until we got home.

"You coming, Liv?" I asked, watching her teeter precariously on the edge of her bar stool.

"Nah witch, I'm exhausted," she hiccupped, waving her hand around in the air as she spoke. "Gonna get Vinnie boy to drive me home."

"Sleep well, witch. Come over after you take the lightweight home, Vin?" I invited Vinnie when he came in; securing the front doors behind him, so no stragglers could follow looking for afters hours drinks.

"I'm all yours, sweetheart." His smile fell when he saw the state Olivia was in. He pulled her to her feet. "Come on, witch, let's get you home before you fall asleep on Mick's floor. Where are your car keys?"

"Oops!" Olivia swayed as she stood, giggling. She leaned one arm on Vinnie to steady herself, while she fished around in her bag for her keys. "Maybe matching Malcolm drink for drink wasn't a good idea after all."

"Good luck!" I called to Vinnie, when she triumphantly jangled the keys in the air.

"Save me some *Jack*, I think I'm gonna need it!" Vinnie snatched the keys, hauled her up into his arms, and carried her towards the door. I was glad he didn't throw her over his shoulder, that could have gotten messy.

Me: After hour's drinks at our place with Uncle Jack.

Nick: No can do, short stuff. Nobody to watch Heath. You come here.

Me: Can't. Something's up with Cam. Need to stay with him.

Nick: Should have known if he got the Jack out. Give him a kiss from me and I'll see you both soon.

Me: He doesn't want your dirty lemur kisses.

Nick: How very dare you! My kisses fucking rock!

I was curled up next to Adam, passing a glass back and forth between us. We stood by our unspoken agreement that all drinks were to be shared. That weird connection was still there too, and I couldn't seem to stop my body from getting all tangled up in his, when we sat next to each other. I twisted, draping my legs over his like they belonged there, and he rested an arm across my knees, massaging my knee affectionately.

"Incoming!" Vinnie announced when he arrived.

"How's Liv?" I asked.

"Unconscious! Who left her with Malcolm all night?" Vinnie enquired, helping himself to a glass, and filling it halfway from the bourbon bottle that was on the coffee table.

"I didn't notice. I mean, I knew she was drinking whiskey, but I only served her two," I said eyeing Mick, who suddenly looked very guilty.

"What? She made a bet she could keep up with Mal. We all know he has more than three on a Saturday night. I had to see her try," he defended himself and downed his drink.

"You're mean, Micka!" I laughed with him.

"Ah, but you love me. I'm totally hot," he said, with mock arrogance.

"That's not what I said. I said the thing where you jumped over the bar was totally hot. Not *you*!" I pointed at him.

"Ah, sure it's the same thing and you know it."

"Is not," I argued, taking the glass from Adam, who was frowning in Cameron's direction.

"Afraid so, witch," Vinnie chimed in. "You think Mick is totally hot. It's only a matter of time before you two Marvin Gaye and get it on, now that Jase is out of the picture. The whole town's whispering about it!"

Silence descended. Vinnie clamped his mouth shut and I stared at him. I 'd been centre of enough town gossip over the years, what with our parent's deaths, and my abduction at the hands of a serial killer. Jase and I had always been well known around the place, but it hadn't occurred to me that people would talk about our break-up. I should have known they would. My heart sank and the cracks began to open.

Adam's thumb smoothed a circle on my knee, through the rip in my jeans.

"The whole town?" I questioned, with a break in my voice.

"Yeah, you've got the rumour mill running at full speed since you became a single witch. Although, my money is on your knight in shining armour." He grinned and gestured to Adam with his glass.

Adam squeezed my knee again, gaining my attention. I looked up into his eyes and saw everything I needed right there. True to his word, he would be my partner in battle. He was there to remind me I didn't need to let the darkness claim me again, I could fight it.

"Witch, ain't you got no home to go to?!" I jokily bitched at Vinnie, he put his hand to his heart, feigning a look of hurt.

"Oh, they're a special kind of crazy in this town, Adam. Regretting that move yet?" Mick jested.

"Not for a second. My life needed shaking up a little," Adam replied. He patted my legs, I moved them, and he stood, taking our glass to re-fil it.

"My sister is off limits!" Cameron suddenly blurted, gaining all our attention, when he slammed his glass down on the table next to him. "I've already got one psycho ex to deal with. In fact, she's damn lucky I'm even letting her out at all!"

Vinnie laughed, a hint of shock in it. "What's eating you tonight, pretty boy?"

"Cam?" I ventured, he didn't respond, just looked at the floor and let out a ragged sigh. That worried me more than the outburst.

"You tell me." I nudged Adam when he sat back down next to me.

"They'll find out soon enough, mate. The press will be all over it by tomorrow," Adam told him.

Cameron shrugged, bowing his head to cover it with his hands, and my stomach tied itself in knots at the sight of him in such distress. I leaned forward and reached out to him, pulling one of his hands away from his face, holding it in mine. He squeezed back tightly but didn't look at me.

"We found the body of a young woman today," Adam said. He went on to briefly explain, to being unable to go into detail, that she had been horribly assaulted, and her throat had been slit.

"No!"

Ice hurtled through my veins at warp speed. My palms became clammy, my breathing sped up, and my head spun with questions. Was she left like *them*? Was it *him*? The gloom was suddenly everywhere, and I felt myself slipping into its embrace. Smoky tendrils reached out their creepy, jagged fingers, and wrapped themselves around me, digging into my skin, pulling me deeper into the abyss.

"Fight it, Angel." Adam's fingers fluttered gently on the back of my neck, and he whispered next to my ear. "Come back to me."

"Shit!" Cameron spat and finally looked up at me, knowing what thoughts were running through my head. He reminded me of his presence with a squeeze of my hand, and I locked eyes with him. "Callie, listen to me, it's not him. He's gone. It's not happening again. You're safe, I swear it. I won't let anything happen to you, twin. But you need to know— The reason I didn't want to tell you yet— Shit! Callie, it's Amy. The body is Amy."

"Amy Donaldson?" Mick asked, shooting a concerned look in my direction, and Cameron nodded, pulling his free hand through his hair.

"No," I said again, shaking my head, frantically and dropping Cameron's hand. "No. There's no way. It can't be her. It's not her. She's fine. Amy is fine. Tell me she's ok."

Adam moved his fingers from my neck and stretched his arm around my shoulders, pulling me into his side. He spoke gently. "Angel, you should know that initial enquiries are pointing to Jase being the last person to have seen her alive. He was taken into custody this morning, to await further questioning."

"Shit!" whispered Vinnie, sitting down hard on the sofa beside me, he reached out to grab my other hand and pulled it to him.

"He wouldn't have done anything to her." I frowned, my lip beginning to tremble as I tried to make sense of it. I clung to my brother's gaze to anchor me, attempting to stay focused, and not lose myself in the darkness. "I'd know if he was capable of that. I would. I'd know. Wouldn't I?"

I was suddenly uncertain of everything. What if Jase had gotten angry with Amy after he couldn't find me? What if he'd gone back and fought with her, hurt her, maybe by accident? No. Not my Jase. But then, he hadn't been *my* Jase for a long time.

"He hasn't exactly been co-operative," Cameron said, the exhaustion evident in his voice. "I can't get through to him, he won't talk to me or Greg. He's being held until Detectives from Lochden Marsh come in to question him tomorrow."

"What about me? I saw her too," I suddenly remembered.

"You'll have to give a statement. But that's nothing to worry about, I'll be with you. The estimated time of death puts you at home, having dinner with both me and Adam. If, as we suspect, she went missing the night you saw her, you were with Adam all night," Cameron explained, going into work mode.

"I can't believe this," I said.

Despite everything, Amy had been my friend and a big part of my life. She was part of the coven, the nick name Mick had given Amy, Liv, Dana, and me. Amy was the one who made Vinnie an honorary member. As much as I might have been angry with her for sleeping with Jase, I would never wish this on her, on anyone. Adam wrapped his other arm around me and held me while the tears fell. There was no resisting it anymore, he was beside me in battle, but I was losing the fight anyway.

Adam: Okay?

Me: Okay.

Pocketing my phone, I set down the cup of tea I'd made for my brother, on the shelf in his bathroom. I perched on the edge of the counter, facing him as he stood, shaving, in front of the mirror. My brother inherited our dad's dark hair and olive skin, in the same way I had, but he had mum's blue-grey eyes. They peeked out from under his thick, black eyebrows, whereas my eyes were the same deep brown as dad's. Cameron had a pouty mouth that any woman would covet, and he wore his hair slightly too long, his untamed curls almost drawing level with his chin. Dad would never have let him get away with it at work, but Jim, his old sergeant had been lenient about it and only told him not to let it get any longer.

"Do you think he had anything to do with this, Cam?" I wondered out loud, not needing to explain who I was talking about.

"I honestly don't know. Greg and I spent most of yesterday trying to get through to him, it was like talking to a complete stranger. I don't know who he is anymore."

"I know that feeling," I laughed, humourlessly. "It's as though he forgot how to be himself. He used to be relaxed and easy going, he was always trying to make me laugh. Lately, he's short tempered and moody. I know we weren't exactly in a good place, but I still care about him. "

"I know you do. We all do. This just isn't the Jase we know." Cameron finished shaving, and wiped his face with a towel, before pulling on his shirt. He changed the subject. "What're you doing today?"

"Not much. Got some reading to do for college. I might try and get hold of Nick. Have you seen him lately?" I separated a strand of my hair from the rest and wove it into a thin braid as I spoke.

"I spoke to him yesterday, he said you two had talked lots." Cameron frowned at me in the mirror.

"Yeah, but I haven't *seen* him for ages. That's not normal. When I ask what he's doing he's really evasive. I don't think I can take any more of my friends going bat shit on me," I joked, half-heartedly.

Cameron shrugged it off. "He's probably busy at work, you know how popular he is. Want to get dinner at the pub, before your shift tonight? I should be done at work by then."

"Sounds good. I'll meet you there." I stood on tip toes and kissed him on the cheek. "Take it easy today, don't let him get to you. Ok? "

"I'll try," he promised, and I left him to finish getting ready for work.

Me: Dude! I just polished the floors. Do you know what this means?

Nick: You need to get out more?

Me: The entire floor is a slip n' slide.

Nick: Be there in ten.

THE TEACHER

They found her. I left her beside a stream, the water gently lapping at her toes. I hope the sound of the running water soothed her. The delicacy of a flower did not suit her wilfulness, so she wore a crown of hawthorns, that will decay with her as she sleeps. The shades of red against white; her hair fanned out on the snow, the cascade of her blood patterning her gown, were more beautiful than I could have imagined. I hope they take many photographs, such beauty ought to be preserved.

She wasn't as easy to shape as I'd hoped in the end. Once she realised her fate, she fought me at every turn. Perhaps, her betrayal of my lady angered me, leaving me with less patience than I would normally have for a student. Still, she knew in the end. She was suitably horrified when I revealed myself to her, berating me for my actions with vulgar words. That was when she died.

Young women should maintain a classy elegance, just as my mother taught. This loutish behaviour that has become the norm is not a sign of strength and equality, as they mistakenly believe. It is a belittlement of what women were designed to be. They need to be taught the error of their ways and I have been more than happy to pick up my teaching again.

There are others that need to learn, before I can be reunited with my lady. I have several potential students. When I have finished teaching, she will be my reward. Mine, for the rest of my life, as she was always meant to be. Until then, I will continue to romance her with my gifts.

CHAPTER FIVE

CALLIE

I gave my statement about the last time I saw Amy. The detectives also grilled me intensively about Jase and my relationship with him. Both Cameron and Adam insisted on being present for my interview, which made for a very pleasant time.

"When did he last lose his temper with you?" they had asked. At which point Adam snapped at them for asking leading questions.

"Has he ever been violent towards you?" Cue snarling from Cameron.

"What did you fight about the night you found Miss Donaldson with Mr Montgomery?"

"What do you think they fought about?" It had been Adam's turn to snarl then.

"Did you see Amy again after that night? Did you confront her? Were you angry?" After which Cameron had seethed that I wasn't under suspicion and had a cast iron alibi.

Being trapped, in an enclosed space, with four dominant male types is not an experience I'd care to repeat any time soon. Testosterone overload!

Jase was released without charge of Amy's murder. That morning, I found another dead rose and a bottle of expensive perfume on my doorstep. It was a strong, heady scent, one I'd worn for him over the years because he loved it, but I preferred a more subtle aroma. The detectives on the case couldn't— yet, they had stressed— connect him to her murder, other than the fact that he was the last person to see her alive. That alone wasn't enough to hold him and without any further evidence, they had no choice but to let him go.

Leaving college after my classes, I wandered, deep in thought and enjoying a brief respite from my usual paranoia, towards the bus stop. I was basking in the sunshine that had made an appearance, despite the snow that still lay on the ground and the chill in the air, when Jase's car pulled up alongside me.

"Feel like getting lunch at a pub out in the country before we go home, baby?" He leaned casually across the passenger seat and talked through the open window.

"Ah... no. Thanks," I told him, trying to hide my surprise at his sudden appearance. I continued walking and he drove slowly alongside me. He must have been waiting for me to come out, I realised.

"I just want to talk, Cee. Please," he begged. His grip on the steering wheel tightened, his knuckles turning white and I could see he was struggling to stay calm. "You know I didn't hurt Amy, don't you?"

"Yes, I do," I answered. Although he was technically still under suspicion, I was almost certain he wouldn't do those things. "I never really thought you did, but it doesn't change what happened with us. You still cheated on me. We're still finished."

"She's gone, Cee. She's not a threat to us anymore, it's not like it's going to happen again." He stopped the car at the curb, idling the engine.

"What?" I halted and stared at him through the open window. *Was he serious?*

A familiar, black motorcycle pulled up in front of Jase's car and I felt the tension leave my body. Nick climbed off the bike, and removed his helmet with one hand, while pushing his floppy, blonde, hair out of his eyes with the other.

"Hello, stranger." He flashed a grin at me then looked towards Jase, the smile instantly dropping. "You ok, buddy?"

"Just fine, Nick. Trying to have a conversation with my girlfriend, if you don't mind," Jase responded angrily. Nick caught my eye and raised an eyebrow at me in question, had he missed something? I shook my head in response.

"Didn't think so," Nick murmured, under his breath. "Why don't you go home, Jase? I'll drop Callie off and then I'll come over later with a few beers. I'll give Nate and Luke a ring, it's been a while since we had a decent session."

"CeeCee?" Jase looked at me. His eyes were cold and unfeeling, and sent a bolt of dread through me. Where had my Jase gone? The one I knew better than I knew myself. The one I'd loved all my life. There was no hint of him left in those eyes.

"I'm not going with you," I stated, unwavering. Jase stared me down.

"When a lady tells you, she doesn't want your company, you really need to listen, Jase," Nick warned.

Jase turned away from me, muttering viciously under his breath, before closing the window and driving away, the tyres of his car screeching on the tarmac.

"Caffeine?" Nick asked, the infectious grin returning. He grabbed my hand, leading me to his bike and set about securing the spare helmet on my head. There was a reason I called Nick sunshine. He never failed to brighten my day, never failed to make me smile, never failed to lighten my mood. He simply was my own personal sunshine.

"Always," I agreed and climbed on the bike behind him.

"Pockets!" His voice rose above the noise of the engine. I wrapped my arms around him and shoved my hands into his pockets, snuggling into his familiar warmth.

It felt like an age since we'd ridden the bike together. Snow and ice had covered the roads for weeks and Nick used his car over the winter months. The recent warmer spell of the last few days, started a long-awaited thaw, and he'd obviously decided it was bike weather again.

Nick was as big a part of my life as Cameron. My parents always loved telling the story of how we became friends. On our first day pre-school, I marched right up to the pretty, little blonde boy, and plonked myself down next to him in the sandpit. He stopped burying his own feet in the sand to look at me, and I announced loudly that we were going to be best friends forever. He pulled my hair, a habit he'd never broken, and apparently was impressed when I didn't flinch or cry but laughed and poked the dimple in his cheek instead. The three of us had become inseparable almost immediately. He was the honorary third twin in our family. My parents had adored him as much as Cameron and I both did.

Nick's dad left them when he was still a child. His mother hadn't been much use after that, drinking herself into oblivion on a daily basis. She died when Nick was twenty. Being over eighteen, he applied to become the legal guardian for his three younger brothers. The system was against him, but he'd worked himself ragged, fighting to prove he was capable of caring for them. He did everything in his power to provide for them and made sure they had everything they needed. In all honesty, it was nothing he wasn't already doing before she died, since she hadn't been capable of taking care of them herself. Finally, a social worker decided to give him a break and backed his application.

My best friend hadn't been given much of a childhood. He'd been forced to grow up far too quickly. All four Warren brothers were regulars at our house, for mealtimes especially, over the years. My own parents took them under their wing when theirs failed them. Nick was there for us when our parents died, and we were there for him in return. Cameron and I, and our other friends, all helped out with the boys when we could. His brother, Ethan, was now nineteen and training to be a mechanic at Nate's dad's garage. The younger two, Danny, who was seventeen, and Heath, who was fifteen, were both still in school full time.

"So, where have you been?" I demanded, giving him my best scowl, when we sat down at a table, in the cafe we'd stopped at.

"Busy trailing Jase, keeping him away from you," he said, as if it should be obvious. He reached a tattoo covered hand between us and pulled on my ponytail, unable to resist any longer.

"Are you serious?" I gaped at him. "You've been following Jase around all this time? And he just let you? "

"He hasn't exactly been predictable since you broke up. Drinking, getting into fights, trying to follow you everywhere. Between him, work, and my brothers, I haven't had much free time," he explained.

"Nick—" I was speechless. As if he didn't have enough to do, and here he was, running around after my unbalanced ex-boyfriend.

"You're welcome." He shrugged a shoulder as the waitress arrived with our coffees. "Honestly? Cam asked me to keep an eye on him, but I would have done it anyway. He doesn't deserve a second of your time after what he did. I just didn't realise it would turn into a full-time job. How're you holding up, anyway?"

"I'm alright. Shocked about Amy, more than anything. Trying not to think about the other stuff," I said, sipping my black coffee. I wasn't a fan of all the fancy frothy, flavoured coffees that my friends loved. Some things just shouldn't be messed with.

"It's hard to believe she won't just come skipping over, and say something crazy, like she used to. After she did that to you though, it's hard to know how to feel about her." He leaned forward and laced our fingers together on the table. "I'm sorry I haven't been around, especially the night you walked in on them. Was it awful?"

"It wasn't the most fun I've ever had. Adam was great, he got rid of Jase for me. I'm not sure what I would have done if it hadn't been for him." I filled him in on everything else that happened that night and life since. Leaving out the parts where I openly and uncontrollably drooled over Adam every chance I got. "Of course, Cam went into big brother mode and barely let me leave the house for a week, but now I realise you were in on that with him."

"Not sorry for trying to protect you. I'm yet to meet this Adam bloke. Heard a lot about him, though. Apparently, he's already making quite an impression. Only been in charge a few weeks and he's got the whole town sitting up and taking notice." Nick sat back and trained his eyes on me while rubbing at his short, neatly trimmed beard.

"Well, someone's had his ear to the ground," I teased.

"You don't miss much in my job. Tattoo studios are worse than hair salons for gossip." Nick winked. "Seems he's earned himself a reputation as your hero, too. A knight in shining armour, no less."

"You shouldn't listen to Liv and Vinnie so much," I laughed and fiddled with the sleeve on my jacket.

"Yeah, maybe there's something in their stories this time." He cocked his head on one side and inspected me through narrowed eyes.

"What's that look for?" I frowned.

"You're so clueless. I've missed you, Moonbeam!" He laughed, shaking his head at me.

"You know where I am." I half-heartedly let him know that I still wasn't entirely happy with him for disappearing on me.

"Like I said, been busy. But I intend to rectify that from right now." He confirmed his words with a nod and his signature grin.

"Well good!" I smiled. "Because I missed you too, Sunshine."

Me: Game night. Tonight. Our place. Be there or be sober and alone, losers.

Nick: I'm in as long as the lemurs aren't.

Greg: Are you two ever going to tell the rest of us this lemur story?

Nick: Lemurs are demonic. That's all you need to know.

Vinnie: I think we all know Nick just prefers monkeys to humans.

Me: You guys in or not? No lemurs, Sunshine boy. Just copious amounts of alcohol, junk food, a coven meeting, and COD for all you toy soldiers.

Mick: In.

Me: Smooth talker! 🖤

Dana: We're in. I'll prep the cauldron.

Me: Good girl.

Greg: Did you add Adam to this message, Cal?

Adam: She did, cous. I'll be there.

Me: 😊

Nick: If Ethan is home then I'm in.

Me: Already cleared it, he'll be home. Bribed him with chocolate muffins.

Nick: Woohoo! It's like being a parent and getting a last-minute babysitter. My life bloody rocks!

Liv: LMAO! Flippin' love you, Nick!

Nick: Back at ya, Liver bird!

Me: Olive? You in?

Liv: When am I not?

Me: If you're out (there)?

Liv: John Legend, witch! That was abysmal!

Me: Fail.

Liv: Epic! That makes me in the lead.

Me: No fucking way! Not after my Maroon 5 extravaganza. That sent me miles ahead!

Greg: ?????????????

EDUCATING CALLIE

Vinnie: Freaks!

Nate: No can do, babe. Sorry.

Me: Ah come on, Nate!!! COD is calling. Your country needs you!

Nate: Next time. Promise. Love ya, babe. Bell me soon. Xx

Me: Will do. Xx

Nate: 😊

Luke: Me neither. Family stuff.

Twin 2: Everything ok, Luke?

Me: You alright, Luca?

Liv: Waving here, Lukie boy!

Luke: Waving back, Liv. I'm fine. Things are just insane since Amy and I can't get away right now.

Me: Alright, Luca, don't be a stranger though, yeah?
Luke: Never, Cal. Xx

Me: Xx

Vinnie: Ooh, kisses! I lurve kisses! Xxxxxxxxxxxxx

Liv: Shut up, witch!

THE TEACHER

It angers me that my lady has been throwing away my gifts. Such ungrateful behaviour is unbecoming of her. Had she completed her education with me, she would know this. Going forward, I cannot tolerate it. There is now a need to add yet more lessons to her growing list. If only she had stayed with me, her education would be over now, and we would be beginning our lives together. Far away from outside influences that could take her from me. Still, I have found a new gift for her. I believe she will be impressed with this one and it will suitably re-enforce the lessons she must learn.

In the meantime, I have found my next student. I will watch and wait for the opportunity that allows her to join me. During my observations of her, I have learned that she is quite the wild thing and I believe I will enjoy taming her very much. She uses the act of sex to gain favour with men. The control she has over them would be admirable, if it weren't for the evil she does with her body. A lady does not use her body in that way. Mother taught that all whores were to be punished. A lady would never touch a man or allow herself to be touched in such a vulgar and personal way. This is the lesson she will learn under my supervision.

My methods are harsh, as were mother's, but they serve a purpose. The world must be rid of whores. A world without women who expose their bodies, in a bid to tempt men, would be a safer place. My work enforces that belief. If a man is not exposed to the sights of the female form, he will not be tempted to give in to the devil's work. Mine is a job I have taken great pride in over the years and I continue to do so.

CALLIE

When the snow finally thawed, Cameron decided to celebrate the occasion with a game night at our place. The boys gathered around the TV screen, drinking beer and shooting each other on *Call of Duty*. The girls gossiped and drank copious amounts of wine in the kitchen. I welcomed the distraction; I was ready to play in the light.

Nights like this were about as close to the *"girl's night"* classification as I got. Not that I was a tomboy in the true sense of the word, I just wasn't a high heels, and frilly dresses kind of girl. I was more of a rock chick— my music tastes and vintage band shirts inherited form my dad. My inner girl never came out to play for very long. I'd always got on better with the boys. Maybe it was Cameron and Nick's influence, since I was surrounded by boys for so long, before the girls came along. Maybe it was just that boys didn't ask as many questions. Still, I loved Liv and Dana with my entire being and I appreciated that no matter the fact I had always gelled easier with the boys, sometimes only your girls could make things better.

"Incoming!" Greg called, as he and Dana walked through the front door and into the living room.

"Hey, you two, come on in." I called back from the kitchen, where I was preparing a plate of nachos. Liv was emptying peanuts into bowls, while casually throwing one at my head every few seconds.

Dana pressed her lips to Greg's cheek, and joined Liv and me in the kitchen, while Greg turned towards the sofa area. Cameron, Adam, and Nick were all gathered around the TV screen discussing teams, weapons, and tactics, like they actually had a clue. Nick and Adam had officially been introduced, and Nick had given me a sly smile and a wink, when he looked at me afterwards. I knew what he meant by it. I had no intention of reacting though.

I poured Dana a glass of fizzy stuff and topped up Liv's and my own. Adam stood and wandered over to us. He said hello to Dana, then picked up my glass and took a sip. My eyes wandered all over him, he wore black jeans and a fine knit, dark grey jumper. Black combat style boots and a chain, draped from the waistband of his jeans, gave the outfit an edge. It seemed he could pull off the bad boy as well as the hot cop really well. I'm sure I had drool running down my chin. *Damn female hormones again. Maybe I should add a drool proof cover to my no swoon zone?*

"Bleurgh! We are *not* sharing tonight, Angel." He winced and took a beer from the fridge instead.

"All the more for me!" I smiled and raised my glass towards him.

He moved in close, crowding my space, tapped the neck of his bottle on my glass, and placed a kiss on the top of my hair. I did not in any way have my eyes on his backside as he walked away. Like I said to Greg, heartbroken, not blind. I turned, doing a very poor job of hiding a smile, to find Liv and Dana staring at me with gaping mouths and wide eyes.

"What?" I matched their wide-eyed stares.

"What?" Liv gasped, looking at Dana. "Is she serious? What?"

I looked between the two of them, furrowing my brow. "What?" I asked again.

Dana shook her head. Her white blonde locks bounced around her face, making her look like a shampoo commercial.

"I mean, Greg mentioned something, but I didn't take him seriously. Now I think about it, Adam *has* been asking questions."

"What?" I screeched frustratedly, drawing attention from the toy soldiers in the living room. They all looked over at us with curious eyes. They reminded me of a group of meercats, the way their heads all turned in unison.

"Nothing to see here! Back to your posts soldiers!" Dana shouted and waved their gazes back to the TV screen. They did as they were told, turning together. Good little meercats.

"Angel? Sharing? Winking? Kisses? You were all over his body with your eyes when he came over here." Liv turned to me and listed the words on her fingers.

"Again, what?" Yes, her observations were correct, but I refused to acknowledge what they were getting at.

"You and Adam!" Dana whispered dramatically, leaning towards me.

"What about us?" I stage whispered back, mimicking her leaning move.

"You can't see it." Liv turned to Dana, lifting her glasses to look underneath them at her. "She can't see it."

"For fuck sake, Liv. See what?" I demanded, loudly enough to draw the men's attention again.

"You alright, sis?" Cameron frowned at me.

Since Amy's murder and all the memories it stirred up, he had, understandably, slipped back into hyper protective mode. He was holding back, barely, on the house arrest thing, but I knew he would attempt to enforce it at any sign of stress from me.

"Just fine, twin. I think Olive might be losing her marbles, but I'm fine." I spoke without taking my eyes off Olivia; she glared at me for using the nickname she hated.

"I can't believe you don't see it." Dana shook her head and made her hair bounce again.

I shrugged my shoulders, giving up on them both. "Can you please stop talking in riddles, because I know I haven't had enough wine to be this confused yet. Or you could just stop talking entirely, that would also work."

"You and Adam," Liv said.

Dana began to make kissing noises. Liv made circles from her thumb and forefinger on each hand and started mashing them together like two mouths. Kissing. I took a step back, crossed my arms, and eyed them both.

"Are you two on drugs?" I questioned.

"Callie! Wake up!" Dana screeched, and then turned to Greg sheepishly. "I'm fine, sweetie."

"You and Adam..." Liv began in a hushed voice.

"You keep saying that!" I helpfully pointed out.

"You're flirting." She put her hands on her hips, as if that backed up her argument.

"Well, yeah. Have you seen him? I mean *actually* looked at him. Damn right, I'm going to flirt with him. I've gone from Jase and his mind-blowing orgasms, to zero action overnight, and I'm feeling just a little frustrated. So, I am absolutely guilty of flirting with the fit new man in uniform! Pretty sure half the female population of the town is guilty of flirting with him," I said, becoming exasperated. I was actually more than a little bit sexually frustrated since breaking up with Jase. For all the other faults in our relationship, sex had not been one of them. So, yeah, I was feeling that loss.

"No, it's more than that. If that's all it was, you'd have rebounded and done the horizontal tango by now. He can't take his eyes off you," Liv said.

"We're friends." I shrugged, trying not to look in his direction. He wasn't an idiot and I was certain he'd know we were talking about him. We weren't exactly being subtle.

"Men don't give women nick names unless they really care," Dana said. "You are totally pushing the friend zone boundaries."

"No, we're not," I argued.

I was happy to admit I thought Adam was gorgeous and I'd definitely flirted with him. But to suggest there was anything more than friendship between us was ridiculous. We were friends. We bonded quickly, but only because of the darkness we shared. He understood me in a way nobody else could. I wasn't about to go into that with them though, it would only hurt them to know I kept so much from them. Besides, I was still stupidly in love with Jase.

"I gave Nick a nickname. Ha! Nickname for Nick! See what I did there?" They looked at me blankly. "And he has one for me. I've always called Luke, Luca. But I have nothing other than friendship love for them both. Mick only ever calls me love or Callie love, has done ever since we met. That doesn't mean anything. Well, it does, but I can't tell you what, only that it's not the obvious. I call Liv, Olive, but we're not getting naked and bumping uglies on a nightly basis. What about Nate? He calls everyone babe, even some men, usually Cameron! A nickname means nothing."

"Rambling, Callie!" Liv pointed out.

"Me thinks the lady doth protest too much," Dana sang.

"I don't protest at all. He's gorgeous, I like looking at him, and we're friends. I admit we became close very quickly, but that's because of the way we met. It was an intense night." I gulped at my wine, not at all desperate to change the subject, much.

"You share all your drinks. That's practically kissing," Liv stated, as if that settled it. Case closed.

"Not tonight!" I held up my glass triumphantly.

"He. Calls. You. Angel!" Dana stressed each word, pointing her glass at me for extra emphasis.

"Snow Angel." I immediately regretted sharing.

"What?" They leaned towards me and I swear I saw their ears standing to attention. I sighed.

"When he first saw me, I was so covered in snow, that he thought I looked as though I'd been lying in it, making snow angels. So, he calls me Snow Angel." I let out the words in one breath to get them over with.

Liv and Dana looked at each other, eyebrows raised. I cringed and thanked my lucky stars that the volume on the TV was turned up high, so we couldn't be heard over the gunfire and grenades going off in the living room.

"She can't see it!" They chorused and clinked their glasses.

"You're going to marry him. We're going to be cousins in law!" Dana declared, pointing a perfectly French manicured finger at me.

"*I* am not marrying anyone. Nope!" I wasn't sure what my future held, but marriage was definitely not part of it. I couldn't bring another person into my shit show of a life.

"You are! You have to be next. It's the order, the way we decided. Me, then you, then Liv. All of us bridesmaids for each other. You can't go back on it now!" Dana sulked.

"We were twelve and we were assuming I would marry Jase." I shook my head at her. I neglected to mention that Liv was meant to marry Cameron in the make-believe scenario we dreamt up as children. My eyes strayed over to the living room and I came up with a way to change the subject. "Screw it, I'll just marry my bestie. Hey, Nick, will you marry me?"

"Thought you'd never ask," he answered with a grin, not looking up from the screen.

"See? All sorted. I'll marry Nick." I grinned at Dana and began to empty a large packet of salt and vinegar crisps into a bowl.

"Incoming!" A deep voice announced, and Mick and Vinnie entered, heavily laden with cases of beer and bottles of wine.

"Mickaaaaa!" I waved my glass around in his direction, grateful for a reprieve in the interrogation. I loved that man and his perfect timing!

"Evening, ladies. For you and your kitchen coven, love" he said, kissing my cheek and setting three bottles of wine and a bottle of Baileys on the kitchen counter. He picked up a beer, nodded to Liv and Dana and went off the join the toy soldiers.

"Witches!" Vinnie greeted us all with kisses, before spotting Nick sprawled across the sofa. "Nicky boy, long time no see. How's it going, gorgeous?"

"'Alright, V!" Nick raised his beer in Vinnie's direction. His eyes only briefly leaving the TV screen.

"Such a waste." Vinnie shook his head and leaned a hip against the island. He was head to toe in black- black cargo trousers, black t shirt and black boots, as he always was for work and he looked like a man you really did not want to mess with. My gaze lingered on the boots, a memory threatening to surface.

"You could always try and turn him," Liv giggled, sipping her wine. I blinked, her laugh bringing me out of the beginnings of a flashback I didn't want.

"Been there, done that. All over the t-shirt!" Vinnie smirked.

"What?" I screeched, for the second time that night, then immediately shook my head and smiled sheepishly in Cameron's direction.

"Straight as they come that one. Mores the pity," Vinnie laughed.

"Oh, my!" Dana sighed, fanning herself. "You two together would be so hot. If you ever change his mind you should sell tickets."

"I'll drink to that!" Liv laughed and clinked glasses with Dana.

"Couldn't talk Nate and Luke into tonight, then?" Vinnie looked towards the meercats in the living room. I shrugged in response.

Nate and Luke hadn't been around much since the whole Jase and Callie fiasco. Then Amy had been killed. Luke was Amy's cousin, so understandably he would be tied up with family and mourning. Nate and Jase had always been close, so he was more than likely with him.

"Anyway, Vin, Adam and Callie?" Liv probed, pushing her glasses back up the slope of her nose.

"She can't see it," Vinnie said, pointing his beer bottle at me. "You've been out of the game too long, sweetheart."

I shook my head and picked up the corkscrew to open another bottle of wine. Vinnie moved over to join the men. My eyes, once again, gravitated towards Adam, only to find him already looking at me. We did the mouthing okay thing and then he winked. I smiled, felt my skin singe red, and busied myself filling the wine glasses.

"Hey, future Mrs Warren, how about a beer over here?" Nick called cheekily.

"Erm, I don't believe I'm at work right now, Mr Warren." I laid my hands on my hips and sent him a challenging smirk.

"Please, Moonbeam?" He sent back puppy dog eyes.

"Ugh! How many?" I gave in.

"Better bring six."

"All of you? Really?"

Grabbing the bottled beers, I shoved one in each of the front pockets of my faded grey jeans and carried two in each hand.

Liv hollered "Catwalk, baby!"

I played along and sashayed my hips, over exaggerating each swing, as I walked over to where the men were crowded on the sofa. Thankfully, I was barefoot, or I might have fallen off my shoes through alcohol consumption.

"Work it, work it!" Dana called and I cackled sarcastically. There was a reason I played football with the boys after school, rather than take ballet lessons, I did not possess the grace to *work* anything.

Mick and Vinnie were playing against each other and I set a beer down next to each of them. Vinnie blew me a kiss, Mick mumbled a "thanks, love" and I handed two more bottles off to Greg and Cameron. Sticking my hip out in Adam's direction, for him to take one from my pocket, I returned his earlier wink.

"Thanks, Angel." He took a sip of the beer and smirked. "Nice walking skills. Putting one foot in front of the other and all that."

"That's talent right there, baby. I'm not just a pretty face." I preened jokily and wiggled my hips at him, my insides warming when he joined in with my laughter.

Nick reached for the last bottle with one hand and hooked a finger trough my belt loop with his other hand. He pulled me roughly into his lap and I landed heavily, letting out a *"humph"* sound.

"Sit with me. I haven't seen you properly in forever and I'm feeling needy." He wrapped his free arm around my waist.

"Five minutes, Sunshine. I'm in the middle of a very important coven meeting." I gestured to the kitchen. "How are the boys?"

"Mostly good. Heath had some trouble with a kid at school, but I think it's all done with now. Ethan is doing great at the garage. He really loves the place. Danny is his usual quiet self, still has no clue what he wants to do with his life. He asked about you the other day. Says he misses you."

"Tell him to come and see me, we can be clueless together. Actually, all of you come for dinner. It's been too long. I'll make brownies for him." I poked the dimple in Nick's cheek when he smiled.

"Thanks, Cal, don't know what I'd do without you sometimes. You keep me sane." He pulled my hair gently, in response to my dimple poke, and kissed my temple.

"Back at ya!" I smiled and leaned my head against his shoulder.

"What was all that screeching about earlier?" Cameron asked, leaning towards me, from his spot in my favourite armchair. He set his beer bottle down, on a pile of my books on the floor, next to the chair, and ignored the dirty look I sent him. I absently noticed the pile had gotten smaller but filed it away to deal with later.

"Oh, apparently, I'm blind." I shrugged.

"What?" He frowned, shaking his head.

"That's what I said!" I pointed at him and called to Liv and Dana. "Hey, witches, Cam can't see it either!"

Dana gasped and came teetering over, as fast as her stupidly high heels would allow. Liv, meanwhile, bent double, choking on her wine with laughter in the kitchen. She grappled with her glasses, which she'd propped on top of her head, and had almost fallen off, in the process.

"You! Shush! You can't talk about coven shizzle over here." She waved her hand around in a circle, gesturing towards the men in the room.

"Shizzle?" Greg looked at his wife adoringly and I sighed at how cute they were. I was never a gushy romantic, but I didn't have to be to see that Greg and Dana were perfect together. Crazy, stupid in love. I'd once thought Jase and I could give them a run for their money. Now, I knew we'd just been playing at it. The real thing had fizzled out for us long ago.

"You heard me." She crossed her arms and gave him a *"don't mess with me"* kind of look. Her white blonde hair, ridiculously long eye lashes, and baby pink sweater dress ensemble, were more of a hindrance than a help with her attempt at badassery. Greg just looked at her like she was a cute little kitten.

"Come on, missy." She grabbed my arm and attempted to yank me to my feet, but Nick held on.

"No. It's my turn with her. We've got Callie and Nick shizzle to talk about, and a wedding to plan," he protested.

"So much shizzle," I mumbled, looking at Dana who tapped her foot impatiently.

"Ok, I won't talk about the fact that I'm blind. Not even with my brother. Should I be calling him bruh, now that we're actively using the word shizzle?" I asked, seriously.

Nick buried his face in my neck and his shoulders shook with silent laughter. Cameron choked on his beer, and Adam patted him roughly on the back, while trying to contain his own laughter.

"Did we go gangsta?" Vinnie asked, sounding genuinely curious.

"I've always been gangsta!" Mick announced.

"Mickaaaa the badass!" I laughed.

"Totally hot badass." He winked at me over his shoulder.

"It was the act Mick, not the man," I informed him, laughing.

"You keep telling yourself that, love." He laughed with me.

"Ask the witches," I said as Dana made her way back to the kitchen.

"Oh, no! I can't take any more witch shizzle tonight." He turned his attention back to the game.

"Too late, Mickey, you're dead!" Vinnie declared. "Adam, get your arse over here. You're up, gorgeous!"

"Yeah, yeah. You just concentrate on your own arse because I'm about to blow shit up. You're going down!" Adam took the controller from Mick and settled in front of the screen.

"I'll go down on you anytime you like. Just say the word," Vinnie flirted.

Adam laughed and I loved how he didn't bat an eyelid at Vinnie's over the top flirting. Straight men didn't always know how to take Vinnie. They became awkward in his company and that was generally the tipping point for us. If you weren't into Vinnie, you weren't into us. We came across it less and less these days, but it was still there. Adam had just fallen into our group dynamic. He fit perfectly.

"So, how do you want to do this wedding of ours?" Nick pulled me closer on his lap.

"Barefoot. On a beach. At sunset." I wrapped an arm around his neck and played with the longer hair on the top of his head.

"Bikini and boards shorts?"

"Yes! And tattoos instead of rings."

"That sounds like us."

"Which beach?"

"Well, if we're talking sunsets there really is only one option."

"San Antonio!" I sang.

"Ibiza, baby!" Nick grinned.

"I love it. We can have the reception at Cafe Mambo." I bounced up and down excitedly on his lap and he laughed.

"Why didn't we do this years ago, Moonbeam?" Nick kissed my forehead and I made a note to tell Dana about how nicknames meant nothing.

"I don't know, we're obviously made for each other."

"Come out on the bike with me, this weekend?" Nick changed the subject "It's been ages."

"It's been snowing, in case you hadn't noticed." My fingers traced the tattoos that lined his arm. Nick's arms and back were covered in ink and I loved looking at it all, it mesmerised me.

"Not anymore." He smiled, wriggling his eyebrows at me.

"I'd like that." I smiled back and stood up.

When I walked past Adam, I couldn't resist sticking a hand in his deep brown hair and messing it up. He held up his beer bottle in response and I took a drink before giving it back. See, just friends. I mean, I'd been sitting on Nick's knee for the last ten minutes, planning our pretend wedding. We had nicknames for each other. Mick called me love, like *all* the time. Nobody ever suggested there was more than friendship with either of them. Nicknames are just a bit of fun, nothing special about them. Nothing.

Nate: *You're coming tomorrow aren't you, babe?*

Me: *Probably. Feels like I should. But I don't want shit to be awkward.*

Nate: It won't be. Be good to see you. Luke wants you there.

Me: I'm thinking about it.

There was a chill in the air, but the sky was clear, and the sun shone brightly, on the morning of Amy's memorial service. It was easier said than done to match my mood to the weather. Amy's body was yet to be released, but her family wanted to do something to bring everyone together. So, they were having a service at the church, followed by a gathering at The Irish Rover. They would have a private funeral at a later date. Everyone was asked to wear purple, since it was Amy's favourite colour. She'd hated black. I wore a purple pencil skirt with a gold belt, a grey top, my faithful leather jacket, and grey suede ankle boots. I thought she would approve.

Adam: Okay?

Me: Okay.

I turned my phone off and got out of the car. I scanned the crowded church yard for the source of that ever-present feeling of being watched. I shivered, seeing nothing as usual, but the feeling stayed with me. Cameron was immediately on one side of me. Nick sandwiched me in between them on my other side, holding my hand and easing my tension slightly.

Cameron, Adam, and pretty much everyone, had told me over and over that I didn't have to go. That I shouldn't feel obligated after what had happened between Jase and Amy. I knew that. Still, something told me I needed to be there. Amy had been my friend before she was anything else. I wanted to show my support for the rest of my friends and for her family. I also was very aware of the fact that Amy and I never had the chance to speak again, after I walked in on her and Jase. She disappeared that night and I had no idea how she had felt about any of it. I would never know. Considering what happened to her afterwards, I doubt it had crossed her mind again.

The first person I saw was Luke. Our eyes locked over the throng of people and I really didn't know what to expect. We'd texted a little, but none of us had seen him since the night I caught Jase and Amy together. It had seemed as though he was avoiding us, despite Nate's reassurances to the contrary. Cameron stiffened beside me when Luke started towards us, but Luke was quiet and sensitive and I really doubted he would start anything, even if he did have a problem. Luke wasn't as tall as the other guys, but still tall in comparison to me. Being in his last year of medical school, he was your typical student type, with messy, dark brown hair, and a cute, wonky smile.

Luke reached out, putting his arms around me. "I'm really glad you came, Callie." His whisper was for my ears only and I relaxed into his embrace. He squeezed me tightly, before releasing me, automatically taking his gloves off and reaching for my hands.

"Me too, Luca." I allowed him to put his gloves on me. I think he did it more for something to do, keeping busy with a familiar, comforting act, than anything else. I breathed a secret sigh of relief that he didn't hate me for this whole mess.

"Miss you guys." He included Cameron and Nick in the conversation. "It's just not the same anymore."

He and Cameron exchanged one of those one armed man hugs, before he moved onto Nick and did the same. Then Luke came back to stand beside me and enclosed my hand in his, holding on as though his life depended on it. I sensed he was in need of an anchor of some kind and let him hold on, while the three of us made small talk.

"Callie," a female voice said from behind us. I turned to see Sally and Natalie, two of Amy's friends from college. We'd been out together a few times and they came in the pub occasionally. Liv knew them, since she worked in the library and had met them there, but I didn't know them very well.

"Hi," I said, again not knowing what to expect.

They both came forward, arms outstretched, and gathered me into a group hug that completely overwhelmed me. Tears flowed from all of us, until my brother protectively peeled me away from them. Then, Vinnie, Nate and Mick were there, and we were suddenly all together again. Minus Amy. I found myself being pulled into Nate's arms, while the others greeted each other with hugs and quiet words.

Nate's brown eyes looked down into mine. "You alright, babe?"

"I'm okay." I reached up, to tug a strand of his dirty blonde hair, with my gloved fingers. Nate usually had his hair tied back in some way, due to constantly having his head in the engine of a car. "I like it down."

After offering our condolences to Amy's parents, Cameron and I moved back towards our friends, who had been joined by Liv, Greg, and Dana. We were taking our seats in the church pews, when out of the corner of my eye, I noticed a familiar figure walking towards us. Our eyes didn't have to meet for me to know who it was. I knew his walk, his clothes, his smell. I could pick him out of any crowd.

Cameron put a supportive hand on my back, to let me know he was there, but my hardened attitude towards Jase crumpled the second our eyes clashed. He was broken, lost and drifting in his own personal hell. It wasn't the time for our relationship drama. I was here for Amy and our friends. Jase was one of those friends. Before I had time to think about it, we flung ourselves into each other's arms. I felt his hand in my hair as though it had never been absent. The other wrapped tightly around my waist and my fingers gripped his shirt.

"I'm so sorry, Cee" he whispered, his voice cracking on my name. The familiarity of his body against mine, my name on his lips, his voice in my ear was comforting in that moment. Like coming home.

"Shh," I whispered, unsuccessfully holding back tears. "It's not important now."

"Jase, over here." Nate called to him as we drew apart, gesturing to an empty space next to him and behind Luke.

"You gonna be ok?" Jase asked. He nodded at Nate and wiped away my tears with gentle strokes of his thumbs.

"Fine," I nodded. "I'm going to sit here, with Nick and Cam."

"Alright." He nodded again, hesitating.

"Will you be coming back to the pub after this?" I asked.

"I told Luke I would, but I'm not sure Mick will want me there."

"It'll be fine." I assured him and rubbed his arm, then I moved away, to take my seat between Nick and my brother.

Nick grabbed my hand as I sat down, pulling it into his lap. "You ok?"

I whispered yes and looked from him to Cameron, who refused to make eye contact with me.

"One wrong word, Callie. One wrong move. I mean it," Cameron hissed through gritted teeth, looking straight ahead.

"He'll behave." I promised and I knew he would.

"The time she let Natalie bleach her hair because she wanted to look like Tinker Bell..." Sally began.

"And it went green!" Liv finished, forcing a watery smile at the memory.

"She didn't speak to me for a month!" Natalie sighed and raked a hand through her own short, bleached blonde hair.

The bar was packed with Amy's friends and family. Kat, our chef, prepared a huge buffet and Mick flatly refused the Donaldson's offer of payment. One of our staff members, Kaden, was working the bar. Mick gave me instructions to stay with my friends and not worry about how busy it got. We were all sitting together in a group at the back of the pub, recalling Amy stories. I was in an armchair with Nick, perching on the edge, between his legs.

"The time she was going to paint my room and ended up painting Cam's instead." I shared a sad smile with my brother. We never had figured out how Amy managed to mix up my room and Cameron's. I'd always had a sneaky suspicion she'd done it on purpose. She never was one to miss an opportunity to wind someone up.

"Five coats!" Cameron groaned and we laughed. "It took five coats of paint to cover that enormous pink flower she painted above my bed."

"When she wore fairy wings every day for a month," Sally said.

Amy loved fairy wings and had worn them every chance she got. She had several pairs and changed them to match her outfits.

"Remember when she convinced everyone she'd married Mick over the summer and that was the reason he had stayed in town?" Luke shook his head with a smile on his face.

"Those purple Doc Marten boots that she painted daisies on," Nat said, her voice cracking.

"Oh, she loved those!" Vinnie smiled, putting an arm around Nat to comfort her. "Never took the damn things off."

"She painted her car to match," Jase added quietly, his eyes finding mine and holding.

"And her bedroom," Luke said, pulling Liv to him when she gave into her tears.

"She was so funny!" Dana leaned into Greg who was beside her. He kissed her gently on the top of her head, as she rested it on his shoulder.

"That she was." I leaned my head back against Nick's chest.

Despite the sadness of the situation, it felt good to have all of us together. Nobody could ever replace Amy. She was unique, a force of nature and we would all miss her. She'd hated conflict and adored her friends, which was why I was so upset and confused when she slept with Jase. Even now, she was bringing us all together. I may never know why she did what she did. Maybe she was in love with him. Who knows? I did know that nothing either of us could ever have said or done after that night, could take away the friendship we'd had for so many years before it. That was real. So, I resolved to concentrate on that, instead of questions I would never know the answers to. Interrupting my thoughts, Mick brought over a tray of shot glasses and a bottle of tequila. Tequila was Amy's drink.

"Let's send our girl off in style ladies and gents," Mick said, pouring a shot for each of us. He raised his own glass. "To the red-haired fairy princess that was our friend Amy."

"Amy!" We all chorused and downed our shots.

Mick poured another round before heading back behind the bar. The memory sharing continued around me, but I zoned out, my own thoughts shadowing my mood. I looked up to see Adam walk in and sit at the bar. Mick set a beer in front of him and they began talking. Mick nodded in my direction and Adam glanced over, catching my eye.

"Okay?" He mouthed.

"Okay." I nodded and mouthed back.

Adam smiled and turned back to continue his conversation with Mick. Their heads were bowed together, their backs turned to block out anyone else. Whatever they were talking about looked serious. I turned away, only for my eyes to clash with Jase's again. He smiled awkwardly and pretended not to have seen the exchange with Adam, but I could tell he had, and also drawn his own conclusions. Conclusions that I could see hurt him. I decided not to put him straight. What, if anything, was going on between Adam and I was our business.

Sitting in the room with both of them, my mind raced in circles. Jase and I were finished. That much I knew. Honestly, after being with him for so long, I wasn't sure I wanted to dive straight into something with Adam, or anyone. Wasn't there meant to be some kind of cooling off period before you were with anyone else? I'm sure there probably was. Not that I was an expert. I'd been in a serious relationship with one person for the whole of my adult life so far. I didn't know what it was like to be single, to not be one half of a pair. Let alone, what was supposed to happen when you suddenly weren't part of that pair anymore.

Yes, Adam was gorgeous, but that was just physical attraction, right? I enjoyed being with him, I almost craved his company. He made me feel safe and content. I didn't have to hide my darkness for him because he saw it, understood it, accepted it, and because of that, my world was a good place when he was around. Maybe that did mean something. Perhaps my feelings for him ran deeper than I wanted to admit. Yet, if he were to hint at anything more than friendship, well, I couldn't guarantee I wouldn't go running for the hills. There was no doubt something kept pulling us towards each other. I was drawn to his spark of darkness, the way he was drawn to the ocean of mine. We had vowed to battle our darkness together and maybe that was enough for us.

Frustrated with myself, and needing to refocus my mind, I extracted my body from Nick's embrace, and planted a kiss on his cheek. I decided to help Mick behind the bar. Cameron, Greg, and Vinnie had already joined Adam and were gathered in a group around him.

"You don't have to be behind here today, love," Mick said, enveloping me in what I called a Mick hug. He wrapped his arms around my shoulders from behind and held me tightly against his chest, resting his chin on the top of my head. I recognised it as an act of possession, Mick was an alpha male through and through, but I didn't mind. He didn't give affection often, so a Mick hug was a very special thing.

"I want to help, it's busy." I slanted my head slightly, to give him a look that told him I needed to be occupied.

He searched my eyes before finally nodding. He planted a kiss on the top of my head and let go of me. I knew he would get it. He always got it. I served a group of Amy's family at one end of the bar and a few others, then Adam beckoned to me. He cocked his head to one side, gesturing for me to follow him to the other end of the bar.

"How are you doing?" He passed me his beer. Adam hadn't come to the service because he hadn't known Amy, but he'd come to the pub to pay his respects to Amy's family, having met her parents and Luke during the investigation.

"I've been better," I admitted, not feeling the need to put on a show for him. I took a drink of the beer from the bottle. "It's a weird feeling. Sad, because we lost her, but it's difficult not to laugh and be happy at the memories we have of her. You almost feel guilty for smiling about it. I'm sure it's a feeling you know all about."

"I do," he said, nodding his understanding. "The whole mess with her and Jase can't help."

"I don't think I'll ever know what truly happened there. Part of me doesn't want to know, like it would somehow justify what happened to her. Another part of me wants to scream and shout and demand answers that she never be able to give me— and I'm rambling."

"I've come to like it when you ramble," he said, smiling. I pushed the beer bottle back towards him.

"It's nice to see Luke and Nate again, and to have Sally and Natalie with us. It's been a while since we were all together like this." I looked over to see Sally and Natalie watching Adam and me. "Ha! They've got you well and truly in their sights."

"Not my type." He pushed the beer back to me.

"How do you know? You've never met them." I laughed.

"I know my type, Angel, they're not it." He winked and my traitorous stomach did a happy dance.

"How come you haven't got a girlfriend?" I decided to distract myself by prodding around in his life.

"There have been women, just none that stick around." He shrugged.

"None that stuck around, or none that you let stick around?"

"You got me," he admitted with a smile. "I'm sure you've seen it with Cam, this job attracts two types. The ones who see the uniform and assume a hefty bank balance goes with it."

"Gold diggers," I laughed. Cameron called them wedding ring chasers.

"And those who see the uniform as a notch on their bedposts," he smirked.

"Uniform collectors," I labelled.

"Yeah, it was convenient for a while."

"And now?" I asked.

"Now, the woman I want stands out a million miles above all those others." He snared me in his gaze, and I wanted to look away, but something held me there. His eyes shone with a certainty that refused to waver and I was suddenly aware that I was that woman.

Later, as the bar was emptying and I was clearing tables, Jase approached me.

"I'm leaving now," he said quietly. The sleeves of his white shirt were rolled up to his elbows. He'd removed his purple tie and unbuttoned the top two buttons of his shirt. His hands were in the pockets of his navy-blue trousers, and his matching suit jacket was pulled through the loop of his arm, hanging over his wrist. He looked good, but then, he always looked good. "Thought I'd say goodbye."

"Ok, well, I guess I'll see you around," I said, setting down the cloth I was using to wipe the tables.

"Look, Cee, can we please talk? I mean, not now, not tonight. But sometime soon?" His eyes were unsure and full of desperation when he looked at me. He knew he'd broken everything good about us and it was hurting him as much as it was me.

"I honestly don't know what you want me to say," I sighed.

"Just hear me out. Please?" Jase ordinarily didn't beg and plead. This was something he truly needed.

"Alright." I gave in, desperate in my own way, to see a hint of the boy I'd fallen in love with all those years ago.

"Thank you." He let out a breath, relieved and hesitantly took his phone from his pocket. "So, can I call you?"

I nodded and took his phone from him to replace my old number.

"Ok, so I'll ring you soon," Jase said, taking his phone back, confidence oozing back into him.

He lifted his arms and moved to hug me. I hugged him back. Not as tightly as we had in the church. I didn't want him to read anything into it, because I knew there was no going back for us. I could never again trust him completely and that wasn't fair to either of us.

That night, I found a copy of Pride and Prejudice on the front porch that I didn't think was mine. I knew I owned the book, because it was my mum's, but I couldn't recall what it looked like, much less figure out why it had ended up on the front porch. I didn't mention it to Cameron. I probably should have, but it just didn't resonate as something important at the time.

Cameron and I spent the rest of the night huddled up on the sofa, watching back to back episodes of *The Flash* until he couldn't keep his eyes open any longer and I ushered him off to bed. My phone did its *TARDIS* thing almost the second he left the room. I picked it up, happy to avoid sleep and the inevitable nightmares for a little while longer.

Adam: You awake?

Me: Always

Adam: Nightmares?

Me: Not yet. In bed with my new book boyfriend. You?

Adam: Nope, you cured me. Do I want to know what a book boyfriend is?

Me: A boyfriend who is in my book, duh. I'm rolling my eyes at you.

Adam: So, a fictional boyfriend then?

Me: It's the way forward.

Adam: Talk to me about your book.

Me: It has gargoyles. Really sexy gargoyles, with wings and they're badass. Did I mention they were sexy?

Adam: Gargoyles do it for you, eh?

Me: Among other things.

Adam: Share...

Me: Vampires, werewolves, fallen angels, demons, witches. An alien or two.

Adam: No humans?

Me: Why would there be humans?

Adam: Not even a badass, tall, dark and handsome human in police uniform? You know, just stepping in to rescue the damsel in distress from the big ugly gargoyle.

Me: How very dare you! I'm appalled! Gargoyles are far from ugly. No woman in her right mind would ever need rescuing from a gargoyle.

Adam: Is it still too early to fall in love with you?

Me: If you're not into gargoyles you're not into me.

Just as I was setting my phone down it beeped again.

Night Cee. J xx

I frowned at the message, uncertain as to whether I should respond. On nights when Jase and I stayed at our own houses, instead of with each other, he always sent a goodnight message before he went to bed. That's what this was. I thought back over the day, trying to find the point where I had given him false hope about us. The truth was, it could be read into many of the things I'd done. Hugging him, telling him it wasn't important when he apologised, eye contact across the room. Everything down to simply giving him my number. As much as I wanted to ignore the message, I knew it would play on my mind all night if I didn't respond. So, I typed out *"Goodnight Jase."* No kisses, no terms of endearment. Then I put down my phone, climbed into bed and lost myself in my current book.

THE TEACHER

I decided to attend the service for the red head. I knew her, after all. I knew her in a way many of them hadn't. It would have been odd for me not to pay my respects. My absence would, no doubt, have been felt. My lady was in attendance, surrounded by her entourage. She may be blind to their feeble attempts to be close to her, feigning comfort and concern, but I see through their actions. Actions that are caused by her own behaviour. That she allows this intimacy enrages me. I see the desire on their faces as they touch her. I am ashamed to admit, jealousy courses through me, each time one of them is near her. When she learns the correct way to behave, the men around her will no longer be in danger of losing control.

The need to take her, steal her away, is overwhelming, but I will resist. Hiding my true intentions has been the most difficult part of my relationship with my lady, but it will be worth the reward. A reward must be earned; a lesson my mother taught well.

While delivering my lady's most recent gift this evening, I took on my next student. She actually had the nerve to flirt with me, believing I wanted from her what all the others want. Her screams invade my thoughts now, but I will leave her to stew for a while. Perhaps I should have gagged her. I hope she bleeds well.

I have also taken another student under my wing in the last few days. One who came to me for advice. While I have no fellow players in my game, I am not against using a person's vulnerabilities to my own advantage. His mind is easy to manipulate. He will play a major role in the undoing of my lady and neither of them will be any the wiser.

CHAPTER SIX

CALLIE

Nick: I wish I was a glow worm, a glow worms never glum. 'Cos how can you be grumpy when the sun shines out your bum?!!

Me: Why are we friends?

Nick: I'm outside.

Me: Woohoo!

I skipped happily out the front door, hopped down the steps, one by one, alternating feet as I went, and practically flew across the road, to where Nick was waiting for me. He sat on his vintage *Triumph* motorcycle— another of Nate's genius finds— laughing at my enthusiasm. As I reached him, he helped tighten the helmet I excitedly pulled over my head, while I bounced on the heels of my black biker boots and grinned madly at him. Nothing was getting me down. Darkness be damned. Today was all about the light. An entire day of adventures with my sunshine boy and on Valentine's Day, no less. Who needs a boyfriend, when you have a best friend?

"You nearly knocked your brother over there, Miss Bouncy." He grinned and flicked my nose. "Hold still, while I do the straps up."

I hadn't noticed Cameron and a frowny Adam standing on our front porch. They were studying something official looking that they held between them. I'd completely missed Adam's car, parked in the road outside our house, too. I was deliriously happy leaving everything behind for the day, that I'd hopped, skipped, and jumped right past them both.

"Oops! Sorry!" I called and blew a kiss to them. Nick started the engine and I climbed on behind him.

Cameron raised his cup to me, an amused smirk on his face. Adam snapped shut the folder he was looking at, and he held a hand up to wave. His frown dropped and he laughed as Nick circled the bike, turning it in the road. I wobbled and had to grab his jacket quickly to avoid falling off. I was laughing to myself as we sped off towards the open countryside and mountain roads nearby.

"Pockets!" Nick yelled over the noise of the engine. I dutifully wrapped my arms around his waist and buried my hands in his pockets.

With a sigh, I turned my head to one side, rested my cheek between Nick's shoulders, and enjoyed the view. He expertly wove the bike along the curving mountain roads. The higher we got the more beautiful the scenery became. Our small town of Frost Ford was nestled in a valley of lush, green hillsides. A patchwork of open countryside, and farming fields, spread for miles around it. I often felt sorry for Nick, not being able to take in the views as well as I could. He didn't seem to mind, waffling some petrol headed nonsense about the thrill of the ride and the feel of the machine on a good road.

After about an hour, Nick pulled the bike over near one of our favourite spots. We made the rest of the way on foot, to a clearing at the edge of the hillside, a place we'd found by accident one day. We'd stopped on one of our rides and ventured into a patch of woodland, discovering that it led to a clearing at the other side with the most amazing view of the valley. We'd spent hours there over the years. We brought picnic food and a blanket to sit on, carried in the bike's saddle bags. We would lie on the blanket for hours, sometimes talking, sometimes just enjoying the comfortable silence, and the beauty around us. That's the beauty of having a male best friend, they never expect you to fill the silences with mindless chatter.

Unknown: Happy Valentine's Day, beautiful. Next year we will be together again.

Me: Who is this?

Unknown: Your future

My blood ran cold when I read the message. I turned to Nick. "How do you block a number?"

He leaned over, took one look at the phone in my hand, and grabbed it from me, reading the messages. "Who is this, Cal?"

"It'll be Jase, trying to fuck with my head. Just block the number for me, will you?" I asked him.

Nick tapped on the screen for a few seconds and then handed it back. "Have you had any unwanted gifts lately?"

"Not for a few days." I told him.

"I want you to tell me if that carries on, okay? I'll talk to him," Nick said.

I nodded and put the phone away to forget about Jase. Nick wasn't quick tempered, but when he blew, you didn't want to be in the area, so I wasn't about to let Jase ruin our day.

"Do you think anyone else ever comes here?" I pondered, twisting a blade of grass that I'd plucked. It hadn't warmed up too much yet, but snowdrops and crocuses littered the grass we sat on.

"I like to think not," Nick replied. He tugged on my hair and leaned back to rest on his elbows.

"Why not?" I turned and lay on my side, facing him.

"Because this is our place." He shrugged, as if it should be obvious.

"You don't want to share?"

"Nope!" He grinned and rolled to his side, facing me. "I've missed this. I miss, you know, just being us. Life gets in the way so much these days."

"Being a grown up isn't all it's cracked up to be." I agreed.

It had always been easy between Nick and me, our friendship required no effort. After my abduction, he somehow instinctively knew when I was having a dark moment and had a way of bringing me out of it. But even he never saw the full extent of how deep my darkness went. I think he knew I wasn't showing him all of it, but he never pushed for more than I was willing to give. He just made sure he was there when I needed him.

"We don't spend enough time together lately," I said. "We used to sneak off from the others all the time."

"And usually get ourselves into trouble," he agreed with a chuckle.

"Like the thing with the lemurs." I remembered an eventful trip to the zoo, that I refused to let him live down.

"Lemurs are arseholes!" Nick was still grumpy about that little adventure, so he changed the subject. "Remember the time we got stuck on Liv's roof and had to sleep out there? I thought Jase was going to kill me when he found us the next morning."

I laughed with him. We were at Liv's house; her parents were away, and we were staying overnight. We could only have been only sixteen or seventeen at the time. Everyone but Nick and I had fallen asleep, always being the last ones awake. There was a full moon that night and we decided to climb out of Liv's bedroom window, onto the flat roof of the garage, to look at the sky. The window locked itself behind us and since everyone else was downstairs asleep, we were stuck until morning. We'd found it hilarious. Jase had not.

"He was so mad," I said, shaking my head.

"I don't think it helped that you'd used me as a pillow." Nick grinned, wolfishly. It seemed I was in the habit of using men as pillows, even from a young age.

"No," I said quietly, remembering the huge argument Jase and I had over it. I'd had to get in between him and Nick to stop them from hurting each other. Jase had always been jealous of my friendship with Nick. Nick went out of his way to be Jase's friend too and they mostly got on fine. Jase just couldn't seem to get it into his head that Nick and I were no more than friends.

"Hey, you ok in there?" Nick tugged on my hair again.

"Things have changed so much," I sighed.

"You miss him." It wasn't a question and I realised he'd brought Jase back up on purpose, to get me to work through my feelings. He was a sneaky one.

"Kind of. I can't explain it, not even to myself, really. I mean, he's been part of my life for so long, even before we got together. It feels odd not to have him around. Like, it would be odd not to have you around, but I don't miss *us*. I don't miss him being my boyfriend. I certainly don't miss the arguing. It's weird, not having that other person there all the time. But not always bad weird—" I looked at Nick and he grinned. "I'm rambling, aren't I?"

"It's what you do best." He pulled me with him as he lay back down on his back. I twisted to the side slightly and rested my head on his chest. We lay like that for a long time, looking at the sky. Not needing to talk.

Later, we sat on his bike outside my house, chatting about everything and nothing. I shimmied around the front of Nick to sit facing him on the bike, my legs draped over his thighs. A noise, in the trees nearby, snatched our attention and stopped our chatter. We looked, scrutinising the area, but couldn't see anything.

"Probably just a rabbit," Nick said.

"Yeah. Hey, you know what we never did?" I said, a sudden brainwave hitting me.

"We're going to die, aren't we?" Nick joked.

"No lemurs this time, I promise." I drew a cross over my heart with my finger. "But what about those matching tattoos we always talked about?"

"You still want to?" he asked, taking my hand and tracing a design on the back of it with his finger.

Sometimes, before he began tattooing, Nick would use a pen and draw designs on my skin, to practice. It was usually when he felt stressed about something to do with his Mum or brothers. It calmed him somehow, more so than drawing on paper. I spent half of our teenage years covered in faded black ink drawings; they were so beautiful, I never wanted to wash them off.

"Of course! But, I'm not sure you've got any room left." I gestured to his arms, underneath his leather jacket. Both of his arms were almost fully covered in stunning inked designs. As were his legs, chest, and back.

"There's always room for you. Alright, let me see here—" He gently took my wrists in his hands and pushed up my jacket sleeves. He indicated my bracelets by rubbing his thumb over them. "Can I take them off for a minute?"

I nodded, trusting him completely. He loosened some of the ties and removed them all. Pocketing my bracelets, he turned both my wrists over and looked at the scars. After a few minutes, he nodded to himself and put all my bracelets back on, in exactly the right order that I always wore them. I was fussy about how they all sat next to each other. I had them sorted so that they rested perfectly against one another to cover the scars.

"I can cover this one pretty easily. The other arm will take something bigger." He told me quietly holding onto my left hand. I didn't miss the emotion in his voice when he spoke. The scarring on my left wrist was slightly smaller and lighter in colour than my right one. I nodded and a single tear trailed a path down my cheek. I liked the idea that he could put something meaningful and permanent over the mark. Nick leant towards me and kissed the tear away from my cheek. Then he smiled and tugged on my hair, making me laugh away the sadness.

"I'll come up with some designs and talk to Popeye, see when he can fit us in. I've already got a few ideas." He referred to the other tattoo artist that worked in his studio. Nick couldn't ink himself, but he would do mine. "Anyway, you and Adam?"

"Ah, not you too!" I groaned, pulling my hand away from him.

"Pretty difficult to miss." He smiled and dragged my hand back into his lap, refusing to let go. "You like him?"

"Yes, I like him. He's my friend. I like you. I like Mick. I like Vin..." I pouted.

"Alright, alright, I get it. You're in denial." He laughed, interrupting my outburst.

"We're friends. That's all!" I crossed my arms, as if that confirmed it.

"You sure?" Nick raised his eyebrows at me.

"No," I whispered, dragging my bottom lip into my mouth with my teeth.

"I knew it!" Nick whispered back gleefully.

"No. You don't. You don't know anything. Shit, Nick, I don't know anything!" I rambled.

"Confused much." He smirked. I hated him.

"One of these days, Sunshine, you're gonna get caught. You're going to fall head over heels and I'm going to be there. Laughing." I poked him in the chest.

"That'll never happen." He shook his head. "So, Adam."

"I don't know. I like where we are, right now. If it ain't broke and all that." I shrugged helplessly, not really sure how to explain myself. There was something different with Adam. I had something deeper than any of my other friendships with him, but I couldn't find the words to explain it. I didn't *have* to put it into words for Adam, he already knew because he felt it too.

"Well, for what it's worth, I've got a feeling about you two."

"Ah, one of Nick the love guru's feelings. Well, I suppose I'd better hire a wedding planner, hadn't I?"

"No, you're still marrying me." Nick laughed with me. "He can have you at weekends. I need you at home to cook, and clean, and look after my brothers during the week!"

"That's all you want me for?" I feigned outrage.

"Yep. Well, that and all the steamy. No point in having a wife if you can't have sex on demand!" He stuck out his tongue at me.

"Cameron would lock us up if we got married." I laughed.

"He'd lose his mind trying to keep us out of trouble!"

"Who's getting married?" Cameron appeared at the top of the porch steps. He was shirtless in only jeans, and barefoot, his wavy, dark hair all over the place. My brother had long ago perfected the art of always looking like he just woke up.

"Don't!" I warned Nick, giving him my best *"one word and I'll break you"* look. He smirked at me and waggled his eyebrows, letting me know he wasn't convinced. "Nobody! Nobody is getting married."

"Erm, *we're* getting married, Moonbeam. Remember, you asked me the other night? Ibiza wedding, baby!" Nick's eyes flashed with mischief. "Wait, it wasn't just the alcohol talking, was it?"

"Ok, well, nobody apart from us." I rolled my eyes, climbed off the bike, and walked up the steps onto the porch. "You been asleep all day, twin?"

"I was tired," Cameron replied defensively, rubbing at his chest. "Nick, you hanging around, bruv? I feel like a barbecue."

"Plan! We can make it an engagement party, honey bun. What do you think?" Nick continued to tease me, I ignored him.

Nick kicked the stand out on the bike and climbed off. He turned, in time to catch the car keys Cameron threw in his direction and walked around to let himself into our car.

"It's February!" I said, glancing between them.

"And?" Cameron replied and I knew better than to continue that line of conversation. A barbecue was happening. I watched him pull his phone out of his pocket and send a group text to our friends.

"Don't forget to invite Adam," I reminded him.

"Done. Nick and I will get beer and meat. You do the salad, pip squeak." Cameron instructed, pointing at me with his phone in one hand. With the other hand, he caught the sweatshirt I threw at him and pushed his feet into trainers. Who says men can't multitask? Then he ran down the steps and joined Nick. "Don't forget the salad!"

Salad? Really?

"Make your own salad, you pre-historic beast!" I shouted after him as the car pulled away and decided to have a shower instead.

THE TEACHER

I am livid. After hours of careful surveillance, I successfully managed to discover my lady's new telephone number, and now I cannot access it. She has somehow blocked me from contacting her. This is not acceptable to me. How can I tell her when she looks beautiful, if she will not allow me to speak to her?

My latest student will take the brunt of my anger, but my frustrations with my lady will linger until I have her again. It's impolite to ignore the attentions of a person. Surely, she must be aware of this? Her manners are not usually this poor.

I collect the poetry book I have for her from the hallway table. My gifts, she cannot continue to ignore. She has shown me that she will not be swayed with flowers, the finest champagne, or divine fragrances. She requires more thought than this, my chosen one is not easy. My Mother taught me well in the art of romancing a lady and I intend to use those lessons to the best of my ability. Patience will be my virtue; I must not rush this. She will come back to me. Mother warned me that a whore will push herself at a man, this is not what I require from my lady. She must remain innocent, demure and pure, only ever mine.

Tonight, is not for her. Tonight, is for teaching. My new student awaits, and I am feeling quite brutal. This one has many lessons to learn about the dangers of sharing her body. Her education may take some time. Mother was explicit in her orders that all whores must be reformed. I will see her legacy through exactly as she wished. Then, I will take my reward.

First, I have a gift to deliver.

CALLIE

"Keats?" I murmured to myself, as I picked up the book and flicked through the pages, after wandering onto the porch after my shower. There were highlights on almost every page and I paused to read a few of them.

Beauty is truth, truth beauty,'--that is all Ye know on earth, and all ye need to know.

A thing of beauty is a joy forever.

The poetry of the earth is never dead.

Do you not see how necessary a world of pains and troubles is to school an intelligence and make it a soul?

The final highlight sent a cold shiver through me and I snapped the book shut. It had been left on the top step of the porch, clearly in view. A niggling voice at the back of my mind insisted there was a strong chance this wasn't Jase's doing. He was aware of my love of books, but I couldn't see it even occurring to Jase to go out and buy me a book of love poetry. Let alone highlight some of the lines. Unable to face the truth, I began to question my knowledge of Jase. Maybe this was him trying to change for me, make more of an effort to acknowledge my interests? I doubted it, but then, what did I really know about him anymore?

Taking the book inside, I added it to a pile on the window ledge, intending to deal with it later. I don't know why I didn't leave it out to tell Cameron immediately. No, that's a lie. I was in denial and I didn't want to worry him. Maybe I was wrong, and Jase was changing his ways, and trying to get my attention with books. If that was the case, I wasn't going to accept them. I intended to give them back and let him know he was wasting his time. I pushed it out of my mind, refusing to allow the niggling voice to grow, and acknowledge the fact that there was more to this than I was willing to think about. The darkness was closing in on me, but I was going to outrun it this time. I had to.

I put the bowl of salad I was holding down on the table with a clatter and scowled at Cameron. He threw his head back and laughed. I hoped the flames singed his eyebrows off. In his defence, he'd returned from the supermarket with a tub of cookie dough ice cream and a jar of red heart shaped sprinkles, for me. Seeing as there was ice cream involved, I couldn't justify staying angry with him for long, but I wouldn't give in too easily, even if he did find it hilarious.

"Incoming!" Liv sang, as she and Vinnie walked up the steps to the front porch.

Cameron and Nick had a raging fire burning at one end. They claimed they had it under control, but I had my phone in my hand, ready to dial 999, at the slightest hint of a spark hitting the wooden deck. Adam followed a few minutes after Liv and Vinnie, along with Dana and Greg.

"For you." Adam handed me a small bag.

"What's this?" I frowned, craning my neck to look up at him.

"Have a look." He nodded towards the bag. I opened it and pulled out a pair of rainbow coloured, striped mittens. I smiled; Adam had officially joined the *Callie needs gloves* club.

"They're not just any gloves, look—" He pulled them all the way out of the bag, to reveal a thread, running between the two mittens, attaching them together. "You thread them through your coat sleeves. No more forgetting or falling out of pockets. They're always there."

"Genius! Adam, you're amazing." I jumped up and threw my arms around his neck to kiss his cheek. He laughed because my feet were no longer touching the floor. Looping his arms around my waist, he lifted me higher.

"You like them then?" He murmured into my hair.

"They're perfect. They make me feel like I'm five again and that was a good year." I rested my hands on his chest when he set me down. "Thank you for thinking about me."

He smiled before leaning down and kissing my forehead. "You're welcome and I think about you a lot, Angel."

I ignored Dana when she giggled and sang the words *"Forehead kisses"* from somewhere behind us. Instead, I grabbed Adam's hand and led him inside to get a drink.

Nick: Prepare to go on lockdown.

Me: ???

Nick: Fair warning.

Me: Are the lemurs coming?

Nick: No, it was touch and go for a while, but I threw them off the scent. Your brother is on his way to you. Go easy on him. I'll come and see you later. xx

Call it paranoia, but I could feel a presence wherever I went. Since I'd given him my number, Jase messaged me daily. Just idle chitchat kind of stuff. I saw no harm in replying at first, then he started turning up at random points during the day. He always seemed to know where I would be. The roses and other gifts were less frequent, but they still came, and he still denied sending them. It was the books that unnerved me more than anything.

The fact was though; Jase didn't have to be watching me to know where I would be. He knew when I worked, when I had classes, when I was at home. We had lived that life together for years, so him showing up out of the blue shouldn't really have surprised me. He did it all the time when we were together, and he wanted us to get back together. I should have known he'd do this. I gave him my number, had I thought he wouldn't use it? Still, this feeling I had was more than that. It was a weird sense of déjà-vu, and I couldn't put my finger on the reason behind it.

Then, the killer claimed another victim and a woman from the nearby town of Lochden Marsh was also missing. As Nick's warning predicted, Cameron, Adam, and Greg were getting watchful on us girls, and refusing to let us go anywhere without one of them. None of them would, or could, go into details. All they revealed was that this one had been worse than Amy and they were almost certain the two were related, along with the missing woman.

Do you know how easy it is to fall into darkness? I stood outside my body and watched myself change; I couldn't stop it. It consumed me. It tore through me, strangling my organs as my heart fought to beat faster, pumping the darkness through every part of my body, until all feeling burned in its scorching fire. I wasn't sad or afraid anymore, I was numb, and numb is so much worse.

"I don't want you going anywhere alone," Adam said.

On autopilot, I served him and the others in the pub. His eyes bored into mine as he said the words. I didn't have to tell him the crazy thoughts running through my head, he knew. They probably all knew what this would do to my already shattered piece of mind. It wouldn't be hard to figure out, I'm certain it was written all over my face. I'd slipped into a kind of living coma. I was alive, operational, but trapped inside my own mind and oblivious to what went on around me.

"And not just with the other girls," Cameron added, fiddling with the label on his bottle. "You need to be with one of us. Especially, at night."

"What?" I gaped at him. Obviously, I knew why he was doing this. He was terrified. The memories were there for him too. I couldn't let him know that I was beginning to lose myself to them again.

"I'll bring her home myself after her shifts here." Mick appeared beside me. He stood close to me, his shoulder and arm touching mine as he bent and leaned his forearms on the bar. His actions were there to comfort me, but he still carried on the conversation as if I didn't exist. "Either that or she'll stay over here, with me."

"I am here, you know!" I snapped, determined to not let the wave of fear that had washed over me show on the outside. *It's not him, it's not him*, I mentally chanted. Mick put an arm around my waist and pulled me against his side. Adam eyed Mick and something passed between them, a silent nod from them both, as if making an agreement.

"I'm serious, Callie. You, Dana, Liv, you don't go anywhere without one of us. I've already spoken to Nate, Luke, and Nick. They're all making themselves available and I'll talk to Vinnie tonight." Cameron was obviously spooked by this if he was rallying the troops. Suddenly, I was certain there was something he was holding back.

"What aren't you telling me? I know that look. I know you. You're keeping something from me." I challenged him.

"I just want you safe," he snapped. We silently glared at each other for a few seconds, silent messages passing between us. He wasn't going to give anything up, Cameron's stubbornness was rivalled only by my own. He could see I was scared and needed to know what was happening, but he had given me all he could, or was prepared to.

"Fine. I'll let it go. But you should know that I don't believe you." I narrowed my eyes at him.

"You need to get on board with this, Angel. I plan on being your shadow until this sicko is caught." He held my eyes in that way of his, the one that told everyone this was going to happen exactly as he said.

"What about college? I can't expect a police escort to and from all my classes, can I?" I challenged Cameron again. My voice cracked and my bravado began to slip. "Why don't I just use the car and you walk to work?"

"You'd still be alone. The last victim was taken between leaving work and getting into her car, which was parked right outside her place of work." He explained as gently as he could, I still shuddered. Mick turned away and poured a glass of brandy which he set in front of me. I resisted the urge to knock it back in one.

"You call Cam or me when you need to go anywhere and if we can't come ourselves, we'll send one of your other friends. Someone you know will be with you." Adam closed his hand over mine on the bar, pausing my incessant polishing with the bar towel. I looked up, silently thanking him for noticing my anxiety.

"Please don't fight me on this, Cal. This isn't just you and the girls. We're publicly issuing this advice to every woman in the area. Admittedly, we're going overboard with you, but I need to know you're safe and this is the best way," Cameron said.

He looked at me then and I saw the worry in his eyes. He was right there with me; I could almost hear the same words running through his head as were on a loop in mine. So, I stopped pretending for a second and gave in, because he needed me to.

THE TEACHER

Hiding my true identity and intentions, as I endeavour to maintain a relationship with her, has proven the most difficult and most important part of our game. Contact with her has been scarce, while her security team shield her from the world. They treat me as they always have, unaware of the danger I pose. Although, not to her. Never to her. Her, I only wish to keep. I miss her when we aren't together and crave our alone time more than ever.

I watch her as she walks towards the waiting car. Head low, steps fast and hurried, her eyes flick nervously around her. She feels me under her skin. We are part of each other, though she seeks to deny it.

Our history consumes her, yet she attempts to hide from the memories. I know her every move. Her every breath, every action, every thought originates with me. She was made for me and I for her. Wy can she not see this? Her happiness is my only desire. I would never force from her anything she wasn't willing to give. She would never need to fear anything again, her lessons would show her that.

My hands ball into fists when today's chauffeur leans across the seats and pushes a strand of hair from her face. She smiles at the words he speaks to her. I cannot abide the way she looks at him, as though he is her entire world. She is luring him, enticing him with her female charms. He is a willing captive, but it will only end badly for him. I will ensure she looks at me that way before her lessons are over. Her eyes will no longer hold fear and loathing. She will always worship me first. She will always love me first. I made mistakes with her in the past, mistakes I will not repeat.

CHAPTER SEVEN

CALLIE

I lay in bed watching the storm rage outside my open window. I loved storms; my mum had always told us it was Mother Nature's way of showing us that even she could have a bad day. The sky was screaming its anger down at me tonight and I was agreeing with every word. There was no point in trying to sleep, the nightmares would only come in force. They became relentless when Cameron and the others took up bodyguard duties.

The white curtains billowed in the wind, and a black cloud covered my mood, as well as the sky. I couldn't stop my mind from wandering to Jase. We used to lie in my bed together on nights like that, watching the storm through the open window. When we were younger, he would sneak in through my bedroom window and keep me company, while we innocently held hands, and counted the seconds that passed between the thunder and lightning. As we got older, he didn't need to sneak in through the window anymore, but he did it anyway. We would lie naked in each other's arms after making love. My head resting on his chest, his fingers lazily tracing patterns on my skin, while we watched the sky light up.

A scuffle at the window caused my heart to lurch into my throat and I sat bolt upright in bed. *It's not him. It's not him.* My mantra kicked in. It's alright, I told myself, Cameron and Adam are in the living room, all you have to do is scream. The three of us eating dinner together was becoming a regular occurrence, but I'd left them to it when the storm began, not being in the mood for company.

"It's okay. It's just me, CeeCee." Jase's voice carried through the window. It was followed a few seconds later by his smiling face. "Hey, can I come in?"

"What are you doing here?" I snapped, my heart rate slowing slightly. "You scared the shit out of me. You know they found another body, right?"

"Shit! I didn't think. I'm sorry, babe." He moved to climb through the window.

"Stop!" I held up a hand and frowned at him.

"It's not him, Cee. He's long gone. You're safe." He paused and ran a hand through his soaked hair. I relaxed a little and tried to control my breathing. "I miss you. I wanted to watch the storm together, like always. That's all, I swear it."

I sighed and nodded, knowing I should send him away. I just couldn't muster the strength to do it. I pulled the covers up to my chin and watched him make short work of climbing in through the window. He proceeded to kick off his boots and shrug out of his jacket. I broke my silence when he reached for his belt.

"What the hell are you doing?"

"I'm drenched, walked all the way here in the rain. Couldn't drive because I had a beer with Dad earlier," he replied.

He continued to peel the wet denim from his legs and yanked off his t-shirt, in that one-handed way men do. Then, there he was. My 6'2, golden skinned, muscle bound, Adonis of a boyfriend. *Ex Callie! Ex-boyfriend!* I hastily reminded myself. I bit my lip, what was I thinking? Why did he have to be so gorgeous? Jase picked up the corner of the duvet and climbed into the bed as though it were nothing unusual. Honestly, it wasn't. He'd spent countless nights in my bed, and it hadn't been all that long ago. I missed him too, but I wasn't about to tell him that.

"Hi," he said, his voice low. He settled next to me on the pillows and tilted his head to the side, to look at me.

"Hi," I whispered.

I turned my eyes to the window and the wrathful storm outside, whose thunderous roars suddenly matched the pounding of my heart. A comfortable silence fell over us. Even after everything that had happened, even though I was questioning myself for letting him in, it didn't feel awkward to be this close to him.

"Jase, please..." I begged painfully when I felt him inching slowly closer. I knew I wouldn't resist him if he touched me.

"I just want to be near you." He stretched an arm out and pulled me to him before I could resist.

I snuggled into him and rested my head on his chest, draping an arm across his bare stomach. We both sighed in contentment. Jase trailed his fingers through my hair, and I closed my eyes, loving the feel of his hands back where they were supposed to be. I don't know why I didn't fight him, push him away and tell him to leave. Yes, I did. I was weak. Weaker than a rich tea biscuit, in a hot cup of tea, is what I was when it came to Jason Montgomery. I'd always been weak when it came to him, letting him take charge and steer our lives in the direction he thought we should go.

"I'm so sorry, CeeCee," he whispered.

I didn't react. I lay silent and still, waiting to see if he would continue. Secretly hoping that he had some magic words that would make it all go away, miraculously setting everything right again. He didn't. It was just a string of clichés.

"I never wanted to hurt you, never meant to lose you. I don't know what I was thinking, if I was even thinking at all. I swear to you, if I could go back, I would never even think about doing it again. I'm an idiot. I was the luckiest man alive and I fucked it up. I lost the best thing that ever happened to me, my reason for living. I can't even give you a reason for it. I'm so sorry, Cee." His voice cracked, and I looked up to see the tears spill over and begin to fall down his face. His eyes met mine when I lifted my head. I looked away hastily, chickening out of the confrontation.

"Is there a chance for us Cee?" he whispered. "Can you forgive me? Can we come back from this?"

"Jay, don't, please." I begged again. I hadn't called him that in forever and I mentally berated myself for doing it as soon as I saw the flicker of hope cross his face.

"I'll do anything," he pleaded.

"Even if I did forgive and forget, I could never trust you again. That's not fair on either of us, we can't live like that." I told him thorough my own tears.

"I'll do whatever it takes to earn your trust again. Tell me you don't love me anymore. Tell me and I'll go. I'll leave you alone. I won't bother you again." He twisted so we faced each other, and held my face gently between his hands, forcing my eyes to meet his. "Say the words, baby. Tell me you don't love me, and I'll walk away."

I couldn't say the words because they weren't true, and I wasn't sure they ever would be. I couldn't guarantee that there wouldn't be a small part of me that loved this man forever. I'd loved him my entire life and it wasn't a case of just switching off. That was why this was so hard. That was the reason I held on so long, even when things started to go wrong between us, because no matter what had happened, how he had changed or what he had done, I never stopped loving him.

"I can't," I sobbed.

He was kissing me before I could register his movement. Gently at first, tentatively, testing my reaction to his lips on mine. I didn't stop him, because just for a minute, just for one, blissful moment, I wanted to be back where we were before. Madly in love and unable to keep our hands off each other. Best friends. Together. Callie and Jase.

So, I kissed him back. His hand moved to the back of my neck, the other wound around my waist, pulling me closer to him. The feel of his smooth, solid chest under my palms sent a hot pulse over my skin. I reached up and tangled my fingers in his hair. Without breaking the kiss, he shifted us, to pin me underneath him. His tongue slid over my lips and into my mouth, my stomach muscles clenched, and I let out a moan. Damn, I missed kissing him.

"You're everything, CeeCee. Everything." He whispered the words as he trailed hot kisses down my neck and across my collarbone. I moaned again, lost in the sensation of his bare skin against mine, the familiar weight of his body above me.

"They could never do what you do, baby. They never meant anything. They could never be what you are to me. they never made me feel the way you do." He pushed the thin strap of my vest top off my shoulder and replaced it with his lips, moving slowly down my arm.

Wait. What?

"They?" I tore my mouth away from his as clarity hit. Breathlessly, I laid one of my palms flat on his chest and pushed, attempting to sit, using the other hand to pull at the straps on my clothes, and cover myself.

"Hmm?" Not noticing my sudden mood change, he leaned forward to chase my mouth with his. I twisted my head away from him.

"*They*. You said *they*." The blissful haze rapidly evaporated, giving way to a black, angry fog. I pushed at him until he got the message and moved back. We knelt, facing each other on the bed.

"Cee, what's wrong?" He frowned. *Seriously?*

"They, Jase. You said THEY could never do what I do. None of THEM ever meant anything. Exactly how many were there?" I demanded, my voice rising gradually with each word.

"Fuck!" He whispered, dragging a hand down his face.

"Yeah. Fuck!" I agreed. "Get out!"

"Baby, wait. Let's talk a bit more. We were getting somewhere. We can sort this out," he argued, his eyes pleading with me.

"No, we can't." I began pushing at him again, until he had no choice but to stand up. The tears streamed down my face as I looked at him. "Even when you spewed every cliché in the book at me, I still thought... Maybe for a second. Just maybe. Because I wanted to believe we were worth it, that we were bigger than that. But we can't. We really fucking can't!"

I stood, drying my eyes with the heels of my hands, and gathered his clothes. When he refused to move, I flung them through the open window, into the flower bed that lay underneath. I grabbed his boots and threw them out too. The irony that my mum used to tell him off, for trampling her flowers, when he used the window and threaten to bury his designer boots in the flower bed, wasn't lost on me.

"Get out!" I was yelling now, and I knew I would get Cameron's attention sooner or later. I just hoped Adam had left.

"Cee, please." Jase looked helplessly at the window, where I'd thrown his clothes.

"No!" I said through gritted teeth. "You almost had me there, Jase. I nearly fell for it. You must have a really low opinion of me to try that shit."

"It's not like that, Cee. You *do* mean more." He moved towards me, attempting to explain and only succeeding in digging himself further in.

"Stop calling me that!" I screamed loudly and put a hand up to stop him coming any closer. "You need to go."

"I'm not leaving until we sort this out!" Jase was getting angry now.

"The fuck you're not!" My bedroom door flew open and Cameron stood in the frame, anger pouring off him in waves.

He moved forward swiftly and grabbed Jase by the arm. Dragging him from the room in nothing but his underwear, he snarled vicious words at him all the way to the front door. That's when I noticed Adam, standing in the living room, a look of pure hatred on his face, aimed at Jase.

"Angel..." he said, when he turned towards me. I couldn't read his expression, but I was in no mood for lectures.

"Don't." I said, throwing a hand up in the air. "I'm weak. I'm an idiot. I know! Cam will give me all the I told you so's I can deal with; of that you can be certain. So, just *don't!*"

I turned and slammed my bedroom door behind me. I climbed back into my bed and cried myself to sleep. I vaguely remember Cameron coming in and gathering me up in his arms at one point. Whether it was due to a nightmare or my tears over Jase, I wasn't sure. I think Adam was there at one point too, a fuzzy vision of him on the fringes of a nightmare lingered when I woke the next morning. The smell of bacon and the sound of voices wafted through the house and I put on a brave face, knowing whoever was here would already know what had happened.

I shuffled, puffy eyed, towards the kitchen, where Cameron, Nick, Adam, and Liv were gathered around the island. Mick stood by the hob wearing my mum's old *"Domestic Goddess"* apron. I rested a hip on the counter close to Mick, needing his unwavering strength. He leaned over and kissed the top of my head.

I let my tear stained eyes meet theirs, waiting for one of them to impart some wisdom. They didn't. No words were needed. Adam came over and handed me his cup. He kissed me on the forehead and stepped away again. Nick reached over and pulled my hair. Cameron winked at me, and Liv wrapped her arms around my waist from the side, resting her cheek on my shoulder.

"Full Irish breakfast, that'll set you right, love," Mick said.

"You threw his clothes out the window," Liv whispered.

"Yeah," I whispered back.

"In the rain," she continued.

"Yeah," I answered quietly.

"You're my hero." She squeezed her arms tightly around me.

Twin 2: You know, you're the perfect height for an arm rest.

Me: I am finding you zero amounts of funny right now, Cameron!

"You sure you're ready for this?" Nick asked, when I climbed onto the bike behind him. I'd been guarded to within an inch of my life for weeks and I was feeling ever so slightly claustrophobic, on top of the paranoia. I needed to let off steam. So, I'd jumped at the chance when Nick called and told me Popeye could fit us in for our tattoos that afternoon.

"I'm ready," I said.

"You know it can't be undone?" Nick warned, smirking.

"What, are we having each other's names inked on our foreheads? Or are you chickening out on me, Mr Warren? You're covered in the things and it's not like it's my first." I reminded him.

A few years earlier, not long after our parents died, Nick inked matching tattoos on Cameron and me. An anchor, on the back of Cameron's ankle, I had a ship's wheel in the same spot. Nick told us I steer the ship and Cameron anchors us in. Not that I was doing much in the way of steering our ship lately.

"Looking forward to it." Nick grinned. "I think I like the idea of my name on your forehead though. We wouldn't have to worry about any more moronic ex-boyfriends, rendering you brainless in the middle of the night, if they all thought you were mine!"

"Yeah, yeah, whatever," I mumbled.

A few hours later, Nick and I lay side by side, on a blanket in our hillside spot, comparing our new matching tattoos. Nick had doodled and played around with a lot of designs, finally coming up with the mathematical symbol for congruence, meaning different yet the same. We'd both instantly agreed that the two, small, horizontal, straight lines, and one wavy line, was just right. The only difference between the two, was a small sunshine next to Nick's symbol, and a tiny crescent moon beside mine. I had always called him my sunshine, but he only admitted to me while Popeye was inking him, that he had started calling me moonbeam because he thought of me as his moon.

"*...because no matter how dark it gets, you still shine bright.*" I may have ugly cried a little when he said that. In front of Popeye.

"They're perfect." I smiled as we held our wrists next to each other, admiring the simple artwork.

"Agreed," Nick said. "But one more brain-dead moment with Jase and my name is going on that head of yours!"

"I'll settle for a ring finger tatt when we tie the knot," I joked.

"Deal. What are you going to do with the bracelets from that wrist?" Nick laced his fingers in mine and brought our hands down to rest on his chest.

"Well, since there are only two from that side, I can fit them on the other arm with those three."

I'd played around with them and figured out which ones I wanted next to each other. I briefly considered removing the one Jase gave me, but something stopped me. It was a string of amethyst stones, meant to represent protection and neutralise negative energy. He bought it from a beach vendor during our first trip to Ibiza. I was being sentimental, but I just didn't feel right taking it off.

"I can come up with something to cover that one, too. If you want. It will have to be bigger though." Nick offered.

"Hmm, I would like more ink at some point, but I'm kind of attached to the bracelets. They all mean something important to me because of who they came from, so I want to keep wearing them."

"You're right. The ink means something special and the bracelets do, too. Besides, you are only allowed matching tats with someone else," he declared.

"Since when?" I turned my head to face him and frowned at him.

"That's your theme. The ink you have matches mine and Cam's. So, I won't put more on you unless it means something between you and someone important." He reasoned, making me smile at the sentiment.

"Love you, Sunshine Boy." I bumped my shoulder against his.

"Love you back, Cal." He pulled a strand of my hair. "Anyway, talk to me about the Adam situation."

"Get over it," I groaned.

"Nope. Not until you see what's right in front of you," he pushed.

"Even if I wanted him, I can't have him."

"Why the hell not?" Nick frowned at me.

"Because I'm broken, and he deserves better." I shrugged. Who was I to put all of my baggage onto Adam?

"Are you fucking kidding me?" I flinched at his tone as he turned on his side and reached over to pull my chin between his thumb and forefinger, forcing me to look at him. "He would be the luckiest man alive to be with you. You are not broken. That piece of shit messed with your head, and you're dealing with it, but you are *not* broken, Callie. If you were, you wouldn't be here right now. You'd be hiding in a corner somewhere, afraid to live your life. You are everything Adam deserves and more. And you deserve someone that loves you like he does, too. You and that stupid brother of yours have saved my life more times than I want to remember. You're the best people I know, nobody deserves to be happy more than you do. You never talk like that about yourself again. You hear me?"

I nodded, feeling a little emotional and overwhelmed at his outburst. He moved his hand to the back of my neck and brought our foreheads together.

"I asked you a question," he whispered.

"Okay, but it's only been five minutes since I broke up with Jase. I can't go out with anyone else yet, even if Adam *was* interested. I don't know if I'm even into him that way."

"Rambling, Cal. It's nobody's business but yours when you choose to go out with someone else. You've got to stop worrying about the gossip mongers in town and live your life, for you. Believe me, I know. If you worry about the gossip, you'll never live the life you deserve. You're the only one that counts." Nick threw an arm around my shoulder as we both sat up fully.

"When did you get so wise?" I peered at him thoughtfully.

"When my parents let me and my brothers down on an epic scale, and I had to fill both their shoes. I've been the subject of my fair share of the town gossip, Cal. You can't let them grind you down." He stood, pulling me to my feet, and we began to walk back towards his bike.

"You're right. Let's get vodka on the way home. Sleepover at yours. I'm in the mood for Warren brother shenanigans." I figured Nick could do with letting off some steam too.

"You want to party on a school night?" Nick put a hand to his chest and feigned shock.

"Let's go wild, Sunshine!" I laughed.

"You don't have to ask me twice, Moonbeam!" He handed me the spare helmet and we climbed onto the bike.

Nick: Do you think I'm ugly?

Me: No. Why would you say that?

Nick: Wait, what did I just text?

Me: Do you think I'm ugly?

Nick: Yes. But it's ok, the lemurs will still take you.

Me: The lemurs only want you, dude!

I put my phone away and went back to my book. I was thankful the lunchtime shift I was working was quiet, mostly due to my fuzzy, vodka head, from the night before. I'd stayed at Nick's place, as planned. He, his brother Ethan, and I, played drinking games until we couldn't string a sentence together between us. Danny and Heath thought we were hilarious. Now, I was convinced a little man with a pickaxe had got stuck inside my head and was digging his way out.

"What's his name?" Adam asked, indicating my book and not referring to the little man with the pickaxe. He leaned towards me across the bar and the subtle scent of his aftershave hit me.

"Zack," I said, smiling back at him and closing the book. He was completely clean shaven. I hadn't seen him without some kind of dark stubble on his face before and struggled to look away.

"Vampire? Werewolf? Gargoyle?"

"Human!" I announced triumphantly.

"Human? That's a big step for you. Are you sure you're ready for this?" His eyes sparkled as his smile built.

"Don't panic, his girlfriend is a succubus," I deadpanned.

"And how's that working out for him?" He feigned seriousness but was unable to hide the crooked smirk that had appeared.

"They're having difficulties with the whole *"her touch can kill"* thing, but they're making a go of it."

"He's got it covered though, right? I mean he's a badass, obviously?" Adam grabbed a menu off the bar and opened it while he spoke.

"Total badass!" I confirmed.

"Well, it's ok that he's human then." He laughed and looked down at the menu.

"You know her books?" Cameron arrived with Adam and had been silently listening to our exchange. I turned to get their drinks and passed their lunch orders to Kat in the kitchen. Ear-wigging their conversation as I went.

"I know what she reads. I haven't read any of it though." Adam hastily let Cameron know that he didn't read the paranormal romance books I loved so much.

"I see," Cameron said.

My brother's lips curved into a smile. He looked from Adam to me and back again. It seemed my brother was no longer blind and could now see *"it,"* just like Liv, Dana, Vinnie, and Nick. *Oh, good!* I mentally checked on my no swoon zone, which was now thirty feet high, and rigged with explosives. *Good luck getting over that you sickeningly perfect piece of man candy!*

"What's that?" Adam reached out and snared my wrist, turning it over to look at the tattoo.

"Shit! How did that get there?" I joked and moved back the dressing over the new ink, to show him.

"What does it mean?" He smiled indulgently but failed to hide the look of annoyance I caught in his eyes. My hackles were raised instantly. How could he have a problem with me getting a tattoo?

"It means different yet the same. Nick and I got them yesterday. The moon is because Nick calls me Moonbeam, his has a sun underneath." I pulled my wrist away from him.

"So, that's why you cancelled in favour of him yesterday. It wasn't just about the vodka!" Cameron teased, knowing I had the hangover from hell. He took my wrist and leaned over to see for himself. "Cool."

"You and Nick got matching tattoos?" Adam frowned at me.

"We've been talking about it for years, but never got around to it. Couldn't find the right design."

"And because Jase wouldn't let you. Mr Possessive couldn't have his girlfriend getting a tattoo to match her best friend, just in case it was secret code for, *we're getting it on behind Jase's back*!" Cameron ranted and stalked over to the juke box with a dirty look on his face.

"Is it?" Adam asked, his frown deepening.

"Is it what?" I threw a frown of my own at him.

"Secret code? You and Jase are over now, that would make room for Nick." His voice was low, and his eyes grew dark.

"No." I wasn't about to go into the whole *'Nick and I are only friends'* speech. If he couldn't figure that out for himself, then it was his problem. "Why do you care anyway?"

"Good to know." He seemed to relax then and his eyes brightened again, although he completely ignored my question. Had it been jealousy I'd seen in those eyes? I hoped not. Another overbearing possessive man in my life was exactly what I didn't need right now.

Back when I was sixteen and didn't know any better, Jase's jealous streak had seemed romantic. He told me repeatedly that he was going to marry me one day, that I would be his for the rest of my life. I'd swooned like the smitten sixteen-year-old girl I was.

As we grew up, the constant questioning grew old. Jase started talking about us getting married as soon as I finished college. That was when I began to see what life with him would truly be like.

I was still reeling after my parent's deaths and I couldn't figure out what to do with my life. He lamented about how I didn't need a career. He would eventually take over his family's construction company, like his father had after his grandfather, allowing me to stay at home. Fine, if that's what makes you happy, but I wasn't cut out to be housewife of the year.

I could have played the domestic bliss game for a while, but I wouldn't have been content with that life for long. Our relationship became fraught with arguments and tense exchanges. He wanted us to buy a house and move in together, get married, have babies. I wanted him to give me the freedom to figure out what I really wanted to do with my life and support those decisions when I made them.

"I like it." Adam's voice brought me out of my thoughts.

"Well, isn't that fortunate?" I snapped, still irritated by his questioning.

"It suits you." He smiled, ignoring my obvious annoyance. "It means something, I don't think anyone should permanently mark their body unless it means something."

"Is that what the frowny face was about?" I asked, might as well be upfront about it. If there was one thing Adam and I did well, it was straight talk. "You thought I'd just randomly mark my body for the hell of it?"

"Yes and no," he said.

"Explain?" I pushed.

Kat brought out his steak baguette, and Cameron's BLT, and set the plates down on the bar. Adam glanced up to thank her, flashing a quick smile, and turned his attention back to me.

"I may have had a little attack of the green-eyed monster," he admitted openly. I raised my eyebrows, silently asking for more information. He paused for a few seconds, as if deciding whether to continue. "I don't like the idea of you being with anyone else."

"Are you serious?" I hissed and let out a frustrated huff. He shrugged and squirted mustard on his food.

"Hey, twin, you want to go out and get dinner after your shift here? I'll be finished around the same time. I fancy a very rare steak." Cameron came back over, ending any further discussion on Adam's newfound possessiveness.

"Sure, Cam." My response was automatic, and I didn't look at him.

I narrowed my eyes at Adam, letting him know I wasn't satisfied with his explanation. He held my gaze, un-wavering, confidence oozing from him. We stayed that way, battling silently, while Cameron mumbled around his mouthful of food about his next meal. I looked away when Adam's eyes hooded, and I couldn't take the sexual tension any longer.

THE TEACHER

The woman whimpers at me through her gagged mouth. This one has been mildly more satisfying than the last. On the surface, she learns her lessons quickly, complying with my expectations. I am not sure she isn't attempting to play her own game with me, in order to escape. This one presents a challenge. She is puzzling and I enjoy toying with her each time she tries to gain the upper hand. The trouble with women like her is, they are secretive, cunning and sly. I cannot tell if her lessons are sinking in effectively enough because she is so adept at faking the results I require.

She became seemingly demure and submissive early on. Her clothes tell a different story. Short skirt, low cut top, leaving virtually nothing to the imagination. My dear mother learned the hard way that this is not the way a lady should dress. She suffered for her mistakes in an entirely different way than my students. I would never lower myself to *that*. Her suffering was at the hands of others. Still, she learned her lessons and passed them onto me, so that I may save these women from themselves. Many branded her crazy, I knew better. Teaching is a calling set as deeply within me as breathing and my mother saw my potential. I am comfortable in the knowledge that I am doing the right thing.

I remove the gag and the student promises to change her ways if I let her go free. She vows to become the lady I require her to be. I contemplate it briefly, but how do I know she will keep her word? A woman who dresses in this manner is incapable of honesty. A woman who shows off her body in this way is a tease, not a lady. She will drive men to commit the crimes that were committed against my mother. The crimes that resulted in my birth. I simply cannot trust her. She needs further teaching. I readjust the gag and sit back to regard her. The tears, washing away the blood on her cheeks, brings me a feeling of peace that I usually only find with the final lesson. This one still has much to learn, but first I have other business requiring my attention.

CHAPTER EIGHT

CALLIE

How are you? J xx

Really? I responded. Was he serious? After he had been thrown out of my house in his underwear?

J: You at work right now?

Me: You know I am.

J: I'm passing by. Mind if I stop in?

Me: It's a public house, Jase. You don't need permission.

J: Is that a yes?

Me: Whatever.

I wasn't over-joyed at the thought of Jase coming into the pub but there wasn't much I could do to stop him. Adam and Cameron went back to work after their lunch and the place was now virtually empty. Kat was cleaning up in the kitchen and a small group at a table in the corner lingered after eating lunch. Mick had gone out that morning for a meeting with his accountant and wasn't back.

"I can take my time clearing down if you like, honey?" Kat offered, when I told her he was coming. "Hang around in the kitchen, just in case."

"No, don't stay any longer than you need to. We live in the same town; I can't avoid him forever. Besides, Nick is next door and Cam is only across the road if I need him."

"Well, I'll be here a while longer yet. I'll let you know before I leave." She smiled and went back to the kitchen. "Oh, if you plan on stripping him down and throwing him out in the street in his underwear, let me know and I'll film it."

"Ha! I'll holler if I need you for that. Thanks. Kat."

I left the kitchen to go back to the bar just as Jase walked in. *Damn!* I stopped in my tracks. How was I supposed to stay strong around him when he looked so good? He might not have done much in the way of growing up mentally, but physically, he was all over it. Working for his family's construction company meant the whole work boots and scruffy jeans look, which he could pull off perfectly. He'd had his hair cut too. My mind wandered, and I remembered the feel of the freshly shaved hair at the back of his hair, whenever he got it cut.

"Hello." He smirked cockily and I silently cursed myself for giving him exactly what he wanted.

"Hey," I replied, cursing myself again, for the moment of weakness that allowed him to hug me, before I slipped back behind the bar.

I wasn't afraid to admit I missed those arms... to myself... silently. You can't blame me though. What woman doesn't like to be held? That brief encounter in my bed was all wrong but it had felt so good. Until it didn't. I needed to give myself a serious talking to. We'd been in the same room for mere seconds and I was ready to throw myself at him like a bitch in heat.

"Drink?"

"I'd kill for a brew, not stopped all morning." He grinned, grabbed a bar stool, and sat down. "You're looking good, baby."

"Thanks," I said awkwardly as I heated hot water in the coffee machine for his tea.

"Sorry, old habits." He noticed my discomfort at the term of endearment.

I shrugged it off and decided I had to confront him about the flowers again. If I did that, I would get annoyed with him and stop drooling. At least, that was the plan.

"Can you please stop with the roses and chocolates? As for the books..." I practically wore a hole in the bar top with my tea towel.

"I told you, I haven't been sending you roses and chocolates. Why would I? You don't like them, and babe, I know you like your books, but I wouldn't know where to begin looking for all that paranormal stuff you read. Even if I did, you've probably read anything I'd pick."

Well that was news to me. Jase knew what I read. Maybe he did know me better than I thought he did. I realised I was fighting a losing battle with him and let it go, once again ignoring that persistent niggle in the back of my mind, that this was something more sinister than I was prepared to admit. I finished preparing his tea and set it down in front of him, dropping the two packets of sugar I knew he would use next to the cup.

"You look surprised," he said.

"Hmm?" I raised my eyebrows in question.

"That I know about what you read? Did you think I didn't notice?" He gave me a disappointed look.

"No. I mean. I don't know." I struggled for the words.

"I notice everything about you, Cee. I always have. It's my job to know. Just because I'm not interested in the same things doesn't mean I don't notice how much *you* love them." He was clearly a little irritated.

"Yeah. So, what's new?" I asked, over perkily changing the subject, in an attempt to ease the tension that had fallen between us. "Apart from the haircut."

"Yeah, saw Dana for a trim, yesterday." He brushed a hand through his hair. "Actually, I have got some news." He grinned over his cup at me. He had the most beautiful smile, even better than Nick's.

"Share," I said.

The tension cleared immediately, and the conversation began to flow, the way it always had with him. We'd been at ease with each other all our lives and it's pretty damn hard to just stop doing something you've done all your life. I found myself pondering how uncomplicated life could be if we fell back into our old relationship.

"Dad gave me my first site manager project this week. I'm overseeing the new school building at Marbledon."

Jase, to give him his due, wasn't afraid of hard work. He went straight into the family business from school and began working his way up. There was a lot of pressure on him to work for his dad, after his older brother made it perfectly clear he had no interest in it and joined the army instead. But Jase stepped up and worked harder than most would to get where he was. He'd always felt he had more to prove, being the owner's son and didn't want anyone telling him it had all been handed to him on a plate.

"Jay, that's fantastic news. Is it a big job?" I asked, beaming. I couldn't help the excitement I felt for him. This was huge, it was what he had been working so hard for.

"The school is set to take three hundred pupils. So, yeah, big enough."

"I'm happy for you," I told him sincerely.

"Yeah, life is on the up." He smiled, meeting my gaze "Only one thing missing."

"Jase—" I began. My smile dropped.

"I miss you, Cee. So, fucking much!" His voice splintered, and I turned away, to blink back tears. I busied myself behind the bar, keeping my back to him, so he couldn't see how much his words affected me. Yeah, it would be so easy. *I can do this.*

"I'm sorry," he said quietly "I shouldn't have said that. I promised I wouldn't do this. Told myself I'd just come over here and tell you my news. Make small talk, be friendly. You were the first person I wanted to tell. I just had to see you; you know?"

"I know." I nodded. We fell silent.

How could I not know? We always went to each other first, with everything, good news and bad. Why did this have to be so complicated? I wanted to be strong and stay away from him, but I just couldn't bring myself to cut all ties. A life without Jase just didn't feel like my life. Maybe I was clinging to the past out of fear of change. The last few years had been traumatic, to say the least, and perhaps I couldn't bring myself to let go of one of the few constants in my life. After losing my parents, I couldn't bear to think of anyone I loved no longer being there, Jase especially, at that time.

"Let's start again?" he smiled, pulling himself together. "So, how are you?"

"I'm good. Working. Studying." I shrugged. Some things didn't change.

"Exams coming up soon?" He lifted his cup top take a drink.

"Yeah, in a few short months I'll be the proud owner of a bunch of qualifications I still don't know what to do with."

"I'm leaving now, honey." Kat called when she came out of the kitchen. She gave Jase the evil eye as she walked past him, but he didn't turn to look at her, his eyes didn't leave me.

"I'll see you at the weekend," I answered before returning my attention to Jase.

"You should take Mick's offer to manage this place, it's what you love."

"You and Mick make the perfect team here. This place would be nothing without you." He finally glanced at Kat as bustled past him and left.

Jase had never been overly supportive of anything I enjoyed or wanted to do. It surprised me that he even noticed what I liked doing. Yet, here he was proving it to me twice in as many minutes. I mused over his words. Mick told me all the time he wanted me to take on a bigger role at the pub. I couldn't deny I loved the place. Jase refused to entertain the idea the last time we spoke about it, but I wasn't really considering it myself then either.

"I don't know, maybe," I considered.

"Don't waste the opportunity, babe." He stood up and pulled out his wallet to pay for his drink.

"It's on me." I waved his money away.

"It's good to talk to you, CeeCee." He leaned across the bar to kiss my cheek.

"You too," I answered dreamily, watching him leave. Blinking myself back to reality, I began emptying the glass washer. "Too damn easy."

J: You looked pretty today.

Me: Stop spying on me, Jase.

J: Can't I pay you a compliment now?

J: It's rude to ignore me.

J: I thought you had better manners. After all we've been through together.

J: I wish you would trust me. I love you. See you soon.

The decayed rose petals crumbled to dust and scattered on the gentle breeze, when I picked them up to dispose of them. There were more chocolates that morning, too. I added the copy of *Great Expectations* to the pile of books on the windowsill and forced it out of my mind. I was going to have to tell Cameron eventually, but I wanted to put it off as long as possible. He was going to be angry and despite Jase denying all knowledge, it had to be him. The other option, the one that told me these were all books that had been on the shelf in *that* house, was one I could not allow myself to entertain.

"Incoming!" Adam called as he walked through the door.

"Adam, you beautiful hunk of manliness!" Vinnie flirted loudly. "Am I glad to see you, bud. I think she's cracking up in there and I've gotta go to work!"

EDUCATING CALLIE

I told Vinnie about the visit from Jase and Adam's reaction to my tattoo. In true Vinnie style, he listened attentively, built both scenarios up to be more than they were, and turned the whole thing into some twisted love triangle, with Jase and Adam doing battle to win my heart. He'd even talked about medieval dresses and jousting tournaments. All before dramatically announcing that I simply needed to get laid.

"I'm cracking up because of *you,* Vincent!" I screeched and threw a cushion at his back as he left, cackling to himself.

"Angel," Adam ventured.

"Did you bring beer? Tell me you brought beer." I turned to look at him for the first time since he arrived; his arms were laden with goodies.

"Beer, pizza, and the *Die Hard* box set." He grinned triumphantly.

"I *love* you, Adam." I knee-walked across the sofa and grabbed the enormous pizza box from him. How could I stay mad at a man who brought me pizza?

"Now, there's something I could get used to hearing." I heard him mutter, while he searched the kitchen drawers for a bottle opener. I checked the walls around my no swoon zone for gaps. Barbed wire, that's what it needed!

Adam and I watched *Bruce Willis* set the world straight in his vest, while we pigged out on pizza, and even though Adam wasn't a pineapple person, I forgave him, because he got half of the gigantic pizza *with* pineapple, just for me. Cameron arrived home as we were about to put on the second movie. I was in the bathroom and came back to hear him and Adam talking in hushed voices.

"Where was this one found?" Adam asked. My skin broke out in a cold sweat.

"Over by the dis-used railway station, the one behind the new school site, in Marbledon." Cameron said quietly.

"Laid out the same way?"

"Exactly like the others."

"Shit!" Adam hissed. "He wants us to know it's him."

"I know it can't be done officially, but I want my sister protected," Cameron stated.

"Fuck officially, nobody is getting within a hundred feet of her," Adam decided. "Everyone is on overtime until we catch this fucker!"

Their voices became whispers after that, and I didn't catch anything else of their conversation, until all of a sudden, I heard back slapping, and more muffled voices, then laughter. Feeling mildly guilty at eavesdropping I went back into the room.

"What are you two whispering about?" I eyed them both.

"You." They both answered. *Oh, good!*

Cameron filled me in, as much as he could, about the body that had been found. Obviously, he'd given Adam more details than he could give me, but the news had come in as he had been leaving work, so he didn't know much anyway.

"It's him," I whispered.

"No, Callie." Cameron had me in a bear hug before I could blink. "It's *not* him, okay?"

"Oh, come on, Cam. You don't believe that. There are things you're not telling me, I'm not stupid. It's the same, isn't it? What he's doing to them? I know it's the same. I know it's him," I rambled hysterically.

Cameron steered me to the sofa and wedged me in between himself and Adam. Adam's hand found mine, he tangled our fingers, and squeezed lightly.

"You're safe, Angel," Adam said, laying a gentle kiss on my forehead. "We aren't going to let anything happen to you."

"Which film are we on?" Cameron asked, picking up the remote. "I'm starving, you better have saved me some pizza."

I saw straight through his distraction techniques, but I didn't have it in me to argue. I might not be a woman who needed a man to survive, but right then I had every intention of leaning on Adam and my brother and allowing them to take over for a while.

I woke the next morning, apparently having again used Adam as a body pillow, on our sofa. He was on his back, his arms wrapped tightly around me, and I was sprawled across him, just as we were on his sofa the night we met. When I apologised, he grinned and told me it was rapidly becoming his favourite sleeping position. Then I had an *"Oh, shit!"* moment and did a runner. But I hadn't had a nightmare.

Me: I did it again

Liv: Oops? I'm excited. I love a good Britney reference.

Me: Major oops!

Liv: Adam?

Me: Used him as a pillow last night.

Liv: So, is he your boyfriend now? Or is he your boy friend?

Me: What's the difference?

Liv: The difference is that tiny space in between called the friend zone.

Me: Shit, I dunno, Olive.

Liv: Blurred lines.

Me: Robin Thicke.

Liv: What rhymes with hug me? (I'm singing) Did he hug you?

Me: All night long.

Liv: Lionel Richie.

Liv: Worst case scenario?

Me: Give it to me

Liv: Timbaland. You're screwed.

Me: Good talk, Olive

Liv: Don't call me that.

Shortly after Liv imparted her invaluable advice, in between our manic song contest, Vinnie sent me a gif of a medieval jousting tournament. I sent back a *"You know nothing, Jon Snow"* meme and thanked the universe for friends who made me smile.

Mick and I sat at the bar after closing the pub. There was something peaceful about being in there after hours, the only light coming from the fridges behind the bar, no noisy chatter, no music. Just Mick and me, with a bottle and two glasses sitting on the bar between us. I was in a funk and sounding off at him about not being able to decide what to do with my life.

"Offer still stands, Callie love, always has always will," he said.

"I know and I appreciate it, but it's more than that." I huffed, lifting my glass to my mouth.

"What if I could offer you more than the manager's position?" Mick ventured, rubbing his chin thoughtfully.

"You proposing, Micka?" I joked.

"In a fecking heartbeat, if I thought you were meant for me." He winked and we laughed.

"Go on then, you've got my attention." I looked over my glass at him.

"I have plans for this place. Well, another place, actually. I'm talking expansion. I could do it on my own, but honestly, I don't want to." He glanced at me, testing the water. "I've been looking for a reason to get my brother over here permanently. I already spoke to him about it. He's interested, but ideally I want you on board as well, love."

"Talk to me." I leaned towards him.

"I'm thinking three equal partners. Jared, you, and me, each with a third share in this place and any subsequent places we open. The nature of any further businesses is up for discussion, but I have a couple of ideas that I'd like both your input on." He was watching my face for a reaction, but I was holding my cards close to my chest and giving it my best Lady Gaga. Going into business with Mick and his brother, Jared, could be exactly what I was looking for, but I wanted details first.

"The two of us are already an excellent team. This place wouldn't be as successful as it is without you behind me. You're good at this and you love doing it as much as I do." His green eyes bored into mine and he leaned towards me as he sold me his idea.

"Can't deny that I love this place." I had to agree.

"All those courses you've taken, they're all relevant to this business." He topped up both our glasses from the bourbon bottle that sat on the bar. That's when I realised, he had been planning this. *He* had suggested those courses. *He* had kept the manager thing at the forefront of my mind. *He* had taught me everything I could ever need to know about running the pub. I grinned and shook my head at him.

"You planned this from the beginning!" I accused, not at all angry. Some might argue it was controlling, but it was just his way of trying to make me see my own potential.

"Maybe not to this degree and I prefer hoped for, not planned. But yeah, guilty as charged," he confessed, not even trying to hide it. He smiled at me, knowing he had me hooked. All he had to do was reel me in. "I saw something in you the first day we met. You came charging in here, demanding I hire you on the spot. You were young, and had zero experience, but there was a quiet determination about you that put me in your corner from the second I laid eyes on you. Of course, with that pretty face, I knew you'd be good for the place. You've put your heart and soul into the rover as much as I have, I think it's time you got something back from it. Something bigger than a wage slip at the end of the month. I've gone over numbers with my accountant and I've been putting together lots of info for you and Jared. We can do this, Callie love."

"You've got it all figured out, haven't you?" I grinned at him.

"It's been on my mind for a long time. You know as well as I do, we could do good things together. You and me, we understand each other. There's no bullshit between us. You're my driving force and I'm yours." Again, I couldn't argue with him and I found myself nodding in agreement.

"And Jared? Is he willing to move over here, permanently?" I asked, plopping a lump of ice into my glass. I didn't give Mick any; he didn't drink it that way.

"It's something we've talked about. Since Da passed, there's nothing much keeping him in Ireland. Etta has her husband and the kids, they're solid, she doesn't need Jared around like she used to." He referred to their sister, who had recently had her second baby with her husband of three years. "Plus, he likes it here. He has friends in town, you being one of them."

I nodded again. Jared and I had gotten along fantastically each time he had visited Mick. We'd also proven we could work together, when he helped out behind the bar during his visits.

"Look, love, there's a lot of details involved and a lot to think about. I'll talk to Jared, get him on *Skype* at some point, so we can all talk together. In the meantime, will you think on it?" Mick put a hand on my leg and squeezed affectionately.

"Yeah. Yeah, I definitely will." I smiled at him and nodded, feeling a lot brighter about things than I had in a long time.

Money wasn't an issue for me with investing. Our parents left both Cameron and I a generous cash inheritance that neither of us had needed to touch. I could well afford to buy into the Rover and anything else that might come along. It wasn't nightmare free, but I slept better that night in Mick's spare room above the pub, content in the knowledge that maybe, just maybe, not everything was so bad.

Dana: The situation regarding your lack of girl status has reached defcon2 we need to rectify immediately.

Me: I'm not going shopping with you, witch.
Dana: I already made the appointments.

Me: We need appointments to shop?

Dana: No, we need appointments for hair and nails.
Me: No, Dana!

EDUCATING CALLIE

Dana: Tomorrow. 9am. Be ready or I'm bringing out the big guns.

Me: Vinnie doesn't scare me.

Operation distract Callie went into overdrive after my little freak out to Cameron and Adam. My brother roped in all of our friends to keep me busy. Liv and Dana ushered me off on a girly shopping trip from hell, with Vinnie along as chaperone. Nail and facial appointments were attended. Dana actually stamped her feet when I refused to have pink nails, going with blue instead. I'd rolled my eyes and silently wondered if she was ever going to accept that I wasn't pink and fluffy. We had lunch at a fancy restaurant, with cocktails and lettuce leaves, and I returned home exhausted, and in desperate need of real food.

It hadn't escaped my notice that, as Vinnie practically picked me up and carried me out of bed that morning, the other guys were gathering at my house, dressed like a demolition team. If Adam or Greg had shown up in their police uniforms, I might have been forgiven for thinking they were forming a *Village People* tribute band and were about to give an impromptu performance of *YMCA* in my kitchen.

I attempted to give Mick the third degree. He's usually on my side on everything, but he actually uttered the words *"Don't worry your pretty little head about it, love."* earning himself a punch in the gut. He laughed, of course. Like my puny fists could do any damage to his concrete abs.

Adam told me to relax and enjoy myself, almost as bad as Mick's Neanderthal response. Luke wouldn't even make eye contact with me. Nick pulled my hair and told me to buy gloves, and Nate had winked and said *"You're having a girl's day, we're having a boy's day. Just go with, babe."* As for my brother? Well, he'd mysteriously vanished into thin air.

I narrowed my eyes at Cameron, as I hauled my bags up the steps, and dropped them on the porch. They were all now sitting around drinking beer and looking suitably pleased with themselves.

"Good day, sis?" His question was innocent, but there was a furrow in his brow that I filed away to interrogate him about later.

"What have you done?" I got straight to the point.

His eyes widened momentarily. "We're just thinking about lighting the barbecue."

"So suspicious, Cal," Nate said. Luke snorted into his beer. Luke. He was my best bet. Only thing was, they all knew it.

"Luca, come and help me carry these bags to my room?" I smiled sweetly at him.

"Oh, no you don't." Nick put his hand on Luke's arm.

"Stay away from him," Mick warned.

"You don't have to go with her, Luke," Cam added.

"Ah, shit!" Luke groaned.

"It's ok, we'll protect you," Greg told him.

"You're not playing fair, Angel." Adam stood, picking up my bags. "I'll help you."

"I'll find out." I warned them all. I followed Adam into the house, still mildly irritated by his earlier caveman behaviour. "There had better be some huge ass steaks going on that barbecue, Cameron. That witch made me eat girl food all day!"

"Stop whining and bring back wine, Callie!" Dana called after me. I stuck my thumb in the air to acknowledge her.

Adam put the shopping bags down on the end of my bed and turned to look at me. "You bought books, didn't you?"

"Always." I crossed my arms and tilted my head when I looked at him, aware that he was trying to distract me.

"You have so many already." He sat down on the end of my bed, looking around at the piles of books scattered on every surface.

"Maybe I'll open a bookshop." I retorted and began looking through the bags. I pulled out a lacy, red underwear set and waved it in his face.

"What do you think?" I asked, doing a little distracting of my own. Two could play that game.

"I think you shouldn't have shown me that!" *Woah! Was that a growl?*

Adam stood and prowled towards me. He snatched the underwear from my hand, and threw it over his shoulder, onto the bed. I got lost in the rush of blood to my head, when he backed me up against the wall, and gripped my hips with his hands, pulling my body against his. His fingers dug into my flesh, pressing just enough to sting, but not in a bad way. He was letting me know he was in control. My thighs clenched automatically, and my breath caught in my chest.

"Why ever not?" I pulled my wits about me and feigned innocence. He let go of my hips, using his body to keep me in place, and caged me in, with his hands against the wall on either side of my head. *No swoon zone? Anyone seen my no swoon zone?*

"Because now I want to know what it looks like on you—" His lips caressed my neck as he spoke. He breathed in deeply, then rubbed his nose along the length of my jaw, levelling his mouth with mine. Wetting his lips with his tongue, its tip skimmed my mouth and I stopped breathing. "—and off you!"

My knees went weak and I inhaled sharply. *Well, fuck!* My kind, considerate, sweet, dependable Adam had just shown me a whole new side of himself, and I liked it. I liked it a lot! I wasn't about to admit that or give into it, obviously. I couldn't go there with him. No way, no how. *Walls? Where the bloody hell have my walls gone? Ah, there they are, all crumbled to dust at my feet.*

He laughed as he pulled away and left the room, knowing not only had he well and truly got my attention, but he had also succeeded in distracting me from finding out about their activities that day. The nerve of him. Backed me up against the wall, sexy growled at me, made me think he was going to kiss me, and then walked away laughing. Nope. Impenetrable.

Twin 2: Why are there dead roses and chocolates on the doorstep?

Me: Just bin them and leave it at that. Please.

Twin 2: How long has this been going on?

Me: Leave it, Cam.

Twin 2: Answer me!

Me: A while. I asked him to stop. He denied it.

Twin 2: You sure it's him?

Me: Who else would it be?

Twin 2: Nobody. I'll deal with it.

Me: Don't do anything stupid!

The gloved hand held my chin firmly in place, forcing me to follow his actions in the mirror, as he dragged the point of the knife down my cheek again. Classical music played loudly in the background, drowning out my screams. His icy stare was fixed on the reflection in the mirror. He watched with fascination, as the blood oozed from the wound he had created, and made its way down my face...

I woke with a frenzied urgency, a silent scream on my lips as I grappled with the bed sheets. At least I hadn't woken Cameron this time. I turned on my bedside lamp and looked at my alarm clock, 3.47am. Yay! I knew it was unlikely I'd sleep again. I eyed my phone, wondering if Adam was awake. He'd told me to text or call him after a nightmare, no matter the time, but I felt guilty doing it. Before I made the decision to risk waking him, the phone made its *TARDIS* sound and I smiled as I picked it up. The sound always reminded me of Adam. My smile quickly faded when I saw the message was from Jase.

J: Why is your light on so late?

Me: Are you kidding me?

J: Why is it on, Callie?

Me: Nightmares. You know how it is. Why are you outside my house at this time?

J: I'm not anymore. I drove past and noticed. You should be asleep.

Me: You're being weird.

J: I care about you, that's all. I don't want you to be tired tomorrow.

Me: Thanks for the concern. Stop spying on me. It's creepy.

J: It's not spying. It's taking care of you. I won't stop making sure you're okay. Not ever.

I wondered why he was suddenly calling me Callie but pushed it from my mind after a few seconds. It didn't matter.

THE TEACHER

I saw her today. She was dressed in ripped jeans, that show her skin, and a rock band t-shirt with a crude saying splayed across her chest. She looked pretty, but while she may almost be a lady in other ways, she needs an education in how to dress appropriately. I didn't get through to her during her brief stay at my schoolhouse.

The breaking of my lady is my art. She is torn apart at the seams and I alone can stitch her back together, piece by piece. Her scars will form a map of our journey to find each other, forever displayed on her body for my pleasure. They all remain clueless as to how much of her life has been controlled by me. She is mine to stitch back together, piece by piece, until she rises like the phoenix from the flames, a beauty more striking than before. What she is now will be nothing but a memory, distant and unimportant.

My time with her draws near again. The anticipation of seeing the blood coating her beautiful skin once more is almost too much to bear. The pleasure it brings me is beyond anything I have felt with my other students. She wears her blood lessons so well. I must, for now, be content with my memories of her. Mother taught me great lessons in patience, it can be a man's most useful trait. I am content to watch from a distance for a while longer. My new gifts will be pleasing her. A lady wants to be courted, romanced properly and my lady deserves no less.

I retrieve my hunting knife, a standard blade, used by many groundsmen and game keepers in these parts. Nothing unusual or fancy that might stand out when purchased. I would give the detectives seeking me no assistance. Mindfully checking that not a trace of blood is left, I ensure the room is pristine for my next student. The last one was a bleeder. I step over my tools with care, so as not to leave any trace of blood on them. The boot covers will ensure no tread is left on the ground. Not that it matters, the boots and my clothing will be gone by morning. I briefly mourn the schoolhouse, my childhood home. Sadly, I had to give it up when my lady escaped it. Using my current home is a risk, but I have always been meticulous in covering my tracks. It's the reason I have remained unseen all this time.

They never see me coming and they never see me leave.

CHAPTER NINE

CALLIE

Unknown: Hey, Cee. Got a new phone. Lost my old one. Hope you're okay. Love J. Xx

Me: You lost it since 3am, outside my house?

Unknown: ???

Me: When you were texting me!

Unknown: Pretty sure I was fast asleep at 3am. Alone, for the record. Lost my phone a few days ago.

Me: Stop fucking with me, Jase. It's not funny!

Unknown: Seriously, I don't know what you're talking about. I'm close, I'll stop in and we can talk. Stick the kettle on.

Me: Stop acting like nothing's changed.

Unknown: It's that time of the month isn't it? Want me to stop for pizza and ice cream on the way?

Me: Fuck you!

Thankfully, Cameron was at work when Jase turned up at the house. He just walked straight in, calling out *"incoming"* as though nothing was wrong.

"What the hell are you doing here? I'm pretty sure *fuck you* translates to *don't come here* in any language, even stupid!" I snarled at him.

"You sounded stressed. I just wanted to make sure you're alright." Jase held his hands up in surrender.

"I'm fine. You can go now," I snapped.

"You don't seem fine. Ten minutes, Cee. Let me stay. Look, new phone." He waved it in my face.

"No!" I answered.

"We can argue this back and forth all day, babes, but the quicker you give in, the sooner I'll be gone." He smiled at me then because he knew he'd win.

"Ten minutes." I caved. Ten minutes was all he was getting though.

"Where's your phone?" he asked, and I gestured to the arm of the sofa.

"Did you save my new number?" he asked, picking up my phone and swiping the screen to open it and scroll through our texts.

"No."

"Look, two different numbers. See?" He came to stand beside me, close enough for me to smell his aftershave, and showed me the numbers.

"Well, duh! I already figured that one out, genius." I refused to play his game.

"Cee, I lost my phone days ago, I don't even know when. I am telling you, that this was the last message I sent you. The rest after that were *not* me!" He frowned, suddenly looking concerned, as he read the messages that followed the one he claimed was his last.

We both leaned over the phone screen. If Jase was telling the truth, the last messages he sent me had been the day he came to the pub, asking if it was ok to stop in. Anything after that, wasn't him.

"Do you expect me to believe this?" I looked up at him.

"Do *you* really think, after everything that happened to you last year, I would mess with you like this." At least he had the decency to look hurt at my accusations. "You know this wasn't me, Cee."

"Do I?" I asked, truly not knowing what to think anymore.

"Really? Fucking really?" He was hurt and angry as he looked at me, a hand on the back of his neck.

"I don't know what to think anymore." I admitted with a defeated sigh and stepped away from him.

"Baby, this wasn't me. It's obviously someone who knows us both, playing silly buggers with my phone. When I find out who it is, they'll regret it!"

"Maybe." I half agreed.

"Look, they call you Callie. I never call you that, not even when I'm talking to someone else about you. You've *never* been Callie to me."

"But if you were messing with me, you'd do exactly that." My head was whirling with ridiculous theories.

"So, you think I would go to the trouble of buying a second phone, just to fuck with your head? After everything I watched you go through. After everything I was by your side for? Listen to yourself, Cee," he reasoned, struggling to remain calm.

"Shit, I don't know—" my words trailed off and I shrugged helplessly.

"Baby—" He stepped towards me.

"Don't, please don't!" I snapped.

I couldn't hear him call me that anymore. That word sounded wrong on his lips. Jase ignored my efforts to fight him and gathered me in his arms. I think I knew he was telling the truth; I just needed an excuse to keep believing it wasn't my worst nightmare coming back for round two. So, I kept questioning Jase's honesty. He'd had gone through it all with me before. But how many times would I fall for his words and trust him, only to be disappointed by his lies again?

"I went out of my mind when you were missing. Then, I got you back and parts of you were gone, lost forever. All I wanted to do was fix you. I did everything I could to be there for you, Cee. I watched you fall apart right in front of me and there was nothing I could do to make it stop. I know I didn't deal with it in the best way, but I saw what it did to you. I would never, *never* use it against you. No matter what's going on between us."

"I know, I'm sorry. I just—" I couldn't hold back the tears any longer. Jase's arms tightened around me and this time I didn't fight him.

"It's okay, baby. We'll figure this out. Someone has stolen my phone; we just need to work out who it is. We'll talk to Cam."

I nodded against his chest and he lifted my chin, so I was looking up at him.

"I know you're freaked out and paranoid with all that's going on, right now, but you're safe, Cee." He looked into my eyes as he spoke. "Talk to me, babe. Tell me what's going on in your head."

There was a time when Jase's presence alone would comfort me, but that feeling wasn't there anymore. That feeling came from someone else now. Someone who didn't need any words from me to know what was wrong. The thought saddened me with its finality. Jase and I would never again have the trust and love that we once took for granted. We were different now and we couldn't change that.

"It's him, Jay. I know it's him. He won't stop until he gets me. I'm what he wants," I said, between sobs.

"Cee, stop, we don't even know that he's back. You can't think like that. That's how he wins." He rubbed his hands up and down my arms.

"It's him," I whispered. Jase pulled me against his chest again and held me for a few more minutes.

"I'm alright. You can go." I sniffed and pulled away from him, gathering my strength back together. I needed to be in control of the situation again. Everything had spun so far out of my control recently, while I stood back and watched it go. I was stronger than that, it was time to start acting like it.

"I don't want to leave you." Jase admitted. His outstretched arm hung in the air as he reluctantly allowed me to move away from him.

"I'm fine, really. I promise. You should go back to work." I wiped my eyes with my sleeves and composed myself.

"Yeah, that can wait. You're more important." He smiled and moving into my space again, he took over wiping my tears away, with gentle strokes of his thumbs. His phone rang, he ignored it.

"Go," I told him, stepping back. "I'm okay. You just got promoted, you need to prove yourself. Go."

"You're sure?" he asked, and I nodded. "I want you to phone me straight away, if you need me. Anything. Any time. Okay? I saved my new number in your phone. Whatever you need, Cee. Promise?"

"Yeah," I replied quietly.

Knowing he wasn't going to be the first person I went to, hurt more than I thought it should, after weeks of not being together. That's when I realised my love for Jase hadn't stopped or disappeared, it had only changed. Somehow, somewhere along the line, it became something else. It hadn't gone away; it was just different now.

"Tell Cam about this. I'll talk to him too." He bent slightly to meet my downturned eyes.

"I will." I promised.

"Good." Jase lifted my chin and laid a sot kiss on the corner of my mouth. He hugged me again and whispered something that I thought was I love you, into my hair. Then he left.

Jase's visit left me reeling. I think I went through every possible negative emotion there is, in less than a minute. I believed Jase had lost his phone, but I also knew exactly who had taken it. There was no doubt in my mind that my tormentor was back, and it was only a matter of time before he came for me. He knew where I was, he was probably watching me that very second. He'd been outside my house, using Jase's phone to send me messages. Until he had me, he would keep hurting the others, he would keep killing. I found myself toying with the idea of contacting him, on Jase's old number, and telling him to come for me, because at least that way, it meant he would leave the others alone. I didn't do it. I didn't do it because I had too many people to live for.

I moved around the house and closed all the curtains, leaving the place in darkness, while I paced the living room. I was so lost in thought, figuring out what to do next, that I didn't hear Cameron arrive home, with Adam close behind. I don't know how long they had been watching me. I screeched and jumped out of my skin, when I turned to see them both standing side by side, silently regarding me, with matching frowns on their faces.

"Shit!" I gasped. "Seriously, you two. Creepy, much?"

"What's going on, Callie?" Cameron demanded and turned a lamp on. Adam came towards me and took my hand, to lead me to the sofa.

"Sit down, Angel," he instructed, when I looked at him quizzically. The concern in his eyes was unmistakeable.

"Want to tell me why I've just received a frantic phone call from Jase, telling me to get home now, and not let you out of my sight?" Cameron dragged the armchair across the oak floor to sit opposite me. My distracted mind told me that Mum would have yelled at him for scratching her floor.

"He spoke to you already?" I asked, frowning.

"About twenty minutes ago. What the hell is going on, Cal?" Cameron was getting frustrated. I needed to fill him in, fast.

"His phone. His old one, he lost it. But I've been getting messages from it. Weird messages, like he was spying on me. I thought it was him, just messing with me. Then he told me he had a new phone. I didn't believe him at first, but he came over and it's not him. The messages call me Callie, not Cee or CeeCee. Jase would never call me that," I rambled.

"So, someone is using Jase's old phone, to send you messages?" Adam clarified and I nodded. He held out his hand and I gave him my phone.

"The one that says I looked pretty, that was the first one after he lost it. After that, it wasn't him. I didn't click at first, but now I can see it's obviously not him, they aren't his words. That's not how he speaks," I explained, slightly more coherently.

"Could Jase have two phones? I wouldn't put anything past him these days." Cameron speculated.

"No." I was adamant. "I said the same thing, flatly refused to believe it wasn't him to begin with. But you didn't see him, Cam. He was angry and concerned when he read the messages, he just wanted to protect me. He knows how much something like this would freak me out. He was there, remember? He wouldn't use that against me."

"The abduction?" Adam confirmed, his brow creasing as he scrolled through the messages.

"Yes. He was here, he saw what it did to me. He was there, in the middle of the night when I was screaming the place down. He knows. No matter what else has happened between us, I believe him when he says he still loves me. He wouldn't do this." I noticed the cringe that marred Adam's face, and the slight shake of his head, but ignored it. I couldn't deal with his Jase issues. I was only barely dealing with my own.

"You know him better than anyone, sis. If you say it's not him, then I believe you. But we have to pass this on to the detectives in charge of the murders. It may not be related but we can't take that chance and Jase is still on their radar," Cameron explained gently.

"We both know who it is. He's coming for me. He's watching, those messages prove that." I wrung my hands together until Adam reached out and took them in his own. He lifted them to his lips and kissed my knuckles, silently calming me.

"He is not getting anywhere near you. We won't be leaving you alone for a second," Cameron said with finality.

"The books." I suddenly remembered.

"Books?" Adam asked, rubbing my hands between his.

"On the window ledge, they were left on the porch with the other stuff. I thought they were Jase too, but I was wrong."

"These?" Cameron stood and moved to the window. Pullin back the curtain, he picked up the books and shared a look of concern with Adam. "Exactly how many gifts have been left here, Callie? I only know of the stuff I found."

"I don't know, I didn't count. A few. Mostly chocolates and dead flowers."

"Dead flowers?" Adam snapped, his eyes meeting Cameron's with urgency.

"Yeah, I thought it was Jase, so I was binning them. There was perfume, but I threw that away with everything else. I don't know why I kept the books. I suppose I knew there was something different about them. Not Jase's style." I filled them in with a shrug.

"I need to take your phone, Angel. I'll get you a new one. The books, too." Adam moved closer and put his arm around my shoulders. He nodded at Cameron who went outside to the car and came back with evidence bags, to pack it all up.

"Any chance there's anything still in the rubbish bin?" Adam asked Cameron, while holding me close to him. I think it was as much of a comfort to him as it was to me.

"Doubtful," Cameron replied walking towards the back door. "The bins were emptied yesterday after I threw the last lot away. I'll check anyway."

"They're probably going to want to come and look over the house. Sweep for fingerprints and other evidence. If there's any chance he could have been here—" Adam trailed off as my tears broke through and he yanked me fully into his arms. "It's going to be okay, Angel. I won't let you out of my sight. Between Cam and me, you will not be left alone. We're going to keep you safe."

"We're going to get him, sis," Cam assured me as Adam relaxed his hold on me.

And just like that, I was under twenty-four-hour surveillance once again.

Bright sunlight shone through the patio doors, in Mick's simply furnished living room. The doors led out onto a small balcony, where I loved to sit in the summer evenings, during my breaks at work. It wasn't warm enough for that yet, so we were sitting in his living room, drinking tea and discussing up-coming events for the pub.

Mick had been filled in on events from the day before and added himself to my elite team of bodyguards. He knew I was a strung-out mess over it all though and attempted to make it as light-hearted as he could. He even jokily stood guard outside the bathroom. I yelled at him that I couldn't pee while he was out there listening. So, he'd started talking about waterfalls and running taps. It was silly and childish but was exactly what I needed.

"Mick? Callie? You up there?" Greg's voice carried up the stairs, interrupting our discussion.

"Come on up, buddy." Mick stretched his arms in the air and sat back.

Greg and Adam both came up the stairs and walked into the room looking serious. Both in uniform, they were obviously there officially, and that set me on edge.

"What is it?" I asked, my eyes pinning Adam's. Something was wrong and my mind immediately went to Cameron. I'd seen him a couple of hours earlier, but I couldn't help my panicked reaction.

"Cam's fine." Adam met my gaze, somehow knowing the thoughts running through my mind. I let out the breath I hadn't realised I was holding. He came towards me and handed me a mobile phone. "All set up, ready to go, same ringtones as the other one. Cam, Greg and I put in all the numbers we had. Charger is in my car; I'll get it for you later."

I smiled up at him as I took it. "You're too good to me, Adam. Let me get you the money for it."

"Don't worry about it," he said and planted a kiss on the top of my head.

"We need to talk to you both about your chef, Katherine March." Greg told us, sitting down in the armchair. Adam took a seat on the sofa next to me.

"Is Kat alright?" Mick asked, concerned.

"Her husband reported her missing. He hasn't seen her since before her shift here on Tuesday," Adam explained. "We know she made it to work, because Cameron and I were both here for lunch that day and saw her."

"What time did she leave?" Greg aimed the question at Mick.

"You'd have to ask Callie, mate. I was at a meeting with my accountant," Mick said.

They both looked to me. Images swarmed my mind and suddenly, I was chained in that damp cellar again, the knife scraping slowly down my arm, the metal cuffs digging into my skin, my throat sore from screaming.

"Angel," Adam whispered against my ear. He grabbed my hand and stilled the movement, where I had begun rubbing my wrist. He squeezed tight to bring me back to reality. "You're not there anymore. You're safe in the pub. Mick, Greg and I are here with you. Come back to me, Angel."

I let out a shuddered breath and blinked a few times, anchoring myself to the feel of Adam's hand holding mine. I looked into his eyes, searching for the light I needed to drag myself back to reality. It was there, strong and certain for me, as always.

"She, erm..." I rubbed my forehead and took a breath. "She worked her shift and left as normal. Actually, no, she stayed a little later than normal, maybe half an hour. So, she would have left around four o'clock, I think."

"Did she seem ok? Nothing bothering her?" Adam asked, leaning forward and drawing my eyes back to his, to keep me with him.

"She was fine. If there was anything wrong, she didn't tell me," I said numbly.

Removing my hand from his, I picked at the frayed rip on my jeans, needing something else to focus on. My mantra was pacing through my thoughts. *It's not him. It's not him. It's not him.* The flowers. The chocolates. The perfume. The books. *It's not him. It's not him. It's not him.*

"When was she due to work again?" Greg asked, his voice soft and gentle.

"That would have been tonight," Mick said, running his hand through his hair, his eyes had become fixed on me. "Are you alright, love?"

I nodded, automatically. I wasn't. He knew it. They all knew it.

"Why did she stay later than usual?" Greg asked and my eyes snapped up. Things were about to get worse.

"Jase." I dipped my head back and sighed. "Jase was here. She offered to stay until he left, so I wasn't alone with him. I told her it was fine, but she hung around anyway. She left a few minutes before him."

I didn't look at him, but I knew what was coming as soon as I felt Adam tense beside me.

"Jase was here? That would be the same day his mobile went missing. The day of his last texts to you?" Adam's voice became cold and he moved back from my space slightly.

"Yes. He was passing and stopped in to say hello." I shrugged.

After he had been there for me with the messages, I wasn't going to go back to the Jase hating tip again. He was in no way connected to any of this. I knew it, I just couldn't prove it.

"He just seems to keep turning up lately," Adam said under his breath. He was clearly annoyed but being there in official police capacity he couldn't exactly show it.

"So, Jase could confirm he saw her leaving?" Greg slid Adam a sideways glance, attempting to gage his mood.

"Yes. He walked out a few minutes behind her," I said.

"Did he speak to her?" Greg continued.

"Not unless he saw her again outside." I shook my head.

"Thanks, Callie. I don't suppose you know where Jase is working at the minute?" Greg asked.

"He's at the new school site in Marbledon. His dad made him site manager over there. That's why he came to see me, he wanted to tell me his news. He was excited. It's his first site manager job," I explained, rambling.

"That's close to the old railway station, isn't it?" Adam aimed his question at Greg. I got the feeling he was tuning me out.

"Sure is. Feel like a drive, Sarge?" Greg asked, getting ready to leave.

"Definitely," Adam replied through gritted teeth.

"Do you think this is connected to the others? To Amy?" I asked quietly. I knew it was, I didn't really have to ask. *It's him. It's him. It's him.* My mantra changed and I couldn't stop it.

"It might not be, but we can't rule it out yet, Angel." Adam reached over and squeezed my knee, suddenly mindful of me again.

"I know this has all triggered some God-awful memories for you, sweetheart," Greg said softly. "I'm so sorry about that."

"No, it's fine. This isn't about me. So, Jase is under suspicion again?" It wasn't really a question.

"He's possibly the last person to have seen Kat, we just need to speak to him. Don't worry, Cal." Greg stood, held out his hand to me, and pulled me up, reassuring me with a hug as I stood.

When Greg released me, Mick came up behind me and enfolded me in a Mick hug. I halted the flashback that threatened. I didn't need to see myself, in front of that mirror, with a masked face behind me in the same way. I leaned back into Mick, grateful for his strength.

"Have you got a lift home sorted for later?" Adam asked, as they were getting ready to leave. His tone was matter of fact, not particularly friendly.

Adam was clearly pissed off about me seeing Jase, but honestly, what did it have to do with him? Even though I was only just beginning to realise it, I'd spent years being controlled by Jase. I wasn't about to make the same mistake twice. If Adam thought he could walk into my life and pick up where Jase left off, he was sorely mistaken. Besides, there were more important things going on than a bruised ego.

"I'm staying here tonight. Cam is on a late shift and didn't want me home alone." I told him, matching his matter of fact tone.

"Good idea." Greg nodded once, backing my brother as usual.

"Will you fellas be in for a drink later?" Mick asked them, tightening his arms around me and resting his chin on my head.

"Probably." Adam nodded and looked at me, demanding my eye contact. I knew, even with his attitude over Jase, he was silently asking if I was okay. He still cared, still needed that reassurance from me. So, I nodded and mouthed the word he wanted to see. He smiled and nodded back.

Damn man was giving me whiplash!

Me: Hey guys, new number again. Love you all. Callie. Xx

Liv: Got it, sweets. Love ya back. Xx

Vinnie: You okay, witch? Heard about everything.

Me: I'm fine, Vinnie.

Nate: What's going on, babe? You at work?

Me: Here until lunch and again tonight, Nate.

Nate: I'll be over in a few.

Me: :)

Dana: Greg told me, honey. I can't believe it. You make sure you are never alone. Do you hear me? Not even for a second. Let the boys protect you. I am not losing you again, witch! Love you so much. Xx

Nick: We've got her, Dana, don't worry. I'll be in before lunch, Moonbeam.

Me: Love you too, Dee. Nick, I made a lasagne for you guys. Ethan picked it up this morning, it's in the fridge at the garage.

Nick: Because you have nothing else on your mind than feeding me and my brothers?

Me: Someone has to do it.

Nick: Love you.

Me: Love you more.

Luke: Saw Cam this morning. You need anything let me know, Cal. Xx

Me: I will, Luca, thank you. Xx

THE TEACHER

I decide that this will be my last student before I finally take the time I have earned with my lady. This one was easy to take. She had no idea. Although she knows me, she never has fully trusted me and thought to fight me. Deluded woman. For that reason, her lessons have been harsh. She has endured much pain and there will be more for her before the end. I enjoy hearing her scream as I drag the knife across her smooth, white skin and watch as the blood seeps out. I'm not finished with her just yet. I will take my time and enjoy my final teachings. I must make them memorable before my lady comes back to me.

CALLIE

Since that morning, I had been escorted back home, and watched like a hawk by an over attentive Nick, until my evening shift at the pub. He then, dutifully, drove me back to the pub and deposited me safely into Vinnie and Mick's hands. I was beginning to feel like the baton in a relay race and it was only the first day. Who knew how long this would go on for?

My phone sounded its message tone. I pulled it from my pocket and opened the message from Jase. Nate had given me Jase's new number, when he came over to the pub to find out what was happening. I texted Jase mine but didn't get a reply until later on, and then it wasn't exactly pleasant.

J: You wanna call your dog off?

Me: WTF???

J: Greg and his cousin

Me: Adam? Did they speak to you about Kat?

J: Accused me of kidnapping, more like. Then your bodyguard warned me off. What's going on between you two?

Me: ???

J: He told me to stay the hell away from you. Reckons you're no longer available. Not that he can stop me. I haven't given up on us, Cee. He can't give you what I can. He doesn't know you the way I do.

Me: *I'm at work. Can't talk.*

I sent one final message, hoping to cut him off, and pocketed my phone. After our chat the other day, I had hoped Jase and I could move on to find some way of existing together, without all the drama. Obviously not. But then, this was Adam's doing, not Jase's. I met Adam's eyes across the bar and saw red.

"What did you do?"

"I'm going to need a clue here, Angel," he answered casually, as he took a swig of his beer and levelled me with his gaze.

Nothing, absolutely nothing seemed to faze this man. I was pissed off with him and he knew. He definitely knew, and he was perfectly alright with it. He was even looking at me as though he found my anger cute. The way Greg looked at Dana when she went off at him. Well, I'm no cute little kitten!

"Jase!" I snapped angrily.

Yes, Jase had been refusing to leave me alone, but I'd asked Adam and Cameron to let me deal with it. It was going to take longer than a couple of months for our relationship to go from what it used to be, to anything that might remotely resemble normal, in the future. Adam had ignored me. He'd gone against my wishes and completely overruled me. My brother doing that was something I expected, but Adam? His protective dominance was both irritating and a turn on. I knew I couldn't have it both ways, but I also didn't want him controlling who I spoke to or spent time with.

"Was that him?" Adam's eyes darkened when he glanced at my jeans pocket, where the top of my phone poked out.

"Did you honestly think he wouldn't tell me?" I hissed. We were attracting attention.

"When did you give him your new number?" He demanded angrily.

Really? Did he think because he bought the damn thing, he had a right to tell me who I could give the number to? If that was the case, he would most definitely be getting the money back.

"This morning, when I gave it to everyone else. And I'm asking the questions here!" I moved away from him, stopping to pass the time with Malcolm, and a friend of his, for a few minutes while I served them. Then, I told Mick I was taking a quick break, and motioned for Adam to follow me into the hallway that led upstairs to Mick's living quarters.

"Why the fuck are you warning Jase off me?" I whirled on him, stopping him in his tracks.

"I don't want him around you," he stated simply, as if it should be obvious.

"And since when is that your decision to make?" I snapped.

"Since you landed on my doorstep, broken and alone, in the middle of a blizzard," he replied, his calmness irritating me.

"Adam—" I began.

"No. Listen to *me*. I'm going to be honest with you here, because I've held back long enough." He moved fast, putting me between him and a wall once again, only millimetres of air between our bodies. I put my hands against his chest, in an attempt to gain back some space between us, but it just made him push closer as his arms caged me in. "I want you, Angel. I want you more than I've ever wanted anyone in my life. I want every part of you, with every part of me."

He brought his hands down and gently cupped my cheeks in them, his voice becoming deep and husky and sending a jolt of heat to my core.

"But the fact that you run every time we get close, tells me you're not ready for us, and I won't be your rebound. I want more than that, much more. So, I'll wait. I'll wait as long as you need me to. But in the meantime, I won't have your ex hanging around, trying to talk you back into bed. I protect what's mine, Angel."

His aqua eyes shone, while he held my gaze intensely, as if he could get his message across by embedding it into my brain through my eyes. For a moment, I just stared at him, stunned, letting his words sink in. Then I snapped out of it as that last sentence embedded itself in my head.

I protect what's mine?

"Oh, no!" I shook my head, fuming. "No, Adam! No! You did *not* just piss in a fucking circle around me!"

He laughed. Actually laughed. Full on, head thrown back laughter.

"Woman, you drive me fucking insane." He hissed, through gritted teeth.

He leaned forward and kissed me tenderly on the forehead, his actions in complete contrast to his words. He paused, his eyes closed, his forehead against mine, for a few seconds, breathing deeply.

"Who the hell do you think you are?" I seethed, through my own deep breaths.

"I'm yours, Angel." He stepped back, letting go of me, and walked back out to the bar, as though nothing had happened.

I drove *him* insane? I wasn't the one marking my frigging territory.

Twin 2: What did you do to Adam? He's in a foul mood!

Me: Why would it be me?

Twin 2: Because you're the only one who can get under his skin. You okay?

Me: He'll get over it. I'm fine, Mick got the brandy out.

Twin 2: I'll pick you up for breakfast in the morning.

Me: Ok, be safe.

Twin 2: Love you, girl version.

Me: Back at ya, boy version.

"You and Adam are on the outs, I see?" Mick questioned. He sat down next to me, on the sofa in his living room, and handed me the one of the glasses of brandy he'd poured for us.

"You don't miss a thing, do you?" I smiled and tucked my legs up underneath me.

"Not when it comes to the folks I care about, love." He leaned back and put his arm around my shoulders. "But in this case, I think the entire town heard you giving him what for."

"He warned Jase off, told him to stay away from me." I sighed and leaned my head against his shoulder, allowing his familiar scent to comfort me. Mick always smelled good, clean and fresh, with a faint, underlying musk of the cigarettes he smoked.

"Nothing I haven't done myself. Or Cameron and Nick for that matter. Pretty sure I saw one of Nick's brothers having a go a couple of days ago. Why is it a problem for Adam to do it?" Mick played devil's advocate.

"Because Adam told Jase I was no longer available and made it perfectly clear that he was marking his territory." I told him, taking a big gulp of my brandy. I closed my eyes and relished the sweet burn as it slid down my throat.

"Ah, I wondered when he'd get around to that," Mick chuckled, drinking from his own glass.

"Are you kidding me? You think it's funny?" I lifted my head and glared up at him. Mick set his glass down on the coffee table and sat back before answering.

"Adam and I are very similar, love. We know what we want, and we aren't afraid to go after it. And you—" he touched a finger to my nose, "—are what Adam wants. He's just letting you, and everyone else, know."

"He's pulling some alpha male bullshit and I don't need it!" I sulked.

"But you like it," Mick teased.

"What?" I whisper shouted. Shit! This man knew me too well.

"First, let's get one thing straight. I'm the alpha around here." He growled playfully and I snorted into my glass. *Classy Callie, that's me.* "Don't tell me you don't find it a little bit exciting, when he tells you he wants you, and only you, and he's not about to let another man get in the way of that."

"Maybe a little," I admitted reluctantly. I couldn't deny the thrill I'd felt when Adam had gone caveman on me. "But it doesn't change the fact that I don't even know how I feel about him, let alone if I want a relationship with him, or anyone, for that matter. He's strutting around like I belong to him and it's a done deal!"

"It will be him, Callie love, there won't be anyone else. You know how you feel about him, you're just not ready to admit it to yourself. Besides, he belongs to you, as much as you do to him. He's been yours since the moment you met."

"What are you, psychic or something now?" I laughed and though back to Adam's words. *I'm yours.*

"Adam and I may have had a little chat," he admitted with a sly smirk.

"What?" I felt betrayed.

"I noticed how he was with you and wanted to be clear of his intentions. I won't have my girl getting hurt again." Mick grinned as I shook my head in disbelief. "He's crazy about you. He's a decent fella. and he'll do right by you."

"Now you sound like Nick!" I sighed.

"Adam understands that you're not ready and he's prepared to wait for you. Do you know how hard it is, for a man like him, not to act on his feelings, especially after he's admitted them? He's laid all his cards on the table, agreed to be nothing more than friends, and now he has to be around you constantly. He'll wait for you, but he won't watch you run back to Jase in the meantime." He pulled me back to him. "None of us will for that matter."

"I'm not running back to Jase. I admit I'm confused about how I feel about him now, I'll never go back to him though. I can't have Adam growling like a rabid dog at every man who speaks to me. I've done the territorial, jealous relationship, I can't do that again."

"There's a difference between jealous and territorial, love. Jealousy is wanting what you haven't got. Territorial is protecting what's already yours. He won't growl at all of them, just the ones who flirt with you," Mick joked.

"Gah!" I groaned, feeling frustrated. "You're no help, Mick. You're just backing him up."

"It's time you stopped worrying about everyone else and put yourself first for a change. I know you, love. That head of yours is crammed full of doubts because you're afraid of what everyone else will think, if you move on from Jase so quickly. Well, there is no rule book and it's none of their bloody business. Answer me something?" he asked, and I nodded. "Does Adam make you happy?"

"Yes. Very much." The answer was automatic, not a single thought required.

"Then stop fighting it. You can be wary and guarded, but don't deny your feelings. Take your time if you need to, and when you're ready, Adam will be there for you."

"And if it's not him I want?" I asked, wondering if I really did want to go down this road with him. What if we didn't work out and we ruined a perfectly good friendship?

"Then be very sure. Be one hundred and ten percent certain. Because you don't walk away from a man like Adam unless you mean it." Mick kissed the top of my head.

THE TEACHER

These men continue to make her forget herself. Too enamoured by her to care about anything other than bruised egos, she is a danger to them. It's only a matter of time until one of them slips, can no longer deny his attraction, and takes her against her will. Just as my mother was taken against hers.

This is why the women I teach need me. A lady needs to know the affect she can have on a man. She must not be rushed, forced into a situation where she could forget how to behave. They are making my job harder. She will require more teaching than I anticipated. I must remember to let her know she suffers because of their actions.

Meanwhile, my associate continues to seek my guidance. His will to take my words as gospel, and sheer blindness to the situation he finds himself in, is almost comedic. He steers her directly into my arms with every action he takes.

CHAPTER TEN

CALLIE

"Dessert?" Cameron asked, wiggling his eyebrows and making me smile.

"Breakfast doesn't have dessert, Cam." I rolled my eyes.

Cameron and I were at the cafe opposite my college campus. When we were young, mum insisted on us all eating a meal a day together, but as we grew up and had lives of our own, she was more laid back. As long as the family ate together at least once a week, she was happy. Cameron and I tried as often as possible to eat together since we lost them.

"It does, we invented it." He grinned and I wondered how on Earth my brother was single with a smile like that.

Women noticed Cameron all the time, but he never showed any interest in return. There was the busty blonde in the pub who couldn't keep her hands off him. He insisted nothing had ever happened and she was too much of a bed hopper for him to go there. A woman who was with a different man every weekend wasn't his idea of a catch.

There was a time, after the abduction, when I wondered if he stayed single because of me, out of some skewed idea that he had to take care of me. He denied it, of course.

"You say that every time." I couldn't keep my smile from poking through.

"And every time I put that lemon drizzle muffin in front of you, you eat it. Every last crumb," he teased.

"Well, I can't let it go to waste, can I?" I laughed.

I spun my cup in the moments that passed, while he went to the counter to order our desert. The liquid sloshed up the sides and threatened to spill over, I kept spinning.

"Talk to me, sis." Cameron interrupted my empty thoughts. I glanced up, he was frowny and suddenly very serious.

"I'm fine." I waved him off and began picking pieces off the lemon muffin.

"No. You're sinking," he observed. "You're doing the cup spinning, and all the other little habits you have when you're anxious."

I had no argument. My so-called love life hassles paled into insignificance next to the thought that terrified me most in the world. I wanted to be the calm, in control woman Cameron and my friends needed to see, but I couldn't pull it off.

"He vanished, Cam. No trace. Not a single clue. Nobody knew who he was or where he went. He could come back at any time. Maybe he's been here all along." I blurted, unable to keep my fears from him any longer. "I might know him. He might come in the pub. It could be Mick, for all I know."

"It's not Mick," he replied.

"How can you say that? Nobody knows anything about this man. He held me in front of that mirror, the same way Mick holds me. He made me look at our reflection. I can tell you all about that mask he wore in detail, but I've got no idea who was under it."

I didn't truly think it was Mick. If I thought about it rationally, I would have been able to pick out Mick's eyes. There was no mistaking those bright green gems. *Contact lenses*, a voice whispered in my mind and I shook my head, ridding myself of the idea. I was emotional and my mind was playing tricks on me. Mick hugs weren't the same as being held in front of a mirror and having a knife dragged across my skin.

"How long have you thought it might be Mick?"

"I don't," I sighed. "Not really. I had a flashback once, when he puts his arms around me, that's all it was."

"I don't think he has that kind of evil in him, but if you really think it could be Mick, I'll look into it." Cameron blinked and levelled me with his eyes. "Of course, if we're going with this theory, then I'll have to look into everyone else, too."

"What do you mean?"

"Well, if it's someone we know, it could be Mick, Greg, Nate, Nick—"

"No!"

"Why not?" he argued. "Greg, and Adam for that matter, would both know how to clean a crime scene. Adam hasn't exactly made a secret of the fact he has a thing for you. Nate and Jase have always had that rivalry over you. Nate turns up, the new kid in school. You're the first one to befriend him, bring him into the group. Then Jase steals you from under his nose. Harbouring something like that could do things to a teenager's mind. Something that could become ugly and sinister if it grew with him into adulthood. As for Nick, well, is it really so hard to believe that he could have been obsessed with you all these years? And we can't forget how the first group of women, last year, all had ink done by Nick."

"The police ruled him out straight away. His alibies were seamless, one of them was *you!* We've known Nick all our lives," I gasped, unable to believe Cameron could accuse our best friend of the crimes.

"We've known Jase all our lives, too. He's not who we thought he was. And it wouldn't be the first time the police got something wrong."

"No!" I snapped my eyes up to look at him. "No. It's not Mick, it's not any of them. I'm emotional. Anxious, like you said."

"Relax," Cameron laid his hand over mine. "I'm just trying to help you gain some perspective. You're panicking."

I nodded and took a deep breath. "It's just all getting to me. The new bodies, and not knowing who's doing it. He's still out there somewhere. He's going to come back for me, sooner or later."

"Cal, even if this is the same man, he won't get within an inch of you again. Between me, Adam, and the others, we aren't letting you out of our sight." Cameron tried to calm my nerves.

"Will you admit you're keeping something from me?" I could read him like a book. "They're the same, aren't they? He's hurting them the same way, isn't he? You think it's him that has Jase's phone. I see all the secret huddles that you and Adam get into. Why won't you tell me what's going on, Cam?"

Cameron didn't have to speak; I knew by the look in his eyes he thought it was *him* and not Jase leaving the messages and gifts.

"Okay, look, I don't want to you to read too much into it now, but I found something. In Mum and Dad's room," Cameron admitted.

"What does that have to do with any of this?" I knew he had been clearing out our parent's room recently. He told me I didn't have to help because I still found it too difficult to go in there and I was grateful to him for that.

"When the murders first began, last year, we thought the killer had been around before. There were similarities to those murders and some others, ten years ago. Remember?" Cameron asked.

"Yeah?" I frowned at him.

"Right. Well, it turns out Dad was looking into those murders."

"But Dad wasn't a detective, Cam, he was just a normal copper. Why would he be looking at them?" I was confused.

"Because he thought his sister, Aunt Caroline, was one of the victims. At the time, they couldn't find enough evidence to say for sure. They put her death down to a burglary gone wrong. When her case was closed, Dad decided to look into it himself. From the files I found, it seems he got pretty close to figuring out who it was. It doesn't list any names though," Cameron explained.

Our Aunt Caroline died shortly after we were born. Neither of us had any memory of her, but that she was murdered wasn't new information for us. Our parents told us her killer had never been found and left it at that. They never spoke much of her death.

"Why did he stop?" I was almost certain I knew the answer.

"Because he died. The dates on the files end a few weeks before Mum and Dad's accident." Cameron was looking at me with concern.

"So, Aunt Caroline was murdered, possibly by the same man who abducted me, and Dad was looking into it on his own time," I thought out loud.

"It looks that way." Cameron nodded. "After Adam and I looked them over, I passed the files along to the detectives in charge."

"Do you think Mum and Dad died because of this?" The idea filled me with dread.

"I don't know." He paused to collect his thoughts, pulling his eyebrows together in a frown. "I reviewed everything on their accident and asked Adam to double check it. There are no holes. The brakes went on the car and Dad lost control. The roads were icy. No signs of another vehicle being involved were found. It's a straightforward accident, on paper."

"On paper..." I whispered.

"Yeah," he answered quietly.

"Why didn't you tell me? You've been dealing with the fact that our parents may have been murdered on your own."

"I've talked to Adam. Plus, it's not definite. The chances are it *was* an accident. For all this to be connected would mean it's been building for years. He would have to be targeting our family specifically and he hasn't shown any interest in me. The fact that he's killed women completely unrelated to our family blows that theory out of the water anyway. Mum and Dad died after the others They had no connection to any of them, except Aunt Caroline, and we don't know that was him either. Her death didn't happen in the same way as any of the other women." I doubt either of us believed his words, but I think it made us both feel better to think that it was still an accident. "All we know for sure is that someone is obsessed with you."

"It's definitely him though," I said quietly. "You can't deny it anymore, don't insult me by trying."

"Twin, we're going to keep you safe." He reached over and stilled my hand, stopping me from picking the muffin to pieces.

"You keep saying that. I know you'll try, and I trust you." I tried to sound positive, but this was about more than just me. "What about the others? Who is going to keep them safe?"

"Don't, Cal. Don't do that to yourself. They aren't not your responsibility." Cameron knew what I was thinking. The writing on the cellar wall had plagued me since I escaped from that house.

"What if that message on the wall truly meant I would be his last? What if he would have stopped after me? If I hadn't escaped, if I'd stayed with him, he might not have hurt anyone else. Amy might be alive now. Who is Callie Wilson, that her life is worth more than anyone else's? Why should I get to live, when they don't? What if I could have stopped it?" I barely held back the tears as I rambled.

My brother's voice was full of emotion and his grip on my hand tightened as he spoke.

"You can never be certain he would have stopped with you. We can't prove it's all connected, and you will never know what was going on in his head. What if he *had* stopped with you? What about the rest of us? Were we supposed to just carry on without you? Like it was ok that you were dead, because he hadn't killed anyone else? Callie Wilson is my favourite person. She is the other half of my soul and I can't fucking live without her! Maybe you could take that into consideration when you're trying to destroy her."

Cameron sat back heavily in his chair and brushed a hand through his messy hair.

"You need a haircut," I said.

"Yeah. You wanna go home? I'm not happy with you being at college with all this going on in your head." A mixture of concern and stress masked his pretty face as he reached across the table to take my hand in his again, this time more gently.

"No. I need to go to college and work. Keeping everything normal helps." It was my turn to be the strong one again. That's what my twin needed to see, so I gave it to him.

"Whatever you want, but promise you'll ring me straight away if you change your mind." He looked weary, as though he hadn't slept in months. This was all taking its toll on him too. Now, with this new information, he had so much more to think about. I was glad he was leaning on Adam. I wished he'd told me sooner, but at least he hadn't tried to take it all on himself.

"I will," I promised him.

"Nick's picking you up, yeah?" he asked as we stood. He was on a nightshift again that night and I knew he didn't want me alone in the house.

"Yep. He can't stay over, before you suggest it. Ethan isn't around tonight, so Nick needs to be at home. I'll lock the doors and windows. I'll be fine, Cam. Go home and get some sleep." I instructed him on the walk to my class. It fell on deaf ears. I could almost hear his brain working at warp speed, putting a plan into action, to make certain I wasn't left alone for a second.

"Nick is going to come inside to your class and collect you, I'll go into the studio and talk to him on my way back. You text him the room number and do not leave without him. Don't set foot outside that building without him, do you hear me? Stay inside, preferably around other people. I'll sort something out for tonight. You can't stay at Nick's with the boys there, we're not bringing them into this." He worked through his thoughts and I had no doubt, as I tiptoed to kiss his cheek, he would be on the phone to Adam as soon as he left me, to get him to stay at the house with me that night.

Adam: Dinner?

Me: Dinner?

Adam: That meal you eat in the evening, comes after lunch...

Me: Rings a bell.

Adam: Tonight?

Me: Tonight?

Adam: Are you just going to keep repeating what I'm saying?

Me: Are you just going to keep repeating what I'm saying?

Adam: You're so fucking sexy. Your body blows my mind. One day soon, you're going to let me all the way in and I'm going to show you exactly what you do to me.

Me: What about dinner?

Adam: Coward! You. Me. Dinner. Tonight. Together?

Adam: Cam's on nights. I can come over, so you aren't alone.

Me: That old chestnut.

Adam: You want chestnuts for dinner?

Me: Yes. I forgot to tell you I'm actually a shape shifter. My animal form is a squirrel.

Adam: I do have nuts.

Adam: You drive me nuts

Adam: But I'm still nuts about you.

Adam: I can keep going...

Me: No. Please. No.

Adam: So, if you're a squirrel what does that make me?

Me: A weirdo with a freaky animal fetish? You should talk to Nick, you two have more in common than I thought. Ask him about the lemurs.

Adam: Are you suggesting I have animal sex with Nick?

Me: Only if you sell tickets.

Adam: Do you want my nuts or not?

EDUCATING CALLIE

Me: Not. But why don't you come over for dinner tonight?

Adam: You drive me insane, woman.

Me: I aim to please.

I wandered out of the IT room in a daze, later that afternoon, feeling drained both mentally and physically. It had been a long day and I couldn't wait to sink into a hot bath before Adam came over. I knew the whole *"you shouldn't be alone while Cam is on nights"* thing was only part of the reason he wanted to come over. Even though my chat with Mick had made me feel slightly better about the situation, I still wasn't ready to confront my feelings for Adam.

"Hey, day dreamer." Nate's voice pierced my thoughts and I looked up to find him leaning against the wall, opposite the room I'd come out of.

"Oh, hey, you. This is a nice surprise." I smiled, letting him take my bag when he reached for it. *Don't let your head go there, Callie!*

"Nick couldn't get here in time. Something about the job he was doing taking longer than he expected, so he asked me to pick you up. Couldn't let the lady get the bus, could I?" Nate chatted, while he guided me towards the exit, a hand on the small of my back. "Serious thoughts, babe?"

"Not really. It's just been a long day." I didn't feel like going into details about Cameron's revelations. I wasn't sure I even could, with it being connected to the investigation, better to just stay quiet. Our conversation had weighed heavily on my mind all day though and I was exhausted. I pushed all suspicions and theories out of my mind when I saw Nate's 1966 Ford Mustang. I loved his car. Of he was trying to kidnap me, all he would have to do was offer me a ride in his car. *Pull yourself together, Callie!*

"Looks like you could use a caffeine boost." I nodded and watched him put my bag in the back seat, then open the passenger door, for me. I hesitated, couldn't help it, then shook myself out of it and climbed in.

Nate got in the driver's side. I smiled when he turned the ignition and the engine growled to life. Nate had always been good looking in a rough, rugged kind of way. His blonde hair was pulled back into the hair tie he used when he was at work. A short beard covered his chin, and upper lip, and his clothes were always oil stained, making him look as though he never spent time anywhere other than on his back, underneath a car. Amy had always compared him to a Viking. I just loved his sense of humour and laid-back attitude to life. If we lived near the coast, I could have seen him as a surfer.

"Still got a crush on my car?" He grinned at me, his eyes twinkling.

"Yep!" I nodded and listened to the engine.

"Want to drive?" he asked.

"You never let anyone drive this beast," I said, wide eyed.

"I trust you." He turned off the engine, got out, and walked around to the passenger side.

"You really trust me to do this?" I asked, climbing across the seats excitedly.

"You're the only person who loves this car as much as I do. I trust you, Callie."

I was in heaven, absolute heaven. Driving Nate's car made me fall even more in love with it. If he ever sold it, I would be chomping at the bit to take it off his hands. All the crazy thoughts left me. We took a detour, through the nearby countryside, and stopped at a roadside cafe for coffee, before driving home.

"You want to eat while we're here?" Nate asked absently, looking around, as he held a chair out for me to sit.

"I'm having dinner with Adam later." I told him with a shake of my head.

"So, are you and him a thing now?" He was curious, a smile tipping up the corner of his mouth.

"Checking out the competition for Jase?" I joked, half serious.

"Haven't seen him since Amy's memorial. Luke hasn't either." Nate shrugged.

"Really? But you, him, and Luke are normally joined at the hip." It was unusual for Nate and Luke not to have seen Jase.

"Not anymore. He hasn't been around for months. Even before you broke up, he was sketchy. We've texted back and forth a bit, but that's all." Nate stirred sugar into his coffee "He's different now."

"You noticed too?" I stared into my cup.

"Couldn't not notice. I don't know what he was thinking with Amy. I mean, I knew she was after him for ages, but he never went there. He kept telling her he loved you and to leave him alone. It really wound him up that she wouldn't go away. He went out of his mind when he couldn't find you the night you walked in on them. Luke suggested he give you some breathing space for a couple of day and he pinned him up against the wall. I thought he was going to kill him. He was gutted with himself and it was genuine, you could see it was. Yeah, he loves you. But everything else? Fuck, I don't know." Nate gave up trying to figure it out.

"That makes two of us," I agreed.

I hugged Nate and kissed his cheek when we got out of the car at my house. "Thanks for letting me drive the beast."

"You sure you don't want me to hang around, until Adam gets here? Cam might kill me if I don't." Nate eyed the house, his eyes flicking over every window.

"No, really. I'll be fine. I just want a hot bath and silence for a while." I assured him. "I'll deal with Cam, if he says anything."

He still insisted on coming in and looking around the entire house, for signs of anything out of the ordinary. After checking the back door and all the windows, Nate was finally satisfied that I would be alright for the two hours it would be until Adam arrived.

"So, we're good for next week?" He confirmed. We'd arranged to have dinner the following week.

"Yep, looking forward to it." I said as I watched him walk down the porch steps.

"I'll bell you, babe. Lock the door," he said, turning to watch, until I went inside and locked the door. Then I heard the rumble of the engine as he drove away.

Adam had a key. Since when did Adam have a key to my house? After I locked the door, I'd been expecting Adam to ring the doorbell. I was still wallowing in the bath, buried deep in the pages of a book. The hot water relaxed me for the first time in days and I'd lost track of time.

"Incoming!" His voice startled me out of the book.

"Shit!" I muttered, when I heard his voice at my bedroom door.

"Angel? You in there?" he called around the door.

"I'm in the bath. Almost done. I'll be out in a minute," I called back, hoping that he didn't venture further into my bathroom. He'd get quite the eyeful if he came in now. I might not be shy about my short pyjamas but naked was another thing entirely.

"No worries, I'll be in the kitchen."

I heard the smile in his voice; I should have known he'd be the gentleman about it. Climbing out of the bath, I dried myself and pulled on a pair of black yoga trousers. I added a white tank top with the slogan *"Property of London"* —a reference to one of my favourite books and yanked a comb through my wet hair, before venturing out to investigate the clattering sounds coming from my kitchen.

I found Adam in the kitchen, dressed casually, in dark denim jeans and a navy blue, V-neck t-shirt. The sleeves clung to his biceps and stretched across his chest, hinting at the sculpted muscle under his clothes. My eyes roamed his body and my mind wondered about those V lines again, as I watched him chop salad vegetables. Why did I have such a fascination about this man's body? I mean, I knew Nick had those lines. Shit, Nick had a fantastic body, but I never found myself wondering what it would be like to lick it. *Because Adam is everything you want, wrapped up in a pretty bow. That's why, Callie!*

"Angel," Adam said, giving my t-shirt a knowing glance. I loved that he didn't have to ask. He pushed a single glass of red wine towards me.

"Hey," I replied taking a sip. "Only one glass? I didn't think you liked wine?"

"I don't like that fizzy stuff, you and the girls drink. This?" He took the glass when I passed it to him. "This is different."

"I see." I watched his Adam's apple bob in his throat when he drank from the glass. Can a man's throat be sexy? Because his was. Not that I was thinking about licking that either, obviously. Nor was I swooning in any way, because I'd re-enforced my no swoon zone that day and now had armed guards surrounding it. Adam Butler was not getting through.

"Cam passed the books to the detectives." He went back to slicing onions as he spoke. "We should hear something in a few days."

"He told me about the files he found," I blurted.

"And how do you feel about the information in them?" He set down the knife in his hand and gave me his full attention.

"My Aunt *was* murdered, and my parents *may* have been murdered, by the same man who locked me in a cellar and treated my body like a chopping board. This could all go so much deeper than I imagined. Honestly, I don't really know how to process it at the minute. I don't want to get caught up in those kinds of emotions, because we don't know anything for sure. We might never know."

"I'm here when you need me, Angel."

"I know. Thank you for being there for Cam, too."

"You're important to me, that makes Cam important too." He watched me for a reaction, always wondering if this was finally the thing that pushed me too far and sent me running from him again.

"Yeah, yeah, don't think I haven't noticed your little bromance going on. You don't have to pretend you're doing it for me," I joked, because it was easier to joke than it was to react to his admission. I eyed the ingredients on the counter in front of him. "What are we cooking?"

"*I* am going to cook *you* good old-fashioned steak and chips," he informed me, picking the knife back up. "You are going to sit there, enjoy the wine, and allow me to wait on you."

"Hmm, caveman food, my favourite." I pulled myself up to sit on the counter and made no effort to conceal from him that I was eyeing him up. "You should be careful; a girl could get used to this."

"That's the plan, Angel." He winked and began to pepper two huge steaks, while I had a mini panic attack about his words.

The panic passed quickly this time though and my mind moved quickly back onto him and how things could be, if I allowed it. If I could bring myself to switch off the guilt over Jase. This man had the ability to tie my stomach in knots and turn my legs to jelly, with nothing more than a look. I knew I was playing with fire, but he was so tempting, and I desperately needed the distraction.

"Are you ever going to show me the bad boy, Adam?"

With very deliberate movements, he set down the knife again, and wiped his hands on a towel. Then slowly, while stalking my gaze, he moved into the space between my legs, and settled his hands on my thighs.

"You're not ready for him, Angel," he warned.

"Says who?" I dared.

"Shall I tell you what would have happened tonight, if I wasn't holding back?" He looked down at his hands on my thighs, squeezed slightly. The movement of his thumbs, travelling higher up the inside of my legs, made me suck in a breath. Meeting my eyes again, he lifted a finger and hooked it under the thin strap of my top, pushing it down my shoulder.

"Tell me," I whispered, letting out the breath I held.

"If I wasn't holding back, I would have walked straight into your bathroom, without a second thought. I would have lifted you out of the water, turned you around, pressed my body up against yours and nailed you to the nearest wall with my cock."

I swallowed the lump in my throat, and watched him lower his lips to my shoulder, and kiss it, once, twice. His mouth was soft against my skin and his voice was low and breathy. There was no attempt to hide his desire for me.

"Then, I would have laid you out on your bed and feasted on this beautiful body all night." his finger trailed a path across the tops of my breasts, just above the neckline of my shirt. "I would have made sure the entire town heard my name on your lips. By morning, they would all know who you belonged to."

"Adam," I whispered, my body crying out for him, heart hammering in my chest.

His kisses, patterning my shoulder, became light, sensual nips, but I wanted more than that. I needed to feel what I knew he could give me, not be teased with it. I wanted him to devour me. Take away the numbness and make me scream his name. My hands fisted in his shirt, pulling him closer against my core. I tightened my legs around his hips, and he growled, deep in his chest.

"And you wouldn't have stopped me. Even though we both know you aren't ready for us to be more than friends yet, you wouldn't have stopped me. I know, because I see the way you lean into my touch. I see your breaths quicken, when I crowd you. I feel your heart beating faster when I align my body with yours. I feel the heat you're pressing against me now and I want in as much as you want me there." His hands slid along my legs again, coming to rest with his thumbs on the inside of my thighs, so close to where I was desperate to feel him. His tongue flicked out to sooth the skin he'd nipped between my neck and shoulder, that same patch of skin where he loved to bury his face so often. "You wouldn't stop me, would you, Angel?"

"No. I wouldn't stop you." I turned my face towards his, the scent of his aftershave intoxicating me, wishing that he would just lift his chin and take my mouth with his.

"But tomorrow morning, you'd have one of your "*oh shit*" moments and run from me. I won't have you run from me. You're not ready for us yet. You will be, but not yet." He squeezed my thighs and placed one last kiss on my shoulder, then lifted a hand and pushed the strap back up. "I won't let it begin, until I know it's never going to end, because once you're mine, I'll never let go."

He lifted my chin, to bring my hooded gaze up to meet his, and smiled that perfect smile. I wanted to argue. Held there, trapped in his eyes, I wanted to tell him he was wrong. Insist that I needed him to throw me up against that wall and fuck me into oblivion, and I think he wanted that too. Sexual tension clouded the air between us. We watched each other, him silently daring me to go there, but I didn't. I didn't say it because he was right. I wanted him, there was no doubt about that, but I wasn't ready to be with him the way he wanted. There was no way I would risk what I'd found with Adam on a one-night stand. He was too important for that.

"So, you should probably cook then. I mean, if you're not going to ravage me." I reverted back to my nerdy humour to break the tension that had expanded into the silence.

Adam laughed and easily fell into our usual routine. "Can I fall in love with you yet?"

"Well, that all depends on how well you cook that steak." I answered, grabbing the towel from the counter and whipping it against his backside, as he turned away from me.

"Slave driver," he winked, flirtatiously, and we both knew then, that our relationship had turned a very important corner.

It turned out Adam was pretty fantastic in the kitchen. He cooked the steak to melt in the mouth perfection and even made his own onion rings. Seriously, the man knew how to make batter. The fact that he had cooked a proper meal and not one of those namby pamby, no more than a mouthful on the plate, meals went a long way in my book.

"That. Was. Amazing!" I said, topping up our wine glass and feeling fit to burst.

"I'm glad you liked it." He laced his fingers through mine, leading me from the kitchen to the living room. We sat, close together, on the blue sectional sofa and talked effortlessly. When it was like that, I could forget his caveman reaction over my seeing Jase, and I got a glimpse of the real Adam. My Adam. Now that we were close together on the sofa though, earlier events were playing on my mind. I needed a cold shower.

"So, since when do you have a key to my house?" I pried.

"Cam gave it to me today. It's a safety precaution. I'm not trying to check up on you, or own you, or anything like that. But, now that the gifts don't seem to be from Jase, and after the messages you got, we're covering every angle." He was quick to defend. "Greg, Mick, and Vinnie also have them. Greg and Vinnie handed out keys to their places too."

"It's strange having to think this way, that we might not even be safe in our own homes anymore," I said. "Thank you, for being there and looking out for us."

"No thanks necessary." He kissed my forehead and lifted my chin to gain eye contact. "Talk to me. All this stuff with your parents coming to light must be so confusing for you. What's going on in that head of yours?"

"You shouldn't try and get inside my head, it's too dark for you." I told him. New information and old whirled through my mind constantly; I couldn't even make sense of it myself.

"Angel, I'm already there. I've been there since the second we met. I'm in your head, the same way you're in mine. We're fighting this darkness together, remember?" Adam already had many of the details of my abduction, more than I'd given anyone else.

"It's him. I know it's him. He's back and it's me he wants," I said quietly.

"We don't know anything for sure." He gave me the usual spiel.

"Don't, Adam, please don't sugar coat it for me. I expect it from Cam, and even Greg, but not you. I can't take it from you." I pleaded with him.

"I'm sorry. I try not to. I just don't want you worrying about this. When I see that haunted look in your eyes, all I want to do is make it go away." Adam pulled me closer to him.

"You help more than you know, just by being here. But I need one person, *you*, to be straight with me. I feel like I'm going insane half the time!"

"There's nothing wrong with a little bit of crazy." He smiled; I didn't return it. "Ok, I promise, from now on, I won't bullshit you. I'm still going to tell you not to worry though."

"Do you believe he's back?"

"I believe there are too many coincidences for it not to be him. Since we found your Dad's files, I'd be a fool not to think there's more to all this than the detectives are picking up." He admitted and rather than fill me with dread, his words actually gave me a feeling of relief. It wasn't just my messed-up head, making up stories and blowing it all out of proportion.

"Did you read them?"

"Yes. Your Dad believed your Aunt knew her killer. There were no signs of struggle in her flat, no signs of a break in. She let whoever killed her in," he paused, a slight frown furrowing his brow. "She lived in Marbledon, yes?"

I nodded. "I don't know where exactly, but yes."

"That's the closest town to the house he took you to." Adam was cautious, watching me to gage my reaction.

"And now he's started leaving the bodies there." I fit together the pieces Adam fed me.

"It still doesn't give us much and it's all circumstantial, but I can't help think it's all connected. Your Aunt's murderer, your abductor, and whoever is killing now are likely to be the same person and…" Adam trailed off making me look up at him.

"What? What is it?" I demanded.

"Your parents. Their deaths are too close to the case for them to be accidental, in my opinion."

"I think so too," I admitted.

"Cam agrees. Your dad passed all the advanced driver courses on offer through the police force. He was accustomed to driving in bad weather. He knew how to handle a vehicle. Accidents still happen, but something about it doesn't ring true. We just can't prove it. Your dad didn't have all the information on who he was looking at. He believed it was someone in town, someone they knew, but that's as far as he seemed to get. The files end on a cliff hanger, like one of your books. It's as if there are pages missing," he explained.

Never having read the files myself, I had no idea exactly what my dad had found out. All I had were Adam and Cameron's conclusions to go on. Buzzing with new information, I slipped into my memories. Adam sat back and gave me a nudge with his shoulder, encouraging me to talk to him. So, I let the words spill from me like a waterfall.

"I don't know what freaked me out more, the fact that I never heard him speak or that I never saw his face. Not that either of those things could have made it any better, but it sticks with me because of the way it made me feel. More so than the pain, more than the isolation, the darkness. The scars from his knife have mostly faded, I don't get flashbacks every time I look at my reflection anymore. The pain, I can forget, but the way he made me feel will stay with me forever. The terror when I heard his footsteps on the stairs. The hollow feeling, in the pit of my stomach, when he turned those empty eyes on me, from behind the mask. My frustration and desperation when I screamed at him to speak, to answer me, at least tell me why. The torment of being left alone for so long, wondering how long it would be before he came back and killed me. The feelings will never fade. And I don't have a reason for any of it or a face to connect it to, to get angry with, or blame."

"Then, I find out there could be so much more to it all than I ever dreamt. I daren't let myself think or feel about any of that because none of it is certain. There's still nothing that allows me to make sense of it all. I keep wondering if it's one of my friends because it seems like I know this person, or at least, they know me. I second guessed myself getting in the car with Nate today. Is one of my oldest friends going to drive me into the woods and slit my throat?" I looked down to where I was wringing my shaking hands together in my lap. Adam reached over and took them. His big hands wound around mine, weaving our fingers together, grounding me and calming the shaking. "I'm a mess, Adam. A paranoid, deranged, broken mess!"

"You are the bravest, strongest, most incredible woman I have ever met." Adam reached out a hand and turned my head to face him, with a hand on my cheek. "You could have given up. You could have crumbled and let the darkness consume you, but you didn't. You fought. You continue to fight, every second, of every day. You refuse to let him win. He didn't break you, because you won't give him that kind of power over you. You were dragged into hell and you fought your way through. You came out the other side an angel. My angel. My beautiful, powerful, snow angel."

How could he possibly look at me and see all that?

"I don't feel strong or brave or any of those things. I'm tired. Tired of living in the darkness. Tired of being afraid. Tired of being strong. Tired of fighting. I don't want to fight anymore. For once, I want to be fought for. Just for a little while," I admitted.

I knew I was allowing myself to be defeated. I couldn't help it. I wanted to step back and let someone else carry it all for a while.

"I'm fighting for you. I'll always be here to fight with you and for you. I will fight every day by your side. I'll stay in the shadows when you want me to, but when you need me, when you get tired, I'll step out of the shadows and protect what's mine. Together, just like we promised." He hooked his arm around me and rested his chin on my head. "You with me, Angel?"

"Always," I whispered.

. . .

I'd done it again. I used Adam as a body pillow. Sprawled all over him. Legs all tangled up with his. Hands bunched up inside his shirt. Yes. Inside his shirt. You heard me. My hands were on his bare skin. I'd pulled a Callie, good and proper. *Holy giant fucking shit balls!*

"Morning!" An amused voice came from above us.

"Cam," I groaned and pried my eyes open. *Even bigger shit balls!*

"Morning," Adam yawned. He tightened his arms around me and pulled me closer, rubbing his hands over my back as though this was a normal, everyday occurrence.

"Good night?" Cameron asked and I could hear the smirk in his voice. *That dick!*

"Perfect," Adam replied, his arms tightening again, when I tried to pull myself away from him. "Going somewhere, Angel?"

I groaned and laid my head back down on his chest heavily. "Obviously not."

"Coffee?" Cameron called from the kitchen.

"Strong!" I replied, refusing to look at Adam.

"Just when I think I'm getting somewhere you close off again. Will you ever stop running from me?" He murmured quietly in his sleepy husk, running his fingers through my hair. I'd proven him right. I wasn't ready for us.

"Is it enough that I want to?" I admitted. I knew he deserved more, especially after I so obviously flirted with him the night before, but it was all I could give.

"It's enough." He leaned down to kiss the top of my head. "You didn't have a nightmare."

"I never do with you," I whispered, relaxing into his chest.

Twin 2: You do realise, sis, that the only time you will ever be the same height as Adam is when you're lying down? Dude is going to have serious back problems in years to come.

Me: Zero, Cameron. ZERO funny!

Me: Oops!

Liv: Again? FFS! Witch, just shag him and get it over with.

Me: Good talk, Olive.

I opened the pub for breakfast that morning; something new Mick and I decided to try. We designed a small, breakfast style menu including tea, coffee, pastries, and fresh juices. I was able to do some of the baking myself, in the pub kitchen, but the pastries we ordered in from Bea, who owned the bakery in town. There was nowhere in Frost Ford that offered anything similar, so, although it was late for breakfast at 11am, we cornered the market and it was doing well.

Adam sat at the bar, having driven me to work. He was on nights that night, so wasn't going into work that morning and stayed for breakfast. Mick sat next to him, reading a newspaper, while I was behind the bar. I was busy laying out a coffee cake and muffins at one end of the bar, for the customers to choose from.

"Morning."

A familiar, heavily accented voice rumbled from behind me, as I placed mine and Adam's shared cup down on the bar. I turned, to find Jared, Mick's younger brother, dressed only in grey track pants, framed in the doorway that led to upstairs. Hair the same dark shade as Mick's, but longer, hung messily around his face. He rubbed his pretty green eyes, squinting, and yawning, then aimed a wide grin at me.

"Red!" I cried and flung myself at him, making a sound I'm pretty sure could only be heard by dogs. He caught me and staggered back a step, laughing.

"Jaysus, are you a sight for sore eyes." He murmured, squeezing me tightly. "Missed you, beautiful girl."

"Missed you more." I grinned like a maniac as we pulled back to look at each other.

"Put some fecking clothes on, brother!" Mick grumbled, without looking up from the paper he was reading.

"Gorgeous as ever." Jared charmed, ignoring Mick.

Jared flirted with girls a lot. He joked that if any woman could turn him it would be me, but we both knew Vinnie was more his type. I saw a spark between them, when Jared was over the last time, but Vinnie denied it completely when I questioned him.

"Hang on a second—" Jared narrowed his eyes and held my face in his hands, squinting at me. He addressed Mick with a turn of his head to face him. "What the hell? What's going on here, Mikey?"

"I warned you," Mick replied with a sigh, turning the page of his newspaper.

"What?" I squirmed in his grasp.

"You never said it was this bad. When did this happen?" I assumed he was still talking to Mick, but his eyes had come back to mine.

"Do you really need an answer to that?" Mick answered.

"Are you two speaking in code?" I frowned, moving away from him.

"Your light went out," Jared said quietly and pulled me back to him. Shit! Not hiding it as well as I thought, after all.

The screech of wood across the tiled floor alerted us to Adam standing abruptly and pushing his stool back from the bar. He grabbed his phone and shoved it roughly into his pocket.

"I've got to go in to work." He turned to leave, not even glancing in my direction.

"Later, mate." Mick frowned thoughtfully at Adam's back, as he walked away.

"Something I said?" Jared joked, rubbing his hand across his bare stomach.

"Ah, of course." Mick looked at me and tilted his head towards the door Adam left swinging behind him.

"What?" I questioned.

"Get after him, woman," Mick said, as if it should be obvious.

"Why? He'll be back later," I said.

"Just trust me on this, love," Mick said, and Jared obviously clocked on to something I was missing.

"Go." Jared slapped my backside playfully. "Then get that sexy arse back here and tell me all about the hot new man in your life."

"It's just Adam," I mumbled and wandered out from behind the bar towards the front door.

Out in the street, I stopped and looked towards the police station, Adam was about to cross the road. Unsure what Mick and Jared actually expected me to do; I called his name and started along the footpath towards him.

"Adam," I shouted, he stopped and turned, waiting for me to catch up. "You okay?"

"Fine," he snapped, and I frowned.

"You erm, you left really quickly. I thought you weren't going into work. You didn't say goodbye. Like, I dunno, you were mad or something?" I fumbled over my words awkwardly.

"Nope, not mad. Stupid maybe, but not mad." He turned to go. I reached out and grabbed his belt loop, hooking my finger through it, and pulling him back towards me.

"Adam?" I questioned.

"I have a mountain of paperwork to do, Callie." He sounded impatient.

"Callie?" I was shocked. I hadn't heard him use my name since the night we met and, in all honesty, it hurt not to hear my nickname from him. I wracked my brains for something to say but came up short.

"Is that not your name?" He looked at me finally, sighing loudly, like I was wasting his time.

"Not to you, it's not," I muttered.

I looked at the floor, my hand fell heavily from his belt loop, and hung at my side. I hadn't realised until that moment just how much the nickname meant to me. It was just a word though, wasn't it? A silly private joke, about the night we met and my ridiculous appearance on his doorstep, in the middle of the night. Besides, nicknames didn't really mean anything, did they? Okay, fine, I could deal with this. He had just well and truly friend zoned me, despite our moment of—*what, Callie? Moment of what, exactly? You attempted to flirt with him, and he turned you down.* That's all it was, but that was alright, that was what I'd wanted all along. *Okay, I've got this.* I didn't have it. I was a mess!

"Look, Adam, I erm... I just want you to know that... Well, thank you," I sputtered, fiddling with the sleeves on my sweatshirt.

"For?" He frowned.

"Everything. I mean, that is, the last few months. Everything with Jase and Amy, the night we met, being there for me. Chasing the nightmares away. Fighting the darkness with me. Protecting me. I don't think, no, I *know* I couldn't have gotten through it without you. You've done so much for me and you didn't even know me. I was just some lunatic who turned up on your doorstep, ranting and raving. You didn't have to do any of it. You didn't even have to let me in, but you did. I know I'm moody and guarded. I take you for granted, I mess with your head, and I'm and not always very nice to you, but you still did it. All of it. Without question. So, I wanted to say thank you and I want you to know that I notice. I notice all the little things you do for me and I appreciate them. I appreciate *you*, Adam. But you don't have to keep doing it, not if you don't want to. I mean, I know in a way it's your job. Some of it, at least, but you shouldn't feel obligated. So, you can stop now. If you want to." I breathed finally, a shaky, emotion filled breath.

How was that for ramble of the century? Nick would be so proud of me. Adam's thumb and forefinger came up and lifted my chin until our eyes met because, apparently, I was still looking at the floor.

"Angel," he croaked, with obvious emotion. I sighed in relief at the sound of my nickname on his lips, not realising how close I'd been to tears. "It's good to finally hear that I matter to you, as much as you do to me."

"You do, Adam. You *really* do. You have no idea how important you are to me." I may have only just begun to realise it, but in the short time since we'd met, Adam had become one of the most important people in my life.

"Save me a slice of that coffee cake, okay? I'll be back in later." He pulled me in for a tight hug and I locked my arms around his waist, not wanting to let go.

"The biggest piece." I promised to his chest, and I heard Dana's giggling inside my mind, when he leant down and kissed my forehead.

"For the record, you'll always be my snow angel." He smiled at me before he turned to cross the road and I felt as though my world was brightening with that single action.

"So, how long can you stay?" I asked Jared as we worked the bar together, while Mick did paperwork in his office.

"Ah, you don't get rid of me that easily. We've got business to discuss, an empire to build. I'm here for good!"

"Really? You're really staying? We're actually doing this?" I bounced on the balls of my feet excitedly. I resisted the urge to mentally berate myself for getting excited. when I would probably be dead soon and they'd be doing it all without me. *Ugh! Get a grip Callindra!*

"That we are. That and hopefully a certain tall, dark, and tattooed someone." He winked at me.

"Vinnie?" I screeched. "Seriously? You and Vin?"

"Shush!" Jared clamped a hand over my mouth. "I said hopefully. Nothing is set in stone. He doesn't even know I'm here yet. Let's just say, I fecked up last time and there's every chance he won't even give me the time of day."

"Mmm-hmm." I nodded eagerly and mumbled against his hand. He laughed and removed it. "How did you fuck up?"

"Got scared and ran for the hills." He shrugged.

"So, man stuff, can't admit your feelings?" I surmised, realising it sounded familiar. Especially after the little epiphany I'd had that morning.

"In simple terms." He shrugged again.

"You got this," I told him. "I mean, look at you. You're gorgeous, smart, funny, loving, and kind and he's just... Well, he's just Vinnie. You two are perfect for each other. You're going to be so good together."

"Yeah, well don't go planning our wedding or anything just yet," he joked.

"Red, you know wedding planning is Dana's thing, not mine." I shoved him playfully.

"She can never know about this," he whispered, eyes wide with horror.

"Never." I drew a cross across my heart with my finger, then mimed locking my lips, and throwing away the key.

"So, tell me about hot cop." Jared changed the subject.

I shook my head frantically and pointed to my sealed lips.

"Ah, no," he laughed. "You don't get off that easily. I told you mine, now you tell me yours. Mick informs me there's quite the story there and I want it all. Spill!"

"Mick's full of shit," I huffed.

"Not where you're concerned. You're his number one girl. If it's caught his attention, then it's big news, so I need to make sure this fella is worthy." Jared raised his eyebrows, a cue for me to start talking.

"Ugh, fine." I caved and gave him a quick summary of the car crash that was Adam and me. "Adam is my friend. Except, friend isn't really a big enough word. He's been there for me. A lot. He wants more, but I'm scared shitless, Red. A bit like you and V, except I have all these fucked up feelings for Jase getting in the way. I don't want him back. I know what I feel for him isn't love in the way it used to be, but I can't just turn off my feelings for him overnight. I feel like I'm leading Adam on. I want to be ready to move on with him, I really do, I just can't bring myself to take the leap."

"So, basically, Adam is in love with you, and you're still in love with Jase?" He decided, a taunting gleam in his eye.

"What? No. I'm not *in* love with Jase anymore, but I do still care about him," I protested. "As for Adam being in love with me, it's nothing that serious. Yeah, he made it clear he wants to be more than friends, but it's not love."

"So, what was that this morning? He saw you and me together and stormed out of here like a jealous lover. Have you seen yourself, woman? You need to let Jase go and let Adam in, that man can put the light back in your eyes." He winked at me. I raised my eyebrows at him. "Ah, Callie girl, it's obvious that man is head over heels for you. He doesn't seem like a fella you'd want to be walking away from."

"That's what Mick says. Stupid, know it all, O'Rourke brothers," I grumbled, walking down the bar to serve Ethan and Nate, who had just come in.

"Morning, Cal," Ethan said. Nate looked up from the menu and smiled.

"Hey, you've still got time for breakfast if you're quick," I told them, knowing Nate liked his bacon in the mornings.

"Nah, we're here for the cake today. I just stopped in at the station and a little bird tells me you made coffee cake. That's what I want." Nate patted his stomach, then peered down the bar at Jared. "Is that Red?"

"Yup." I nodded, cutting Nate a large slice of the cake and putting it by his spot at the bar, while he went to say hello to Jared. "How about you, Ethan?"

"I'll take one or two of those chocolate muffins." He grinned at me; the boy had a serious chocolate habit. "Unless you've got brownies hidden away somewhere?"

"Not today, but I can make some for after dinner tomorrow night. You're coming, aren't you?"

"Wouldn't miss it. Dan will be in heaven if you make brownies. No vodka though, I'm still hung over from the last time!"

Me: Hey, how's work?

Adam: Quiet. It's 3am, Angel. Are you okay?

Me: Fine.

Adam: Nightmare?

Me: Hmmm...

Adam: Wanna tell me about it?

Me: Same shit, different night.

Adam: Need my arms?

Me: They're not here.

Adam: They can be.

Me: No. I don't want to disturb you at work just for a hug.

Adam: You can always have a hug, it's never a disturbance.

Me: Ha! If it were a disturbance, you'd have to arrest me.

Adam: And now my head is full of innuendos about you in handcuffs. I'll be there in 10

Me: I'll make coffee. You can tell me handcuff jokes.

Ten minutes later, true to his word, I was pulled into Adam's strong arms when he let himself into my house. He came into the pub later in the day for the cake I'd saved him, but it was busy with lunchtime customers by then. We hadn't hired a new chef since Kat because we were still hoping she was coming back to us. Instead, we reduced the menu and Kaden and I took turns in the kitchen. That's where I was when Adam came back in and we hadn't had a chance to talk much. Though Jared had cornered him and given him the third degree. Adam told me about it, saying Jared wasn't the first person who had demanded to know his intentions towards me. I knew Mick and he had had that conversation, but I wondered who else. Cameron was probably a good bet, maybe Nick, but Adam wasn't telling. It was against the man rules, or something.

Sitting on the stools in the dimly lit kitchen, we shared our cup of coffee. We spoke in hushed voices, careful not to wake Cameron, about nothing and everything. I loved these late-night conversations with Adam, when we slowly uncovered all the tiny little details about each other. Yet, although Adam had told me he was happy to wait for me, I couldn't help but feel as though I was leading him on.

With my feelings for him getting stronger, but my feelings for Jase not waning, I felt as though I was running around in circles. I knew I couldn't move forward with Adam until I was completely over Jase, and that, I reminded myself, wasn't going to happen overnight. I felt terrible for running hot and cold with Adam all the time. Poor man probably didn't know whether he was coming or going with me. It never seemed to bother him, but he was a man after all, it must be getting to him.

"I can hear you thinking over there. What's wrong?" He poked a finger into my knee.

"We can't keep doing this," I decided, not willing to mess with his feelings any longer.

"Doing what exactly?" He frowned, and it bothered me that I was once again the reason for his frown.

"This. Us, Adam. I don't want you to think I'm leading you on. I feel like such a bitch." I sighed heavily and hated myself for sounding like a drama queen, because self-inflicted drama had never been my thing. "I'm messing you around."

"Angel—" he began.

"No, Adam, seriously. We have to stop. It's not like this can ever go anywhere."

"What?"

"Let's face it, the probability of me even being alive this time next year is slim. I won't bring you into that. I can't let it go any further, whether I want it to or not. I—"

"Stop! Stop, right now!" His voice was harsh and dominant, and it made my eyes go wide. I'd heard him use that tone at work, and with Jase. He meant business.

"Adam," I began, but he cut me off again.

"Was I speaking a different language last night? If you hadn't been completely honest with me about the way you feel, then yes, that would be leading me on. I know you're not ready for us to be more than friends and I'm still not going anywhere. I'm under no illusions about where I stand with you and I'm choosing to be here anyway. I'm choosing you. Every time. It's always going to be you. As for the abduction and its aftermath, I'm not afraid of that either. I didn't vow to fight by your side on a whim, Angel. I know what I'm getting into. Stop pushing me away because you think it's for my own good. I'm a big boy. I get to decide what's good for me. Unless, this is your way of telling me to get lost, but I don't think it is. Am I wrong?" He reached out, pulling me off my stool and resting his hands on my hips, as I stood between his outstretched legs.

"No," I breathed. I never wanted him to go anywhere. "You're not wrong."

"Good." He smiled and pulled me closer. "I came here wanting to clear things up about today with you, not listen to you make up another bullshit reason for us not to be together."

"Clear what up?"

"My tantrum over Jared. It wasn't the first time I got jealous over you and I'm not proud of it. I'm sorry. I was on cloud fucking nine after the night we had together. Seeing you react that way to another man flipped a switch in me. I should have trusted you and got the full story, but sometimes, I lose my head a little bit where you're concerned. But let me be clear, there is absolutely, no fucking way, I am giving up our time together. So, stop letting the darkness rule your head, stop pushing me away, and trust that I am exactly where I want to be. Okay?"

"Okay," I whispered.

Adam: Morning, Angel.

Me: Afternoon. ;p

Adam: Comedian. Night shift remember? ;)

Me: How could I forget? Good sleep?

Adam: I dreamt about you.

Me: Do I want to know?

Adam: It was a good dream. Maybe I'll show you one day.

Me: Maybe I'll let you one day. You working tonight?
Adam: No, dinner with Greg and Dana to look forward to.

Me: Is Dana cooking?

Adam: I hope not. Pub later?

Me: Doubt it. Cooking for Nick and the boys.

Adam: Call me if you need my arms again.

Me: I always need your arms. They're the best.

Adam: They are pretty awesome. They're also yours, just say the word.

I cooked pork chops, at Nick's request, his favourite, and then Cameron and Nick argued their case for not clearing up. Apparently, they were both of the opinion that, whoever made the mess should clean it. I knew they were ganging up together to wind me up, it was what they did. I was simply getting ready to bang their heads together.

"Thought we were going to the pub?" Nick asked. "Ethan said he'll take Dan and Heath home for me. I'm a free man!"

"Yep, you should go out," Ethan encouraged.

"We *are* going to the pub," Cameron said, clapping his hands together. "And the boys can clean the kitchen up!"

"I'm not going," I said. "I spend enough time there as it is."

"Behind the bar, not in front of it, that's the point. You need to spend time with us, Moonbeam," Nick argued, downing the remainder of his beer.

"What are we doing now then, if not spending time together?" I argued.

"You're coming," Cameron decided. "You are not staying here alone, and I want to have a drink with my sister. Adam will be there."

"So?" I raised my eyebrows at him.

I was already aware Adam was going to be there, but despite his assurances I was still feeling a little odd about seeing him. Something had shifted in our relationship in the last couple of days and I was in complete confusion over the whole thing. I needed time to sort my messy head out and get Jase out of it once and for all.

"So, you know you want to see him. Don't deny it, twin." Cameron winked at me from across the table.

"Why would I give a fuck if Adam is in the pub or not?" My reply was a little too sharp, which of course, didn't go un-noticed.

"You give so many fucks they're visible from space, Cal." Cameron laughed and shook his head at me.

"You've got a whole *Great Wall of China* made of fucks given for Adam Butler." Nick joined in and Ethan laughed with them.

"Why do I keep you two around?" I sighed, going back to my plan to bang their heads together.

"You'd never manage without us," Cameron stated simply with a shrug.

"Yep, we're awesome and you need us for life stuff." Nick backed him up.

"Besides, Adam always wants to see *you*." Cameron pushed, that evil glint he got when he was winding me up had appeared in his eye.

"And?" I was exasperated.

"And you love him!" Nick sang at me.

I bit. "What? Don't start all that love guru shit again, Nick. Adam and I are not together. I don't know what's going on there, okay? It's messy and complicated and it hurts my head to think about it. Are you happy now?"

"Rambling, Cal." Nick reached out and put a finger on my lips, to shush me.

"Don't you shush me!" I mumbled around his finger. He laughed. So, I opened my mouth and sucked that finger of his. Hard.

"Had that hand wrapped around my dick before I came over here," he said, straight faced.

I gagged.

"Although, having felt the power of that suck, I'm thinking your mouth could do a better job than my hand," he joked.

"Shut up! Shut Up! Shut up!" Cameron put his hands over his ears and whined. "That's my sister, dude. Fuck, she's practically *your* sister!"

"You're sick. That's what I'm calling you from now on, sick Nick!" I reached over and pushed him off his chair, onto the wooden floor.

"I thought we were getting married? I see what's going on here.

You're dumping me for Adam. Don't leave me, darlin', you're my life. Who will wash my dirty underwear, if you leave me? How will I ever get over the power of that suck? My hand just won't cut it now! We can work it out. I love you so much, Moonbeam. Give me another chance!" He managed to spout his lame jokes between guffaws, while rolling around on the floor.

Jared was working behind the bar that night. He served us our drinks and we joined Luke, Nate, Liv, and Vinnie at a table. There was a definite stand-off happening between Vinnie and Jared. I eyed Vinnie as I sat down, letting him know that we would be having a chat about it soon.

"You're going to come aren't you, Cal?" Liv jumped down my throat as soon as we were seated.

"Where?" I asked, curling my legs up underneath me in my chair.

"Dana's having a sleep over, next weekend. She invited Sally and Natalie. Girls only," she explained, pushing her glasses back up her nose.

"Aren't we a bit old for that?" My brow furrowed. I knew exactly how a sleepover at Dana's would go. It would be an alcohol fuelled, group counselling session, with nail painting, and facemasks. Nope, not entering that hell dimension, thank you very much. "And, we're not allowed to do anything girls only anymore. Actually, *I'm* not allowed to do anything without my own personal bodyguard anymore."

"Callie!" Cameron warned. We shared a look that let him know I was only joking and let me know he just wanted me safe.

"It's on Saturday and your own personal bodyguard will be in residence. Greg and Adam are both off work and will be upstairs, in Adam's place." Liv glared at me, in a way that told me without words, I had better get my arse there or she'd never speak to me again.

"Which is exactly where I will be, if I get my way," Natalie announced as she and Sally joined us, sitting either side of Liv on a sofa. Cameron and Nick both looked expectantly to me for a reaction. I just raised my eyebrows at them. Natalie took a sip of her vodka and coke and looked at me. "Come on, Cal. I mean I know you had Jase, who is sex on a stick, even if he is mentally unstable, but even you have to have noticed, Adam is hotness personified!"

"She's noticed," Vinnie confirmed with a sly smile.

"And he has definitely noticed her," Liv giggled.

"He hasn't noticed anyone *but* her," Vinnie agreed.

"Are you and Adam—" Luke leaned forward in his seat to look at me.

"Friends!" I interrupted and Luke held his hands up in surrender.

"Oh, you are so much more than friends." Liv shook her head.

"Talk of the devil." Nate nodded towards the bar, where Greg, Dana, and Adam were ordering drinks.

"Well, if you're not going to make a move on him, I will." Natalie stood and walked towards the bar.

"Say something!" Liv shot forward in her seat and spoke through gritted teeth.

I shrugged, and watched with interest, as Natalie sidled up beside Adam, and spoke to him. He turned, looked down at her, and nodded once, before seeking my eyes out with his own, and making a beeline for me. Sally snorted into her drink. Natalie caught my eye and we both burst out laughing.

"Witch, that man is like your own personal heat seeking missile." Vinnie fanned himself dramatically. I had to admit, Adam's reaction made me feel a little bit warm and tingly inside.

"Angel," Adam greeted me with eyes only for me and an intimate smile.

Sitting down on the arm rest of the over-sized chair I was curled up in, he laid an arm across the back of the it, and planted a kiss the top of my head, before greeting the others. He obviously wasn't going to be hiding his feelings anymore. More like he was putting his claim on me. *Nope, not thinking about it now. It's all good, nothing to panic about.* Natalie reached across him and fist bumped me when she re-joined us and sat down with Greg and Dana.

"A sleepover?" I asked Dana, a hint of accusation in my voice. I mean really, were we ten?

"Yeps!" She nodded, making her curls bounce.

"Nopes!" I countered. Cameron couldn't contain his choked laughter.

"Oh, don't be such a negative nelly. It'll be fun. They won't let us have a girl's night out, so we'll have to have to improvise," she chirruped, excitedly.

"What did she just call me?" I blinked and looked up at Adam. He squeezed my shoulder but failed to hide his smirk. I turned my attention back to Dana. "Are we going to wear *my little pony* pyjamas, and have pillow fights, and midnight feasts, like when we were ten?"

"I'll take a ticket for the pillow fight. Ringside," Nate quipped. I narrowed my eyes at him.

"No, it's going to be a sophisticated affair. Since we can't go out and get busy on the dance floor, we'll bring the party to us." Dana didn't bite.

"Right, so we're going to wear little black dresses, and heels, hang a disco ball in your living room, and dance around our handbags?" I listed, to laughter from the men.

"*You* don't do that on and actual night out, Callie!" Sally accused, pointing a finger at me. "*You* shoot tequila with the hot barman all night!"

"That was *one* time!" I defended myself, hiding a smirk behind the Guinness that Adam and I were now sharing.

It had been one of the last nights out we'd had with Amy. I'd had a rough day and argued with Jase. So, when the good-looking bar tender paid me some attention, I'd lapped it up. Shallow, I know, but it had given me a boost, and made me feel better for a couple of hours. The sad fact was, he'd recognised me from the pub, and we were talking shop, mostly. Adam raised his eyebrows at me, and I looked away quickly.

"Anyway, we're going to paint each other's nails, and colour each other's hair, and share secrets, and sing, and laugh, and drink cocktails, and eat chocolate, and dance, and cry," Dana announced, flicking her hair. Just as I thought, my own personal dimension of hell.

"Sounds mind numbingly perfect!" I rolled my eyes again. Adam chuckled and squeezed my shoulder again. Dana knew I didn't mean it.

I just wasn't as girly as her. Not that it ever stopped her from trying to convert me at every opportunity.

Adam grabbed my hand later, as we were leaving, and locked our fingers together. He walked me backwards when I turned to face him, until my back was against the wall outside the pub, and his body was flush against mine. The familiar tingles that overrode my senses when he was close set in, and I sucked in a harsh breath of cold air.

"Come back and have coffee with me. I didn't think I'd get to see you tonight and I'm not ready to say goodbye yet."

"It's late, Adam. I've got an early start and a really long day tomorrow. I don't think I need caffeine." I had an early business management class, a stock take to do at the bar, and an evening shift the next day.

"Hot chocolate then," he bargained "And it's me that's picking you up for your early class, remember? I've got brandy..."

"You don't play fair, Mr Butler." I caved, mentally slapping myself on the wrist for being so easy. Who was I kidding? I wanted to be with him. I wanted to be with him every second of the day.

"I'll never play fair where you're concerned."

After Adam assured Cameron that he wouldn't let me out of his sight, we walked with Greg, and a very chattery Dana, towards their place. Adam refused to let go of my hand, despite my wriggling and attempts to put space in between us. Quite why I was still fighting it, I didn't know, but I was. Maybe it had become a habit.

"You guys coming in for a night cap?" Greg offered when we reached their door.

"No," Adam answered bluntly, without looking at them, and led me straight past them to his own door. Dana giggled. I called goodnight to them over my shoulder and was practically dragged up the stairs to his loft apartment.

"That was rude, with Greg and Dana." I scolded him half-heartedly, throwing myself down on his sofa.

"I've shared you enough tonight." He set a cup of hot chocolate and the brandy bottle between us on the coffee table.

"If we keep this up, we'll have to buy bigger cups." I laughed and topped the cup off with the brandy. Mick had dropped off everything Adam needed from the pub, but we were still sharing.

"Or you'll have to stay longer, so we can share more than one drink." He smirked.

"Ulterior motives?" I mocked.

"Absolutely." He put an arm around me and pulled me into his side.

"You looking to be my pillow again, Butler?" I narrowed my eyes at him.

"Ah, you saw right through my cunning plan, Wilson!" He laughed, then became serious. "Will you try and do something for me?"

"Anything, you know that," I replied. He paused, looking at me thoughtfully, as though wondering whether his words were going to break me.

"Even if what I want you to do is for us?"

"Tell me."

"We're going to end up together, we've made that clear. We're taking our time getting there, but we both know where this is going, Angel."

"Okay..."

"I want you to relax. Stop questioning it. Stop looking for a label. Stop worrying about gossip. We're good together, and things will progress for us when you're ready. I won't push, but I won't pretend I don't have feelings for you either. I intend to remind you every day that you mean the world to me." He put his fingers under my chin and raised it until our eyes met, then leaned in to kiss me on the forehead.

"No labels. No questioning." I thought aloud, deciding to ignore the last part of his declaration. I could do that. Couldn't I? It had to be better than what I was doing then.

"No more *oh shit* moments and running away from me." He suggested and we both laughed. "Just us. Walls down. Fighting the darkness together."

"Just us," I agreed and suddenly felt a weight lift from my shoulders. As soon as I decided to stop worrying about it, it felt right and as though things had finally fallen into place. I couldn't help but wonder what I'd been running from in the first place when it came to Adam.

When I woke the next morning, well rested, and sprawled across Adam's chest, there was no panic and rush to move. Just an overwhelming sense of contentment. I was actually aware of how good it felt to wake up in his arms, rather than bursting head long into an *"oh shit"* moment.

Of course, I wasn't amused at having to get up stupidly early, so we'd have time to go back to my place to shower and change, before college. Adam offered me the use of his shower, but with no clean clothes to change into, I'd opted to go home. He hadn't missed the opportunity to inform me, with a huge grin on his face, there was always room in his wardrobe for some of my things, if I wanted it. Sometimes, I think he said those things to deliberately terrify me, for his own amusement.

Twin 2: You'd better have stayed at Adam's.

Me: What if I didn't?

Twin 2: Don't make me lock you in the cells, Cal.

Me: Relax. I was with Adam. I'm sorry you were worried.

Twin 2: Just text in future, before you fall asleep on him.

Me: Who says I fell asleep on him?

Twin 2: It's Adam. That's what you do with him. He makes your nightmares stop. I'm thinking of asking him to move in. ;)

Me: Haha! Love you, idiot.

Twin 2: Love you more, shit head.

"I despise mornings!" I dragged a comb through my wet hair and threw my phone on the table. Cameron was already at work when we got to the house, so I texted him good morning and got a lecture in return.

"I know." He smiled at me over our shared cup of tea.

"You'll come to hate me in the mornings," I told him. "Everyone does."

"I'm sure I can come up with a way of waking you up that ensures you won't be grumpy. Evidently waking in my arms isn't enough, but at least you didn't run. That's progress right there, Angel," he teased.

"One of these days, we'll actually sleep in a bed. *That* will be progress," I grumbled.

He rose from the stool he was sitting on and moved around the kitchen, to where I was standing. His arms snaked around my waist from behind and he gathered me against him. His cheek grazed mine with that sexy day-old stubble and my stomach tied itself in knots. This man pulled reactions from me that I had no idea I was capable of.

"When I finally get you in a bed, we will *not* be sleeping," he whispered into my hair. His breath was hot against my neck and sent shivers down my spine. It was a good job he was holding onto me because I'm pretty sure I lost the use of my legs. "Now, are you going to put some clothes on, or is my right arms going to get one hell of a work out later?"

"You... work out over me?" I glanced down at my bare legs, wearing only a t-shirt after my shower.

"You like the idea of that, Angel?"

"Maybe," I smiled.

"Oh, you and I are going to have so much fun," he teased and tugged the hem of my t-shirt. "I know you have a crazy day today, but I want us to spend some time together."

"We'll see each other loads today; you've got Callie sitting duty, remember?" I reminded him, pulling myself together.

"I'm talking about real time. A few minutes here and there in between work and college isn't that. Spend the day with me tomorrow?"

"Alright." I smiled when I felt his hands flex on my waist.

"What, no arguments? Excuses? Running at speed in the opposite direction?"

"I think... No, I know, I'm done with the running." I twisted in his arms and looked up at him, resting my hands on his chest. "I'm not saying that I'm ready to move this on any further, but I'm not going to run away from you anymore. I was being ridiculous, running from the one person I've never had to hide from. The person who saw me and my darkness right from the start and never once expected me to pretend it was any better than it was. You didn't try to fix me, you vowed to fight alongside me so that I can fix myself. You accepted my darkness, didn't judge and weren't afraid of it, you matched it with your own. That's something I should never have run from and I won't be doing it anymore."

"Angel," he smiled. "You never have to hide from me, and I will never hide from you. All those things you claim I've done for you; you've done for me in return. When I'm with you, it's the only time I feel like I can finally breathe again. You wear your darkness like a badge of honour, it strengthens you and you've taught me how to do the same. You saw it in me from the second our eyes met, and you acknowledged it, not verbally, but in the look you gave me in that split second, you accepted me and *my* darkness. You give me the courage to fight it because you're right there with me to do it. I haven't given you all of it yet, but I will. It's yours when you want it. Just as yours is mine."

His phone rang, ruining our moment completely.

"Well, that ruined the mood," I said with a smile.

He laughed and pulled me in for a hug but ignored his phone. "We should go."

"Ugh!" I groaned.

"Well, at least you're not about to go into work, with a bunch of men, while visions of you, under me, in my bed, float around my head." He reminded me of our earlier conversation as he buried his face in my hair. And there went my legs again.

Adam: Music? Music is always a good start to the day.

Me: Silence is golden.

THE TEACHER

They're passing her around, like a joint to be shared by many. My mother suffered the same fate, at the hands of men who never pretended to care. She was determined I would not become that kind of man and I am certain she is proud of her son. At least my lady's lapdogs have the decency to feign their concern for her. Of course, it is nothing more than want and desire on their part. A cruel con to meet their own selfish needs. I see that. It's a shame she cannot. She goes nowhere alone anymore. More thought must be put into our reunion. I'd prefer it if she came willingly, as was my original plan, but I'm no longer certain she would. These ridiculous men have made her paranoid, but she has no reason to fear me, I will take extra special care of her this time.

The pretty cook from the pub occupied me for a while, but like all the others in the end, she refused to continue her learning long enough to meet my expectations. She grew accustomed to the pain, the screaming stopped, and I tired of her then. She has merely been a distraction; she was, conveniently for me, in the wrong place at the right time. I hadn't specifically planned on her, but as it turned out she has been the perfect addition to my plans.

Her resting place was a change to my plans. I would not normally have left her in the same place as another, but it appeared the most obvious way to send the message that I am here. They could find me, if they weren't so incompetent. My lady would stand a better chance, if she were to put her mind to it and spend less time fretting over events she cannot control. Her focus should be on saying goodbye. Her future is mine to deliver.

CHAPTER ELEVEN

CALLIE

The thing that disturbed me most about Kat, was that I wasn't surprised or shocked when she was found in the same place as the last two women. I think I had somehow subconsciously accepted she was dead before she was found. That acceptance enabled me to maintain a thread of sanity, when I realised another of my friends had lost their life because of the same man who had taken me. Her death pointed the police in Jase's direction once again, which in turn, pointed the killer back to me.

I numbed myself to the details, so that I could hear them. Maybe it was twisted of me to want to know, but it was something I felt I should know. She sustained many of the same knife injuries as the others. She had also been killed in the same way—her throat slit and left to bleed to death— a detail that hadn't been released to the public, but I knew because I insisted Adam told me and, as much as he didn't wanted to tell me, he had promised not to sugar coat it anymore.

EDUCATING CALLIE

None of the victims died where they were found, Kat was no different. She held a bunch of wilting wildflowers and wore an ankle length, white nightgown. Her feet were bare and black with dirt that was ground into her skin. Her hair was fanned out behind her, like a pillow, and her eyes were closed, as though she was sleeping. If it hadn't been for the knife wound across her neck, you wouldn't have known she was dead.

Why was he suddenly leaving them in the same place? He'd never done that before. Was he leaving some kind of message? My mind briefly glossed over the idea that he was deliberately trying to frame Jase for the murders. It made no sense, why would he do that? Kat's murder only added to the theory that this was someone we knew, making the possibility that my parent's deaths were connected even more likely. A fact I had no strength to deal with.

Jase told the detectives he hadn't spoken to Kat outside the pub the day she disappeared. No one could confirm that, but he did have an alibi for the rest of the day, a construction site full of builders could vouch for him. He was also at work at the time of her death. That was proof enough for me, even if it wasn't enough for them. Plus, if this did go back as far as we thought it might, Jase was only a child when the first murders happened, and he was definitely not the man who had abducted me.

Cameron helpfully suggested this could be a copycat killer. That could definitely put Jase in the frame. He had argued that someone could have become obsessed with either me or the original killer. It wouldn't have taken much to find out details from the case and copy them; the media had been full of stories, despite my refusal to speak to them. I just could not believe Jase had anything to do with it. Adam said he believed the detectives on the case weren't fully convinced; they just didn't have anything to hold Jase on. He tactfully withheld his own opinion.

Frost Ford, being the gossip mill that it was, hummed with theories and suspicion. Women weren't leaving their houses alone and many were finishing work early, returning home before dark each day. The police were inundated with calls about suspicious men, mostly fake or brought about through sheer fear and paranoia. We began to live in a police state, while the authorities from all the nearby towns were put on high alert, and a distinct police presence was seen on the streets, until the killer was caught.

In true *"keep calm and carry on"* mentality though, the pub remained busy. Customers still came to drink and stayed late, deep in conversation and sharing theories on the investigation. Mick installed CCTV inside the pub and made it a policy that no woman would be permitted to leave alone. Nobody complained.

"Evening Mal." I attempted to smile through my sombre mood, as I joined Mick behind the bar and made conversation with the regulars. "You staying for the band tonight?"

"No, these old ears can't handle that kind of noise." He nodded towards his drink. "I'll be on my way after this one."

"Well, you enjoy your evening," I said, turning to serve Ethan and his group of friends, who always came in when Frost were playing.

"You too, Callie," Mal replied.

The mood lightened when Frost began their set. I think we all needed a distraction. I spied Sally and Natalie, at the front of the crowd. Nat had a bit of thing for one of the band members, but I didn't know which one. She looked like she was on full form tonight, dancing around in front of the stage, and I briefly felt sorry for the poor fella, then I smiled and thought go girl!

Mick and I had challenges we set for each other when it was just the two of us working. That night, during the band's interval, we played the tequila challenge. This involved each of us taking it in turns to get on our knees behind the bar, while the other poured tequila into our mouths. The customers timed us and whoever lasted longest won. If I won, all the women in the bar got a free shot and if Mick won, the men got a free shot.

I was pouring tequila from into Mick's mouth, having just lasted sixteen seconds myself. Mick signalled me to stop at thirteen, but I carried on, stopping at sixteen. Mick stood, a sly grin on his face and prowled towards me. I stood my ground, challenging whatever he was planning. He grabbed my face in his hands, tilted my head back and kissed me— passing tequila from his mouth, to mine. He let go and laughed loudly, taking a bow, to cheers around the bar. I half choked on the tequila, laughed, and hoarsely declared a draw, while wiping my mouth.

"Free shots for everyone!" I called, ringing the bell and grinning at Mick.

"You'll pay for all that tequila, Callie love," he said winking at me.

"I'll add it to the cost of my investment!" I replied. He began to line up the shot glasses along the bar.

"Step back, fellas. Ladies first in this establishment." Mick addressed the men closest to the bar.

"Because we is proper like that," I mocked, deliberately messing up the English.

"Posh, that's us love, practically a wine bar!" He began to pour out the shots.

As the ladies finished, we set out more glasses, and the men moved in to take their free shot. I slid past Mick and moved to join Adam, who was beckoning me, from the other end of the bar.

"How are we going to share this one?" He indicated the tiny glass on the bar. "I like Mick's idea, but I'm afraid if I do that, then every other man in the place will want the same treatment and I can't have that."

"No, couldn't have anyone else marking *your* territory, could we?" I picked up the shot and downed it, before re-filling it and passing it to him, with a wink that made him laugh. "Same glass, two shots. Problem solved."

"Things are looking better over there." Mick observed, when I walked back towards him, leaning into his embrace, as he put an arm out for me to step into.

"Yeah, it's funny how you suddenly find answers when you stop asking questions." I smiled.

"It's good to see, love You deserve some happiness." Mick squeezed my shoulder affectionately.

I ventured out into the mass of people to hunt down some empty glasses, since we were running low. Luke and Nate had joined Ethan and his friends, so I chatted to them while I cleared a table at the back of the pub.

"We still good for Tuesday, Cal?" Nate asked, grinning at Ethan's wolf whistle and goading while he spoke to me.

"We certainly are," I confirmed. Nate cancelled our original plans. He'd been cagey about why, avoiding my questions, but we'd made other arrangements.

"Good, got a surprise for you." He grinned again.

"Oh?" I pried.

"Well I'm not going to tell you, am I? Then it wouldn't be a surprise." He slung an arm around my shoulders.

"Coming on to my girlfriend, Nate? I thought we dealt with this years ago?"

We turned to see Jase's angry face glaring at us, his mouth down turned in a snarl. Ethan turned to one of his friends and said something, speaking quickly into his ear, the friend then disappeared into the crowded pub. I assumed he had been sent to get Vinnie.

"I'm not your girlfriend anymore," I snapped. Jase was practically swaying on his feet, obviously having had a few too many to drink. "Nate and I are friends. Friends have dinner together."

"And are you having dinner with Luke the following night? Vinnie the next? Oh, and let's not forget your new bodyguard. Are you having dinner with him as well, CeeCee?" Jase turned his anger on me, causing Nate to drop his arm from my shoulders, and move to stand slightly in front of me.

"I have no plans to, but if they asked I would!" I stood my ground and gave him the same warning I would give to any other customer who was causing a problem. "Jase, if you want to stay, you need to calm down or I'll have security escort you out."

"When will you learn, CeeCee? We are *not* finished. I am *not* going anywhere." I moved to walk away, and he grabbed my arm. "I really thought we were getting somewhere, when you let me in the other day. I thought we'd turned a corner when I had you in my arms again, comforting you. But now you're back to being a cold-hearted bitch!"

"Let go of her, Jase." Nate warned, moving to fully put himself between Jase and me.

"Take your hand off her arm. Now." Adam's low, calm warning resonated from behind me and it made me glad I wasn't on the receiving end of it.

"Make me, pretty boy!" Jase instigated, side-stepping Nate and dragging me with him. "You won't touch me, you know what will happen if you do, *Sergeant*!"

"It would be unwise of you to threaten a police officer, in front of witnesses." Adam leaned in and spoke quietly in Jase's ear. "You'd be surprised how far I'm willing to go to protect her. Don't challenge me."

Cameron and Vinnie appeared around us. Jase's grip on my arm tightened. Adam saw me flinch in pain and moved so he was toe to toe with Jase. Their eyes burned into each other, a hush overcame the pub and I watched as they stared each other down.

"It's time you left," Adam said, calmly.

"Not without my girlfriend," Jase sneered.

"She's not yours!"

"Is that right? Let's ask her about that, shall we?" Jase flicked his eyes to me. "What do you say, Cee? Does he know you as well as I do? Can he replace me so easily? Does he know about all your freaky little ways? All the dark little cravings you have in the bedroom, and out of it? Could anyone else give you that? I don't think he's got what it takes."

"Jase, stop it," I pleaded.

"Does he know what it feels like to be inside you?" Jase pushed, tightening his grip on my arm.

"You're hurting her," Adam gritted out, clearly struggling to hold his temper.

Realisation hit and the sneer on Jase's face became a look of dismay. His grip loosened, Adam saw it and snapped a hand out to guide me towards him. I moved with him, turning my back to Jase and following Adam's gentle push to move behind him, towards Cameron.

"I'll be right with you, Angel," he whispered, as I was pulled against my brother's chest.

Cameron encased me in his arms, deliberately shielding me from whatever was taking place between Adam and Jase. I heard Jase's apologies and pleas to be heard grow distant, drowning in the noise of the patrons, as they returned to their conversations, after the drama.

"Are you alright Callie? Did he hurt you? Let me see?" Luke fussed, going into full on doctor mode, and trying to pry me away from Cameron, so he could look at my arm.

"I'm ok Luca." I reassured him, shakily.

"Let him look," Cameron insisted. He bent to talk into my ear, but his eyes were looking over my head and across the crowded pub, at whatever was happening behind me.

Both Adam and Vinnie had disappeared, presumably escorting Jase off the premises. I let Cameron and Luke steer me towards the bar, Nate following closely behind.

"Take her upstairs," Mick said as he pulled a pint, obviously aware of what happened. "First aid kit in the hallway."

In the lounge upstairs, I removed my long-sleeved shirt, revealing a white tank top underneath, with the slogan, *"Bollocks"* across the chest, to raised eyebrows and smirks from Cam, Nate, and Luke. Their amused looks turned to anger when we saw the large, red fingerprint marks that were forming along my upper arm. Luke examined it quickly and gently, confirming it was only bruising.

I smiled and leant over to kiss his cheek. "Thank you, Luca."

Sally poked her head around the door frame. "Put this on it, Luke. It'll take the bruising straight out." She threw a tube of arnica cream to Luke, who caught it and applied a thin layer to my arm. Sally was a nanny to three small children and carried all kinds of weird and wonderful potions and lotions in her bag. Apparently small children fall down a lot.

"Come on, let's get you a drink. Doctor's orders." Luke smiled and I let him take my hand.

Adam was at the bar, talking to Mick. His eyes darkened when he saw the marks on my arm, but immediately softened as they lifted to meet my gaze. He lifted a hand, opening his arm to me and I eagerly moved into his embrace, sighing when he fastened his arms around my waist, and kissed the top of my head.

"What did you do to him?" I asked quietly.

"Don't defend him, Angel," he warned.

"I won't," I said.

Once again, just as I went back to thinking I knew and could trust Jase he was proving me wrong at every turn. It was time I washed my hands of Jason Montgomery for good.

"Vinnie and I just sent him on his way, that's all. Are you alright?" He lifted my chin so he could see my face.

"Luke fixed me up." I nodded and rested my head back on his chest.

"Thank you," Adam said to Luke.

"That's him finished in here, love," Mick said. He handed a beer bottle over the bar and I twisted in Adam's arms to take it. "He got a second chance because you vouched for him. He fucked that up and he won't be coming through that door again."

"You won't hear me argue." I agreed with him, sadly.

"Fucking psycho!" Liv joined us and pointed at my shirt with a grin.

"You ok, sweetheart?" Sally asked, moving to stand next to Luke, and hooking her arm through his.

"I'm fine, really." I told them.

I leaned into Adam's side and wrapped my arm around his waist, sticking my hand in his back pocket. He slipped his thumb under the hem of my shirt and rubbed the bare skin on my hip, making my skin tingle.

"I'm just sorry I didn't get to look totally hot jumping over the bar again." Mick winked at me cheekily.

"The act, Mick. The act."

Adam: Breakfast in bed?

Me: You mean the sofa? Since we don't sleep in beds?

Adam: Breakfast on the sofa/bed?

Me: Crumbs and sofa/bed are never a good mix.

"Where are we going?" I asked Adam the next morning.

He was reluctant to leave me the night before, but I reassured him that I was fine and that I needed a good night's sleep, in a bed, in order to prepare for our day together. He cheered up at that thought, and left me in my brother's capable hands, with instructions to be ready bright and early. I'd complained at that, obviously, but he just grinned at me, and I knew he was thinking about our previous conversation about waking me up in ways that would make me happy. I was sure there was a bad boy lurking in there somewhere, but Adam kept him well hidden.

"Somewhere you love, but rarely visit," he said me cryptically. I screwed my nose up and stuck my tongue out at him. He laughed.

"What will we be doing?" I tried, as he ushered me towards his car.

"Well, the place we're going has a very specific set of rules. Rules that must be followed exactly, in order to enjoy it to its fullest."

Adam opened the passenger door and stopped me before I got in the car. He put a hand on the roof of the car, to block me from getting in, and cupped the side of my neck with the other hand. I looked up at him, quizzically. He smiled and leaned down, to drop the lightest of kisses on my lips, leaving behind a tingling feeling that made me smile happily. He closed the door when I got in and walked around to the driver's side.

"Not sure how I feel about rules," I grumbled, fiddling with the radio tuner.

"Don't worry, they're good rules. But the main one being, no darkness. Not today. Today, we play in the light."

He gently pulled my fingers away from the radio and lifted them to his mouth, kissing them. Then he plugged a memory stick into a port in the car. *Guns n' Roses, Paradise City* filled the car's speakers. I looked at him and grinned. He had remembered a story I had told him one night, about how it was my dad's favourite song, and he would always play it repeatedly on long car journeys. It wasn't until we had been driving for almost two hours, and sung along to *Paradise City* countless times, that I began to pay attention to the direction we were heading.

"We're going towards the coast," I observed, turning to him, a slow smile tilting my mouth.

"We are." He smiled, glancing at me sideways

"Are we going to the seaside?" I demanded excitedly, jumping up and down in my seat.

He laughed, shaking his head at my antics. "That we are Angel."

I clapped my hands together, grinning a grin that could rival that of any Cheshire cat. I absolutely loved days at the seaside. Our parents often used to surprise us, with days out on Saturday mornings, if Dad wasn't at work. Another detail of my life I had shared with Adam, during one of our late-night conversations. We'd made a list of seaside rules, things you absolutely *had* to do when you went there. And he had remembered. He'd listened to me. He'd been listening to me right from the beginning. Adam, I realised, knew me. And through those same conversations, I knew him.

In true British tradition, the sky was dull and grey when we arrived, but it wouldn't be a day at the seaside if it didn't rain a bit. None of that could wipe the smile from my face though. There's a chance I may have been jumping up and down, like an excited child, when we got out of the car.

"Can we ride the pier rides? Can we get candy floss? Can we buy tacky souvenirs? I can't leave without a sugar dummy for Cam. He loves those things. You need a *kiss me quick* hat. You'd suit one of those; it's in the seaside rules." I rambled excitedly.

"Well if it's in the rules. But first..." Adam laced his fingers though mine and led me to a stall at the edge of the beach, where he bought a bucket and spade, before walking us down the steps onto the sand.

We wandered out across the sand dunes, towards the wetter sand, where we knelt and built a huge sandcastle, with turrets, and seashell decorations, and a moat that led all the way to sea. Adam stopped an elderly couple walking on the beach and asked them to take a photo of us with our creation.

"You're such a pretty couple. I can see that you're very much in love," the lady said with a smile, when her husband handed back Adam's phone. We smiled politely; the complications of our lives not worth going into with strangers

"Fifty-four years ago, I married this woman. Let me tell you, young man, if your girl makes you as happy as mine makes me, you make sure you never let her go." The man told Adam.

"I don't intend to." Adam smiled at them and put his arm around me.

We watched them walk away, hand in hand. I couldn't help but smile at them wistfully. What would it be like to have a peaceful life?

"How beautiful, to still be that much in love, after all those years together." I mused.

"Yeah," was all Adam said, watching me watch them, with a smile on his face.

When they were nothing more than specs on the beach, Adam grabbed my hand and pulled me towards the sea, where he sat on the sand. He pulled me down next to him, and took off his shoes and socks, revealing those ugly feet of his. He wasn't kidding, they were freakishly big, and hairy. "Stop staring at my feet and take your shoes off!"

"But they're..." I struggled for words.

"Is this going to be the breaking point in our relationship? Do I need to get cosmetic surgery? Because I'll do it. Can we get past this, Angel?" He teased and I couldn't help but laugh.

"I'll cope, as long as you don't make me look at them."

"Good, now get your feet naked!"

"Are you nuts? It's freezing!" I said, shaking my head at him.

"You can't come to the seaside and not paddle. It's in the rules," he said, rolling his jeans up.

I laughed and joined him. I was right, it was freezing, and I screeched when the water hit my skin, but soon we were splashing around at the water's edge. Running away from the waves, kicking water at each other, chasing each other up and down the beach, until eventually we collapsed on the sand, laughing happily. I couldn't remember a time that I had felt so relaxed and carefree.

"You know what else is in the seaside rules, don't you?" He looked up and down the length of the beach.

"Donkey rides?" I asked. Although, I thought we were a bit too heavy to be doing that. Donkeys should be ridden by children only.

"Fish and chips," he announced, collecting our shoes and pulling me to my feet.

"Ooh, yes!" I agreed, suddenly famished.

We walked barefoot off the beach. Adam stopped to give our bucket and spade to a little boy and girl, who were coming onto the sand with their parents. They ran off, shrieking gleefully, to build a sandcastle of their own. After brushing the sand off our feet, and my mini rant about sand between my toes, we found a chip shop. We sat on a bench, overlooking the sea, eating fish and chips with lots of vinegar and mushy peas.

"What do you want to do next?" he asked, when we finished eating.

"Shouldn't we head back?" I thought of the drive and the fact I had to work that night.

"You're not working tonight," Adam said with a grin, as if reading my mind.

"Yes, I am." I frowned, confused.

"I spoke to Mick. He agreed you deserved a day off. Jared is covering your shift."

"We don't have to leave yet?" I asked, my eyes lighting up.

"Nope," he confirmed.

"Adam. You are the best." I threw my arms around him and laughed when he agreed with me.

We continued to walk along the promenade, towards the pier, stopping to look in every tacky souvenir shop along the way. They had everything from painted rocks, to snow globes, and those little plastic windmills that fall apart before you get them home.

"Oh, oh, oh!" I spied a pair of *Supergirl* socks hanging on a rail.

"Did you just have a nerdgasm?" Adam laughed when I vowed payback on my brother for sharing that little piece of information.

"They've got capes on them. Actual capes," I stated, very seriously.

"Then you must have the *Superman* socks." He said, picking them up.

"Super*girl* Adam. They're Super*girl* socks. Seriously, if we are going to have any kind of future together, you're going to have to get in the know about your superheroes!" I put my hands on my hips and faced him.

A smile brightened his face. He reached out and pulled me towards him by my t=shirt. "You're talking about our future together, Angel. You know how that makes me feel?"

"Erm, super?" I smiled up at him and he laughed, squeezing me tighter.

"How can you tell, anyway? They both wear the same colour." He indicated the socks.

"Because *I'm* a girl. If I were a boy, they would be *Superman* socks. But I'm a girl so they are *Supergirl* socks," I explained.

"You're a geek," he announced and went inside to pay for them.

"Thank yooouuuu!" I sang.

He handed me a small bag containing the socks. I looked up to see he was wearing a black cowboy hat with a ribbon around it that read *"Kiss me quick!"*

"Well?" he said.

"What?" I grinned.

He pointed a finger at the hat. I rose up on my tip toes and planted a quick kiss on his lips.

"Shame they don't make one that says kiss me slow." he said, as we began walking again.

"What makes you think I would have obliged?" I flirted.

"Well, I could always have gone and found that lovely old lady," he said.

"Noo, she was too smitten with her husband to notice you." I told him, reaching for his hand.

"She was giving me the eye and you know it," he said.

"She was not!" I argued.

"Jealous, Angel?" he teased.

"Jealousy is wanting something you don't have." I quoted Mick with a coy smile.

"Ah, so you have this, do you? Now who's sure of themselves?" He waved his hand up and down his body.

"Just pointing out that I don't want something that I don't have. Therefore, not jealous." I smirked at him cheekily.

"Of course, Angel. That's exactly what you were doing." He pulled me closer by my hand and kissed the top of my head.

EDUCATING CALLIE

I swung our hands in between us and we made our way to the pier, where we spent ages dropping 2 pence coins into the slots, trying to get the piles of copper coins to topple. We placed bets on the horse racing game and shot hoops through the basketball ring. Of course, Adam was better at that, being tall. Cameron would have had a field day with the short jokes, but I did manage to sink a few baskets of my own. To which I cheered loudly, and Adam picked me up and swung me around cheering with me. We got some funny looks, but it didn't matter. Of course, I made him promise not to tell anyone at home that he'd had to lift me up, so I could get the ball through the hoop in the first place.

Outside, we stopped to take pictures in the face in hole boards. Then, at the end of the pier, we climbed the twisted stairs of the helter skelter, and at the top Adam abandoned his own mat, pulling me down to sit between his legs, on my mat.

"Ready?" he asked, when he wrapped his arms around my waist.

"Yep!" I nodded and he pushed us off.

We whizzed down the spiralling slide, landing in a tangled heap of arms and legs at the bottom. I got up first and yanked Adam to his feet, both of us laughing hysterically. The man with the tokens shook his head at us but cracked a smile all the same.

We bought ice creams, with chocolate flakes and strawberry syrup, and leaned over the end of the pier, shivering and looking out at the sea while we ate them.

"What's next?" he asked, as we watched the waves batter the pier legs beneath us.

"Hmm... Oh, the grabber machines, the ones with the teddy bears." I made a grabbing motion with my hands

"Of course," he agreed, and we went off in search of the machines

Several attempts later, I had won a little brown dog with huge eyes and a wonky mouth, and Adam had a small white teddy bear holding a red heart, with *"Be Mine"* written on it. We swapped prizes, and Adam made me promise to sleep with the bear every night that he wasn't with me.

On the way back to the car park, we bought sticks of rock in every flavour, not forgetting a huge, red, sugar dummy for Cameron, and a painted beach rock for Mick, with the slogan *"You're my rock"* on it. I couldn't resist. At the car, Adam opened the passenger door for me, and I reached up to kiss his cheek.

"Thank you." I whispered.

"Thank *you*." He turned my words around.

"What did I do? This was all you." I frowned.

"You stopped running, Angel." He lowered his forehead to rest it against mine. "For the record, I would have kept chasing."

"Good to know." I grinned and we got into the car just as the rain started. It might have been a dull, grey typically British day, but Adam and I had spent it playing in the light.

Dana: Relationship update after yesterday?

Me: Lots of hand holding. A souvenir teddy bear. Supergirl socks and two very quick lip kisses.

Dana: Oh, my! he's courting you like an old-fashioned gentleman. It's so romantic. He's your Mr Darcy.

Me: Have you even read Pride and Prejudice?

Dana: What's that got to do with anything?
Me: Mr Darcy?

Dana: Yes, Mark Darcy from Bridget Jones.
Me: Wow!

Dana: Never mind that, have you acquired the sweatshirt yet?

Me: Oh, ye of little faith. I acquired the sweatshirt on the first night.

Dana: You make me so proud.

Adam picked me up from college on the Tuesday. We ate lunch in his office, at the police station. I ignored Greg's wolf whistle and threw the sandwich he'd asked us to pick up for him at his head. Adam led me straight past the other officers in the station and into his office, without saying a word to anyone. Cameron was nowhere to be seen. I assumed he was still out on patrol somewhere.

"So, you're going out with Nate tonight?" Adam asked. We sat at his desk, eating turkey salad sandwiches.

"Mmm-hmm." I nodded.

He watched silently, while I opened up my sandwich, and squirted the little packets of mustard and mayonnaise into it, before topping it off with salt and vinegar flavoured crisps.

"That's disgusting!" he observed, frowning at my food.

"I'll convert you," I teased.

"I doubt that," he replied. "Where are you and Nate going?"

"Oh, I don't know, Nate said it was a surprise." I paused and looked up at him, "You're ok with this, aren't you? I mean, Nate and I are friends, that's all. Apart from that one time—"

"What time?" His eyebrows flew up.

"Shit!" I whispered. "It was nothing. We were kids. Nate was my first kiss. Before Jase and I got together. It was one kiss, that's all. Look, if you don't want me to go, I won't."

"I'm not going to start telling you who you can and can't spend time with. I just wanted to make sure you won't be alone at any point; you need to stay with Nate at all times." He turned his concerned gaze to me, and I realised what he had been getting at.

"I'm sorry. I suppose I'm just used to Jase and his constant questioning." I shrugged. "He would never have let Nate and I go out together alone."

"The fact you've got history with Nate took me by surprise, but I can tell the difference between kid's stuff and the real thing." His voice became quiet and I realised my comments had hurt him. "I'm not him, Angel."

"No, no you're not. But honestly, Adam, Jase and I were together for so long, I'm afraid I don't know how to be with anyone but him." I sighed.

"Then let me teach you." He reached over, smiling, and laced our fingers together on the desktop then joked. "I won't take kindly to goodnight kisses though."

"Ah, I see, you're doing that territorial thing again." I grinned.

"I believe the term is pissing a circle around you," he teased. "And you like it. All your book boyfriends do it."

"Yeah, I kind of do when it's you." I admitted and we both laughed.

THE TEACHER

Today was a good day. For both of us.

CHAPTER TWELVE

CALLIE

Adam: Tea in bed. Strong, with a splash of milk. A thermal cup with a lid. No spills. Tea stays hot. No food. No crumbs. No music, complete silence. I believe I have everything covered.

Me: Hmm...

Adam: And I'll allow your latest book boyfriend to share the bed with us.

Me: There's a bed this time? An actual bed?

Adam: There is definitely a bed in our future.

Me: Beds, tea, and book boyfriends, I think you may be onto something there.

Adam: Of course, the day would have to start earlier, to give you that quality time with your book boyfriend.

Me: You ruined it.

Cameron lifted the lid on the slow cooker and inhaled deeply. "Chilli?" he asked, his eyes lighting up. I nodded. "Awesome, I knew there was a reason I kept you around."

I smacked him in the chest, and he looked me up and down.

"You almost look like a girl there, twin," he teased.

"I always look like a girl, these things kind of give it away!" I pointed to my chest and he laughed.

"Could've brushed your hair though." He gestured to my messy ponytail. "And dropped the man boots."

"Stop picking on me," I whined.

"Or what?" he challenged.

"I'll tell Mum!" I announced. "You know she'll come back and haunt your arse if you upset her girl!"

Cameron laughed and pulled me in for a hug. As we had suspected, nothing more had come of Dad's files on Aunt Caroline's murderer, or our parent's deaths. So, despite the fact both of us, and Adam, thought there was more to it, Cam and I had agreed to move on from it until, or if, any more evidence came to light. We still had the books, and Jase's stolen phone, to go on. Maybe they would uncover something.

"So, Adam is ok with you going out on a date with Nate?" Cameron asked, releasing me and stepping back to lean a hip against the kitchen counter.

"It's not a date and why wouldn't he be ok with it? Adam and I aren't together. We're just seeing how things go," I rambled.

"Got your wet suit on under there, twin?" He motioned to my clothes.

"Huh?" I frowned, looking down at myself.

"Because you're surfing the sea of denial and are about to take a dive off your board, dude!"

"Wow, where did that come from?" I teased with a grin.

"Quite the deep and sensitive thinker, me," he said.

EDUCATING CALLIE

"Yeah, if it involves holding a beer in one hand and the TV remote in the other." I gathered my purse and phone together. I made a show of waving my phone in Cameron's face, to prove that I had it with me, before shoving it in my pocket.

"Profound is my middle name." He winked. "Just don't go giving Nate the wrong impression."

"Why would I do that? We're friends. He knows that."

"Does he?" Cameron asked sceptically.

"What are you talking about?" I demanded.

"Well, you *were* each other's first kiss and if it weren't for Jase... You know," he said with a shrug.

"We were kids!" I gaped at him.

"Come on, Cal, you know Nate and Jase fought over you for months after Nate kissed you. Jase made him promise to stay away from you. They had that stupid agreement that neither of them would ask you out. Then Jase got sneaky and asked you out anyway." he told me as he reached into the fridge for a carton of orange juice.

"I didn't know that," I said quietly. There had been a time when things could have happened between Nate and me, but I'd never seen it as serious. It certainly wasn't something I thought would be an issue all these years later.

"Yeah, you did. Everyone knows." He opened the juice carton and drank straight from it.

"Not me," I snapped, crossing my arms. "After Nate and I kissed, we barely spoke again for months, I didn't know Jase had anything to do with it."

"Incoming!" Nate called, entering the house.

"Nate," Cameron greeted him, looking over my head at him. *Stupid, tall men!*

"Babe." I could hear the grin in Nate's voice as he greeted Cameron, who laughed in response.

"Hi," I turned to face him, and he smiled and winked at me.

"Well you kids have fun. Watch out for sharks, sis! Maybe I'll give Adam a bell and see if he wants to help me out with that chilli you made." Cameron began to walk, backwards, towards his bathroom, and I had no doubt Adam would be there when I got home.

"Sharks?" Nate asked.

"Don't ask." I shook my head, "He's an idiot!"

"Fair enough. Ready to go?" Nate asked.

"Yep!" I smiled and told myself it was fine, I've got this. Nate knows we're just friends. Then I felt his arm wrap around my lower back, and his hand rest on my hip as we descended the porch steps, and I wasn't so sure.

Nate, it turned out, had found out about a drag racing event at a track not far from Frost Ford and had managed to get tickets at the last minute. There were a lot of vintage American cars competing and he knew I shared his love of muscle cars. We watched race after race, and cheered loudly when our favourites won, while feasting on nachos, and cheese fries. I was glad I'd worn my trusty boots, since we were standing in a muddy field.

As we made our way back to the car park, after the final race, Nate tossed me his car keys. I grinned at him and climbed into the driver's seat whispering, "I love this car."

"We should go to an auction, see if we can get you one. I can help you fix it up," he offered.

"Really? You'd do that?" I glanced at him. "That would be amazing!"

"Of course. I'll keep an eye on the lots and let you know if anything comes up."

We sat, side by side, on the porch steps talking in hushed voices, after we arrived back at my house.

"I had a really great time tonight, Nate, thanks," I told him.

"Me too. It's nice to be able to spend time with you at last and not have Jase breathing down my neck," he replied.

"Did he do that a lot?" I asked, recalling my earlier conversation with Cameron.

"Constantly. I've wanted to take you drag racing for years because I knew you'd love it, but he'd never let it happen. Any time I mentioned doing something with you, he would make damn sure it either didn't happen, or he would be there too." Nate explained and then he looked at me and sighed. "You really have no idea, do you?"

"About what?"

"Mine and Jase's history over you?"

"Actually, Cam mentioned something before you got here tonight. I never knew how bad it was back then though," I said, looking down at my boots. "I mean, I knew Jase had a problem with you and I spending time alone, but I thought it was just because he knew about the kiss."

"We fought over you for so long," he said, a regretful smile on his face.

"Why didn't you tell me about the agreement you made? After you kissed me, and then wouldn't speak to me, I thought you regretted it, or that I was a horrible kisser. We weren't exactly experts, but thirteen-year-old girls don't need to be thinking they can't kiss, Nate. It was traumatic!" I attempted to joke.

"We clashed noses, my lips hit your chin before they got anywhere near your mouth, and you head butted me!" Nate remembered.

"We were so cool," I laughed.

"I never regretted it for a second! Best decision I ever made was losing my kissing cherry to you. And believe me, you can kiss, once we finally got our act together. I've compared every girl I've ever kissed to you, none of them match up." We both laughed. "Luke and the girls tried to get me to tell you I liked you. But then Jase asked you out and you seemed so happy. I assumed it was because you obviously liked him more than me. So, I asked them all to keep it quiet. As long as you were still my friend, I was happy. But Jase never allowed us to get too close. You'll always be my one that got away, Callie."

As I thought back, I began to remember that Nate and I, when he finally started talking to me again, had never really been left alone together. Nick and I had done so much alone together, despite Jase's protests. I'd spent time with Luke, too, but never Nate. Jase was always there if Nate was. And there was me thinking he only ever had a problem with Nick.

"You have to know; I wouldn't have put up with that if I'd known." I looked up at him, suddenly mournful of the friendship we hadn't been allowed to have. Nate and I had a lot in common and we'd missed out because of my controlling boyfriend.

"Of course I do, Cal. But it's ok, really. Jase made you happy for a lot of years. There are people in this world who never get to feel that.

I'm glad that you did." He put his arm around me, and I rested my head on his shoulder. "Would it have made a difference?"

Oh, shit moment pending...

"I would have been majorly pissed off," I said, carefully.

"I know that. But would it have made a difference to us, if I had told you? What if I'd asked you out first?" he probed.

"It's in the past, not like it can be changed." I blurted quickly, not looking at him.

The truth was, if Nate had asked me out before Jase, I would have said yes. I might have been crazy about Jase for most of my life, but I had the biggest crush on Nate after that kiss. He had been so gentle and sweet; and after the initial fumbling, he made sure it was every girl's perfect first kiss. I couldn't tell him that now. I adored Nate, but we would only ever be friends. I didn't really think he felt any differently than that towards me either, he was just caught up in the memory, in the same way I was.

He squeezed my shoulder. "No, I suppose not." he murmured.

"Well, Jase isn't an issue anymore and we're still friends, right?" I asked.

"Always," he agreed.

"So, we can do those things together now. Just us, or with the others, whatever way we chose." I concluded, looking up at him finally.

"You're right. All those bands we wanted to see that only you and I liked? Back on the list, babe. We've got some catching up to do." He smiled down at me, a glint in his eye. Suddenly, his lips were sealed to mine and I couldn't move. I was temporarily shocked into motionlessness. Finally, I got my wits about me, and gently but firmly pushed my hands to his chest. He drew back, still smiling at me.

"Nate, I didn't mean—" I began.

"It's ok, babe, I know you didn't." His smile turned cheeky. "I just wanted to kiss you like a grown up, without all the headbutting!"

"Nate!" I screeched, slapping his shoulder. He laughed, I joined in, leaning against him.

"Still a great kisser, by the way," he joked.

We were still laughing when the front door flew open, and Cameron and Adam came charging out, both looking ready to kill.

Nate and I stood up too quickly. I stumbled, almost falling backwards down the steps. Nate caught me, pulling me against his body and holding me steady, causing us both to laugh even harder.

"Okay?" Adam looked at me, his eyes scanning me up and down, for anything out of place.

"Okay." I nodded, as I extracted myself from Nate's hold, wiping the tears of laughter away from my eyes.

"What's going on? We heard you scream, Callie." Cameron gave me the same once over Adam had. *Crap!* They had heard my scream and thought the worst.

"No, no, it was nothing." I hastily reached out, and allowed Adam to take my hand, and lead me up the rest of the steps. He was eyeing Nate suspiciously.

"It was just a joke," Nate said, apologetically.

"What kind of joke has my sister screaming, Nate?" Cameron snarled.

"Cameron! Calm down. I didn't scream. Well, not the way you think," I scolded.

"I kissed her." Nate confessed.

"You did what?" Adam demanded icily and stepped in front of me.

"Adam." I moved to stand beside him again, hooking my fingers into his back pocket, and pulling slightly until he stepped back.

Nate held both hands in the air defensively. "I kissed her, and she pushed me away, and then we laughed about it. It wasn't serious. Just a history repeating itself kind of thing. You've got nothing to worry about, Adam. I know she's with you. Callie and I are just friends, no blurred lines here."

I put a hand on Adam's arm, and he exhaled, turning to me. "Is that what happened?"

"Yes, that's what happened. You can trust him," I said. He nodded once.

"Don't kiss her again." Adam looked at Nate and I rolled my eyes.

"Understood." Nate nodded, but I saw the twitch of his lips at my eye roll. "Ok, so I'm gonna go."

"No, come inside, have a drink with us," Adam relented.

"Yeah, come in, buddy. Sorry about that. We're all a bit on edge, at the minute." Cameron held his hand out and Nate shook it.

"My apologies." Adam then held his hand out and Nate shook it, too.

"No worries, I get that you were just protecting your girl. But you should know, there are a lot of us that care about her." Nate told him, making it clear that he wasn't going anywhere, and I was glad he stood his ground.

"I see that. And I'm glad she's got so many good friends around her." Adam smiled.

"Well, I'm glad she's found herself a decent bloke," Nate replied, and they walked into the house. So, was this going to be a three-way bromance now?

"That's fine, you just carry on, talk about me like I'm not here. Not like I can hear you or anything," I mumbled.

"Rambling, Cal." Cam put his arm around me as we walked towards the front door, "You're going to be explaining that kiss to me later."

"Nope." I laughed.

Adam: Morning foot rubs?

Me: I can tell you're trying desperately to remain a gentleman with these ideas. It must be killing you. Let the bad boy out, Adam.

Adam: Angel, you aren't ready for him yet. If I let him out, neither of us would be wearing clothes and I would be inside you.

Me: So, foot rubs? In our bed?

Adam: OUR bed? I think I might be getting to you.

Me: Will there be book boyfriends? I like it when there are book boyfriends.

Adam: I'll dress up as your book boyfriend of choice during said foot rub.

Me: Role-play in bed? You never told me you were kinky. This could swing things in your favour. I'm on werewolves this week.

Adam: Can I fall in love with you yet?

Me: Wouldn't want you peaking too soon, wolfman.

Cameron was sitting on the end of my bed, while I stood in front of my mirrored wardrobe, brushing my hair. He'd just told me the books had brought back nothing that could be used to identify the person who left them. This killer was evading them at every turn, they literally had nothing. The bodies were clean of any trace of him, there were no witnesses that had seen him take any of the women, the gifts he left me were clean. Our dad's files had told them he thought it was someone who lived in Frost Ford, but that was five years ago, so not really helpful because there was no way of knowing if he still lived here. And, unless they were prepared to investigate every single person in town, there really wasn't much they could do with that information. They just couldn't find anything that might even hint at his identity.

"Nothing at all?" I looked at Cameron in the mirror.

"Nada. Not even a partial fingerprint. Nothing at all to identify him, they're completely clean." Cameron explained.

"And the phone?" I asked.

"They tried to use Jase's old number to trace the phone, but we haven't heard anything about the results. If they were successful, we'd know by now." He didn't sound hopeful. "They searched Jase's flat, to see if it was there. Obviously, they found nothing. Whoever this is, he's careful, like OCD careful."

"Well, I suppose if he's got OCD, at least that proves it can't be Jase. He's the messiest person I know. I doubt he could have been bothered with the effort of wearing gloves to make sure he didn't leave fingerprints." I attempted to laugh it off. Ignoring the fact that there was no longer any doubt in my mind, that the killer was the same man who taken me before, and that he was coming back for me. Truth be told, there hadn't been any doubt in my mind for some time now. Especially since Adam and I had talked about it.

"Don't do that, sis." Cameron came around to the side of the bed and sat back down on it heavily. "You know I can't stand it when you do that."

"What do you want me to do, Cam? Get hysterical? Run around screaming and tearing my hair out? Cower in a corner and be afraid to live my life? Please enlighten me here, because I really don't know what you want from me!" It's safe to say, I lost my temper. "It's not exactly a normal life experience, having a serial killer stalk you. Constantly looking over my shoulder. Dissecting every situation I find myself in, through sheer paranoia, because it was only ever a matter of time before he came back for me. I'm sorry if my reactions aren't to your liking, but I really don't know what the fuck I'm supposed to do!"

I was crying by the end of my rant and Cameron was there in an instant, pulling me to his side and dragging me into his arms.

"I can't do it, Cam. I can't do this again."

"I'm going to keep you safe." He said the words, but I didn't think either of us really believed them.

CHAPTER THIRTEEN

THE TEACHER

I watch them all, dressed in black, pretending to mourn a woman they barely knew. I knew her. I knew her inside and out, by the time my teachings were complete. They gather around her husband, feigning concern and sadness at her death. They do not know that she died a better person. She died with the knowledge of her mistakes. And that was my doing. They ought to thank me, not hunt me.

Flanked by her ever-present bodyguards, my lady remains out of reach, for the duration of the service. I fight the desire to step in, take over as her chaperone. They would be none the wiser; it would alert them to nothing. I have remained hidden among them for so long now, it wouldn't occur to them to look in my direction. However, she is weak at the moment and it would irritate me immensely to be in her company while she is in this state. I no longer feel she is able to control her guard dogs in my presence. I will wait for her a while longer. Our time is coming my lady.

CALLIE

The sound of the *TARDIS* landing filled the room. I reached for my phone, on the kitchen island, where I'd left it. Cameron slid it across to me with a flick of his wrist and I opened the message. We all went back to our house after Kat's memorial service. Mick had offered, but her family hadn't wanted a gathering at the pub, so we closed for the night, as a mark of respect.

J: I need to see you.

I ignored it. I wanted nothing to do with him. I put the phone down. Cameron was frowning at me.

"Hey, Cal, play list for our sleepover? What do you want on it?" Sally called from the sofa. Her and Liv were going through all mine and Cameron's music, taking out what they wanted.

TARDIS.

J: It's important!!!

I ignored it again, putting the phone face down on the island, also ignoring the heat of my brother's gaze.

"Cal?" Sally called again.

"Hmm? I don't know, whatever you guys want," I said, distractedly.

"You're going to ditch us, aren't you?" Natalie said with disappointment. "You're going to get Nick to come and rescue you from our girl's night, and take you off on his bike, to do whatever crazy shit it is that you two do together."

TARDIS.

I didn't look at my phone.

"Well, I hadn't planned on it, but now you mention it..." I looked at Nick and he winked at me.

"Just don't get lost this time," Cameron warned. Nick and I laughed.

"Lost?" Sally wanted to know.

"The last time Dana tried to organise a girl's night, Callie and Nick took off. They were meant to be going to Stonehenge, but they got lost. Fuck knows where. For three days!" Cameron was shaking his head, but there was a trace of a smile on his lips.

"Hey, it wasn't an entirely wasted exercise, we learned how to swear in Dutch," Nick argued. I nodded enthusiastically, agreeing.

"Callie! Don't you even think about it!" Liv screeched and pointed at Nick. "Nick, you are not, under any circumstances, allowed to take her. I don't care how much she begs. Don't make me take your bike hostage!"

"Do not touch my bike, Olivia." Nick pointed at her.

"Chill, Olive." I told her.

"Don't call me that!" She stuck her tongue out at me.

TARDIS. Cameron raised his eyebrows at me. I ignored him, and the phone, again.

"I'm not ditching you, ok?" I sighed.

Admittedly, a girly sleepover wasn't high on my to do list at that time, but I knew they were all excited about it, so I would be there.

"Good. Because if you even try, I will have you handcuffed before you can blink." Dana pointed a corkscrew at me, then went back to opening the bottle of wine in front of her. "I can do that! I'm married to a copper. I can get handcuffs!"

"Now, there's an idea..." I murmured quietly, wondering if Adam took his handcuffs home with him.

"For the record, I am very much in favour of where your mind just went, Angel." His voice came softly at my ear.

I looked at him sideways and smirked, as his arms snaked around my waist from behind, and he pulled me tight against him. The thought of all things I could do to Adam if he were in handcuffs made me giggle. I rested the back of my head against his chest and closed my eyes.

TARDIS.

"Oh. for fuck sake!" Cameron and I raced to reach for my phone. My fingers skimmed the edge, sending it spinning in his direction. It slid across the island and he got it before I could stop him. He slid his thumb over the screen and opened the messages.

"Is he fucking serious?" My brother ground out the word through gritted teeth and his face darkened as he looked at me.

"Just ignore him." I brushed it off.

"You've been ignoring him, Cal! We *all* have, at your request. And guess what? He hasn't gone anywhere, so that worked out really fucking well, didn't it?" Cameron was pissed off, seriously pissed off.

Adam held out his hand for my phone and Cameron passed it to him. I had no problem with either of them reading the messages; I just didn't want to deal with their reactions. I was sure if I ignored Jase, he would eventually get bored and go away. Eventually.

"It's fine. I'll just block his number. You can do that, can't you? Of course, I have no idea how, but it can't be that hard. I can *Google* it. It's about time I learned how to use—"

"Rambling, Cal." Nick interrupted, leaning over Adam's shoulder, to read the messages for himself. "I thought you were going to tell me if this carried on?"

"He did stop. For a while." I answered Nick's accusation.

The hand on my waist got tighter as Adam silently scrolled through the messages. There was a chilled edge to his scowl that I hadn't seen before. I knew I needed to calm him down somehow. I turned and laid my palms on his chest; he relaxed into my touch instantly and brought his eyes down to mine.

"You're going to ignore him and he's going to get bored and give up."

"He's got no intention of going anywhere, Angel." His voice softened when he spoke to me, but I could still pick out the anger in his tone. Adam passed my phone to Mick who was waiting to read the messages.

"I'll talk to him," Luke said, walking into the kitchen.

"No, Luca. He's your friend. You're not getting involved." I pushed out hastily.

"Not anymore. Not after what he did to you, the other night in the pub. But he *has* listened to me in the past." Luke looked at Nate, who had followed him into the kitchen and was now leaning against the wall.

"That was then, mate. He's lost it even more since." Nate shook his head at Luke.

"What are you talking about?" I asked, turning in Adam's arms again. His fingers, digging into my hips, indicated he had no intention of letting me go any time soon. I didn't mind.

"I talked him out of doing something stupid, after you two broke up." Luke shrugged, refusing to make eye contact with me.

"Luke?" I questioned, needing more.

The room stilled, everyone focused on Luke. I laced my fingers with Adam's on my waist and felt more of the tension leave his body. He rested his chin on the top of my head and inhaled the scent of my hair.

"He was going to do something he'd regret. Luke talked him out of it." Nate rushed out, pleading me with his eyes to drop it. This was obviously something he hadn't wanted me to know about.

"What was he going to do, Luke?" I demanded.

"He wasn't thinking straight. He'd messed everything up between you two. His head was all over the place and he was desperate to get you back," Luke explained.

"Luca..." I said quietly.

"Spit it out, fella," Mick said.

"It wasn't long after you broke up. He couldn't get you on the phone. I tried telling him that you'd lost it, but he didn't believe me. He said he just wanted to know that you were okay. We told him you were fine, but he wanted to see for himself. Nick was doing his best to keep him away from you, but he couldn't watch him all the time." Luke breathed in deeply. "When he got here, you were already asleep, the lights were all off. Nate and I followed him, he was around the back of the house, at your bedroom window."

"You sleep with the window open, so he was going to climb in." Nate took over when Luke went quiet. "He wanted to slip into bed next to you and hold you for a while. He said he'd done it before, lots of times."

"What?" I whispered.

I tried to lean further into Adam, but there was no space left between us. I wanted to attach my body to his somehow, to climb inside him where it was safe, and never come out. He leaned down and kissed the top of my head. "Easy, Angel," he murmured into my hair.

"Creepy much." Liv murmured.

"That's exactly what we told him. I said that you would be terrified, it was different before. You were together and you'd expected him to do it." Luke looked at me and I nodded.

Jase had climbed in my window before, many times over the years. But like Luke said, that was different because I knew he was likely to do it. I shuddered, wondering what he would have done the night of the storm, if I had been asleep.

"Anyway, I told him that if he did it, he'd scare you and there was no way he would ever get you back after that. It took a while to talk him out of it. Nate pushed your window closed so we didn't wake you up." I frowned at Luke's words, remembering a night when I had woken from a nightmare, convinced I heard something outside my window. I looked to Cameron, who nodded his agreement, he remembered too.

"Jase kept saying it would be fine, because you guys had been together for so long, you could never be afraid of him. You spent practically every night together, blah, blah, blah. Anyway, eventually I got him to see sense, and we managed to get him home." Luke finished.

"I'll kill him!" Cameron growled.

"I think there's a queue," Dana said quietly, leaning her head on Greg's shoulder.

"He has to be told once and for all, Callie. What with everything going on, Jase is just one thing we really don't need to keep dealing with, right now." Cameron hesitated over mentioning my current stalker situation, but we all knew what he meant.

"Cameron's right, love. This is one problem we don't need at the minute. We're all doing our damndest to keep you safe, having to look out for Jase on top of that isn't helping matters." Mick attempted to soften the blow.

"You alright, Cal?" Nick asked me.

"Yeah. I just—" I sighed and looked at my best friend, "What happened to him, Nick? How did this happen to him, without us realising? We should have noticed sooner. *I* should have noticed!"

"You did notice, baby girl." Vinnie leaned forward, resting his elbows on the countertop. "You'd been noticing for over a year."

"But I didn't help him. I didn't even try. I was just thinking about myself and how I could end things with him." I shook my head.

"Did he ever get violent with you, before the other night?" Nick asked, running a hand through his hair and looking agitated.

"No." I reached out to squeeze his hand and reassure him. It took a lot to push him over the edge, but when he went... Well, let's just say, you didn't want to be on the receiving end of Nick's temper. "It was just the control thing, wanting to know where I was, who I was with, all the time. I thought it had only come on over the last couple of years. I never noticed he had always been that way, too young and dumb to see it, I suppose. We argued a lot the last year or so, it's no secret, you all knew. There was a lot going on, not just him changing, but my stuff, too."

"Your demons were not a factor in his behaviour, Callie. That's all on him." Jared told me gently.

"I'm amazed you put up with it as long as you did." Nat said, drawing her knees up into her chest, and wrapping her arms around them.

"Every time I tried to confront him about it, he showed me the old Jase again and I'd second guess myself. I thought it was all me. My head wasn't in the right place to figure it out properly. I was too wrapped up in my nightmares. I didn't know who *I* was half the time, let alone who he was becoming." I shrugged and she smiled sadly at me.

"*Not* your fault, Callie! *Never* your fault! NEVER!" Dana burst out; the memory just as painful for her as it was for me. Greg pulled her closer to him. She looked at me through tear filled eyes. "He should have been there for you after what happened, not the other way around. You were suffering and all he did was use it to control you."

"I wish we had been closer then, I would have staged an intervention." Nat said. I laughed and some of the tension left the room.

"Ok, look, there will be no ex-boyfriend killing tonight. Tonight, is about Kat." I looked around at them all.

The men in my life looked about ready to head out and hunt him down. I couldn't let that happen. Reluctantly, they all agreed and slowly conversation started back up around the room. I took Adam's hand and led him to my room, knowing he craved the alone time that I wanted too.

"Sit." I told him and pointed at the bed.

"Angel?" he questioned, moving first to the window, closing and locking it.

"Sit!" I told him again. He sat on the end of my bed and I stood close, facing him. "I don't want you going anywhere near him. You, Greg, and Cam, he would use your jobs against you in a heartbeat."

He reached out, hooking a finger through my belt loop, and pulling me to stand between his legs. "Don't worry. When we see him it will be official, all above board."

"No, Adam. Not even then. He can be ignored. He's proven that tonight. I ignored him and the messages stopped. He'll stop and he'll leave me alone." I rested my hands on his shoulders.

"Vinnie turned your phone off." He looked at me. "It's been five months. He's getting worse, not better. An official visit may be just what he needs."

I thought for a minute, trying to see his point of view. He felt a need to protect me, it was in his nature. Just as it was in Cameron's, and Greg's, and had been in my dad's, it's why they did what they did.

"Alright, look, leave it for now. See if he gets the message. If he does anything else, you can talk to him. Please? I can't have this blow up on top of everything else right now, Adam. I don't know how to cope with anything more. I'm already on the edge."

He searched my eyes, looking for something, I don't know what. I didn't look away. I let him search; in hope that he found what he was looking for. After a few minutes, he smiled. "Alright, we'll do it your way. But I'm serious, Angel, one more foot out of line and I take over. I deal with him once and for all."

I nodded my agreement and Adam moved his hands around to my back, slid them into my back pockets. He squeezed slightly and pulled me a step closer, lowering his head, and resting his forehead against my stomach. I moved my hands across his shoulders, up his neck, and into his hair, holding him close to me, relishing the feeling of him in my arms.

This man had come into my life at the worst possible time, but it felt right. Who's to say how long you should go, between relationships? Who decides whether it's too soon, or not? Where's the book on that? I knew what was happening between Adam and I was happening fast, but I also knew it was right. Yet, still something was holding me back. It wasn't my feelings for Jase, I realised. I still loved him, but the love I felt for him had changed. It wasn't that all-consuming, romantic, I can't breathe without you, love anymore. It was more like. I care about you and want you to be ok, love.

Closure, there's a word. I wondered if that was the key to my being able to move on with Adam. Nothing about my relationship with Jase had been resolved. I had no answers about him and Amy. I might have told myself I didn't *want* them, but perhaps I *needed* them.

"Woman, let me love you." Adam groaned against my stomach and lifted his head to look at me.

Abruptly, he stood, picking me up as he went. I wrapped my legs around his waist, pulling his body into mine. His words sent a shiver rippling all over my body, as he backed me up against the door, and buried his face in the hair that fell around my neck, inhaling deeply. Music blared loudly from the living room suddenly and someone hammered on my door.

"Come on, lovebirds, we've got a playlist to sort out and I need your back up, girl or it's going to be all boy bands!" Nat yelled through the door. "You can canoodle with hotness after we've all gone home!"

When Adam moved his mouth, to kiss the space between my neck and shoulder, I moaned, tilting my head to the side, to give him access. The butterflies in my stomach did a happy dance at the feel of his lips on my skin. I loosened my legs, but he didn't let go. He raised his head to look at me and gave me a wolfish grin. "We could sneak out and go to my place."

"There would be no sneaking, we have to pass them all to get out of the house." I reminded him, smiling. He kissed me lightly on the lips and rested his forehead against mine.

"One day soon, I'm going to kiss you properly. I can't wait to taste you, Angel, but I'm going to take my time and give you the attention you deserve. It won't be just a quick stolen moment, we're worth more than that," he promised, releasing his hold on me.

"I'm going to hold you to that." I promised back with a grin and led him into the living room, where Liv and Dana had blind folded Vinnie, and were spinning him in a circle.

CHAPTER FOURTEEN

CALLIE

Me: S.O.S

Nick: Dude! You haven't even been there ten minutes.

Me: It feels like days! I can't do it. I thought I could, but there's just so much pink. I know I'm weak. I'll climb out the bathroom window. Pick me up.

Nick: No can do, Moonbeam. The lemurs are closing in. Need to stay off the radar.

Me: You're lying. There hasn't been a lemur sighting in weeks.

Nick: You can do this. Be strong. I have faith in you, little warrior.

Me: I'm revoking your best friend status if you don't get here right now!!!

Nick: Shit, Cal! The lemurs found me. There's too many of them. I'm not going to make it. Tell my brothers I fought until the end...

Me: Traitor!

"Black. Like my soul!" I said, dramatically. The sleepover had begun in earnest and I was trying. I really was.

"No! You're going to be a lady! And your soul is anything but black, Callindra Cecilia Wilson!" Dana snapped; hand on hip and tapping her foot impatiently. Little did she know.

We were choosing nail colours. The others were all going with pink, and peach, and gold, because the weather was getting warmer, and it was almost summer. I, on the other hand, wasn't doing pink or peach or any of those colours, not even to keep my beloved Dana happy. I did purple, and blue, and red, and black. Silver at a push.

"Here," Nat said. She rummaged around in her bag and handed me a shiny, green bottle. I took it and unscrewed the cap, examining the colour. Not quite the *Hulk's* shade, but it would do.

"Yep, I can do green." I nodded.

"Alright, I suppose, but only because it's sparkly." Dana conceded gracefully.

Liv laughed. "You were never getting pink on her, Dee, you know that."

"I had to try!" Dana pouted as she yanked my hand into her lap and got to work.

Between you and me, I didn't mind pink all that much, I just didn't want pink clothes or pink nails. Although, I did have some pretty awesome bright pink boots, that looked fantastic with my black jeans.

I was wearing *Bat Girl* pyjamas and looked completely out of place among Dana's pink polka dots, Sally's unicorns, and Nat's butterflies. At least Liv looked more like me in her *"Don't let the muggles get you down"* t-shirt with red striped pyjama bottoms. I didn't care, I loved my *Bat Girl* pjs, the logo glowed in the dark. Pure nerdgasm material!

EDUCATING CALLIE

"I'm out of club soda for the mojitos." Sally appeared in the doorway, a jug in one hand and a bunch of fresh mint in the other.

"I put it in Adam's fridge, I'll grab it in a sec." I told her; quietly glad of the excuse to make my escape before the face masks came out.

"Help me, *Obi-Wan Kenobi*, you're my only hope!" I stuck my head around Adam's door.

We'd left all the interior doors in the building open, so we could holler if we needed Adam and Greg. I secretly thought the guys just wanted to listen in on the girl talk. It's a known fact, men are bigger gossips than women.

"Get in here, Leia." Adam laughed and looked up as I went in, his eyes taking me in from head to toe.

"Nice Batma... girl pyjamas." He corrected himself, remembering our conversation about the *Supergirl* socks. Such a quick learner.

"The logo glows in the dark," I announced, proudly.

"Geek," he said, shaking his head at me with a grin, and I bowed theatrically.

"How's it going down there?" Greg asked, pulling two beer bottles out of the fridge and handing me one. Our friends had embraced mine and Adam's drink sharing by that time, and only ever offered one between us.

"I've had my hair streaked purple, my nails painted, and my eyebrows waxed. I'm currently undertaking a top secret and very dangerous mission in face mask avoidance." I informed him, gratefully accepting the beer and taking a long drink.

"I figured we'd be seeing you, sooner or later. I knew you'd have to escape at some point." Greg laughed. "How close are you to ringing Nick?"

"Nick is dead to me, that traitor, he already sold me out!" I told him. They both laughed, I didn't find it funny. "They'll come for me if I'm gone too long. If they send Nat, I'm screwed."

"She seems even less girly than you." Adam observed, sliding an arm around my waist, hooking his thumb in the waistband at the front of my pyjama bottoms, and pulling me against him, my back against his front. Maybe I could just stay here?

"Actually, you'd be surprised, she's no match for Dana, but she doesn't mind all that stuff." I said, inspecting my nails.

"Green?" Adam asked.

"They wouldn't let me have black." I leaned back against him, "This was a compromise because it's sparkly."

"You let her do it because the *Hulk* is green, didn't you?" He smiled knowingly and ran his fingers gently through my new purple streaked hair.

"Yes, but you can never tell her that." I tilted my head to look up at him as I relaxed into his touch.

"You two need to stop denying you're together." Greg pointed his beer bottle as us, then grinned, and walked out of the kitchen, shaking his head.

"I better go." I took a big gulp of the beer, ignoring Greg, handed the bottle to Adam, then gathered the three bottles of club soda out of the fridge. I stretched up on tip toe to kiss Adam on the cheek, he leaned down to meet me, but he turned at the last second, so I caught his mouth instead and he smirked at me. I rolled my eyes at him, my stomach may have held a butterfly convention, too.

"Later Greg," I called as Adam followed me out into the hallway.

"Have fun!" Greg replied sarcastically.

"My sofa is available tonight, if it gets too feminine down there for you later," Adam said when we reached the top of the stairs.

"And will you be on it?" I asked, smiling.

"Only if you are," he flirted.

"Save me a space." I called over my shoulder.

I paused at the bottom of the stairs and heard Adam groan as he went back inside. Greg's voice travelled down the stairs and I couldn't help but overhear.

"Shit, cous! You're a walking hard on around her." He laughed and I smirked to myself, happy in the knowledge that it wasn't just me that was affected by our closeness.

"Tell me about it." Adam's pained voice followed, and I felt a twinge of guilt.

"I've never seen you like this over a woman before."

"That's because it's never been her before."

"Are you going make a move?" Greg asked.

"She's not ready yet. She knows how I feel, but this has to come from her. If I push her, it won't last," Adam said.

"You're really serious about her then?" Greg asked. "This isn't just a fling for you? Because I don't want to see her hurt again, and Dana would probably kill you in your sleep."

"I know she's your friend, cous, but you don't have to worry. I'm playing for keeps. There's no way I'm letting that woman go once she's mine. She's everything I never knew I wanted." Adam told him and my stomach flipped.

The witches were in full on disco mode when I got back downstairs. They were dancing in the middle of the room to a Grease medley. I pulled out my phone and texted Nick a picture of a lemur with bulging eyes and the caption *"I own you"* before heading into the kitchen to mix more cocktails.

"*Karaoke!* Get the machine out, Dana." Liv squawked excitedly. She was getting her happy drunk on again.

"Yes!" Nat and Sally agreed, bouncing up and down.

"You gonna sing us a song, Cal?" Dana asked.

"Yeppers!" I said.

Singing and dancing like an idiot was something I had always excelled at. I was in high spirits after overhearing not only Adam's confession about how he felt about me, but Greg making sure his intentions were good. I had the best friends and it was time I started to enjoy them again. Since the darkness came, I hadn't involved myself in any of this stuff as much as I used to. Aside from messing around at work with Mick, I avoided it. I knew I needed to make an effort to get that part of me back, even if I was on borrowed time.

A few minutes later I was belting out *"Living on a prayer"* like a pro. A screechy, slightly tipsy pro, who sounded like they had a sore throat, but a pro, nonetheless. My voice wasn't exactly singing calibre since my abduction and the damage to my vocal cords, but I could carry a tune, and I gave it my best shot. We took turns choosing songs for each other and of course, Dana got *"Barbie Girl"*, which she fully embraced. Liv did a surprisingly tuneful version of Natalie Imbruglia's *"Torn,"* and Sally and Nat shouted their way through *"Girls Just Wanna Have Fun,"* before Liv picked out *"Before he cheats"* for me, which turned into a group sing along. It was a real girl power moment that made Dana's night.

Eventually, we collapsed on the sofa and lapsed into gossipy girl talk which, obviously, centred on mine and Adam's relationship status. Exactly what I was hoping to avoid but I went with it, ready to cut them off the minute they got too deep.

"I heard Nate tried to get in the way," Dana pried, raising her eyebrows at me in question, and twirling the straw in her drink.

"No, he didn't." I said sternly, waving my glass around hazardously, one finger pointed at her. No way was I having Nate brought into mine and Adam's drama. The rumour mill had obviously been running since Nate and I went out, but I was happy to remain ignorant of the details, as long as Nate's name didn't get dragged through the mud.

"But he always did like you. He was your first kiss after all," she pushed.

"Ancient history, Dee. Nothing to tell. Although, I am pretty pissed off that none of you told me what was going on with him and Jase in school." I looked between her and Liv accusingly.

"If Nate had asked you out before Jase, would you have said yes?" Liv asked, diverting my irritation.

"Fuck yeah!" I grinned and they all cackled, like the witches they were.

"But you and Adam?" Dana wanted to know.

"We're figuring it out," I said, carefully. "I'm not jumping into anything with him, but I like him. A lot."

"And he more than likes you," Dana remarked. I looked at her questioningly. I knew how Adam felt, he hadn't exactly made it a secret, but I wondered if he had spoken to Dana about it. She nodded towards the front door. "He was head over heels the second he found you out there. Couldn't stop talking about you, asking all kinds of questions."

"He did?" I asked, suddenly curious.

"Yup! What's she like? Do you think she'll get back with him? He even wanted to know your favourite pizza topping!" She frowned, and I laughed knowing exactly why he had asked about pizza. "Is it mutual, Cal? Because he is very serious about you."

"I think so." I nodded. I knew it was, but I really thought Adam should be the first to hear that, when I was ready to admit it out loud.

"You *think* so? How can you only *think* so with *him*? He's practically perfect in every way. How does he keep that body of his in shape? That's what I want to know, he doesn't seem like a gym rat." Nat spoke with a gleam in her eye and I couldn't help laughing at her.

"He's not." I told her. Adam told me about his love of martial arts, karate in particular, and how he had competed in a lot of competitions as a teenager, even taught it for a while. He still used it to keep fit now and wanted to teach me. I hadn't yet, but I knew I would give in eventually. "Karate is his thing. He wants to teach me, but I've managed to avoid it so far."

"For someone who isn't your boyfriend, you certainly know an awful lot about him." Sally observed with a smile.

I shrugged. "We talk. I ran away from him a lot to begin with, put walls between us. I was afraid of how he made me feel. It seemed too soon. I don't know *how* to be with anyone but Jase and looking back now, I realise I lost myself a little when I was with him. I let him take control and the thought of that happening again scared the shit out of me. But Adam is so not Jase. We talked about it and I'm done fighting it. It feels right. So, we're taking it slow and figuring it out as we go"

"And Jase?" Sally asked.

I just shook my head, the texts demanding to see me were still coming, but I was ignoring them. Cameron and Adam wouldn't be happy that I hadn't told them, but I wouldn't have them getting into drama at work over my messed-up love life. They felt a need to protect me, but I needed that for them too.

"He keeps trying to talk to me, saying he wants me to hear him out. And part of me thinks I need to, but the bruises he left on my arm tell me I don't want to go anywhere near him. It kills me that he's not the same person I fell in love with, but I don't know how to help him." I told them, sadly.

"Did Amy really like him?" Liv asked Sally and Nat, they both nodded.

"She was obsessed with him though, it wasn't healthy." Nat said with a shake of her head.

"No, it was freaky. One minute she'd be all guilt ridden and avoiding him because of you, the next plotting to come between you," Sally explained. "She would ring and text him constantly and turn up at his place every time she knew you weren't around. He always turned her away and she would go into a deep depression over it. As far as we know, they were only together that one time. He refused to be in her company before that."

"I don't want to know." I shook my head. "Amy might not have been the friend I thought she was, but I don't want to think badly of her. I can't. Not after what happened to her. Nobody deserves that."

"Do you miss him? I mean it must be weird, you were together forever," Sally prodded.

"She misses the sex!" Dana giggled. She wasn't wrong and I nodded with a wry smile.

"Ooh, come on, dish the dirt. How good is he?" Nat wanted to know.

"Well, it's not like I've got anything to compare it to, he's all I know." I defended, reluctant to give details.

"You still know whether he's good or not though. I mean, how often did you have to fake it with him?" Nat pushed.

"Erm, never," I said.

"Never? Seriously? He made you come every time?"

"Yes, Nat, fuck woman, do you want a demonstration?" I laughed. "I mean, obviously not at the beginning. We were seventeen and neither of us knew what we were doing. But we practiced. A lot. And it got good. Really, really good!"

"How often did you do it?" She wasn't giving up.

"Often enough." I admit, sex with Jase had been pretty fantastic and I grabbed every chance I got with him.

"Oh, please, it's no secret. They were at it like rabbits, every second of the day. Our Callie is quite the little nympho and Jase was *more* than happy to oblige. They were hot as sin!" Liv spilled her alcohol infused guts.

"Thanks, Olive," I groaned, making a note to drop her in it the next chance I got.

"Any time, any place..." Dana sang.

"No, like where?" Sally gasped.

"You name it." I shrugged and they all collapsed in giggles. I couldn't actually think of a place Jase and I hadn't had sex.

"Shit! How the hell do you go from raging nympho to born again virgin overnight? You must be so frustrated!" Nat looked at me with wide eyes.

"Let's just say *Duracell* won't be going out of business anytime soon," I confessed and downed my drink.

"Adam is going to be in for a real treat when you finally give in to him, witch. I should warn him." Dana smirked over the top of her glass at me and I shook my head at her.

"You'd better hope he's got stamina!" Sally giggled.

"Well, I'm glad you and Adam are giving it a go. You're perfect together. And when you marry him, we'll be related. Cousins in law are a thing, right?" Dana said and we laughed.

"Alright, Cal and Adam are a done deal, we all know that. What I want to know is, if Callie has ever done the deed with Nicky the golden boy!" Nat announced.

"Oh, absolutely we're getting married." I laughed, as did Dana and Liv. Nat and Sally wanted more though. I sighed, ready for the interrogation to end. Why could people not just accept that nothing had ever happened between Nick and me?

"Come on, Callie, we need this stuff," Sally pushed. "We'll dish our own dirt, too."

"Alright ladies, switch your ears on because this is a onetime only speech." I cleared my throat and took a breath. "I love Nick. I've loved him from the second my pig tailed; two-year-old self set eyes on him. I always have and I always will love Nick. I love his smile, I love his sense of humour, I love his kind heart, I love his art, I love when we laugh together at nothing, and do crazy shit, I love all our stupid private jokes.

I love his sense of loyalty and the way he takes care of his brothers. I love that he loves me exactly the same way as I love him. I love us. But I'm not *in* love with him and he is not in love with me, there *is* a difference."

"Aww, that was beautiful Callie," Liv smiled mushily at me. "I love you and Nick too."

"Me three," agreed Dana.

Thankfully, they all moved on to the Vinnie and Jared situation after that. Then Nat started talking about her drummer boy. I'll admit to being curious about Nat and whichever member of Frost she had her eye on, but I'd had enough girl talk for one night, and snuck outside, leaving them to it.

I sat on a bench on Greg and Dana's deck and allowed the cool night air to surround me. The deck backed onto the forest, sitting there was peaceful and calming. After a few minutes, I heard feet on the outside steps leading up to Adam's place. I didn't need to turn around to know it was him.

"Angel," he said, sitting next to me, and handing me his cup of hot chocolate. "You shouldn't be out here alone."

"You're awesome," I said indicating the hot chocolate. I could smell the brandy it was laced with, just the way I liked it. "And I'm not alone, anymore."

"You knew I'd come down," he said putting an arm around me and pulling me closer as I nodded. Of course, I'd known. "All done with the girly bonding session?"

"There's only so much interrogation of her life this girl can take," I told him. "I actually believed Nat was going to water board me, for not sharing enough information at one point. I'm surprised your ears weren't burning."

"We're the hot topic of conversation then," he laughed, unzipping the navy-blue hoodie he was wearing and handing it to me. "It's cold, put this on."

"Thanks. You have no idea, they're relentless." I gave him the cup and pushed my arms into the sleeves, wrapped the material around me and breathed in his scent.

"Did you just smell my jacket?" He laughed lightly.

"It smells like you," I defended and really, says the man who sticks his face in my hair, every chance he gets.

"I'm hoping that's a good thing?" He took a drink and passed the cup back to me, before wrapping his arm back around my shoulders and pulling me closer to him.

"Yep." I nodded as I wrapped both hands around the cup and leaned into his embrace. "I like your smell. It makes me feel safe. Definitely a good thing."

He twirled a piece of my hair around his finger and spoke softly. "That first night, when you fell asleep on me, your hair was still damp from the snow and I could smell coconut from your shampoo all night. It became my favourite smell very quickly."

I smiled sadly, his observation provoking a memory. "I used to smell like cherries, Jase loved it. When... *he* took me, the bathroom at the house had all my products in it. Everything I used, right down to the same toothpaste. So, as soon as I was back home, I threw everything I had ever used away. All of it. Then I made Cam insane, when I stood in the shampoo isle of the supermarket for an hour, sniffing all the bottles for something that was nowhere near the smell of cherry."

"Well, I'm glad you picked coconut." He sighed deeply and pulled me tighter.

Moments of silence passed between us and I felt his mood become heavier. I twisted towards him, put the cup down on the bench and cupped his cheeks between my hands so I could see into his eyes.

"You've gone dark on me, Wolfman."

"A little," he admitted, holding my gaze.

"James?" I asked about his brother, recalling that it was around this time of year he had died.

"I don't think anyone has ever been able to read me like you do." He smiled down at me and reached out to lift my legs, shifting me into his lap. I sat sideways on him, with my legs dangling over the arm rest of the bench and leaned my head on his chest. He coiled his arms around me tightly and rested his chin on my head, breathing deeply for a few seconds before he began to speak.

"I've already told you a lot about him, about the who he was and his personality. You know he was three years younger than me, the same age as you and Greg. They were close. Greg and I never really became close as friends until he joined the force, too. It was always him and James whenever the family got together. He hung around with you a few times, I think. When we visited Greg's family."

"I do remember him," I said. "He played football with us. I think I remember you, too. Sitting in the car when your parents dropped him off with us."

"Yeah, I remember seeing you that day," Adam replied. "You were laughing, with Nick. I thought you were beautiful even then."

"You don't have to say that," I laughed.

"It's true," he insisted. "I questioned Greg about you when they got back. That's where he got his thing about you and I getting on from."

"Really?" I frowned, twisting my head up, to look at him.

"Cross my heart," he said. "That first night, you mentioned us meeting before, I already knew we had, but I couldn't tell you then, it would have been stalkerish.

"Yeah, you're right. Go on," I encouraged. "Tell me about James."

"James and I were very close. I took him everywhere." He laughed quietly. "It was an ego boost to me, really. He had this big brother, hero worship thing going on. He would brag about how good I was at sports and was determined to join the police force. He came to all my karate tournaments, cheered louder than anyone else. He looked up to me, but he always believed he was somehow inferior. He didn't think he would ever be able to live up to people's expectations of him, because they thought he should be like me. I told him he was enough and only ever had to be himself, but I'm not sure he ever believed it. We were more or less inseparable, until I joined the force. What with training, and then finally going out on the job, we spent less and less time together. He began to resent me, avoided me whenever I was at home. I can see it now, but I was oblivious at the time, caught up in living my dream."

Adam paused and I looked at him. He stroked my cheek with his fingers and sighed.

"He got involved with a bad crowd, as the saying goes, and started doing some stupid things. Little things that built up and got worse over time. I went on duty one night to find him in the cells. He'd been arrested for drunk driving. I was so fucking angry with him, told him he was soiling my reputation on the force, making me look bad. We didn't speak for a few weeks. Eventually, I realised how selfish I sounded and tried my best to support him. He assured me it wouldn't happen again."

"A few weeks later, he was taken in for drug possession. He made more promises. Mum was devastated, Dad was just silently disappointed. He's never been a man of many words; his actions speak louder. Anyway, gradually things escalated, until it got to the point where if James got caught again, he was facing prison time. He made all the promises again, did everything he needed to do. He got a job, even talked about going to college and getting some qualifications. Our parents believed he had actually done it this time and were supportive. Not me. I got harder on him. I did believe him, but I never told him. I was brutal and constantly gave him grief, threatening to disown him if he put another foot wrong. But he did it. He pulled it out of the bag and things were better for him. I was so fucking proud of him. But of course, I didn't tell him, I continued to let him think I wasn't there for him."

"The last time I saw him, he told me he would prove me wrong. And I wanted to tell him he already had, but something held me back and I didn't say it. Instead, I told him he hadn't done enough yet, a few months of good behaviour, staying off the drink and drugs, and a college place wasn't enough. I was so hard on him because I thought it would make him try harder to stay on track." Adam ran his fingers through his hair and drew in a ragged breath.

"You can stop, if you want to. You don't have to tell me all in one go." I told him, sitting back and seeing the pain on his face. He reached out for me and wrapped me in his arms again, pulling me close.

"I just need to feel you, Angel. Need to feel you close, to know you're here." His voice was stained with emotion.

"Always," I whispered before he continued.

"I was on a night shift when the call came in. Armed robbery in progress at a 24-hour pharmacy. My partner and I weren't close by, so we left it to other units to respond and continued with our own patrol. Twenty minutes later, I got a call from my sergeant to say James was involved. I all but exploded. I knew instantly he'd broken his promises. It had all been lies. So, I decided there and then, I was washing my hands of him. I wanted nothing more to do with him. No more lies and empty promises. I ignored my partner's advice to go over there and insisted we carry on with our duties. It wasn't part of our area; we weren't required to be there, and this was one mess James could get himself out of."

"The next thing I know, my sergeant is yelling down my radio to get my arse over there, right away. James had been shot. I've never driven so fast in my life; I'm amazed we even got there alive. The entire journey is still a blur. I could guess what had happened. James had gone into the pharmacy desperate for drugs, and held up the cashier, and our own armed response team would have taken him out when he looked like he posed too much of a threat. I knew as soon as we got there, I was too late. He was gone. But I couldn't have been more wrong. He hadn't been robbing the place. He had died trying to take the gun from the drugged-up fucker that was holding the cashier up. The weapon went off in the struggle. Armed response took the junkie down, but not before he took James." The tears that now streamed down my cheeks matched Adam's own.

"The junkie lived; he was shot in the leg." Adam continued. "When it came to court, he was going to get away with time served, because he had other, mental health, issues. I couldn't have that."

"What do you mean?"

"I'm not the person you think I am, Angel," he admitted. "I pulled strings, called in favours, did everything I could to make sure that fucker served his full sentence. He's locked up in a secure ward somewhere. Deemed too far gone to serve time in a prison, but he's away and that's all I cared about."

"Anyone would have done the same in your shoes," I insisted. "I know Cam would. My dad, too."

"My superiors backed me when it came out, ensured I kept the job, even pushed me to take the sergeants exam. They agreed he shouldn't be released, helped me prove he was a danger to the public, but we didn't do it legitimately. I don't deserve this job anymore. I used my position to my own advantage. I should not be on the force, let alone in fucking charge."

"You're good at your job, Adam," I said. "Do you plan on doing it again?"

"Honestly? If I could get my hands on the bastard that hurt you, I'd do whatever it took."

"You and Cameron both," I said, gently. "What you did doesn't matter, it's done, you can't change it. It's what you do next that matters. You're a good copper, Adam, earn it back. Make yourself feel worthy of it again."

"That's the plan," he agreed. "That's why I took this job. I needed a fresh start. I would have handed in my notice if I'd stayed where I was, couldn't live with the guilt."

"And now?"

"It's getting easier since the move," he replied.

"I'm sure you're not the first and I doubt you'll be the last."

"I never told him." He went back to James. "Never got to tell him I believed in him. Because I did. I really did. I was just too fucking stubborn to admit it. Too fucking stupid and prideful to stand by him while he turned his life around. Now, he'll never know. *Fuck!* I worshipped that kid, Angel. And he'll never know." Adam sobbed, burying his face in my hair.

"He knows, Adam. I promise you; he knows. He always knew. You were his big brother; nothing takes that away." I told him as I held him.

"I took it away," he replied, quietly.

"No. You never took your love away. Never that. You proved that by being so hard on him. He wanted to prove you wrong and he would have known that was your way of pushing him to do it."

"You think so?" He looked up at me, tears staining his cheeks.

"I know so. The people we love always know, even if we don't say the words. There are so many ways to say I love you. So many actions, without ever having to say anything. My brother carrying spare gloves around for me? That's him saying he loves me. The way Nick pulls my hair? That's him saying it. When I call Liv Olive, I'm saying it to her.

Being tough on James was you telling him you loved him and that you wanted more for him. He took your love and was determined to do something with it. The fact he wanted to prove you wrong tells me he knew, undoubtedly, that you loved him, and his own actions, changing his life, and proving you wrong, that was him telling you he loved you back."

"When we ask each other, Okay?" He grinned cheekily, regaining some of his composure.

"That too," I admitted with a smile.

Adam held my eyes with his as he contemplated my words. "Thank you for fighting with me, Angel."

"You know I always will." I smiled and reached up to wipe the tears from his cheek.

A crooked smile lit up one side of his face. "Can I fall in love with you yet?"

"Not if I fall in love with you first." I smiled back and wrapped my arms around his neck in a tight embrace. The kind he had given to me so many times before. My stomach tumbled when I felt his lips on my neck, and I sighed in pleasure, and anticipation of that kiss he had promised me.

The warm fuzzy feeling iced as a noise at the edge of the woods startled us both. The unmistakeable sound of a person running through dead leaves brought us both to our feet.

"Did anyone come out here with you?" Adam asked, scanning the tree line for signs of life, all emotion gone from his demeanour. He snapped into protection mode in a split second and was suddenly all business.

"No." I shook my head and took the hand he held out to me.

"Go upstairs and tell Greg I went to check it out. Then go back to the others and lock the doors. Don't let anyone in but us," he instructed me.

"Adam—" I hesitated, concerned for him.

"I'll be fine." He kissed my forehead and let go of my hand. "Get Greg for me, ok?"

Dana and I were the only ones still awake when Adam and Greg came back. They found signs of someone being out in the forest behind the house, but whoever it was disappeared fast. Greg decided to stay downstairs in his own place, after all. He had planned on staying at Adam's, but they both now thought it was safer for him to be at home. I said I'd take the sofa, rather than sharing with Dana as originally planned, allowing Greg his own bed. Dana piled the sofa with pillows and blankets, and gave me a sly smile, before leaving Adam and me alone in the living room.

"Okay?" He asked. He sat down next to me and reached across to pull me, sideways, into his lap.

"Okay." I nodded and rested my head against his shoulder. He pulled a blanket over us and wrapped his arms around my waist. "Aren't you going upstairs to bed?"

"No. Staying right here with you." He buried his face in my hair, nuzzling my neck as he did so. I smiled contentedly and fell asleep.

Of course, I awoke wrapped around him the next morning. I didn't have an *"oh shit"* moment and run for the hills. I snuggled in closer and enjoyed the moment.

"Hmm, definitely my favourite sleeping position," he murmured, half asleep, when I stretched in his arms. He pulled his arms tighter and I settled back down on him. It was my favourite sleeping position, too.

THE TEACHER

My lady continues to be taken in by those boys. She belongs to me, she always has. I must nip this in the bud, before one of them defiles her. I cannot allow that. I did not wish to be hard on her, but she leaves me with no choice. She will suffer in unimaginable ways before her lessons are learned, all because of her so-called friends, her family. I know I can use her feelings for them to my advantage. I will turn her against them. They will know soon enough that she does not belong to them. That she has always been mine.

CHAPTER FIFTEEN

CALLIE

Adam and I were at the supermarket, picking up barbecue supplies. In typical British style, summer was taking its time in making an appearance, but the weather was getting slightly warmer, considering it was already June. Not that my twin and his trusty sidekick needed good weather for a barbecue. Cameron and Nick, after spending an entire evening binge watching *YouTube* videos on the fine art of barbecuing, decided they wanted to do a Sunday roast on it. They sent us off with strict instructions to buy the biggest joint of beef we could find, because they'd invited everyone we knew. I foresaw a lump of meat that was burnt on the outside and raw in the middle, but they were insistent, and to be fair, most of their adventures in barbecuing were successful. We were in the car park, loading our shopping into Adam's car when I heard him.

"CeeCee." The voice came from behind me and I froze instantly. I'd known things had to come to a head eventually between Adam,

Jase, and me, but I'd been happy to continue in my little bubble denying anything was wrong.

"Get in the car, Angel," Adam said, his voice low and commanding.

"Cee, please look at me," Jase pleaded.

I didn't want to, but I had to turn around to get in the car. I took a deep breath and turned, making my way towards the front of the car. As Jase stepped into my path I halted. My breath caught in my chest when I saw his face. His eye was swollen, and black. Bruises ran along his jaw, there were grazes across his nose and cheeks, and his lip was puffed up, and split across the middle.

"What the—" I breathed, reaching up to his face on impulse, and snapping my hand back before it made contact.

"Ask your bodyguard," Jase spat venomously.

Adam came to my side, he took my arm, and steered me around the car to the passenger side. In shock, I allowed him to sit me in the car. Jase continued to rant, and I turned to Adam. I looked at him wide eyed, as he got in the driver's side, unable to conceive that he would do anything like this.

"Cee, he did this. It might have been dark, but it was him. You know it, as well as I do. Who else could it have been, Cee?" Jase managed to call out his accusation before Adam slammed the door shut.

Jase hammered on the window. Adam sighed. He took the keys from the ignition and calmly got out of the car. He closed the door behind him and spoke to Jase. Adam kept his distance and remained calm. I couldn't hear what was being said, but I could see by the look on Jase's face that Adam wasn't getting through to him. Jase had been horribly beaten. His movements, and the way his arm was curled into his side, told me there were other unseen injuries on his body.

Could Adam have done this? I shoved the thought away as soon as it came to mind. Yes, he admitted to me that that there were things he'd done to bend the law, but none of those things were violent. To deliberately and maliciously beat someone just didn't hold true to the person I knew Adam to be. Then again, he hadn't denied it, he hadn't said a word, and he plainly hadn't wanted me to see Jase in that state.

That could just be Adam protecting me, I'd grown used to that from him.

Jase could take care of himself. I'd never known anyone get the better of him. Not that he was a big fighter, but he'd earned himself enough of a reputation, when he *had* been in that kind of situation, that word got around, and people knew not to mess with him. I was pretty sure, aside from Mick, Adam could be the person who finally did take on Jase and come out on top.

I watched their exchange through the windshield. There was no yelling or physical contact. They looked like two men having a perfectly normal conversation. Jase turned and looked at me through the window. He paused for a few seconds, then turned back to nod at Adam, before walking away, his head hanging low.

Adam got in the car and started the engine, without a word. The drive home was filled with a tense silence that neither of us broke. When we got there, I went straight to my room without speaking to anyone. Cameron and Nick didn't seem to notice, and Adam joined in with their preparations. I wanted to know what happened. I wanted to give Adam a chance to tell me. But the fact that he hadn't even opened his mouth, or tried to come after me, told me that he didn't want to talk. Besides, there was that much going on in my head at that moment, I don't think I would have given him a fair hearing.

When the others arrived for the barbecue, I ventured out of my room. Adam occasionally slipped an arm around me or kissed the top of my head. I didn't shy away from the contact, I wanted it, needed it as much as he did. We shared our drinks as normal, but it wasn't normal and we both knew it. We needed to talk and neither of us was about to do that with everyone else around.

"I'm gonna get going." Adam came to be in the kitchen. I was sitting alone at the island, nursing a glass of wine that I didn't even want.

"Alright." I nodded. I wanted to ask him to stay, to just hold me and keep the darkness away, the way only he could, but I didn't say it.

"We'll talk tomorrow, ok? I'll pick you up from college after your exams. About six, yeah?" he asked.

"Fine," I said, watching my glass as I turned it in circles.

"Do you need me to take you in?" He pushed a strand of hair from my face, trying to get me to look at him.

"No. I'm having breakfast with Nick first, he's taking me," I supplied numbly.

"Look at me, Angel," he whispered, the pain evident in his voice.

I did, searching his eyes. I knew this man. At least, I thought I did. He wouldn't do this. Maybe he thought I should automatically know that, without question. But I wanted, no needed, to hear him say it. I tried to let him know that as we looked into each other's eyes. He sent his own message back, one that told me I shouldn't have to ask. That I should just know and that I could count on him. But neither of us said the words the other needed to hear. We were at a standoff.

"Good luck with the exams. I'll see you tomorrow." He leaned forward and pressed a soft, gentle kiss to my lips, lingering a few seconds longer than he had before. I closed my eyes and savoured the fleeting seconds that our lips touched, when I opened them, he had walked away from me.

I sat on a bench in the emptying college car park. Only two cars remained. Adam was running a few minutes late leaving work. He texted to say he was on his way.

Wait for me Angel, he'd sent.

Always, I sent back.

I wasn't going anywhere. I was ready to talk. I'd lain awake all night. My heart and my head were in agreement that Adam hadn't done those things to Jase. I didn't know who had, but I knew it wasn't Adam. I was desperate to apologise; I'd been wrong to doubt him. I wanted to set everything straight between us. *Us*. I was ready for us. I wanted that kiss he had promised me. The brief kisses weren't enough anymore. I wanted Adam in my life. I wanted Adam, and I wanted us. I smiled to myself while I waited, my heels scuffing the ground as I bounced my knees in anticipation. When the darkness came, I tried to fight it, but it was strong and overpowering. I had no choice.

CHAPTER SIXTEEN

CALLIE

"No!" I startled awake, instantly knowing I was back there. Back with *him*. In the darkness. He had come back and he had found me. The way I'd always known he would.

"My lady awakes." A deep, gravelly, and somewhat familiar voice sounded from the corner of the dark cellar, and I instinctively turned towards it.

My eyes, not yet adjusted to the dim light, made out a tall, dark figure, lurking in the shadows. Chains clinked on the concrete floor as I moved. I was shackled to the wall. Everything was all exactly the same, except this time, he had spoken, and he was still speaking.

"I knew you would come back to me, sweet lady of mine. I just had to bide my time. Your teachings were cut short last time. I still owe you punishment for leaving me, but that will come. You will learn new lessons now and you will become a lady, just as you were always meant to be. This is it, sweet Callie. This is the end. You are my reward for a lifetime of teaching. I will show you the life you can have when you choose me, and we will be happy together. Now is our time."

As my eyes fully adjusted, the figure moved slowly towards me. A familiar form took shape. I breathed in sharply, my breathing halted, and I connected the voice to the man. I knew this person who had caused not only me, but so many others such pain. I had known this man all my life. I trusted this man. It couldn't be.

"You?" I whispered.

"That's right, sweet Callie. It's me." Malcolm crouched beside me on the cold floor and reached out to tuck a piece of my hair behind my ear. His touch was gentle and over familiar. I flinched away from him. "My dear, sweet, Callie. It has always been me. I am your destiny, as you are mine. Let me show you."

He stood and turned his back to me, flicking on a ceiling light, fully illuminating the room. I looked around me in horror. Photographs of me covered every inch of space, on every single wall. Some, I recognised from my last year of school, some more recent. Most of them close ups of my face or me alone, walking to work or sitting on our front porch, with a book. Others with Jase, or Cameron, and Nick. Several with Adam, one of us wrapped in each other's arms, in Greg and Dana's garden the night of the sleepover. My stomach lurched and I retched, bending to let out what I could on the ground, but nothing came up. My stomach was empty. I absently wondered how long I had been there.

That happens in situations like that. Your mind can't help but pull you back to rationality every now and then. You find yourself thinking about things that really shouldn't be on your mind at a time like that. I think it's your way of keeping yourself sane. Bring a bit of normality into a far from normal situation, to help you cope, and not lose your shit.

"Two days, sweet Callie. We have been together for two days. Your stomach is empty, I will feed you soon." His salt and pepper hair hung just below his chin. It swung when he turned to smile at me, a hand scratching at his thick grey beard.

I squinted in the darkness at him, unable to fathom that this kind, gentleman had been the one to hurt me. The one who killed those women, my friends. He was an unassuming, regular in the pub. The man everybody knew and had time for.

"They're looking for you. That mangy police dog and his pups. The Irish thug, the biker, and his brothers too. Even the doctor and the mechanic. All of them, tearing the town apart in your name. They will never find what rests right under their noses. They have proven as much, with their incompetency at finding me, over the years. They have no clue and neither did your father before them. I don't even need to be that careful, really. They never look in my direction. I'm just a lonely widow, living out his life in solitude," he gloated, before continuing as though all of this were perfectly normal.

"Later this evening, I am going to cook you a very special meal. Our first of many, I feel we must celebrate our reunion. I intend to tell you my story, and answer your questions, over time. Since you have proven in the past that you are not to be trusted, you will be taking a nap whilst I'm out. Just remember, you brought this on yourself, my sweet Callie. You must not fight me. That sort of behaviour is not becoming of a lady. You will learn to understand that, when you behave badly, I must correct that behaviour. I must teach you the right way. If you behave correctly, I will no longer have to teach you." His words were soft, gentle, like a father scolding his child, but there was a tone in his voice, one of malice, and excitement at the thought of punishing me. His eyes danced like that of a crazed lunatic, and his smile was manic. This was a man on the edge, not the man I knew him to be. There was even a difference between him and the version of him that had taken me the first time.

I barely had time to fathom what was happening, and sift through my thoughts, when the sweet sickly smell that haunted my nightmares engulfed me, and I was in darkness once more.

TEACHER

They think I am here to show my support. I put on a good performance for them, asking for news, offering words of condolence, and joining the search parties, just as I did the last time. I listen discreetly to their conversations in the pub. Her brother is distraught, and their librarian friend desperately attempts to console him.

"She will come back to us. Do you hear me, Cameron? This is Callie. *Our* Callie. She never gives up. She never stops fighting. She came back to us before and she will again. You will *not* fall apart, Cameron. You will *fight*. You're will fight just like she does, every single day of her life! That's what she needs from us and that is exactly what we are going to give her!" She stands on her tip toes, her hands on his face as she speaks quickly, and anxiously, to him.

A glass smashes against the wall and the Irish thug roars in anger. "How the fuck is this happening again?" He demands from nobody in particular.

His long-haired brother and the door man snuggle closely in a corner. My lady will be glad she has brought those two together. I must remember to tell her the good news. Perhaps, I will keep that little gem as a reward for when she pleases me.

The biker sits with his head in his hands at the bar. I cannot be sure, but I think he is crying. I always thought he was too sensitive to be a real man. His brothers are close by, murmuring words of comfort.

"I won't lose her. I will not fucking lose her, Ols!" Her brother growls at the librarian and yanks her close to him, clinging to her like a life raft.

Their attention turns to the door, as the police mutt and his pup come through it. Cousins apparently, although I see little resemblance.

"Anything?" One of the biker's brothers, the middle one I think, asks hopefully. The pup shakes his head and moves into the arms of his *Barbie* doll.

The mutt says nothing but lays a hand on the biker's shoulder and squeezes slightly, before taking the stool next to him. The mutt himself, is a mess, even more so than the others. I can see the stress and lack of sleep etched into their faces. This would not make my lady happy. She would want them to take better care of themselves. It makes me delightfully happy, however. It means my lessons have extended to them. If they had treated her correctly, taken care of her in the way she deserves, ensured her behaviour never wavered, I would never have had to teach her. They only have themselves to blame.

The mutt accepts a drink from the thug, and they converse quietly. The brother and the other pup move in beside them and listen, leaving the two girls to cry together.

"I'm getting her back. I won't stop until I have her back in my arms." The mutt is telling them, with a determined edge to his voice. "I don't care what I have to do. I'll tear the whole fucking world apart if I have to, but I will find her, and I will bring her home safely."

The thug puts a hand on his arm and speaks. "We're right there with you, fella. Whatever it takes."

CALLIE

"Good evening, sweet Callie." He drew the knife along my arm, just enough to draw blood. His voice held a calmness that unnerved me more than the hint of craziness I'd heard before. "I have not yet decided upon your punishment for leaving me. That will take some thought. I have, however, observed your recent behaviours at the hands of the excuses for men that you surround yourself with. It may not be your fault, directly, but still, you must learn from these mistakes. We will begin there. First, I intend to give you a taste of our future, the life we can have together. You will dress for dinner. I will return to escort you in no more than twenty minutes. Do not shower, you will keep the evidence of your lesson with you for the meal. Tricks will be punished. It is not ladylike to keep me waiting."

I was no longer in the cellar, but a bedroom. He must have carried me, while I was unconscious. It was almost identical to the one in the abandoned house. The same pink patchwork bedding on the pine framed bed, the same chair, and bookshelves in the corner, the same mirrored wardrobes, the same green velvet curtains, the same dressing table, laden with the same creams, and cosmetics. Ones I no longer used, to my relief.

Cameron may have only mentioned it in passing, but he hadn't been wrong about the OCD. Everything was meticulously placed. We should have known. We should have realised it was him. The fact that he sat on the same stool, at the same bar, at the same time, every single night, and drank the same amount, of the same whiskey, each time should have roared at us to take notice. This was a man who lived his life by the minutest of details and he had passed right under the radar for years. I instinctively knew he hadn't brought me to the same house. He wasn't going to make that kind of mistake. That would be the first place they searched.

Hanging on the front of the wardrobe, was a long, black evening gown. Again, almost identical to the last one. It was all happening the same way. I was reliving my nightmare, but this time I knew there was no way out. On auto pilot, my mind numb, I changed into the dress. As before, when he returned, he stood me in front of the mirror and forced me to look at my reflection. There was no silent glare this time, this time he spoke. This time he answered the questions I had screamed at him before.

"Do you see the cuts I made on your body, sweet Callie? They are the evidence of your lessons. Each time you forget yourself and behave in an unladylike manner, you will be taught a lesson. You will carry your lessons with you, until your behaviour is once again suitable. Then, and only then, will you be allowed to clean and cover your wounds. And be warned, my dear, these are not harsh lessons I am teaching you. I have no desire to teach you those particular lessons, but if you insist upon behaving in the way you did before, I will be forced to resort to more painful methods." He turned, looping my hand through his at the elbow, and escorting me like the gentleman I had always believed him to be.

"Let us eat," he announced and led me down the stairs, into the dining room.

It was then I realised we were in his house. A house I knew well. We visited Malcolm and his wife often with our parents. Cameron and I played in the garden as children, while Malcolm and my dad barbecued, and my mum and Irene gossiped over wine. Looking back, without my childhood innocence, I could see the all times that Malcolm's gaze had lingered too long on me. I remembered the innocent excuses to play with Cameron and I, and the way he would always find a way to get rid of Cameron, giving him a task to do elsewhere. He never touched me. He never made me feel uncomfortable, but I could see now that it wasn't normal behaviour.

Had my dad suspected it was his friend, all those years ago? The files Cameron found told us he was getting close, but no name was mentioned. This is what Malcolm meant by them not finding what's under their noses. He was keeping me minutes away from the pub, from Adam's place, and the police station. Shit, Jase's house was right on the corner of the same street, mere seconds away.

"Now, sweet Callie, I seem to remember you not enjoying your caviar the last time we had dinner together. No matter. These are things we will learn about one another; over the years we spend together. This evening, we have salmon en croute, a dish my dear, departed wife perfected over the years. It is considered a little old fashioned now, but a classic, in my humble opinion. Please sit." He pulled out a chair at one end of the table in the familiar dining room. I scanned my surroundings half-heartedly for escape routes, knowing I would find nothing. He had made mistakes last time; he would not make them again.

"I know you were brought up well, sweet Callie. I know your parents began teaching you how to be a lady, and I thank them for that, even if they did attempt to become the bane of my existence. It will serve you well in your lessons with me. However, the men in your life have been unhelpful recently. They have caused you to forget yourself. Not your fault. I can help you remember and teach you how to correct your behaviour. I'll have you back on track in no time. Then we can begin our lives together. We're going to be very happy together, my sweet Callie. I will show you how a real lady ought to be treated, unlike that dim-witted ex-boyfriend of yours. I showed him what happens to a man who hurts his lady. He will wear those lessons on his body for some time to come. My only regret is that I was unable to pin the deaths of my recent students on him. That would have brought things together nicely."

He talked easily, in a light and friendly tone as he ate, as though he made no more than polite dinner conversation. Even though he had just admitted to beating Jase and attempting to frame him for murder. That he could be so nonchalant about killing someone made my stomach churn.

"Is your meal to your liking, sweet Callie?" he enquired.

"Yes. Thank you." I nodded.

I had little energy for anything other than playing along with his game. He obviously had a thing for ladylike behaviour, and I was no fool. I realised my best option was to go along with it, for now. His smile widened at my response and he began to speak again. For a man who sat in the pub, barely saying two words all night, he was certainly making up for it.

"Now, I am aware you must have questions for me, and I have every intention of answering them. I will tell you my story, one in which your family play a very prominent role. But we have plenty of time for that. A lifetime no less, sweet Callie."

He made more small talk while we ate, it was like an incessant rattling in my ears. I pretended to listen, continued to go along with it, nodding and replying in all the right places. I excelled at mindless small talk due to working in the pub. I ignored the sick feeling in my stomach at each mention of my parents. The increasing knowledge that he had been behind their deaths danced at the corner of my consciousness, but I didn't want to let it in. I didn't want to accept that part of this scenario yet.

"You will find new clothing in the wardrobe in your room. They will all fit, I made certain of that when I checked your clothing size from your wardrobe at your house. Your measurements haven't changed from the last time we spent together. You may change into sleeping attire before I leave you for the evening."

He escorted me back to the bedroom. He had been in my house. The police had suspected this the first time he took me, due to his knowledge of the products I used. But he was obviously meticulous in covering his invasion, as no trace of him had ever been found. But then, he had been in my house as a guest of my parents that many times that if they had picked up his presence, it likely wouldn't be looked on as suspicious. I struggled to keep the small amount of food I had eaten down now, as I realised his hands had been on my clothes.

He had been in my bedroom. What had he touched? If I ever got out of this, I was going to make Dana so happy, we were going on one hell of a shopping trip!

"Thank you. I will be out in a moment." I responded, dutifully, my voice shaky.

He was leaving me. Of course, he would have to go to the pub and keep up appearances. If he dropped his routine suddenly, people might notice and come to the house, concerned for the man they all thought so much of. So, of course, he had to go and sit at the bar and make small talk with Mick. Mick. The tears welled in my eyes at the thought of my friend. I'd have given anything to be at work with him, joking around, playing our silly games, dancing like idiots to the juke box.

I found a white, floor length nightgown in the dresser drawer, obviously his idea of how a lady should dress for bed. I shrugged out of the dress and pulled it on, going through the motions. Subconsciously, I knew I was shutting down, giving up. I knew I should fight, but I couldn't find a reason to anymore. There was no way he was letting me go a second time. This was it for me, this was my ending. Deep down inside me somewhere, a tiny voice screamed at me to not let it happen this way, to at least go out fighting. But I was done. That voice was becoming quieter, more distant, by the second. I was giving up.

"Why don't you choose a book to keep you company this evening?" Malcolm appeared in the doorway and I spun to face him. "Do not fear me, sweet Callie, I am your future. I am here to teach and protect you, not harm you. Regretfully, I must lock you in the cellar when I leave. Until you prove yourself to be trustworthy, it is the way things must be. This will be your room to use as you wish, after we establish that trust once more. Come." I took the hand he held out towards me, my skin crawling at his touch, and allowed him to lead me downstairs to the cellar. "I had thought to add a few creature comforts for you in here, but I don't want you to feel too at home in this room. You must aspire to the bedroom, you see. I will not chain you this evening, but rest assured, if you try anything, the chains will go on and will remain for the foreseeable future. I do not think you want that do you, my sweet Callie?"

"No." I shivered at the thought of the hard metal around my wrists and looked over to the wall where the chains hung from hooks.

"Good. We will discuss the permanent markings on your skin at a later date, but needless to say, I was not impressed by them. Now, you have a simple bathroom here. Lavatory and sink, you need no more, at present. There is bottled water in the fridge beside the bed and there are blankets to keep you warm. The ceiling light has now had the bulb removed, but you do have the lamp, that will provide you with enough light to read. I will never deny you your books, sweet Callie, but living simply in this room will teach you to appreciate the finer life that I will provide for you, in the future. You will learn to be thankful for everything I give you over time and you will see in the end that a life with me is a rich and fulfilling one."

During his speech, he had ascended the stairs, and now he closed the door as he left. I listened to a key turning in the lock. Footsteps sounded above me as he walked across the wooden hallway floor. A dull bang vibrated through the house when the front door closed and then his footsteps faded down the concrete garden path. I was alone. Should I make a noise? Hammer on the walls and windows, like last time? Is it worth the effort? My mind wandered to the pub and I thought of all my friends. Would they want me to give up? Knowing the answer, I hauled myself to the tiny window and banged on it with my fist. It had been painted black, as was his routine. It was smaller than the last one, so even if I could break it, I wouldn't have fit through.

I banged as loudly as I could but, as I feared, I received no response. Since I had no way of knowing how long he had been gone, I knew I couldn't keep it up indefinitely. It didn't help that my voice could no longer gain enough volume to shout for help effectively. The odds were against me. So, I sank back down on the bed, hammering on the walls and pipes as I went, for good measure. It was a half-hearted attempt, but I had done something. I lay down and cried myself into oblivion.

THE TEACHER

Ah, this ought to be interesting. The ex-boyfriend is here. I watched the two of them grow together. Young and believing themselves in love. The two were once innocent souls, who reminded me of my wife and me in our beginnings. He used to worship her, but somewhere along the line, he lost his way and became unworthy. He hurt my sweet lady with his infidelities. I attempted, for a while, to assist him in reinstating himself with her. My motives were, of course, for my own gain, but the thought was there. I have already given him a beating, but I didn't feel he learned anything from it. He didn't know it was me, he thought it to be the mutt. I would quite enjoy it if he knew I was his punisher. Particularly, if I were to reveal that I had also in fact left my previous students close to his workplace on purpose, encouraging the police to look at him, and leading them away from me. Not that they had ever gotten close to me.

He thunders into the pub, all guns blazing. "What the fuck are you doing in here when you should be out looking for her?" he yells accusingly at the police mutt, who is hunched at the bar.

The mutt stands, slowly, to his full height and gives him his undivided attention. These two have had dealings before and despite the mutt not being worthy of my lady, he can most certainly handle himself. My money would be on him, if it were to become physical between the two. A watch worthy fight, for sure.

"Not now, Jase." The biker comes between them, always the peace maker.

"What the fuck do you mean not now, Nick? She's been gone for days and he's just sitting there, feeling sorry for himself. Has he been looking? Because I fucking have. Non fucking stop!"

The mutt takes a step towards him, his voice low and deliberate, as usual. "I haven't stopped looking for her, Jase. Not since the second I knew she was gone. Cam, Greg, Nick, Nate, Luke, Vinnie, Mick, and Jared have all been looking, too. Along with as many police officers as I could get, many of them volunteering to give up their free time. Greg and Cam are out there now, as are Vinnie, Jared, and Nate. So, you can be sure that I will find her, and I will bring her home."

The thug intervenes. "Come on now, Jase, we're all a mess over this. We all care about her and we're doing everything we can. Adam hasn't stopped, and you can bet your arse he'll be straight back out there searching, the second he leaves here."

The ex turns to him. "I fucking love her, Mick, that's the difference."

"And you think I don't?" The mutt explodes, grabbing the throat of the ex and bending him backwards over the bar. His shouts command the room around him to silence. I don't believe I have ever seen a truly angry reaction from him in the past. It's nice to see he has emotions, as he tightens his hold on the ex's collar. "I thought you and I had gone over this, Jase? She is everything to me. Do you understand me? EVERYTHING! You can be angry, Jase, angry that she's missing, and angry that you fucked up and lost her. And you can look for her, along with the rest of us. But I am telling you again, just to be clear, Callie is *mine*. You had your chance and you fucked up. And *when* I bring her home, *I* will be the one spending the rest of my life keeping her safe. *I* will be the one making her happy!"

The ex turns to leave, when the mutt roughly lets go of his collar. "We'll fucking see about that." He snarls on his way out.

If there is one thing the mutt and I agree on, it is that the ex-boyfriend is not worthy of my sweet lady. And so, I decide to take her a gift. One that will show her just how much she means to me.

CHAPTER SEVENTEEN

CALLIE

"Did you know, I am a teacher, my Callie?"

I shook my head, looking at him vacantly across the table while we ate breakfast, like normal people, rather than captor and hostage. Why would I have known that he was a teacher? As far as I knew, he'd been retired for years. I quickly discovered he didn't mean teacher in the same way the rest of us do. He had woken me that morning with the hunting knife on my face. Just a tiny warning mark he said, apparently, he didn't want to mark his future wife permanently. That had made my mind wander to Nick and all our crazy wedding talk. I'd earned another scratch with the knife for not paying attention.

"I believe every young woman should have the opportunity to learn how to be a lady. That is what I teach. That is what those who came before you failed to learn. Their failure is why they had to die. That is what you will learn." He smiled at me. "You are the special one. I see a wife in you. Your parents began your teachings well, their involvement gave my path a focus, an end to aspire to. I will help you to complete what they began. Eventually, you will see what I can offer you and you will choose not to return to your previous existence, but to stay with me, just as Irene did. Together, we will have a happy life."

"Why?" I whispered.

I wasn't sure he had heard me, until he laid down his cutlery and stood. With his eyes on me, he rounded the table slowly and pulled out the chair beside me to sit down.

"Now, Callie, I already told you I fully intend to tell you my story. As a matter of fact, my intension is to do so over dinner this evening. Unfortunately, my dear girl, you questioned me. I cannot have that kind of behaviour. A lady never questions her man. Come." He gently took my arm, his calm demeanour making me nervous, and led me up the stairs to the bedroom.

How could he handle me so softly, when we both knew what was coming? Once in the bedroom, he ripped my shirt from my body, discarding it on the floor, and arranged me in front of the mirror. I wore only a plain white bra and a pair of black trousers. He held my chin in place and took out the serrated hunting knife from the back pocket of his trousers.

"Now this can all stop, Callie, just as soon as you learn the lesson. Eyes on your reflection." I did as I was told. I didn't want to, I tried to hold it in, but the pain was sharp, and took me by surprise. I cried out as the knife point dug in and tore the skin on my shoulder. He dragged the blade, drawing blood, in a long line all the way to my elbow. "You remember how this works, don't you? All the marks I put on you will fade in time. I will never mark you so deeply that it will remain visible for long, just enough to drive your lessons home. Tell me why we are here, Callie."

"I don't know," I whimpered, and the knife went back in at the top of my shoulder, making me wince with the pain.

"Yes, you do, Callie. What is your lesson?" The gentleness of his tone disappeared and was replaced with that harsher, more forceful one.

The knife drew another line directly parallel to the first and my arm burned as I felt my skin splitting open all the way down. The blood spilled from the wound, dripping from my fingertips. I didn't remember the burning last time. Thinking back, I'm not sure I was conscious enough, from all the chloroform he fed me, to really feel the pain.

"Why are we here, Callie?" he repeated angrily. He always dropped the sweet from my name when he was angry with me. He hadn't used it since I questioned him in the kitchen.

"Because I questioned you." I told him, without emotion, what I thought he wanted to hear.

For so long, I had known that this was coming, that he would come back for me. I would once again stand in front of the mirror with him, so I'd surrendered myself to what was happening. Still, that tiny voice was still trying to be heard, and so my mind was flipping from numb to terrified and back again, at a rate of knots.

"Why shouldn't you question me, Callie?" I felt the knife at my shoulder again.

"I'm sorry, I just wanted to know why you're doing this. I thought you wanted to tell me." I began to ramble.

"Concentrate! Why shouldn't you question me?" He punctuated each word with a short scratch of the knife on my arm. I screamed, my legs becoming weak beneath me. His grip on my chin tightened in a bid to hold me upright. I could practically feel the bruises forming. "Think now, Callie. You know this. Why shouldn't you question me?"

"Be... Because a... A lady never qu... questions her man." I finally got the words out between heaved sobs and deep breaths.

"There it is. I knew you would learn fast, my sweet girl. I picked well in you. Irene always said you were a good girl." Relaxing his grip on my chin, he laid both hands on my shoulders, the knife now gone, and turned me to face him. "Now, you may take some time to reflect on your lessons. Stay in your room until I say otherwise."

He turned and left the room. The key turned in the lock on the other side of the door. I let out a staggered breath, sunk to the floor, my back against the mirror, and sobbed.

I must have cried myself to sleep because when I woke, I was on the bed in the cellar. I wondered how he was managing to move me around like this in my sleep. I wasn't a heavy sleeper and normally woke at the slightest noise or movement. He must have been drugging me somehow, perhaps in my food or water? Because all I knew was that I constantly felt exhausted. A grunt in the corner of the cellar startled me from my thoughts. I looked over to see a hunched figure in the darkness. Fumbling around for the lamp I knew to be there, I switched it on. A low glow lit the dank and gloomy greyness of the room.

"Hello? Malcolm?"

I stood and ventured away from the bed, moving slowly towards the section of wall I knew the chains were attached to. The figure jumped at the sound of my voice and backed up against the wall. The chains rattled as the figure moved and I realised they were attached to whoever this was. Fear pooled in the pit of my stomach as I realised, he had taken another woman. Why? When I was supposed to be the last?

"Hello? I won't hurt you."

I continued to move towards her, and a deep masculine groan came from the figure. A man, I realised with a jolt. Why would he take a man? He had never done that before, at least not that I knew of. It had always been women. I crouched low beside the form and reached over to remove the hood that was covering his face. Bile rose in my mouth, my stomach rolled, and I gasped. I scampered back, crouching nearby as I uncovered the man.

"Oh, no. No, no, no, please God no. No. No. No." I keened and rocked back and forth on my heels as I recognised Jase's beaten and bloody face in front of me. He began mumbling incoherently, and pulling on the chains, yanking hard, his eyes wide and disorientated. I moved to his side quickly snapping out of my shocked state.

"Shush, Jase, it's me, it's CeeCee. It's ok. I've got you. Hush, baby, please. We're going to be ok. Jay, please listen to me, hear my voice Jay, it's me." I cradled his face between my hands and tried to soothe him with words, tried to get him to hear my voice.

If there were any noise down there, it would bring Malcolm down those stairs, and that was never going to be a good thing. I began planting chaste kisses on his cheeks, and forehead, whispering words of comfort in between, knowing that I had to calm him and fast. After a few minutes, Jase's eyes eventually focused on me and he began to calm.

"CeeCee?" he croaked.

"Yes, it's me. Hang on..." I moved quickly to the fridge and brought back some water. Opening the bottle, I held it to his lips. "Here, drink some of this."

"Where are we?" he managed to whisper hoarsely, after drinking some of the water.

"In Malcolm's cellar," I said, hearing how ridiculous it sounded.

"Malcolm? What? I don't understand." Jase pulled on the chains as he reached for me. I moved closer and took his hands in mine. "What the hell is this?"

"Tell me what you remember," I prodded his memory. "What happened to you?"

He shook his head and squeezed his eyes tight shut for a second. "The last thing I remember, was coming out of the pub after yelling at Mick and Adam. Nick was there too. Malcolm in his usual spot. He followed me out. I assumed to calm me down, he's been giving me advice about you, since we split up."

"Advice?" I whispered.

"How to get you back, that kind of thing."

"What else?" I pushed. If Malcolm had been schooling Jase's behaviour, that would explain a lot.

"Nothing, until I woke up here." He moaned as he tried to move to a more comfortable position. "Your arm Cee."

"It's fine. Nothing. You know, it's what he does, doesn't even hurt anymore." I rambled in an attempt to calm him.

"Malcolm did this to you? And the last time?" Jase began to put everything together.

"It was him all along. He took the others. He took me the last time. He never went anywhere, Jay. He was here the whole time. Watching. It was him that hurt you, not Adam. Him who took your phone. He told me he was purposely putting the bodies close to your workplace to try and set you up, too." I sank down on the cold floor, beside his long legs.

"I knew it wasn't Adam. Malcolm told me if you thought it was

Adam, it would look bad for him." Jase attempted to shrug, but I could see it hurt him to move. "I didn't know who it was though. It's starting to make sense though."

"He's been controlling you," I said.

"Come closer, Cee." Jase pleaded. I moved in as close as I could get to him and rested my head on his chest. "Tell me everything."

"I don't know much. He hasn't told me why he's doing it. Just that I am meant to be his reward for a lifetime of teaching, or something. It's fucked up. He has some kind of obsession with women behaving like ladies. He insists I dress a certain way, picks out clothes for me to wear. Every time I do something he considers unladylike, the knife comes out. He calls the cuts my lessons. He keeps hinting at my mum and dad being involved somehow, but he hasn't said how yet. I think he killed them, too, Jay," I explained.

"Shit!" Jase pulled me as close to him as the chains would allow.

"We're definitely in his house. I've been upstairs and I remember it, from when we used to visit with my parents. All the windows are covered, nobody can see in. He locks me down here when he leaves. I've banged on the window, but I can't break it like before. I screamed until my throat gave out. He's not making any mistakes this time." Weakening, I let the tears come.

"It's okay, baby. I'm here. We'll figure it out. You do not end this way." Jase crooned into my hair and I let the comfort wash over me, no matter how temporary I knew it to be.

We sat in each other's arms like that and let the minutes tick by silently. There was no doubt this was one of Malcolm's twisted lessons for me. I would fight for Jase, I decided. I couldn't let him suffer for me. This wasn't his fight. It was all somehow connected to my family. It was up to me to make sure it ended with me and didn't involve anyone else.

The door at the top of the stairs creaked open and a dark silhouette appeared at the top. He descended slowly, every creak on the stairs chilling me further.

"Ah, sweet Callie, I see you have found your gift. Unfortunately, you have un-wrapped it too early. I so wanted to see the surprise on your face when you discovered my trinket for you. You should have waited for me. A lady waits for her man." His voice dripped with ice and Jase's arms tightened around me.

"Stay the hell away from her, you bastard!" Jase shouted at him.

Malcolm laughed loudly. "And in what position are you exactly to be giving orders, I wonder? Come to me, Callie!" He extended a hand in my direction, but his steely eyes never left Jase.

With effort, I pushed Jase's arms away. He looked at me, confused and I pleaded with him with my eyes to stay quiet and let me go.

"It's okay. If I don't go to him, it will be worse for both of us." I whispered and he shook his head frantically. I kissed his cheek and looked away quickly as the tears appeared in his eyes. Rising on unsteady legs, I moved towards Malcolm.

"Good girl," Malcolm praised. He took my hand and rested it on the banister at the bottom of the stairs, his eyes telling me to stay. He moved towards Jase, goading him as he went. "Do you see this Jason? See how she comes to me? Responds to me? Don't you wish you had taken better care of her now? She could still be yours if you had treated her like a real lady and not defiled her at every opportunity. You did not know how to treat her, none of you did. Not you, her brother, not the Irish thug, or the biker, and most certainly not that mangy police dog! Not even my advice could help you. You all failed her and now it is left up to me to fix her."

"You're going to take a little nap now, my boy. She will return to you later, when I have finished with her." He crouched beside Jase and I saw the tell-tale rag in his hand. Jase pulled at the chains, growling angrily. Malcolm covered Jase's face with the chloroform filled rag, he struggled for a few seconds before the drug rendered him unconscious.

"Come now, my lady, it is time for your lessons." Malcolm led me up the two flights of stairs, towards the bedroom, and once again I was in front of that mirror.

The knife worked its path down my arm for the third time. I knew what he wanted to hear, but I wasn't giving it up. This time I was angry. Doing this to me was one thing, but hurting someone I loved to teach me one of his sick lessons? No. I would not give in to that!

I held out as long as I could while he silently repeated the pattern from shoulder to wrist, over and over, until I lost count of how many scars I would be left with. I could no longer see the marks he had made for the blood that covered them. Staring blankly at my reflection, I became mesmerised by the crimson river that trailed down my arm, and dripped onto the carpet, forming a pool of red against the beige material under my bare feet. *That'll be a bitch to get out,* I thought to myself humourlessly. We stood there, in front of the mirror, countless seconds passing as he forced me to watch his actions. I was numbing myself to the pain, but I knew I would soon pass out.

"Come now, Callie." He spoke at last. "Don't make me give your lessons to your little friend downstairs instead. Tell me what you have learned."

My eyes had been closing, but I jolted back into consciousness at the mention of Jase. Finding my legs, I stood straighter, despite the weakness I felt. I could not, would not, let him hurt anyone else because of me. Jase and I may not have been on the best of terms, but he didn't deserve this. My fight returned, and I gathered the strength I knew I had to muster, in order to play this maniac at his own game.

"I should have waited for you to open my gift." I told him coldly. My voice was weak, but I said the words without wavering. I could do this, I knew what he wanted to hear, it was easy to give him exactly what he wanted. I could play his game; I knew the rules.

"Ah, there she is. My lady is coming back to me. Yes, yes, you should have waited. You ruined the pleasure for me, Callie." The sweet hadn't returned to my name, he was still angry. "When I bring my lady a gift, it gives me joy to see the look on her face. By opening it without me, you ruined my surprise entirely. You robbed me of my joy. I think, perhaps, I should destroy your gift, take it away from you as punishment. That would be fitting."

"No!" I snapped out quickly. "Please don't hurt him. Please. I will do whatever you want. I'll be who you need me to be. Just please don't hurt him anymore."

"I only need you to be a better version of yourself, my sweet girl. I approve that you wish him no harm, particularly when he treated you so poorly. This is how a lady behaves. She forgives the mistakes of others. Much better, sweet Callie." He dropped the knife from his gloved hand, into the sheath he wore strapped around his waist, and met my eyes in the mirror. "You will rest here, in your room. Take the time to reflect upon your lessons. Do not shower or tend to your wounds, they are not deep enough to require bandaging. Dress for dinner. I will come for you then."

CHAPTER EIGHTEEN

CALLIE

Malcolm returned to collect me for dinner, for which I'd dressed as instructed, another full-length dress, picked out by him, in the perfect size. This time, it was jade green and flared from the waist to the floor. Lace covered my shoulders, and upper back, and formed cap sleeves across my arms. It couldn't have been any less something I would have worn. I sat through the meal he prepared, but I couldn't recall now what it was he cooked. I don't know that I even ate anything. During dinner, he made small talk, telling me about his day, of which I remembered little other than making the required responses when he expected them. Then he led me to the living room at the back of the house.

I imagined the house form the outside. No different to the way it always was. I passed it daily, on my way to work, as did Cameron. To look at it, nobody would guess it held such horrors on the inside. It was a pretty house, with an immaculately kept garden. Roses climbed the front wall and framed the doorway. The downstairs window always displayed freshly cut flowers. It was a cleverly disguised house of horrors. Maybe the fact Malcolm believed he was doing nothing wrong was part of its deception. He carried on life as normal, while he tortured women in his cellar. Such a lovely house couldn't possibly be home to anything like that. That kind of thing only happened in run down, abandoned buildings, where nobody thought to look beyond the outside. But nobody thought to look beyond the outside of a perfectly respectable house either.

While Malcolm prattled on about getting to know one another, I was desperately trying to come up with a way to get Jase out of there. Only one of us needed to get out and get word to the police about the other. Jase would have told me to run for it if I got the chance and send the police back for him. I would rather he got out because I thought there was less chance of Malcolm killing me, if Jase got free. If I left Jase in the house alone, he wouldn't live long after my departure. Still, if by some miracle, the opportunity arose, I would take it. What other choice did I have? So, I kept searching and scheming, whilst playing Malcolm's twisted game.

I took the seat he indicated, a large floral armchair, had been his wife's, with a mahogany side table next to it. He placed a glass of brandy on the table, then took his own seat on the other side of the unlit fireplace, whiskey in a crystal tumbler clasped in his hand. The curtains were drawn, but I expected the windows were painted over, and two small table lamps provided the only light in the room. The room was set for a cosy night in. What the outside world couldn't see was the torturer and his victim behind the facade.

"Have a seat, sweet Callie. I think it is time you heard my story."

"I'd like that." My response was automatic, robotic even, but my mind was working at warp speed.

"Relax and listen, then. I will answer your questions at the end. You will not interrupt; I do not wish to return to your lessons this evening. I have an appearance to make in that God forsaken pub."

"I understand," I agreed timidly, in the manner I hoped he wanted to see. His smile, which I didn't return, told me I had pleased him.

Malcolm took a sip of his whiskey and settled himself in his chair.

His demeanour relaxed and calm, as though about to tell a perfectly normal story, not one of how he became a serial killer.

"My mother was a formidable woman, beautiful, elegant, and graceful. A strict disciplinarian, she was a force to be reckoned with. We lived in a grand house, deep in the woods, you have been there. It was where I first took you. Sadly, thanks to your antics, I may no longer return there. Although, due to the assistance of an acquaintance of mine, I have been able to hide my ownership of the property. Perhaps, in a few years, it may be possible to go home, after you have chosen me." He paused to collect his thoughts.

Mummy issues, I thought to myself, are you fucking kidding me? All this suffering, all those women dead because his mother was a bitch? I adjusted myself in my seat and did everything I could to contain the anger raging within me. Just listen to him, Callie, I told myself. Give him the audience he wants and keep Jase safe. That's all you have to do.

"Please do not fidget, sweet Callie, it is not ladylike at all." He glanced at me before continuing. "Now, as I said, Mother was a strict disciplinarian and demanded suitable behaviour at all times. Bad behaviour was punishable by a number of methods. She required me to be a gentleman, without exception, and her lessons in the subject were impeccable. My own pale in comparison. Of that, I am certain. She raised me with the knowledge that one day, if I became the gentleman she was teaching me to be, I could find myself a lady of my own. A future I, naturally, aspired to." He took a sip of his drink and gestured for me to do the same, before continuing. I picked up my glass and drank, the burn of the amber liquid bringing my senses back to life.

"Of course, I misbehaved, as any young boy does. My mistakes were few and far between, since I had been instructed from such a young age, but when I made them, I was punished— usually through lack of food and water, only physically if my behaviour was extreme— and afterwards, I was given a period of reflection. During this time, I was chained in the cellar of our home. Much like you, and the others, and as your Jason is now. My reward being my return to the house and all the comforts Mother provided for us. My childhood was a happy, contented one, but sadly when I came into my teen years, Mother became ill." He paused to smile wistfully.

"Now, to fully appreciate my story, you must know a little background on my mother." He watched me carefully, as I lifted the glass and looked at it, an idea forming. "If you intend to attack me, I would suggest a knife, at dinner. A smashed glass will cause you more injury than me, my sweet."

I snapped my gaze up to meet his, setting down the glass carefully. I hadn't realised I was leaning forward and eased back into the chair. Malcolm nodded, approving of my actions and continued talking.

"My mother was raped. Many times, but many men." Malcolm smiled wistfully at a memory that should have repulsed him. "I was born of that encounter."

I floundered, manners insisting I say something. Sympathise, empathise. Nothing came. He didn't seem to notice.

"She fully accepted her part in her downfall. Mother knew she was to blame. Working in a pub, wearing short skirts, flirting with these men. She also realised she was lucky to escape with her life. She fled Frost Ford, her hometown, and began again in Dublin. Her recovery came with the friendship she found in the Catholic church. A priest was her saviour and my birth, her gift. In me, she was granted an opportunity to educate not only her child, but the women of this world. Some would argue she was traumatised by the events. She wasn't. My mother taught with a clear head. She educated women to acknowledge, that there was a certain way they behaved that would endanger them."

"As I grew into my teenage years, and began to look at women differently, she increased her lessons. Assisted by her priest, she taught me the evils of sex. No lady will ever offer sex to a man. She will keep herself pure. No gentleman will ever demand sex from a lady, nor would he want a woman who offered it."

"She conditioned you to believe sex is wrong," I blurted.

"I suppose that is how a therapist might look at it," Malcolm smiled. "But aren't you glad I have the self-control not touch you in that way? Doesn't that make you feel more comfortable in my presence? Can you not see, that this is how a man and woman should be?

Only whores have sex! Whores should be punished and taught the error of their ways."

I stayed silent while he ranted. I didn't voice the questions or opinions I had on what he was telling me. While my sarcastic side wondered if his mother was trying to wipe out the human race by outlawing sex, the rest of me knew he wasn't really looking for my opinion on it all. He didn't want a conversation, or to tell me his feelings on love, and marriage. He merely wanted an audience to listen to him spew his warped beliefs. I wanted to ask if his mother had killed the women she took in, before he became involved. I was afraid of the answer though. How long had this been going on?

"The day I joined my mother in teaching came about after observing a particularly harsh lesson with one of her students. I came upon the most bewitching young woman. She was only fifteen years old at the time, I was eighteen. I began to go out of my way to catch a glimpse of her, until one day, I found her with a boy, behind the school bike sheds, of all places. The things she was allowing him to do to her were not becoming of a lady and I knew instantly, it was my job to rescue this girl, and teach her the error of her ways."

"I befriended her and waited for the perfect time. I told Mother I had found my lady. She, of course, reminded me that I must ensure I taught the girl well. She must respect me and choose to stay with me. Eventually, the opportunity to take her arose and I did so. It took some time to fully immerse her in the ways of being a lady. It was a turbulent time, what with Mother's worsening illness. During those years, both of the ladies in my life had good days and bad. I believe the turning point was Mother's death. I wasn't sad at the loss of my mother; she spent many months prepared me for the time. I didn't cry or become emotional as I took her life. I didn't like losing her, though. It left me elated, knowing I had granted her the freedom she never truly found in life."

"When my lady saw the change in me, she began to respond more quickly to her lessons. Her wounds were treated quicker and she spent less time in the cellar, earning more and more freedom each day. By the time she turned eighteen, she had chosen me. We were married at the earliest opportunity and spent many happy years together. You know her as Irene, my beloved wife." He paused again, to let his words sink in.

I desperately tried to control my reactions, knowing an outburst would not be the right way to respond. He had taken Irene when she was just fifteen years old and subjected her to this her entire adult life. It was unfathomable. She had seemed so happy and in love with him. They were the couple we all looked up to as kids, absolutely devoted to one another. Irene never showed any signs of distress or unhappiness. She had loved Malcolm. I breathed deeply to calm myself, although my stomach rolled, and I wanted nothing more than to fling myself at him and claw out his eyes.

"I know what you're thinking."

I wanted to scream at him that he had no idea what I was thinking, because he didn't think like a normal person. He was a lunatic. Just keep Jase safe, I kept telling myself. Stay numb, play the game.

"You're wondering about children," he said, drinking from his glass, and licking his lips. "Couples fall in love, get married, have children. A woman's body, after all, is designed to birth children."

"Why didn't you?" I felt compelled to ask. He obviously wanted to tell me.

"While I had no desire to partake in any sexual act with my wife, we attempted artificial insemination, several times. It was not to be."

My stomach churned. Somehow, I knew he didn't mean insemination by a doctor, in a clinic.

"Now, let me continue. Over the years, despite my loving marriage, I began to realise something was missing from my life. Of course, it was my calling to teaching that I was craving. Teaching in Dublin, while satisfactory, never really fulfilled me the way it had with mother. Something was missing. A... let's say, unsavoury character, made me an offer I could not refuse, allowing Irene and I to return to my mother's home of Frost Ford."

"My mother's family home still stood, in the woods, as you know. But Irene wanted to be closer to town, so we found this house. I gave my failed ladies the ideal reflection period, eternity to think about their behaviour. Your Aunt Caroline was a turning point in my life. She gave my teaching meaning. Her wild ways appealed greatly to my nurturing personality. Too free spirited and vulgar to ever be a lady. Not that it mattered, the unsavoury character I mentioned wanted her dead. She was my first steps on the path to my reward."

Malcolm had an accomplice. I tried to commit everything he was telling me to memory, so I could unravel it later, but the questions fought with the facts and I struggled to make sense of any of it. Who wanted my aunt dead? Who was this other man he referred to?

"I took her like I did the others, only she was easier because she knew me. I became her brother's trusted friend, in anticipation of her demise. I won't bore you with the details of her death, except to say it was beautiful and most definitely not a waste of life. There are other factors, concerning that third party I mentioned, that you will know eventually. Now is not the time."

I reached up to rub my temples and he frowned. "Are you unwell, my lady?"

"No, it's just, a lot to take in." I smiled, weakly. *Play the game, Callie!* "Please, carry on, though."

"We are almost done." He smiled back at me and gave me a long, thoughtful look before he continued. "Sadly, your father began to look too closely at her death. He became convinced she was one of mine and refused to let it go, despite the investigation stating that her death was not related to my students. He was good, he really ought to have become a detective. He got too close in his investigations, sweet Callie. I am not certain whether or not he made the final connection, but I could not allow him to continue. It pained me to deal with him."

"Your parents were rarely parted, so very much in love, they shared everything, and so it transpired that your mother knew about your father's activities. I realised with regret; I would have to take them both. It was quick and painless. You have my word they did not suffer. Until that time, I had valued their friendship, and it was a shame events had to happen that way. But their deaths were not in vain. You see, before them and your aunt, my path was nothing more than a way to pass on my mother's teachings, no real purpose other than that. Your family, by way of my un-named acquaintance, gave my path the focus it was missing. With you, I have the ability to come full circle and end my journey. To receive the reward my work has earned."

"Caroline was the reason I came to Frost Ford. You are the reason I stayed. I promise you this, sweet Callie, you will have my love and respect as Irene did. I will honour you in every way when you choose me. For you, and you alone, I will retire from teaching. We will have a wonderful life together." He stopped talking, at last, and began to stand.

"Now, I must make my nightly appearance. You will remain downstairs. You may tend to your Jason, as a reward for listening well. I believe it will serve as a suitable reflection period for your earlier misbehaviours. Come." He held out his hand for me to take and helped me stand.

"Malcolm, thank you for telling me your story." I ventured, playing along with him, my head was heavy with the weight of his revelations, but I needed to push it all aside for the moment, and find a way to help Jase. He smiled in approval at my gratitude. "May I take some food for Jason? Would it not be considered rude to allow our guest to go unfed?"

"Ah, but of course you are right, my sweet lady. You may prepare him a plate from the fridge while I change. I won't be long, sweet Callie, be ready to go downstairs as soon as I return."

I nodded and moved to the kitchen, quickly finding a plate, and throwing cold meat, bread rolls, and fruit on it. Then, taking care not to make a too much noise, I opened the drawers around the kitchen, hoping to find something to use as a weapon. There were no knives sharper than a butter knife or anything else I might use. I laid one of the blunt knives on the plate, anyway, hoping to make it look natural. I'd known finding anything more useful was a long shot, but I had to try.

Then, I noticed Malcolm's coat, hanging on the back of a chair at the kitchen table. I crept to the door, stilling to listen and make sure he wasn't coming back. When I heard no sign of movement, I moved stealthily back to the table to check the pockets, finding a large ring of keys. Trying to stop them from rattling in my shaking hands, I scanned them for what I thought might be the key to the chains that held Jase. There was one, smaller than the others, almost like a padlock key. I quickly removed it, my hands fumbling. I winced in pain, when my finger slipped, and my nail snapped while trying to pry the metal apart to remove the key. A quick glance revealed a nail napped at the quick, and blood pooling in the wound. I shoved the finger in my mouth, to suck away the blood, and yanked up my dress with my other hand, securing the key in the waistband of my underwear. I put the key ring back in the same pocket and composed myself, to wait for Malcolm.

THE TEACHER

I am pleased with my lady's behaviour. We enjoyed a delicious meal together and she listened patiently to my story, giving it the attention it deserved. Her reflection period will leave her with questions, no doubt, but that is a conversation we can have when she has had time to reflect.

I sit at my spot in this pub, second drink in, and listen to the goings on around me. They are all in and out, as usual. This seems to have become some kind of command centre for her search. Police in uniform and detectives roam around the town, but I know from previous experience they will scale down the search soon enough. The mutt and his pups, I expect, will continue forever more if they can get away with it, but the others will have to return to their normal duties.

"Nick, have you heard from Jase since last night?" The mutt addresses the biker without pause, as he strides through the door purposefully.

"No. Is something wrong?" the biker responds.

"His father called into the station earlier. He says they haven't heard from him since last night, and his phone is dead. Cameron and Greg are checking his workmates now."

"CCTV?" the biker asks.

"We should be so lucky in this town." The mutt huffs a sarcastic laugh. "If this place had CCTV, we would have picked this fucker up months ago. Apart from this pub, there's not a camera in the county!"

"The joys of living in the middle of fucking nowhere!" The biker runs a hand through his hair.

The mechanic joins them. "Do you think Jase disappearing is significant?"

"It could be. He was a suspect for a while, the detectives never ruled him out. I can't imagine he would disappear if this was all down to him. He'd want to be seen, keep up appearances, but he hasn't been thinking straight either. Either way, I'm following every lead we get."

The mechanic tells him. "There was a time I would have said, if he had her, he wouldn't hurt her, but after what he did to her arm, I don't know."

The biker stands abruptly and his stool scrapes across the floor. "I'm going to check his place. Feel like joining me?"

The mutt stands, too. "I can't do it officially. No until he's been gone twenty-four hours."

The biker holds aloft a key ring. "I've got his spare key. Granted, he changed the locks, so I had to kick the door in, but I'm just checking up on a friend, worried about him."

The mechanic stands now. "Let's go."

After a brief word between the police mutt and the Irish thug, the three of them leave the pub. I congratulate myself. Not only did I bring my lady a wonderful gift, I have her would be rescuers running in circles.

CALLIE

"Jay." I knelt beside him and pressed a hand to his cheek. "Jay it's me. I need you to wake up." He murmured as I hurriedly reached under my dress, to find the key. "Jay, I brought you some food, you need to eat, and drink some water. The chloroform will have you feeling shitty, but I need you to fight it for me."

"Cee?" He blinked several times and tried to focus on my face, bringing his hand up, but unable to reach me because of the chains.

"Hang on. I think I might have the key." I held his hand still and tried the key in the lock. It was a little stiff, and it took a few tries because my hands were shaking. With the movement, the dry blood that caked my arms crumbled, leaving my skin sore and inflamed. I ignored the pain, and the wounds that were opening back up, and eventually the key turned. The lock clicked and the chains fell to the ground. "Yes!"

Jase's arms came around me fast and he pulled me to him. "You're amazing, how did you get that?"

"Pure luck! I need you to eat and drink something. Then we've got to try and get out of here. He went out, so we probably only have about an hour and a half until he's back." I explained quickly.

"Alright," Jase croaked and took the bottle of water I offered him. He drank deeply, but only managed a few bites of the food. "I can't, Cee, I'll throw up."

"Okay, look, you just rest there for a while. I'm going to try making some noise, he's got neighbours, someone *has* to hear me." I stood underneath the small window and began hammering on it for all I was worth. My fight was back, and I was determined at least one of us was getting out of there. After a few minutes, Jase was behind me, standing on shaky legs, but standing all the same.

"The pictures, Cee." He looked around the walls at the photographs.

"Don't look." I told him, unable to follow his gaze.

"I'm going to see if I can do anything about that door. You keep banging, okay?" I nodded and he leant down to kiss my cheek. "I'll get you out of here."

Minutes ticked by. We both tried everything we could. Jase's battered body didn't have the strength to kick the door in. He could barely stand straight, let alone put enough force behind himself to get the door open. He had rib damage, leaving his movements painful and limited. We both searched, to no avail, for some kind of tool to pick the lock or break the window. The blunt butter knife I brought downstairs was too big to use as a tool. Malcolm had, ironically, learned his own lessons and left nothing that could be used to help us escape. Eventually, exhausted and hoarse from shouting, we collapsed onto the tiny bed and huddled together in defeated silence.

Lying there, in Jase's arms, only made me think of Adam. Something I had been desperately trying to avoid. I loved him; I had loved him for some time. I couldn't pinpoint when it had happened, but it had. I thought back to the conversation we had about his brother James. When I was gone, would Adam remember? Would he remember all the ways I told him I loved him without saying the words? Without even realising myself I was saying the words. I hoped so. I hoped he would realise, too, that I had never really thought he could have hurt Jase. I now knew it to be Malcolm, but I hadn't really needed that confirmation.

"We were alright, weren't we, Cee? At least for a while." Jase whispered in the dark, his hands tracing circles on my back.

"We were more than alright, for a very long time." I told him, truthfully. We hadn't been perfect, but who was?

"I've loved you for as long as I can remember, you know that. I don't remember a time in my life when I haven't loved you." There was a sad smile in the sound of his voice. "Even back when I couldn't say your name. You know, I don't ever remember calling you anything else after CeeCee. When I could have said your name easily, you were still CeeCee, to me. I wouldn't let anyone else say it though. Even then, when we were kids, I was trying to own you and I had no idea what I was doing."

"I didn't mind," I told him. "I liked that only you called me that."

"I need to tell you about Amy and some other stuff," he whispered against my hair.

"No, Jay, I don't want to hear that. When we get out of here, we can talk all you want," I answered.

"No, baby, I have to say these things to you. I don't know if I'll get the chance again."

"Don't. We are *going* to get out of here, Jay!" I snapped.

"I love it when you call me that. Always did. I avoided her for years..." He began, his hand in my hair, stroking gently.

"Please..." I begged, on the edge of tears.

"Let me, Cee. I need you to know this," he pleaded. I nodded silently.

"I avoided her as much as I could. I knew she liked me, but I never saw her as anything more than a friend. I only ever had eyes for you. She would ring, and text, and turn up when you weren't there. The first few times she came over we hung out, I thought, just as friends. I'd make her a brew and we talked, like you and Nick. Then she began to make it clear what she really wanted. I started to steer clear of her after that. About a year before... Before you were taken the first time, I began to realise I was losing you. I started to get desperate. I wanted a ring on your finger and a baby in your belly, as fast as I could get them there. I even started hiding your pills." He paused and I couldn't help the laugh that came. It wasn't funny at the time, but now it seemed insignificant.

"I remember." I told him. I'd thought it was my own stupidity, forgetting my pills. I'd gone to the doctor and switched to an injection that I only had to remember every twelve weeks.

"I thought if we had a baby you wouldn't leave me, as though it would somehow fix us. I was constantly paranoid about what you were doing, all those men that were around you when you were working. I knew that Matt bloke, from the band, was into you, had been since school, and it drove me insane." He sighed and I squeezed his bicep, in an effort to comfort him. "I couldn't stand the thought of a life without you, Cee. That's also when the arguments started. The night you went missing, we fought, before you left for work, and again after. I hated what I was doing to you, but I couldn't see a way to keep you. After we found you, we just fell back into us, like nothing happened. It was good again for a while. I thought we'd be ok. Then you went into yourself, struggling to deal with what had happened to you. And what did I do? I stifled you again, refused to give you what you needed."

He stopped for a few minutes, just holding me, as we breathed together in the dim lamp light. "The night, with her, with Amy, she turned up after you left for work. I always sent her packing. Again, we'd argued before you left. When I saw her on the doorstep, I just thought, why the fuck not? You didn't want me anymore, she did. I'd been drinking. Nah, I was hammered, and it seemed logical in my head. But when we were there, with it actually happening—"

"I don't need a blow by blow, Jay," I joked, shallowly.

"Sorry. All I could see and think of was you. It wasn't her in my mind, it was you wanting me again. You, giving me what I craved from you. You, letting me make love to you, the way I always had. I chased you, and Adam refused to let me anywhere near you. He was protecting you, even then. When I got home, she was still there. I yelled at her. Told her she was disgusting, and I wanted nothing to do with her, that you were the only one I would ever want. I said unforgiveable things to her. She ran off into the night screaming and swearing at me. Fuck, Cee, if I had known what was going to happen to her."

"You could never have known that, Jase. Nobody could. It wasn't your fault." I attempted to comfort him, but I felt the same guilt over Amy that he did, so I guessed it fell on deaf ears.

"Losing you was worse than anything I had ever felt, CeeCee. It was fucking torture. I drank. A lot. I'm sure Nick told you, since he was on my tail the whole time. I was in a club in Marbledon one night, and there was this woman who looked like you. At least, to me she did. Maybe I was just seeing you everywhere and I wanted her to look like you, but I saw what I saw. I took her outside and fucked her up against an alley wall, then I walked away from her. Didn't even ask her fucking name, I think I might have even called her Cee." I winced at his words. "I'm not proud of it. My only defence is that I was falling apart over you and that's a thin defence at best. She was the only other one. Her and Amy. That was it. I didn't want you to think there were all these other women, the whole time we were together, because I was true to you, Cee. All those years before that, you were mine and I was yours. Completely. I didn't even look at another woman. I promise you. I lost the best thing in my life and I will never forgive myself for hurting you. I'm so sorry, CeeCee, so fucking sorry. Please believe me." He was crying now.

"I believe you, Jay." I leaned up to kiss his cheek, my own tears mingling with his. I did believe him. I wanted to say more, to tell him I forgave him, and that although we were no longer together, I would always care for him deeply, but I didn't get the chance.

The front door slammed and we both jumped up, not knowing what to do next. He would come down here and see Jase out of the chains. He'd know I took the key. I was in for mirror time, that was a given, but what would he do to Jase? The door at the top of the stairs opened. At a slow and deliberate pace, his steps echoed off the bare walls. Jase turned to me and held a finger to his lips; he stood, picked up the butter knife from the plate, and moved silently to the shadows at the bottom of the stairs. I wanted to tell him to come back, not to challenge Malcolm. Malcolm would use his own knife. But I couldn't warn Jase, without letting Malcolm know, too. As Malcolm reached the last step, Jase didn't hesitate, he pounced on our captor, tackling him to the floor and they both went down grunting.

"Run, Cee! Get out! Go!" Jase yelled at me.

Hearing the pain in his voice, I knew I had to make this count, so I fled up the stairs. I ran through the kitchen, and straight into the hallway, to the front door. Of course, it was locked, and the thick, wooden door had no glass to break. I looked around for Malcolm's coat, but it was nowhere in sight. He must still have been wearing it, which meant no keys. Frantically, I began to thump the door, screaming and shouting as loud as my voice would let me. I ran through all the downstairs rooms, banging at the windows, all of them locked. Turning in a circle, in the living room, my eyes landed on the side table next to the chair I sat in earlier, I lifted it and took it to the patio doors at the back of the room. I swung the table, like a baseball bat, at the window. Swinging and hitting, over and over again, until the glass cracked. My hair was yanked from behind and I fell to my knees.

"I trusted you," he ground out, pulling me to my feet by my hair, and dragging me through the house, back towards the cellar. "You have been deceiving me, playing a very dangerous game with me. Now you will learn, my Callie. Now you will learn."

He flung me through the cellar door and down the stairs. I landed in a painful heap of tangled limbs at the bottom of the cellar steps, flinching as the footsteps followed me down. Once again, I was dragged to my feet by my hair, and pulled across the room to where Jase now lay in a heap, a pool of blood rapidly forming around him.

"No!" I screamed. My mind refused to register the damage to my body from the fall, my only thought was Jase. I reached for him. Malcolm yanked on my hair to pull me back.

"I was going to allow you to keep him a while, see if we couldn't teach him, too. But not after this betrayal. You think to steal from me, Callie?" he bellowed. He was losing control; I heard the change in his voice. "You think to deceive me? Fool me once, Callie, fool me once. Your punishment my dear, *sweet,* Callie, is to watch your first love die. The wound I have inflicted will allow him maybe fifteen minutes, possibly less. Say your goodbyes. Tomorrow, we leave this town and everything in it!"

He threw me to my knees. I landed in the sticky pool of Jase's blood. Malcolm turned and left the cellar, mumbling to himself as he went. I crawled to Jase's side and searched for the wound, finding a tear in his t shirt at the side. I tried in vain to apply pressure and staunch the bleeding, but the blood covered my hands in seconds.

"CeeCee," he groaned.

"It's okay, Jay, you're going to be okay. I'll fix this, I'll find a way." The blood continued to seep from the wound. I tore at my dress, somehow finding the strength in my weakened arms, to rip off long shreds, and wrap the wound. I tore Jase's shirt and packed it up at the open stab site, before wrapping the pieces of my dress around him and tying them, as tightly as I could. I was no nurse, and had no real clue what I was doing, but I would try anything.

"Now you want to get naked with me?" Jase joked, as he coughed and struggled to breath.

"Old time's sake, eh?" I tried to laugh with him, but it was more of a sob. I was losing him, and I knew it.

"Just hold me, Cee. Hold me until it's over." He shivered and I moved to lie alongside him, putting one arm under his head for support, and the other across his middle. I pressed myself against his side and got as close as I could. He turned his face towards me and those hazel eyes I loved so much met mine.

"This isn't it, Jay. You're not going anywhere. I won't let you," I cried desperately. "You stay with me, you hear me? Don't you fucking dare leave me, Jay!"

"We both know that's not true, babe. Nobody knows we're here. Just—" He coughed, and I told him to take slow breaths until he could speak again. "Promise me something, Cee."

"Anything," I vowed.

"You *will* get out of here. Cam and Adam will find you. They won't stop until they do. And when they do, I want you to be happy." His voice cracked with emotion and another wave of tears washed over me. "Adam loves you."

"You loved me first, Jay" I choked back the tears.

"I did and I never stopped. I never will. I've only ever loved you, nobody else. I loved you first, Cee—" He struggled to take a breath. "But he loves you better. I was so focused on keeping you, I didn't notice I was suffocating you. He won't do that, baby, he'll love you the right way. He'll let you breathe."

"I love you, Jay. I'll always love you." And it was true; there would always be part of me that loved Jason Montgomery. Nothing could change that. Nothing. I had to make sure he knew.

"I know, babe. I love you, too. My, CeeCee," he spluttered.

Then he was gone, and I screamed, and wailed at the side of his body, until the darkness consumed me.

THE TEACHER

My anger and disappointment knows no bounds. Once again, I trusted too swiftly. This woman catches me off guard. She plays me She defies and deceives me, and I continue to allow myself to be taken in by her at every turn. Mother would be crestfallen with my behaviour. I would have been punished in the most brutal manner. The punishment is not mine to suffer this time.

My lady's bag catches my eye from where it lies, forgotten, in the corner of my bedroom. I discarded it on the nightstand, the evening I brought her home. I empty its contents onto the bed and begin to look through them, for what, I don't know. Perhaps, I am searching for a clue that will help me get closer to her, something to break down the barrier she puts between us. Her mobile phone, turned off, draws my attention. I took it from her bag and turned it off as soon as I had her in my car. I turn it on now and wander downstairs. I am certain there will be many messages for her; perhaps I can use them as a reward in her future lessons. I once saw a documentary about positive reinforcement. I certainly need to re-think my methods with her.

A knock at the door startles me, and I continue down the stairs, where I set the phone down on the hallway table and answer the door. The brother stands on the doorstep, in uniform. I compose myself quickly. A rapid glance over my clothing, as I discreetly remove my gloves, tells me I have been careful enough, no blood has touched my clothing.

"Cameron, any news? Please tell me good news."

"No, Mal, nothing. Look, I'm sorry to bother you, but we had reports of a lot of noise and glass smashing coming from your place late last night. I have to check it out."

"Of course, of course, come in. I can assure it was nothing more than a broken window, my boy. In here." I usher him inside and lead him to the lounge.

His eyes scan everywhere. I doubt his distracted mind is truly seeing the knocked over table, and other mess, that his sister left during her escape attempt. Still, I briefly work out a plan to take him, should the need arise. It would be far from ideal, the mutt likely knows where he is, but I can make it work, if need be.

"Silly old fool that I am, left my step ladders set up overnight, by the patio doors after I cleaned the windows. Heard a fox going through the rubbish bins out in the back garden and chased it. Shouting and hollering, I was. Bloody thing ran straight into the ladders, got itself tangled underneath, and knocked them into the window." I laugh as he looks at the window.

"You got someone coming out to fix it up for you, Mal?" So concerned, such a good boy.

"About to give them a call now, son," I lie easily.

"Alright, well if you need a hand," he offers.

"Wouldn't dream of it. You get back out there and find that sister of yours. More important than this old man."

He nods and walks back towards the front door. My lady's phone chooses that moment to make an horrific screeching noise from the table.

"Didn't have you pegged as a sci-fi fan." He frowns and the phone continues to scream.

"Ah, you know, I have no idea what that is. Your sweet sister did that for me one night in the pub. She said it was cool. I just let her get on with it, never could say no to her. I don't half miss her antics behind that bar, Cameron." I know I'm floundering, but I think I still have him. I even manage to push a tear out.

He eyes the phone momentarily, an unreadable look crosses his features, and then turns to me. "Me too, Mal. Me too. I'll leave you in peace."

I sigh in relief when he finally leaves. That was a close call. I turn my attention to fixing the damage my lady caused, deciding to let her stew in her first love's blood, until this evening. The water she drinks down there will keep her drowsy, I have seen to that, and I have little desire for her company at present.

CALLIE

Loud noises pulled me from my slumber. Heavy footsteps overhead. What on Earth was going on up there? Stickiness pulled at my skin and I remembered.

"Jay," I whispered.

His lifeless body lay next to me. I raised my head to look at him. His eyes were closed, if it weren't for the blood, I could have made believe he was sleeping. At home, in his bed. Peaceful.

The noises and movement above me grabbed my attention again. I looked towards the stairs. There was shouting, more than one voice.

"What the...?" I whispered, my bruised and stiff body fought me as I tried to sit.

Voices hollered from the top of the stairs. The door seemingly flew off its hinges. Feet thundered down the stairs, and a figure came hurtling towards me, halting suddenly. One word.

"Angel?"

The sound that left my body was inhuman. The gurgled, blood curdling, cry of a dying animal as it surrendered to its pain. In a split second, he was on his knees pulling me to him, my body shaking involuntarily.

"Adam?" Another beautiful voice called from the top of the stairs.

"I have her, Cam. She's alive." His voice rumbled in his chest as he pressed me to him. "You better hold on for me, Angel. I only just found you, there's no way I'm letting you go. You hold on for me, okay?"

"Okay," I whispered.

CHAPTER NINETEEN

CALLIE

The light hurt my eyes, even though they were closed. I tried to turn my head away, but it was everywhere. There was a chemical smell, not *that* smell, not the one that would haunt me for the rest of my life, but a clean one. My head felt heavy and woozy. I tried to lift it; I don't think I succeeded.

"The blinds," someone said. There were scuffling sounds and the light dimmed. Fingers wound themselves through mine and the bed dipped on one side. I pried my eyes open slowly.

"Welcome back, twin." My brother's voice cracked as he spoke.

His bloodshot eyes met mine and his slightly too long, wavy hair pointed in all directions on his head, as though he'd been running his hands through it, over and over again. There were bags under his eyes and what I thought must have been a week's worth of beard adorned his chin. It was the most beautiful face I'd ever seen. He bent forward, slowly, taking care not to jostle my body, and gently took me in his arms while the tears came.

"My anchor," I whispered through my tears. It hurt to be held, but I welcomed the pain. It meant I was alive.

"Hey, witch." A voice came from the other side of the bed. I pulled back slightly, to see Liv's blotchy, tear stained face, smiling at me. I smiled through the tears. My smile became a wince as a cut on my cheek re-opened. Liv sobbed while she hugged me. "I have never been so happy to see anyone in my life."

"Awake at last." A nurse appeared at the door, smiling. She entered, and busied herself checking on me, and making notes as she bustled around the room.

"How long was I asleep?" I croaked, my voice still hoarse, barely more than a whisper. The nurse gave me some water before answering.

"Just under twenty hours. You had quite the bump on your head and we had to pump a lot of drugs out of your stomach." She told me, in a matter of fact manner. I didn't have the energy to ask what drugs she was talking about. I didn't really care, maybe later I would. Right then, all that mattered was I was alive and away from *him*. The nurse looked between Cameron and Liv. "Now, I know you have all been worried sick, but not everyone at once, alright? I'm breaking the rules letting them all wait outside the room as it is."

"I'll go and tell them. Give you two a few minutes." Liv kissed my cheek and left with the nurse.

"I was so scared, Callie. I thought I'd lost you. Again!" Cameron climbed up on the bed and held me close again. "I'm so sorry we didn't find you sooner. And Jase, fuck, Cal!"

"Cam, stop. You couldn't have known. Nobody did. I'm fine. I hurt, but I'm ok. You found me and I'm here." I let the tears fall freely. Tears of relief and tears of grief for Jase.

"He's dead," Cameron said quietly.

"Mal... Malcolm?" I stammered, confused slightly. Cameron gave me an apprehensive look, trying to gage if I was ready to hear it yet. I needed to know. "Tell me."

"Malcolm's neighbours reported some kind of disturbance. They said there was shouting, screaming, and loud noises the night before last. I went to check it out and he passed it off as some crazy shit with a fox, and a broken window. I almost believed him, but there were signs of a struggle in his living room." Cameron huffed a laugh. "Then the fucking *TARDIS* landed in his hallway. I knew instantly it was your phone. He told me it was his and you had put the sound on it for him. He was clearly lying; you would never have known how to do that."

We laughed quietly at my inept technology knowledge. Who knew that would be the thing that saved me?

"I got on the phone to Adam. He called in the detectives, they brought in armed response. I wanted to go straight in there and get you out myself. Adam did too, but we knew he was armed, so we had to wait for back up. They surrounded the house. He must have seen them. It all happened so fast. He shot a police officer, one of the detectives from Lochden Marsh."

"He had a gun?" I gasped.

"Hunting rifle. As soon as he fired, they fired back," Cameron concluded. "The second they took him out, Adam, Greg, and I were in there tearing the place apart looking for you."

He was dead. I didn't know what to do with that information right then, so I shoved it aside to deal with later.

"The detective? Is he alright?" I asked, wondering if it had been one of the ones I had met.

"Took a shot to the leg, but he's ok." Cameron told me, smiling at my concern for the stranger. "Lee Garvey, he interviewed you after Amy went missing."

"I remember him," I said.

The door opened and in walked Mick and Nick.

"Callie love," Mick breathed, taking my hand and pressing my palm to his lips, before leaning up, and placing another kiss on my forehead. His unshed tears spilled over and rolled down his cheeks, his grip on my hand tightening.

"My rock." I smiled, leaning into his kiss. His tears dripped into my hair when he rested his chin on my head.

"You'd better hurry up and get better, Moonbeam. I can't justify pulling your hair when you look like this," Nick joked and bent to kiss my cheek. He was on the other side of the bed and Cameron, reluctantly, moved back to let him come closer.

"Do it. Make me feel normal, Nick." I pleaded through my own tears and smiled up at him.

He hesitated, eyeing the bird's nest on top of my head, before finally reaching out, and very, very gently tugging on a strand of hair, then tucking it behind my ear. He leaned over me and buried his face in my neck, his shoulders shaking with his silent tears.

"My sunshine," I whispered and reached up to hug him.

"Don't ever do that to me again. Not ever, do you hear me, Cal? I can't take it. It will kill me to lose you!" Nick sniffled against my neck.

"Are you covering me in snot?" I joked.

"Payback for making me insane," he laughed.

The others all filtered in and out after that. Dana and I sat on the bed and held each other for ages when her turn came. I promised her the shopping trip of a lifetime to come. Cameron begrudgingly went home to shower and change, after I told him he stank. We talked a little about what had happened, but I told him we needed to really talk. Confirming to my twin that our parents had been murdered, wasn't something I could do casually from a hospital bed, but I needed him to know before the detectives swooped in for their interviews.

After the doctor detailed my injuries to me— the shallow stab wounds on my arms, a sprained ankle, endless cuts and bruises from being thrown down the stairs, a couple of bruised ribs, blood loss from a deeper wound on my leg that I hadn't realised I had— the nurses helped me to shower, and change into my own pyjamas. I finally began to feel a bit more human. I was standing by the bed, trying to drag a comb through my wet hair, when a knock at the door sounded. I turned as it opened and a tall, dark figure filled the frame. *At last.*

"Adam," I breathed.

He stood there, for a minute. His eyes moving slowly from my head, all the way down my body and back up again. And then he was in front of me. I don't think I even saw him move. His hands came up to cup my cheeks and his eyes locked with mine.

"I'm so sorry, Angel," he whispered, his voice cracking on my nickname.

"Not your fault." I rested my hands on his chest, looking up at his handsome face, and taking in every single detail.

"I should have been there or sent someone else when I knew I was going to be late." He shook his head.

"No." I put a finger to his lips. "He would have got me anyway, he wanted me all along. It was always about me."

"He told you that?" Adam asked.

I nodded. "There's a lot to tell you."

"Angel," he whispered

"But first, you promised me a kiss." I smiled.

"I did." He finally smiled and it lit up my world.

"I think I've waited long enough," I said.

He looked over my face, concern filling his eyes, they finally rested on my lips. "Okay?" he asked.

"Okay." I assured him. "Very, very, okay."

He lowered his head slowly and tenderly brought his lips to mine. The lightest brush of his mouth against mine sent tingles through my body. Softly, he pressed his lips to the corner of my mouth, and I smiled against them. He gently swept his tongue over my bottom lip and the tingles intensified. Then finally, Adam claimed my mouth with his own.

I ignored the pain from the cuts on my cheeks, and bruised jaw, and I kissed him back with everything I had. He groaned and deepened the kiss, sliding his tongue between my lips, his hands moving into my wet hair. It was the sweetest, most beautiful kiss I had ever experienced and so very worth the wait.

I clasped his shirt and pulled him closer, desperate to feel his hard body against mine. He feathered a trail of kisses along my cheek, jaw, behind my ear, and down my neck, before moving back to my mouth and I sighed with pleasure. He eventually moved back, when he realised it was beginning to hurt for me to keep standing on the sprained ankle.

"You're in pain," he said, when I pouted and tried to pull him back to me.

"I can live with it," I said, eagerly.

He slipped an arm under my knees and lifted me carefully, to place me on the bed, propped up on the pillows. I smiled when he picked up the bear, he had won at the seaside that day, and set it down on the nightstand. It had been there when I woke up, I don't know who brought it, but I'm glad they did.

"Can I fall in love with you yet?" his eyes shone with unshed tears, making the blue brighter and more beautiful.

"I'm going to fall in love with you, too. You know that, don't you?" Wanting him close I shuffled over and patted the space next to me. He didn't hesitate.

"It's been my plan all along, Angel." He sat next to me on the bed.

"Soon," I said.

"Let me help you." He reached up to take the comb I'd resumed dragging through my hair. I moved forward, and he sat with one leg either side of me, and pulled me back, to lean against his chest, while he slowly teased the knots from my hair. "I'm sorry I wasn't here when you woke up. I had to be at work while everything was tied up. I got away as soon as I could."

"I know, Cam told me everything. It's ok," I said, briefly wondering why I hadn't had detectives hounding me for information. I had a feeling Adam had something to do with keeping them away. "Was it you? Was it you who found me? I thought it was you, I think I remember hearing you say my name, but—"

"It was me. I shouldn't have moved you, but when I saw you lying in that pool of blood, I was sure I'd lost you, that we hadn't found you in time. Thought it was your blood. All I could think of was that we'd been angry with each other. I couldn't stand for it to end that way. Then I realised you were moving. Fuck, Angel, I've never felt relief like that in my life. I just wanted you out of there. It didn't even register that there was anyone else there." He leaned down and placed a kiss on my shoulder.

"It was Malcolm. He told me he beat Jase. I already knew it wasn't you, but I was being stubborn, I wanted to make you say it. I was stupid and I should have just told you straight away that I knew it wasn't you," I rambled.

"I was stubborn, too. I knew you needed to hear it, but I wanted you to *not* need that. I wanted you to just know," he said.

"I did know. I'm sorry, Adam," I told him.

"I'm sorry, too. How about next time we do what we do best and talk about it, instead of sulking?" he bargained, and I nodded in agreement. "I'm so sorry about Jase. I can only imagine how you're feeling about it. Just know that, when you're ready, I'll fight that darkness with you. All of it. Together."

"I know you will. Thank you." I rested my head on his chest and we fell into silence.

The nurses must have decided to let us break the rules, because when I woke the next morning I was lying on Adam's chest, his arms securely around me. Instead of an oh shit moment I had an *"I want to wake up like this every day for the rest of my life"* moment.

"That can be arranged," he murmured sleepily.

"Did I say that out loud?" I whispered and he moaned happily as his hands found their way underneath my top, caressing my bruised skin so softly. "We're actually in a bed."

"Yeah, not exactly what I had in mind, Angel." He smiled as I lifted my head to look up at him.

"Me neither," I agreed.

"Oh, really?" he asked looking down at me and smirking.

"What? You didn't think you were the only one thinking about it did you?" I teased.

"Tell me everything," he demanded, the smirk becoming a grin.

"Are you sure you can handle my chaos?" I said, turning serious.

"Angel, you flew into my life on that blizzard and ripped off the bandages that were covering my secrets. You gave me your strength and stood beside me, so I could fight again. I'd given up before you. You made me breathe again. You brought me back to life. You gave me back the light. I fucking live for your chaos." He brought his lips to mine and I never wanted him to stop.

"Ahem!" Cameron cleared his throat in the doorway.

"Hey." I turned stiffly to smile at him. Clean shaven and with fresh clothes, he looked much better, and happier than the night before.

"Morning," Adam said, removing his hands from inside my shirt, but making no effort to move from the bed.

"How are you feeling, twin?" Cameron asked He nodded at Adam, and came to the other side of the bed, so I wouldn't have to twist to look at him.

"Sore. Aching. But I don't care." I told him happily, resting my cheek on Adam's chest.

"Only you could come out of something like this and be happy to be in pain." He laughed, shaking his head at me.

"I'm just happy to be feeling anything at all," I said, and Adam's arms tightened around me.

I had honestly thought I would never feel again after Jase died in my arms. The numbing darkness had taken me, and I hadn't wanted to fight it. I wanted it to swallow me, so I never had to come back from it.

Cameron briefly explained that between him, Greg, and Adam, they had managed to keep the detectives at bay for a couple more days. I was glad of that as it would give us time to talk at home.

"I take it you two are finally official?" Cameron smiled and looked from me to Adam.

"We always were, I was just too stubborn to see it," I admitted.

"Well, it's about time," Cameron said. "Do you know what a nightmare he was to work with, when you were giving him the run around?"

We all laughed, and Adam mumbled something about not being that bad.

"Doc says you can go home, as long as you promise to stay in bed." Cameron told me. "Like that'll happen."

"I can help with that." Adam winked at me.

"I don't want to know," Cameron moaned, but he was smiling.

CHAPTER TWENTY

CALLIE

I woke feeling as though the world had reset itself somehow. There was no underlying paranoia or feeling of dread at the day ahead of me. I felt refreshed, as though I'd actually slept, for the first time in ages. I was in my own bed, a firm, muscled, and very naked chest underneath me. After a night of being waited on hand and foot by my friends, Adam had carried me— I protested, but not very much— to my bed and made it perfectly clear he wasn't going anywhere.

"Morning, Snow Angel," he said sleepily, while lazily sweeping his hands up and down my back.

"Morning," I murmured happily and couldn't help the smile that graced my face.

"Made it to a bed again," he said.

"Twice in as many days, we're getting good at this." I agreed, my hands exploring his chest. Why had I waited this long to get my hands on him?

"How are you feeling?" he asked.

"Fantastic!" I lifted my head and grinned up at him.

"The truth!" He grinned back at me, knowingly.

"That is the truth. I'm waking up in an actual bed, not a sofa in sight, and I'm with you."

"Angel," he groaned and pulled me closer, whispering the only name I ever wanted to hear from his lips. I began to trail kisses across his chest, pausing to swipe my tongue in a circle around his nipple. Suddenly, I was on my back, under him and he was looking down at me hungrily. "Woman, you don't know what you do to me."

I smiled, wickedly. I knew exactly what I was doing. "You have me, Adam. Under you, in a bed. Show me what I do to you."

He moaned and pushed his knee between my legs, separating them. He met no resistance from me. He kissed along my neck, his mouth was a weapon and he used it to batter down the walls of my no swoon zone. It crumbled to dust under his assault. I wouldn't be needing it again. My mind wandered back to the night before, when he kissed me to within an inch of my life and we fell asleep in each other's arms. Things had gotten steamy, we had stripped each other down to our underwear, before Adam put the brakes on, to my frustration. That underwear was all that separated us now. Too thick a barrier for my liking. I slipped my finger into the waistband of his boxers and whispered for him to take them off.

"You're still healing, Angel," he protested between kisses. "Barely out of hospital."

My body hurt, but not as much as it ached for him. "I'm fine. I want you, Adam."

"Say that again," he demanded, with the growl he reserved only for my ears.

"I want you, Adam," I repeated with a smile. Then, because I knew what it would do to him, I added, "make me yours."

His kisses went from gentle and searching, to hot and demanding. I tugged at his waistband again, and he knelt over me on the bed, so I could watch him. I licked my lips at the sight of him, reached out my hand to touch him, but he backed away, smiling.

"There will be time for that later," he murmured.

He moved lower, hooking my own underwear with his fingers and pulling, kissing each centimetre of skin as the fabric skimmed its way down my legs. His touch started a chain reaction in me, each one making me crave the next. Dark desire built inside me and flooded out to the edges of my senses. My stomach tightened and the air was sucked from my chest when his lips closed over my centre. He pulled my orgasm from me with only a few sweeps of his tongue, but I needed more. Wanted to feel every part of him, deep within me. I wanted the bad boy.

"Let him out, Adam." I reached for him, my fingers tangling in his hair as I pulled him back up my body.

There was something animalistic in the way he looked at me, a primal urge to make me his. It ignited my excitement.

"You don't want polite, and gentle, do you, Angel?" I shook my head. "You never wanted that. You want a darkness only I can give you."

"Yes," I whispered, pulling him towards my mouth.

Our tongues battled, not for dominance, that was all his and I was happy to let him take it, but for the need to display the love we felt for each other. I threw my head back and gasped, all pain erased from my mind, when he filled me, he groaned and buried his face in my hair, his back arching over me. Our bodies merged and we rode out the feeling slowly, sensually, drawing out the pleasure of our first connection, knowing it was so much more than physical.

"I want all of you, Angel," Adam growled. "Your anger, your fears, your darkness, your light, your chaos. All of you. Mine."

"Yours," I agreed.

"And I am yours," he vowed.

Afterwards, he rested his head on my stomach and traced patterns across my skin. I stroked his hair and held onto him like my life depended on it. He held me like he would never let go.

"So, is *this* a way of making sure you don't wake up grumpy?"

"It's one possible option." I smirked.

"Oh, don't you worry, I've got a lot more ideas for you," he replied and went back to kissing my stomach, moving lower. I squirmed and laughed as his hair tickled my hip. "I am never letting you out of my sight again. I'm going to be pretty unbearable for a while, Angel."

Adam would have his own darkness to fight. Not being able to get to me in time the night I was taken, would be an horrific case of déjà-vu for him. But like my own, we would fight his darkness together and win. It's what we did.

"If this is what never letting me out of your sight entails, I think I can live with it." I smiled as he moved back up my body, resting his arms either side of my head and looking down at me.

"Can I fall in love with you yet, woman?" he asked.

"It's almost time," I said, knowing perfectly well that I was already in love with him.

"Surprise!" They all yelled as Cameron opened the door to our parent's old bedroom.

Feeling nervous, I walked in slowly and looked around, turning in a full circle. I was lost for words. The dread I felt at entering the room evaporated when I looked around me. Shelves lined the walls, crammed with books, from floor to ceiling. My books. I hadn't been losing my mind when I thought they were disappearing; they had been brought in here.

Underneath the window, a seat had been built, with cushions, and blankets, in varying shades of purple. A beautiful old pine desk was the centre piece of the room, laden with stationary, and a reading lamp.

I spun in a circle again, taking it all in. I moved to one side of the room and reaching out, I ran my hands along the spines of the books. Everything from *John Milton* to *Stephanie Hudson* adorned the shelves. It was beautiful. The most amazing thing anyone had ever done for me. I knew it was Cameron's idea, but I could see touches of all of them in that room.

The bright pink fluffy cushion, from Dana. The framed pencil drawing of Nick and I on his bike— I'd know his art anywhere. The silver drinks tray, with a crystal decanter full of what had to be brandy, knowing Mick. The gargoyle bookends had been Liv's doing, without a doubt. The little toy *Mustang* on the desk was Nate. The tiny cauldron, resting in front of my *Mayfair Witches* books, had Vinnie written all over it, and the shelf full of *Marvel* comic books was Luke to a tee. I ran my hand over a picture of all of us that was taken on our last day of school. I was standing next to Jase, his arm slung casually around my shoulders. We were looking at each other and laughing hysterically at something, I wished I could remember what. Amy was sitting, cross legged, on the ground in front of us all, wearing her fairy wings and purple daisy boots.

"I can't believe you did this." I looked at them all in turn as they crowded into the room. I ran at Cameron and threw myself into his arms, crying like a baby. "You're all so sneaky, and amazing, and I love you so much. Every single one of you."

"Early birthday present, twin." My brother smiled down at me. Our birthday was on Halloween, so a very early present, since we were only just entering July.

"Taking Mum and Dad's rules a bit far, don't you think? What the hell am I supposed to give you now?" I smacked him lightly on the shoulder.

"You, being here with me is more than enough. That's all you ever need to give me." He hugged me close.

"I love you, twin." I told him.

We still needed alone time, to talk more about our discoveries involving our parent's deaths, but that time would come. Finding out that Malcolm was part of our lives in such a sinister way for so long had opened old wounds, and our grief had resurfaced. That was something we needed to come to terms with, but we both knew that just like before we would get each other through it.

"Love you back, twin," he replied, squeezing lightly once more, before letting go of me.

"I can't believe you had no idea this was going on under your own roof!" Vinnie laughed and I hugged him next. "Remember our shopping trip from hell?"

"Of course!" It fell into place.

"You deserve it, babe." Nate pressed a kiss to my forehead as I hugged him, and then Luke.

"You're the amazing one." Liv sniffed when I got to her.

"No, you," I argued.

"I'm jealous is what I am." She looked around with envy at the books. She might work in a library on a daily basis, but I knew she would love something like this.

"We can share, Olive." I smiled.

Mick came up behind me, and pulled me into a Mick hug, kissing the top of my head. No words passed between us; we didn't need them. He knew. I knew.

Adam handed me a small package. "To add to your library." He winked at me and I raised my eyebrows at him.

"Don't keep us in suspense, love." Mick grinned, loosening his hold on me and stepped away.

"Yeah, this is where he proves himself worthy in front of your family and shows us all just how well he knows you," Liv crooned, dreamily.

"It's so romantic!" Dana joined in.

I tore off the paper. "Oh!" I breathed. "Oh, oh, oh!"

"Nerdgasm!" Nick announced loudly, to laughter around the room.

"Is that...?" I gasped looking up at Adam. "Is it?"

"It is." He smiled at me, eyes sparkling.

"It's a book," Jared said. "I don't get it."

"It's her *favourite* book, you idiot." Liv nudged him, wiping a tear from her cheek.

"But surely you already have, it if it's your favourite?" Jared frowned. Bless his clueless cotton socks.

"It's a first edition of *Interview with the Vampire*." I knew what it must have taken for him to get hold of the *Anne Rice* book. Originally published in 1976, they weren't easy to come by, especially one in such good condition. I opened the cover and squeaked. "It's signed!"

"Multiple nerdgasm! You're good, Adam." Luke grinned and Adam laughed, sticking a hand in the air to accept the high five Nick offered him.

"I thought your own library deserved something a little bit special." He caught me, laughing again, as I threw myself at him.

"Ok, that's enough. I'm already in tears here," Liv blubbered.

"Drinks!" Greg announced, turning and heading to the kitchen.

"Tunes!" Dana followed him.

"Oh, Cal, before I forget. Found the sweetest *Dodge Challenger* up for auction next week. Black. 1970. It's not a *Mustang* but, feel like checking it out?" Nate came up beside me as we were all leaving my library. I had a freaking library.

"Damn right I do!" I grinned.

I looked around happily at all my friends, from where I sat, in Adam's lap. We were in my favourite armchair, passing a beer back and forth between us. For hours over the last few days, I'd been in a room at the police station, re-telling the events that had taken place in that house. Answering question after question, until I was drained, mentally, emotionally, and physically.

Adam and Cameron were present throughout. I couldn't have remained strong enough to go through it without either of them. The good thing to come from those interviews, was the knowledge that, once they closed the investigation, the house be demolished, along with the abandoned one in the woods, which they had finally managed to trace back to Malcolm's grandmother. I thought I might throw a party that day.

"The Teacher" as Malcolm was dubbed by the media was gone. All of the families he had torn apart with his sickness could now begin to bring their own darkness into the light. Irene, sadly, had no living relatives left to mourn what had happened to her. I wasn't sure if that was a good or bad thing. I suppose we would never know her entire story and the reasons she accepted the life he forced upon her. Part of me thought her story deserved to be told and part of me believed it was better to bury it, along with Malcolm and all his evil.

Although they weren't the twisted lessons he intended for me to learn, Malcolm had taught me to cherish every single moment given to me, and not to waste my life in darkness. He also taught me how to forgive. Jase's death was still raw, the hard part still to come in dealing with that, but he had given me the closure I hadn't known I needed to be able to move on. If we hadn't been in that situation, I'm not sure we ever would have talked in the way we did. I had a lot of healing to do where he was concerned. There would never be a day when I wouldn't miss him, but Adam, and Cameron, and all the others, would be there for me. We would get through it together. Jay would always be part of us.

Adam and I spent every possible second together. We both felt the need to be close, after coming so near to losing something we almost never got the chance to have. We were taking nothing for granted. Adam taught me to stop hiding and running from life. He taught me how to let my friends in completely and allow them to help me heal. Although, he insisted we learned that part together, perhaps he was right. He had also taught me that nicknames most definitely do mean something.

"You're beautiful," Adam whispered, stroking my cheek with the back of his knuckles.

"I'm bruised and battered." I rolled my eyes at him with a smile.

"You're always beautiful to me. I thought it the second I saw your face, all covered in snow." He kissed me. I wrapped my arms around his neck and pulled him tight against me, wanting to devour him.

"Careful, Angel, I'll be throwing you over my shoulder and carrying you off to bed, if you keep that up." He pulled away, grinning.

"Promise?" I asked.

Adam, true to his word, had come up with many imaginative ways to make me a morning person during the last few days. That morning being no exception.

"Woman, I can't wait to get inside you again. I never want to be anywhere else," he whispered roughly in my ear and a flush spread over my body like wildfire.

"Hmm, I love your dirty mouth. I knew there was a bad boy in there somewhere." I told him with a smile. His words never failed to get me hot and bothered.

"Oh, he's there, he only wants to come out and play with you though. But I have to share a while longer yet." He flicked his eyes to the side, indicating the others in the room.

We were gathered to say our own personal farewell to Jase and Amy, just our group of friends. A feeling of contentment washed over me as I looked around the room. Mick bantered back and forth with Jared and Vinnie, who had become the couple of the moment, thankfully taking the spotlight off Adam and me. Mick, Jared, and I had put our business plans on hold for a while, but things were still very much going ahead. We had some fantastic ideas that we were all excited to get started on. I doubted it would stay on hold for long.

Nick and Nate were laughing loudly at something Cameron had said. It was good to see my brother's fun side coming back out. Sally and Luke looked cosy together, and I wondered if something might be going on there, I hoped it was. Greg and Dana were dancing together in the kitchen, not a slow, romantic dance, a silly, hysterical dance, that looked a lot like the birdy song. And Liv and Nat were deep in conversation over a bottle of wine.

"But I don't want to share *you*. Look at them, they're fine, they don't need us," I pouted, waving my hand around the room at our friends.

"You never have to share me. I'm yours, Angel, always," he said. Nope, couldn't wait, needed him right there!

"Can't we sneak off when they're not looking? We can be quick," I pushed, undoing the top button of his shirt.

"There is nothing quick about what I plan on doing to you." His growl turned my stomach into a contender for gymnastic gold at the next *Olympics*.

"Come on, love birds, join the party," Nick called. I stuck my tongue out at him and he flashed that infectious grin of his back.

"Is this what I'm going to have to live with? You two all over each other every second of the day?" Cameron grumbled, winking at me.

"Are you up to the challenge, Adam? She's insatiable," Dana giggled.

"I think I can handle her," Adam replied, his lips pulling up into a grin.

"Got a bottle of tequila with your name all over it, love." Mick waved the bottle temptingly at me and I nodded my approval.

"Shots witches!" yelled Vinnie.

"Adam?" I whispered, hooking my arms around his neck.

"Hmm?" he replied, burying his face in my hair.

"You can fall in love with me now," I said

He lifted his head, kissed my lips, and replied, "Way ahead of you, Snow Angel."

EPILOGUE

"This had better not be a forehead tattoo, Nicholas Warren!" I narrowed my eyes at him, from where I sat, on the black leather chair in his studio. He had insisted Adam and I meet him that morning. The chair was more of a bed, with an adjustable back rest, and it was high off the floor, so I was swinging my legs back and forth, while I waited for Nick to tell me what he had planned.

"Forehead tattoo?" Adam wanted to know. He looked worried and a little bit sexy, sitting in Popeye's chair, with his shirt off. Okay, a lot sexy. Those V lines I'd wondered about? Yep. He had them, alright. I had decided the V stood for *Very lickable* one night, while I was busy getting to know every inch of his body. I'm sure there was a proper name for them, but I liked mine and Adam seemed quite happy with it, too.

"No foreheads, I promise." Nick mimicked a boy scout salute and laughed. He'd never been a boy scout. "Shirt off, Moonbeam, and lie on your right side, left arm in the air. You can assume the same position, Adam."

"Shirt off?" I asked, suspiciously.

"Callie," Nick began patiently, rolling his stool closer to me and fiddling with his inks. "Do you remember when I told you I would only ink matching tats with someone else, on you?"

I nodded. "You said that was my theme."

"Right, well that's what this is. Blindfolds on," he announced.

"Whoa! Wait a minute, you can't expect us to do this blindfolded," I screeched.

"You trust me, yeah?" Nick looked at me with those puppy dog eyes of his.

"Of course," I caved. I trusted him with my life.

"I'm not sure I do," Adam grumbled, but there was a hint of amusement in his tone.

"You want her marked as yours forever, or not, Caveman?" Nick demanded with a sly grin.

He had taken to calling Adam the nickname frequently, over the last few weeks. Something to do with an altercation Adam and Jase had, while I was missing. They both refused to go into detail. I'd get it out of them eventually.

"Wait, what?" I demanded. Adam laughed that arrogant laugh of his. The one he knew drove me insane.

"Don't worry, Moonbeam, it'll be beautiful. Now, blindfolds on and let us get to work," Nick instructed.

Reluctantly, we both gave in and allowed ourselves to be blindfolded. Well, I was reluctant, Adam was suddenly all over the thought of me being marked as his forever. He assumed the position without another murmur.

Just over an hour later, Adam and I stood in front of the floor to ceiling mirror, in Nick's tattoo parlour, sideways on, him behind me. Nick and Popeye removed our blindfolds simultaneously. My eyes moved to my left side, where I now had an intricate angel wing, stretching from the top to the bottom of my ribcage, the feathers reaching around to my shoulder blade. Along the edge of the wing were the words, *"His Angel"* in beautiful, cursive script.

I gasped in awe and looked at Adam's reflection. In exactly the same place, he had an arrow. The feathers on the end matched those of my angel wing, and there was a tiny angel charm hanging from the tip of the arrow. The tip pointed up and the words *"Her Guardian"* were in the same script along the length.

I turned to Nick and Popeye, tears forming in my eyes. I did a lot of happy crying lately. "Thank you, they're perfect. Just stunning."

"Agreed," said Adam, desire laced his voice, as he continued to look at my ink. He reached out and pulled me towards him, catching me in a searing kiss, that left me in no doubt as to what was on his mind.

"Ugh! Guess the weddings off then, Moonbeam," Nick chuckled from behind us, and Popeye laughed loudly.

"Home. Now," Adam growled. Who was I to argue?

Declan Murray tossed the brown police file onto the passenger seat and sighed. It had been a long, complicated, and hazardous journey, but he finally saw an end in sight. He hadn't planned on taking out the killer he'd hired years earlier, but the man had become reckless, and was threatening to leave a trail that would implicate more than just himself. He was making mistakes, and although the deal had been that he was on his own after Caroline was killed, the eejit thought he could hold Declan over a barrel. When you try to play a Murray at his own game, it never ends well.

His contact in the Marbledon police force had assisted in making sure *The Teacher* never made it out of his house alive. It was a simple task, all it required was one man's word that the maniac had fired first, and a sneaky shot at another officer. Malcolm Grainger was no longer an issue.

Declan didn't have a man in Frost Ford, so getting his hands on the files pertaining to the girl's parents, and Caroline's death, had been more difficult to arrange. Of course, he never had any doubt that he could get them, it merely took a little planning.

He started the engine of the hire car, with a satisfied smile. Thoughts of his wife entered his head and he became eager to return to Ireland. After weeks away, he felt an urge to spend time with his family. His sons were in place, nothing remained that could connect the serial killer to him, his work here was done. It was time to go home.

Frost Ford could rest, for now...

THANK YOU'S

To my husband and children,
I'm sorry for the days I forgot you existed because I had moved to Frost Ford in my head. I'm sorry for the days when you went unfed and had to fend for yourselves. I'm sorry for the days you thought you were a single parent, Felipe. Hey, after all those years in the army bubble, I figure you owed me. ;)
But also thank you.
Thank you for not giving up on me and silently supporting me, even though it seemed I had checked out of reality. Thank you for not getting upset at my snappy attitude when you interrupted me when I was "in the zone." You're all beyond awesome. I am lucky to have you and I love you all more than anything.
To my friends and family whose messages went unread, unanswered, and who wondered if I had dropped off the face of the Earth, I apologise. I know I'm bad at that stuff anyway, but I sucked for a while there. You know what, if this works out, I'm afraid I'm going to suck again. Sorry. I do love you all though. Okay? ;)
To Kat.

THANK YOU'S

Thank you. Just, thank you. Without your encouragement, this may well have remained a dream that I never saw through. Your friendship means the world to me and I'm so happy that we could pick up where we left off after twenty years.

P.S. I'm sorry I killed you off.

To my Facebook and Instagram families, thank you for all the support in the build-up to the release. You have all shown me that sometimes you don't have to know a person in "real life" for them to be your friend.

And finally, to everyone who has read this and got caught up in Frost Ford, you are awesome. Thank you.

Before I go, I have a secret to tell you, Frost Ford may be a human series, but its roots are very deeply buried in the paranormal world. To discover the beginnings of my dark and creepy little town, grab The Witch and the Wolf completely FREE via Bookfunnel.

https://dl.bookfunnel.com/htvguez8b4

ABOUT THE AUTHOR

Emma had a dream. It took a long time to realise that dream and when it finally happened, it came via a career as a pre-school teacher, becoming a Mum of three, and 15 years as an army wife, following her husband from posting to posting across the UK and Europe as he served his country.

Emma and her family have now left the army bubble and settled in their forever home of Spain, where she has fully embraced her inner hippie and at last, sat down and listened to the voices in her head.

Emma likes her beer cold, her feet bare and her words uncensored.

https://emmajaynemills.wordpress.com/

OTHER BOOKS

SECRETS OF FROST FORD

Educating Callie

Now including the paranormal romance Frost Ford Origins story, ***The Witch and the Wolf***

---♥---

A Claddagh in the Clover

---♥---

Coming Soon: ***Bleeding into Ink***

THE MORRIGAN PROPHECIES

The Raven Queen

The Spellbound Queen – Book Two Coming in 2020

CLIFF EDGE COVE

Wildflower

Printed in Great Britain
by Amazon